THE ASSASSIN'S WRATH

BOOKS BY R.S. MOULE

LEGENDS OF THE SHADOW
The Assassin's Shadow

THE ERLAND SAGA
The Fury of Kings
The Hunger of Empires
The Madness of Gods

THE ASSASSIN'S WRATH

R.S. MOULE

SECOND SKY

Published by Second Sky in 2025

An imprint of Storyfire Ltd.
Carmelite House
50 Victoria Embankment
London EC4Y 0DZ

www.secondskybooks.com

The authorised representative in the EEA is Hachette Ireland
8 Castlecourt Centre
Dublin 15 D15 XTP3
Ireland
(email: info@hbgi.ie)

ISBN: 978-1-80550-075-9
eBook ISBN: 978-1-80550-074-2

For my nephew, Gabriel.
Heroes are not born; they are wrought.
May you remain magical.

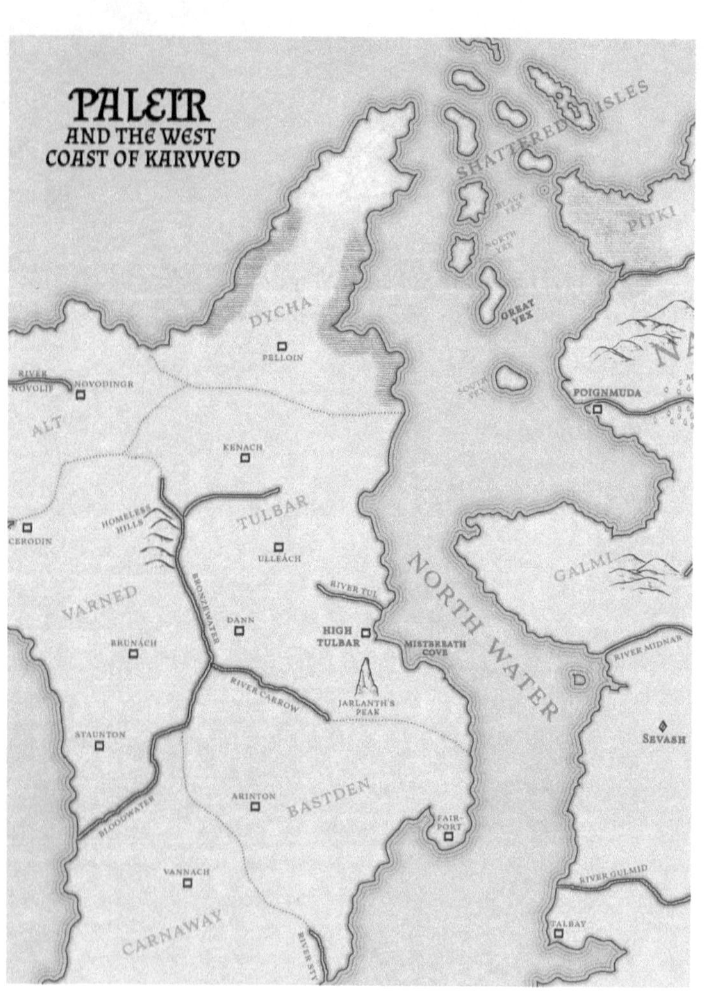

PALEIR
AND THE WEST
COAST OF KARVVED
SHATTERED ISLES
PITKI
EAST YEX
NORTH YEX
GREAT YEX
SOUTH YEX
DYCHA
PELLOIN
POIGNMUDA
RIVER NOVOLIF
NOVODINGR
ALT
KENACH
CERODIN
HOMELESS HILLS
TULBAR
ULLEACH
GALMI
VARNED
RIVER TUL
BRONZIWATER
DANN
HIGH TULBAR
MISTBREATH COVE
BRUNACH
NORTH WATER
RIVER MIDNAR
RIVER CARROW
JARLANTH'S PEAK
STAUNTON
SEVASH
ARINTON
BASTDEN
BLOODWATER
FAIR-PORT
VANNACH
RIVER GULMID
CARNAWAY
TALBAY
RIVER STY

CHAPTER 1

The slain rose from the battlefield, with vacant eyes and dead flesh scarred by dragon breath. They journeyed in their hundreds, with saltwater dripping from their hair and still bearing the wounds that killed them, teeming over the shores of Midding like a pestilence. For each man we had slain, we had lent strength to the necromancer's army of the undead.

A nightmare to stir a man from even the deepest slumber, and yet it pales in comparison to the dream of death that woke me. A song of seawater and dragons, her voice as sweet as honey. The flash of a blade and blood on the stairs. I like to believe the years have numbed my heart to the loss, but when I wake in the chill of the night the guilt still has the power to overwhelm me.

As the first light of dawn creeps through my window, I find myself once more in my study, laying ink to parchment in the hope that this act may bring some measure of peace. I began this account as a record of my travels with Locan A'Shadow, but this is as much my tale as it is his. A tale of youthful innocence grown old before its time. Of lost love and false friends. Of dragons and death.

When last I wrote, it was autumn on the edge of winter in the second year after the Abomination King's fall. My brother Javvian was dead, the final victim of the vampyre Solis Deadhand. My father had disowned me, and having fled my comfortable existence as a prince of the Harkken dynasty to seek adventure, I was left to forge my own path in the world. There would be no going back.

With my brother's blood still fresh on my hands and the grief still raw in my heart, I took a ship south, headed for the distant city of Rameon with the assassin Locan A'Shadow. I could, if I chose, tell you of how the unforgiving weather trapped us in the north for the winter, but I find my memory rushes ahead to the first dawn of the new spring, when our peaceful season at the court of King Wexl of the Shattered Isles was broken by me fleeing for my life.

I raced from the long hall with King Wexl's warriors at my heels. Fierce men with wiry strength, garbed in heavy furs, with braids in their hair and eyes rimmed with paint of a fierce, coppery red. Only the day before, I had been glad to call them my friends and sparring partners, but there was no camaraderie in the war cries that burst from their lips; to avenge the honour of their lord only my blood would serve.

If I could reach Morvolt, my horse, there was some chance I could reach the safety of the *Red Fiend* before the men of Great Yex could overwhelm me. They might take me alive, but the evidence of how the otherwise affable King Wexl treated those who wronged him was blazoned through his hall, the flayed skins of upstart lords turned to grisly banners that flapped from the high beams.

Fear lent speed to my feet. I charged outside, only for a strong arm to seize me around the neck before the hall's high double doors slammed shut behind me, followed moments later by the beating of angry fists against the inside.

I knew a moment of panic before my assailant spun me

round, and the twinkling blue eyes of Huretio Palomino met mine. The flamboyant captain of the *Red Fiend* looked as out of place in the ice-dappled landscape of Great Yex as a peacock among sparrows. His fingers dripped with jewelled rings, a heavy medallion shone amidst the thornbush of dark chest hair that blossomed from his shirt, and his purple tricorn hat was among the most absurd garments I had ever laid eyes on. He had been in the frigid climes of the north for the best part of half a year, but the grey weather had done nothing to diminish the bronze of his skin, earnt from half a lifetime spent at sea evading imperial patrols and customs agents.

'We are leaving then, Master Cetrik?' Even in the low light of dawn, Huretio's grin glittered with knowing amusement.

I offered him a weak smile in return. 'King Wexl does not seem in the mood to listen to reason.'

Behind him, five crewmen of the *Red Fiend* were battling with the doors to hold the horde of Wexl's warriors at bay. The *Red Fiend*'s diminutive second mate, the unfortunately named Pisspot, shoved a pair of swords through the handles, holding it in place while the natives of Great Yex continued to shake the wood with their fists and scream promises of what they would do to me.

'That won't hold them long,' shouted Pisspot, as Huretio shoved me towards the forest path leading to the jetty half-a-mile away where the *Red Fiend*'s dinghy was berthed. The *Red Fiend*'s second mate was three fingers short of five feet, but what he lacked in height he more than made up for in pugnacity. 'What in the Underrealm did you do?'

'It seems that young Cetrik has been dropping his anchor in the warm waters of Wexl's daughter,' said Huretio, urging me to a run. Behind us, fists continued to rattle the door to the long hall, threatening to dislodge the pair of swords. The settlement was waking, women rising to gather water from the river as men staggered bleary-eyed from the undergrowth where they had passed out in the early hours after yet another night of feasting and carousing to mark the Ostara, the coming of spring. We drew strange looks as we hurried away, but apparently nobody was loyal enough to King Wexl to get in the way of seven armed men. 'Our esteemed host was three sheets to the wind, so much so that he apparently did not realise I was at his table when the servant came to whisper in his ear. It is lucky I was there, else we would have been breaking our fast on your cock and balls.'

That at least explained why Huretio and his crew had been ready for my escape. 'I didn't touch her!' I protested. 'That's what I was trying to tell them.'

It was the truth. I had felt Spindle's dancing emerald eyes on me almost from the moment we had set foot on Great Yex. I had convinced myself I must be imagining it, until the regularity with which Spindle found reasons to touch my arm or to take the place of a servant to pour my ale became too much to ignore.

However, I had never held any intention of acting on this – Spindle was as wild and beautiful as mountain heather, but King Wexl had welcomed us into his hall and gone above and beyond the duties of a host. As tempting as Spindle's overtures were, I had resolved that under no circumstances would I disrespect his generosity. My adventure in Narlond had been marred by my unrequited affection for Urlissa, the beautiful elfling sorceress of the Bucani tribe, and I had no intention of allowing my amorous feelings to lead me astray again.

Wexl knew the legend of Locan A'Shadow, and after hearing how we had defeated the vampyre Solis Deadhand, he had insisted that we spend the cold season at his court. A jovial, genial man on the cusp of old age, quick to laugh and with every night a different tale to tell. Even that the settlement of Poignmuda, Wexl's foothold in Narlond, had been claimed by my father did not seem to trouble him: 'The southern man may sow the north by spring, but come winter there will be naught for him to reap,' he told us. The army of Guiland would head south, and when the weather turned, Wexl would claim the spoils.

Every evening had been spent in the warmth of Wexl's hall, feasting on gull eggs and buttered pike, all generously garnished with seaweed, and every day I had trained with his men until I was in the finest shape of my young life, still lean as a spear but now muscled, hardened by the cold and the sparing food of the islanders.

As it turned out, my unwillingness to sully our host's hospitality had made no difference. My polite but increasingly desperate refusals of Spindle had led to an angry red handprint on my cheek and her leaving my chamber in a black mood. Presumably, she had not troubled to correct the misapprehension of the servant who had seen her leaving. With the benefit of hindsight, I would have been better off succumbing to temptation and allowing her to stay in my room.

Spindle had reached me with the news that her father had ordered my death mere minutes before Wexl's warriors arrived at my door. I delayed long enough only to strap my sword belt on and lay a passionate, longing kiss on her mouth. If I was to be executed for a crime, I wished at least to be moderately guilty of it.

The tall pines of Great Yex stared down at me in silent judgement for my folly as we hastened towards the water. Where the path split, I slowed my pace and said to Huretio, 'I need to fetch Morvolt.' My loyal if belligerent steed had a temper as black as his hide and as fiery as the mane of red hair that ran down his back. He had caused such skittishness among Wexl's small stable of stout, shaggy ponies that I had been forced to leave him in a meadow deep in the forest. Against the cold, his coat had thickened until it resembled the woolly fleece of a sheep.

'I already sent Ed and Han to fetch your black beast,' said

Huretio, refusing to break stride and shoving me in the back to force me onwards. 'I knew you would not leave without him.'

Relieved, I quickened my pace. Despite a long night of drinking and feasting, the *Red Fiend*'s crew were likely fit enough to outpace a coterie of Yexan warriors ladened with shields and heavy axes. Huretio was at least two decades my senior with a stomach that was ever threatening to burst the buttons of his shirt, but he showed no signs of slowing. Even Pisspot was keeping pace, his stout legs moving like the skittering paws of a mouse.

I found myself admiring the captain's shrewdness. Edlin Eight-Fingers was a fine hand with animals, and Hanrik Denseneck was a towering, taciturn Ilssian, perhaps the only crewman strong enough to handle Morvolt if he was in one of his black moods.

How we would get Morvolt back aboard the *Fiend* was a matter that would have to wait. It had taken half a pound of dreamshade stirred into his food to get him drowsy enough that he would allow himself to be rowed from the ship to Great Yex. Something to be worked out once we reached the jetty.

'What about Locan?' I asked.

'He said to meet him at the water,' replied Huretio, not breaking stride. 'He had a full cup of whisky when I left him.'

I felt a flash of annoyance. I had been moments from a violent death at the hands of Wexl's warriors, and Locan A'Shadow, the man who had once been my hero, had been more concerned with staring into the swirling vortex of his whisky than turning his talents to saving me. I ought not to have been surprised. As was Locan's wont, he had spent his days on Great Yex drinking. He had emerged from the long hall only occasionally to watch me spar against the Yexans and offer what he considered to be helpful instructions, but which were mostly caustic insults aimed at my skill, courage, and manhood. Wexl was a great drinker himself, a corpulent bear of a man, and the quantities of ale, ice wine, and whisky they had consumed together were no less than heroic. It stood to reason that Locan would be more concerned with finishing his drink than coming to my aid. When I had last seen him, he had been engaged in a contest with men of the Odingr, hard-bitten reavers from the far north who were also being hosted by Wexl before they headed south for the raiding season. Locan would heed his conscience only under protest when it was screaming bloody murder in his ear.

I felt a breath of air on my neck as something thrummed past me, and an arrow fletched with grey goose feathers embedded itself in the trunk of a nearby pine. My head whipped round in alarm, and just as the path curved, I caught a glimpse of a dozen Yexan warriors in hot pursuit, axes slicing through the air as they galloped after us, the sight of their quarry drawing an extra burst of speed from their legs.

Huretio gave a cry. 'Last man to the dinghy shares their hammock with Hanrik for the next fortnight!'

'Fucking run, you mongrel sons of whores!' crowed Pisspot.

Lungs burning, I quickened my pace, loosening my sword in my scabbard as I ran in case we were forced to turn and fight, relieved that I had paused to claim it before I fled. We burst from the cover of the trees, and the full breadth of the North Water spread out before us. The crimson hull of the *Red Fiend* waited only a few hundred metres offshore, a beacon of salvation amidst the roiling grey sea, the crew running from bow to stern like eager ants as they prepared for our departure.

Hanrik and Edlin were pacing nervously along the jetty, but at the sight of us emerging from the forest, they leapt into the waiting rowboat and claimed the oars.

However, there was no sign of my horse.

In my dismay, I stumbled over the boards of the jetty and nearly lost my footing. 'Where's Morvolt?' I shouted to Huretio.

'Look again, my friend!' With sweat streaming down his

brow, the captain pointed towards the *Red Fiend*. 'Your horse is cleverer than both my brothers!'

I did as Huretio suggested, and saw a black shape bobbing towards the *Fiend*. Morvolt, swimming frantically for the ship, where crewmen were already lowering a net into the water to haul him aboard. Given the close confines of the dinghy – it would have been impossible to fit all nine of us and a horse aboard – Morvolt's decision to take his chances with the icy chill of the North Water had likely been the wisest course.

Together, we leapt into the rowboat, landing in a tangle of limbs that set the small boat bobbing in the water while Hanrik and Edlin cursed and sought to row us away from the jetty. Huretio sliced through the mooring rope with his sword and kicked us away from shore just as the Yexans reached the jetty, shaking their axes in their fists in fury as the pirates waved and hooted.

'My dear friends, please give my thanks to your King Wexl!' cried Huretio, waving his absurd hat in farewell. 'And also to his daughter, Spindle, for Wexl's generosity is exceeded only by hers!'

These words were followed by a further round of guffawing from the sailors, and Pisspot even dropped his trousers to wave his manhood towards the Yexans as they stood impotently on the jetty. I did not join them – I had enough fondness for Spindle that Huretio's jest did not please me.

'Any sign of Locan?' I asked Edlin.

The sailor shook his head. 'None.'

That was troubling. I looked back towards the jetty, scanning the forest as if at any moment Locan might burst from the trees. As matters stood, he would be trapped on Great Yex; there was little prospect of Huretio going back for him now.

'Take over, would you?' said Edlin, holding the oar out towards me. 'Ain't easy rowing with only eight fingers.'

Edlin played the fiddle as well as any court-trained musician – his missing fingers seemed to trouble him only whenever there was a task he did not feel like doing. Nevertheless, I claimed the oar and sat down on the bench.

That decision may have very well saved my life. Another arrow whizzed past where my head had been a moment earlier, landing in the churning water. Just because we had left the solid ground of Great Yex did not mean that our pursuers were prepared to let us go free. I immediately put my whole back into the oar, struggling to match the strength and ferocity of Hanrik's strokes.

'These northern bastards don't give up easily,' said Pisspot, moving to place himself behind the bulk of Black Gil, a muscled sailor whose shaved head was fully tattooed in the fashion of the Narlish tribes. 'Make yourself small, lads.'

'Easier for some than others,' said Huretio. He was watching the jetty, and I heard his intake of breath as he realised the lengths to which the Yexans would go to see we did not escape the island.

The archer had flung his bow over his shoulder and was now striking a piece of flint against his knife, aiming to set light to a cloth shoved into the neck of a bottle of whisky.

'Oh, shite,' breathed Huretio. In the sea breeze, they were struggling to get the cloth to catch a spark, but once they did they would be able to launch a flaming projectile that, if it caught us, might send the whole vessel up in flames.

'Put your bloody back into it!' Pisspot yelled in my ear. 'Unless you want to end up a charred corpse in the belly of a razorsquid!'

There were stronger rowers aboard, but there was no time to change over, so I threw myself into every pull of the oar, looking back every five strokes in the hope that the silhouette of the *Fiend* would grow larger.

We were a hundred or so yards offshore when at last the Yexans sparked a strong enough flame to set their makeshift wick alight.

'None of them have a hope of throwing it that far,' said Huretio.

But the Yexans did not waste their new weapon so easily. The archer tied a rag to the shaft of an arrow close to the tip, then laid the projectile against his bow. He dipped its point to the bottle, and a lick of flame caught the fabric. The man leant back, aimed, and sent a flaming missile flying straight for us.

The arrow fell into the water ten yards short of our boat. Its blaze went out with a hiss, but there followed no cries of mockery from the sailors, only a pale, wide-eyed worry that it would not take long for the bowman to find his range. Already, the Yexan was repeating the process with another arrow.

'Move.' Black Gil grabbed me under the armpits and shunted me out of the way to claim the oar, quickening our pace as on the other side Hanrik rowed for all he was worth.

The archer pulled his bowstring back. 'Hanrik,' said Huretio, 'when he launches, still your oar for two strokes.'

The bowstring snapped, and a second fire arrow arced across the sky towards us like a red-tailed shooting star. Hanrik followed Huretio's command, altering the dinghy's course by a couple of degrees before falling back into sync with Black Gil.

The arrow plopped into the water with a hiss two feet to our starboard side, right where we would have been if not for Huretio's evasive action.

The captain gave a bellowing laugh of triumph. 'Great work, boys!' He removed his hat and waved it jovially towards the scowling Yexans on the shore. 'Same again! But this time, Gil, you pause for three strokes.'

But the Yexans did not seem in the mood to entertain Huretio's trickery. Before the archer had even released his arrow, three more men had removed shortbows from their backs and strung them while the others prepared several more fire arrows. They worked quickly, and soon no fewer than four men had their bows ready and aimed for our small watercraft.

Huretio paled. 'They're too far,' he said, but then with a look towards the *Red Fiend* added, 'If the boat goes down, we will swim.'

The Yexans though seemed prepared for this. Several men had claimed a second dinghy from the other side of the jetty, which was now swinging around the end of the wharf. They had no hope of catching us, unless we were forced to swim. Then they could pick us off one by one from close range. I looked back – the *Red Fiend* barely seemed to be getting any larger.

The archers were leaning back towards the sky, their bowstrings drawn back as far as they would go. If they missed, we were free. If even one of them hit, we would be easy prey in the icy water.

Just as I was sure they were about to release, a knife sent a spray of blood fountaining from the side of an archer's neck, sending his arrow skittering harmlessly off his bow and into the air. The man nearest him turned, and a second blade sprouted from his eye, sending him tumbling into the surf.

A figure stood at the other end of the jetty. He was so lean he was almost frail, as if his sallow flesh had found something objectionable about his bones and melted away. A small, mean mouth was fixed in a sneer, beneath a hooked nose with cavernous nostrils, a pair of eyes so flinty and dark that they seemed to rob the light from his surroundings, and a mess of greasy hair black as raven wing. He was short and appeared some way into his fifth decade, nobody's idea of a fighting man, but he strode down the jetty with the easy prowl of a tiger, clever hands already reaching into the folds of his cloak for more blades, each of them whetted to the keenest edge and tipped with a promise of death.

Locan A'Shadow. An assassin whose legend had traversed more than half the known world. A man, it was said, who had only two friends – sharp blades and hard spirits – although sometimes I wondered if I might count myself a third. At the very least, much like Morvolt, he tolerated me.

Two Yexans raced down the boardwalk towards him with their axes raised. A feint, a side-step, and a flash of a knife later, both men slipped from the jetty face down into the water. The two remaining archers turned their bows towards this new arrival, their flaming arrows casting another man's silhouette to Locan's feet, and in the breath of a blink the assassin slipped away in a flicker of molten darkness, reappearing at the back of two axemen and drawing a blade across their throats as the arrows flew harmlessly past where Locan had stood a moment before.

Of the men who had pursued us, only the two archers remained, their hands frozen on their bows. Locan had killed six men quicker than it would have taken them to give him their names.

His mouth curled in a sneer, and on the wind, I caught a single contemptuous word spill from his lips. 'Run.'

The two surviving Yexans did as he suggested, throwing down their bows and sprinting for the forest as if demons dogged their steps.

Locan shrugged his blades back into the folds of his cloak. Our oars had stilled, every man of Huretio's crew spellbound by events on the shore. When he needed to, Locan's magic allowed him to slip into shadows, but when he stood as flesh and blood his presence was magnetic, a scowling, simmering oddity that even the wind seemed to fall silent to stare at.

The bottle the Yexans had used to light their arrows still stood on the jetty. Locan pulled the flaming rag from its neck and cast it aside, then tipped it back and drained the contents down his neck.

'Are we going back for him?' asked Edlin.

Locan looked at the bottle, then at the still-burning rag. He reclaimed the piece of cloth and shoved it back into the bottle's neck.

'What is that lunatic doing?' murmured Huretio.

Locan hefted the bottle, measured the distance, and hurled it out to sea as hard as he could towards our boat, drawing gasps of fear from the sailors.

No sooner had the bottle left his fingers, Locan disappeared in a swirl of darkness.

I cannot claim to have ever fully comprehended his magic, but as best as I understand, if Locan could touch a shadow he could disappear into it, then reappear in any place connected to his original position by an unbroken chain of darkness. Locan claimed it worked best with crisp, dark shapes cast by bright sunlight, but I had seen it work in firelight and weak daylight as well. I had travelled with him this way only once, by mistake, and I was not in a hurry to repeat the experience.

The bottle arced over the water. I could not see the shadow its flaming tongue cast against the waves, but it was enough for Locan. Such was the strength in Locan's arm, it landed only ten feet short of our vessel, and Locan reappeared in a billow of shadow, spluttering and furiously waving his arms as he trod water.

'Back!' shouted Huretio. The two rowers reversed their oars and propelled us back towards a thrashing Locan.

Together, Huretio and I seized him by his waterlogged cloak and hauled him into the boat. We landed in a heap.

'Locan!' said Huretio, greeting him as jovially as if they had just come across one another by chance in a favourite tavern. 'Are you trying to get us killed? That bottle could have sunk us!'

'If I wanted to hit you, I would have,' growled Locan,

turning to spit a mouthful of saltwater back into the sea. 'Some thanks I get for saving your sorry arses. You could have told me you were leaving. Had to get through a whole tribe of Odingr berserkers to get out of the hall. If they hadn't been so drunk they could hardly see, I might have been in trouble.'

I doubted that. Locan could have fought his way through several score of common warriors without getting a mark on him.

'You seemed more interested in the contents of Wexl's whisky store than in the fate of our young friend here,' said Huretio, slapping his palm down on my shoulder as we hastened to untangle ourselves and sit back down on our bench. 'You are a most resourceful man – I placed my trust in your powers of survival.'

'Good whisky here. I won't taste the like of that again,' said Locan, coughing up another dribble of seawater, then putting his thumb against each nostril in turn to clear the contents of his nose. His black eyes found me with a gaze that was somewhere between fury and admiration. 'Heard you were caught tupping Wexl's daughter. Took your bloody time. Got tired of seeing you staring at each other like your nether regions were made of sugar. Maybe think about locking the goblin-fucking door next time.'

'I didn't—' I closed my eyes and sighed. There was no point correcting him. The details of mine and Spindle's courtship would be of no concern to Locan. 'A servant caught her leaving my chamber.'

'Throw her out the window next time. Arse that size, the girl would bounce.' Locan swept his cloak from his shoulders then began wringing the water over the sides. 'At least you waited till spring – I'll give you some credit for that.' He looked to Huretio with a knowing glint in his gaze. 'Where are we headed, Captain?'

Huretio's eyes twinkled. He swept his tricorn hat back onto

his head. The rowers had resumed, and the high, crimson shadow of the *Red Fiend* rose up at our bow. 'To where there is a willing woman in every window and the river runs black with sweet rum. To Rameon, my friend. We will set our course for Rameon.'

CHAPTER 2

'You planning to apologise ever?' came Locan's voice from behind me. 'Might have stayed on Yex until summer if you'd been able to keep it in your breeches.'

I was at the port rail, staring out at the Dreadveil, a fiery, dark miasma of eldritch magic that shrouded the west coast of Midding and much of the North Water.

Midding had once been the most fertile of all the three Karvved kingdoms, ruled wisely from the city of Brightwater by my family's vassals, the lords Mancellin. Until the rise of the Abomination King. Four hundred years earlier, Brightwater had fallen to become the dark tower of Sevash, where he had forged the darkness of the Dreadveil. Even now, almost three years after the Abomination King's death, it still lingered. It was wise not to stare too long; it was said that the wraiths that had risen in its hazy depths upon the demise of their master would beckon you to your doom. To avoid getting too close, our course was shadowing the east coast of the island of Paleir.

'I thought you'd be glad to be on our way to Rameon,' I replied. Locan had never made entirely clear why he wished to return to the city he had once called home. Once he had been a favoured blade of Rameon's emperor. Now he was an exile, like me, and depressingly perhaps the closest thing to family I had in the world. I could tell he was grumpy from a lack of drink – in our hasty exit, there had been no opportunity to take on supplies, and Huretio had granted Locan only the same rum ration as his crew – and my childish inclination was to bait him rather than to appease him. 'Isn't heading south what you wanted?'

'Once I was good and ready.' Locan joined me at the rail, scowling. 'I didn't mean for us to run like thieves in the night just because you helped yourself to Wexl's daughter.'

I shook my head. It had been only a matter of days since our departure, but already I was weary of making denials which nobody seemed minded to believe. I pushed myself away from the rail to cross the deck to the starboard side. Locan followed me, as I had known he would.

Even shrouded in mist, the shore of Paleir was close enough to be visible, a craggy coastline of high headlands and unwelcoming beaches of stone and shingle. The lesser neighbour of Karvved was a quarrelling patchwork of petty kingdoms, at any time anywhere between four and eight warlords fighting over its rolling hills and mud-dappled rivers. A land of wild men and wilder magic. It was said that Halagrim the Deathmistress, the most frightening of the Abomination King's acolytes, had hailed from Paleir.

The island's northern provinces had been divided from Guiland by the Dreadveil for centuries. The last direct contact between my country and the four northmost kingdoms had been when the Mórs of Tulbar still ruled as High Kings of Paleir, their alliance with the sea dragons granting them mastery over land and water and sky.

Occasionally in my childhood, one petty king or another

from southern Paleir had stopped warring long enough to arrive in Keystone, claiming some distant kinship and begging my mother for the men to make the whole land his own. Big, fierce men, and ever disappointed when my mother refused them.

Tales of their brethren in the northern kingdoms were as rare as they were uncertain, but all seemed to agree on one thing: even in the wild lands of Paleir, the dragons were long gone, and the island's unity had fallen with them.

'Not a place you want to be landing,' said Locan. 'No matter how low Huretio's supplies are running. You could wade through the deepest sympathies of a Palishman and not get your ankles wet.'

'You've been there?' I asked, slightly envious. Travel, even to Guiland's closest neighbouring lands, had been denied to me by my parents.

'Killed the Mór of Carnaway some fifteen years back. Emperor Vurash's cousin had to buy his granddaughter back from the slave market there, and Vurash liked the man enough to take revenge.' Locan's lip curled in a sneer. 'That's the Palish for you. They'd make a slave of you soon as look at you.'

Of Paleir's fondness for slavery he was not lying. The dragons might be dead, but the island's thirst for human flesh was not. Every year, the Odingr of the deep north sailed from their frozen lands down the western coast of Paleir to raid as far south as Ceretis and as far east as Ilssia. Most of those they captured ended up in the markets of Carnaway and Varned to be sold back to their families, if they were lucky.

'Let me tell you about the Palish,' said Locan. 'Your Guilish peasants – they'll bow their heads as you and yours ride past, and if they catch a noble rooting their wife, they'll ask his lordship if he'd like any refreshments. Subservience comes as naturally to them as breathing. The Rameans are different – they'll accept an overlord as long as it suits them, but there's many a patrician who's overestimated the patience of his underlings and gone to an early grave for it.

'The Palish though. They call it the Land of a Hundred Kings for a reason, and it ain't because they've got so many of them. Every Palishman reckons he's a lord, and they'll treat the rest accordingly, like dirt on the bottom of their boot.' Locan snorted and spat violently over the rail. 'That's for Paleir. I'll break no bread with slavers.'

Occasionally, Locan still had the power to surprise me. His morality was an edifice built on shifting sand – you could never be sure whether he would regard a thing as agreeable or abhorrent. I had never met a slave – slavery was still legal across much of the known world, but not in Guiland.

'What do you suppose waits for us in Rameon?' I asked, eager to focus on the path ahead. Paleir was too close to Guiland for my taste, and I knew Locan would divulge no more of his contempt for slavery without several drinks in him.

Locan shrugged. 'Well, there'll be nobody putting out the bunting for my return, but I still have a few friends in the city.' His face flickered uncertainly. 'Close to friends anyway. If little Vurash still wants me, he can come and find me. Better than waiting up here to die.'

Locan had been great friends with the former emperor, Vurash IV, or at least something close to friends, but his son and heir, Vurash V, was an old rival, and his ascent had forced Locan to flee the Dominion.

'It might be spring, but it's still pissing cold,' grumbled Locan, pulling his cloak tighter around himself against the sea's frigid salt breeze. 'No one's happier than me that you finally got your pecker wet – might freeze and fall off in this weather – but did it have to be Wexl's goblin-pissing daughter?'

I had liked the brash, affable Wexl. It troubled me that he might spend the rest of his life thinking I had betrayed his hospitality. I had liked Spindle too, but not enough that I would risk bringing dishonour on us both. There had been none of the mad, sleepless lust I had felt for Urlissa, perhaps because the bruise the elfling woman had left on my heart had still not faded. Locan though was the last person I could share that with.

When I did not reply, Locan gave a creaking bark of laughter. 'Keep your secrets then.' He clapped me on the shoulder and turned to leave. 'I'm going to find a pirate who's up for gambling his rum ration.'

I could have offered him mine. My evenings were usually spent with Pisspot, the second mate, named, I had discovered, for a night in his youth when he had been drunk enough to imbibe the contents of a chamber pot and the next day sworn off liquor for the rest of his life. Usually we played Pillars, a complex game of circular tiles on a square board at which Pisspot was something of a master. I was determined to beat him, and I stood a better chance of doing that if I remained sober.

But, if I'd given my ration to Locan, he would have stayed, and I needed to be alone. I enjoyed Locan's company – sour, crass, and drunken as he was – but sometimes a man must keep his own counsel. The melancholy of the grey, chopping waves and the moist mist that soaked the horizon made the deck of the *Red Fiend* as good a place as any for a man to contemplate his life and the direction it was taking him.

I had left Guiland in search of adventure, and in that I had more than achieved my goal. Few men can say they have fought a wrorc, lived among the Bucani tribe, and been pursued by a bodmin and lived to tell the tale. Fewer still can name themselves vampyre-slayer. But there had been a price – the life of my brother, Javvian. Dead on a nameless Narlish hill. We had reconciled our childish quarrels, but with his death the chance for me to truly know him was lost. Now, for as long as my father lived, my homeland was closed to me.

On my departure, I had imagined I might never return, but rarely does the truth of a thing live up to the imagining. I was not an adventurer. I was an exile, condemned by family and roundly cursed by my countrymen. Even now, the tale of my hubris would be spreading through the inns and markets of my homeland, my name a byword for disgrace.

The deck swayed under my feet, the coast of Paleir rising and falling with the swell of the waves. With Locan's condemnation of slavery still burning in my ears, I might have returned to the port side, but the funereal haze of the Abomination King that still hung over Midding was all the more unsettling for being a reminder of how I had come to reach Narlond, and all I had left behind.

Where did I belong if not in Guiland? Narlond had given me no answers. My path did not have to follow Locan's. He may not wish to set foot on Paleir, but that was not to say that I could not. I was no master swordsman, but I was skilled enough with a blade to find employment among any of the divided nation's warring petty kings. If I survived long enough, I might make enough of a name for myself, and my father's anger might cool sufficiently that I could return to Guiland, in honour rather than disgrace.

After a time, I heard footsteps behind me. The evening sun that hung beyond the mist over the outline of Paleir blinded me, so I felt rather than saw the presence of Huretio. He came to stand beside me, the jewellery that adorned his neck and fingers glinting in the late sunlight, his wide-brimmed hat almost blotting the light from my eyes.

'I shall have to bar my crew from gambling against our friend,' he said by way of an opening gambit, his eyes twinkling. 'He has secured himself three additional rum rations for this evening.'

'Perhaps you should just give him what he needs,' I replied, keeping my face to the horizon. I had long tired of trying to understand or moderate Locan's ceaseless drinking.

'Better that he has to work for it, else there will be none left by the time we reach Rameon and he will end up killing half my crew.' Huretio placed a hand on my shoulder, the same place Locan had as he departed. 'You are sure you wish to come with us?'

I shrugged. 'There is nowhere else for me to go.'

Huretio gave a hearty laugh. 'My young friend, there is a whole world for you to go! Is Locan's company so dear to you? Did you not cross Midding with no more than your horse and your wits for company? I have seen far more of this world than Locan – the wonders that a young man such as yourself might behold are beyond counting: Rintland, where they serve the wine fresh from the grape, so honeyed that it will sing upon your tongue, sweeter than any fare to be found in Rameon; the Red Water, where the waves climb so high they could drown the city's golden walls; Ilssia, where in summer the sun never sets, and all the lands east of there, where no wind has yet blown me.'

I looked into Huretio's craggy, tanned features with a knowing smile. 'You are lying.'

The captain's grin glittered with devilment. 'And you are learning. Yes, there is nowhere like Rameon, nowhere more beautiful nor more dangerous.' His smile fell slightly. 'At least, nowhere more dangerous for Locan A'Shadow, and therefore, if you go with him, for you.' He shrugged. 'If your mind is made up, I will say no more. But you need only say the word and we will divert our course to Keystone and you may fall at your father's feet and swear your undying obedience.'

'It is too late for that,' I muttered, turning away to face the water. Even if this had not been so, I would face every threat Rameon had to offer before I would prostrate myself before my father. I would never return to Keystone as long as he lived.

Huretio shrugged. 'So be it.' He brought his fist down on the rail as if this settled the matter. 'It is not wise, but I respect you for it. I know about fathers. The last time I saw mine, it was only my mother that stopped me laying the old man out.'

It was odd to think of Huretio having parents, and only slightly stranger that he might care what his mother thought of him. He strutted about the deck of the *Red Fiend* as if he had emerged into the world fully formed with an eyeglass in one hand and a ship's wheel in the other. 'Because you didn't want to upset her?'

'No, she punched me. No man I've ever met hits as hard as Jevana Palomino, Seamstress protect her.' Huretio made the sign of the needle, tapping his chest twice and then his forehead. 'I woke up in the physician's house having the three teeth she knocked out glued back in.'

When Huretio's mouth did not crack a grin, I realised he was serious.

'What was Locan like in Rameon?' I asked. I had never heard any tales of him from someone who knew him, and there had never seemed a good time to ask Huretio on Great Yex.

The captain gave a wry smile. 'I tell you of my mother, and still you care only for Locan A'Shadow.' He shook his head in mock disappointment. 'The young Locan... Rarely have I met a man so full of his own brilliance. The new emperor did only what the men of Rameon had been dreaming of for years. Even then, he drank as if he believed the barrel would run dry the next day. It made him fearless, which he could afford to be. The Locan I knew then would carve apart the Locan of Narlond like a butcher preparing meat.' Huretio gave a wistful shake of his head. 'Young men... they live on wine, women, and song. I fear that our friend Locan never grew out of that. He has all the cynicism of an old man and none of the sense. The wine that once made him fearless makes him slow, and in Rameon a man like him cannot afford to be slow. And when they come for him, they will take you as well.'

I held my silence, listening to the waves and the clatter of the rigging and the furious commands of Stye-eyed Shiv, the first mate. Even before my adventure in Narlond, I hope I would not have been so naïve as to take Huretio's words at face value. As much as I liked him, the pirate was the sort of man who would steal your purse, pilfer its contents, then return it and claim a finder's fee. While Huretio knew that I had fled a quarrel with my father, it was to my fortune that Locan had not divulged to him that I was a Harkken, a son of Queen Trelaina of Guiland.

Locan was not slow. Only days earlier, he had killed six men to save our rowboat from sinking. I had seen him kill wrorcs, cytrolls, and most importantly of all, Solis Deadhand.

'You are not listening.' The pirate captain let out a regretful sigh. 'I have no more to say. But you would be wise not to place too much faith in Locan A'Shadow. How many times in Narlond did he betray you?'

That was a matter for debate. He had thrown me to a group of bandits, but only with a view to saving the children they had stolen. Later, his hubris had set a vengeful, flesh-eating spirit known as a bodmin on my tail. He had tried to kidnap me in Poignmuda. Finally, he had surrendered me to my father and fled.

Huretio was smiling. 'Enough times that you have to count is too many.'

'He saved my life as well,' I replied. 'Several times.' Not least when he had returned to slay the vampyre Solis Deadhand when all had seemed lost.

'And on how many of those occasions was it Locan who led you into danger in the first place?' Huretio raised an eyebrow. 'You are too trusting, Cetrik Harkken.'

My whole body stiffened. How had Huretio learnt my

name? Slowly, I slid my right hand closer to the dagger sheathed in my belt.

Huretio merely chuckled. 'You are suspicious though. That is good. Suspicion will serve you well in Rameon. The city is a den of vipers. Half would steal your purse, and the other half would kill you and take it from your corpse. Know that your birth means nothing to me – as a ransom you would not be worth the trouble, to me at least.'

I relaxed slightly.

Huretio was shaking his head. 'You cannot know, Cetrik, the coin I would pay to be your age again. Youth...' He let out a regretful sigh. 'You do not understand, but you will, if you live long enough. Nineteen summers old, a vampyre-slayer, and pretty as a summer rose. The world is yours to claim, Cetrik. The girls in Rameon will be scaling the walls just to share a smile with you. It is to our fortune that none of my crew have thought to try and share your bunk.'

The image Huretio conjured killed the blush that had been rising on my cheeks. Some of his crew were terrifying – men like Hanrik Denseneck whose cold black eyes seemed to follow me across the deck. I said a quick prayer to the Seamstress and the Swordsman, the twin deities who had saved humanity from the rule of Dagin, Lord of the Underrealm, that I would never have to fight any of them.

'What is it you want, Huretio?' I asked. 'Are you here to scare me or just to blow smoke up my arse?'

Huretio laughed with gusto enough to show two rows of perfect pearly white teeth. 'You may feel like you need Locan, but you should know that he needs you far more than you need him. He may pretend he does not care, but it suits him to have you hanging on every filthy word that falls from his mouth. And do not trust him. Ever.'

I was about to tell Huretio that I knew Locan's nature well

enough, but a shout from the crow's nest forced the words back down my throat. 'Captain!'

Huretio and I looked up at the sailor shadowed against the sky pointing towards the stern. 'Storm! Looks like a big one!'

We turned. The still evening had promised a calm night ahead, but to the north, the sky was darkening. Storm clouds rolled over the slate-grey sea, driven by an ill wind, and a flash of purple lightning was followed several seconds later by a crack of thunder.

CHAPTER 3

The storm hurtled out of the north like a wayward spirit rushing free of the Underrealm. It howled and thundered, strafing the *Red Fiend* with heavy hail and setting the North Water churning. There is little that will remind a man of his own mortality so well as his first great storm at sea, when for the first time you learn that the fickleness of the gods will kill you just as surely as the cold blade of a mortal.

Below decks, Locan and I huddled within our cabin. I lay in my hammock, feeling every roll of the waves and listening to the shouts from above. Every crewman had been summoned to help keep the ship on course. The *Red Fiend* ran a narrow path, with the Abomination King's lingering death haze to port and the coastal reefs of Paleir with the risk of running ourselves aground to starboard. Over the commotion, I could still hear Huretio shouting himself hoarse, so loud it was as if he meant to drown out the storm.

Inside his own hammock, Locan clutched a pilfered rum bottle. He had sworn he would not die sober, and so had stolen the liquor from Huretio's private stores. An abandoned Pillars board lay on the floor between us. Locan had lost interest and, in any event, with the motion of the ship, it was near impossible to keep the pieces where they ought to be.

'We should get some sleep,' I said, eyeing the lamp that swung from the ceiling. The storm had fallen upon us some hours ago, and it was now deepest night.

Locan hacked up a laugh. 'You're welcome to try. I give it five minutes before this storm throws you out of bed.'

A wave struck our portside like a thunderclap and bounced me so high that my head nearly struck the ceiling. From deeper within the *Red Fiend* came a violent neigh of fear and rage. I felt a rush of guilt. Morvolt was secured in a different part of the ship. It spoke to his bravery that he had come aboard at all. After this, I might never get him close to water again.

Thunder cracked, and when the next wave hit I swear the *Red Fiend* was lifted several feet in the air. It was not Morvolt's scream of distress I heard this time, but my own. I realised how tightly I was gripping the edges of my hammock, my knuckles turned bone white.

'Seamstress's teats, grow a pair, would you?' Without warning, Locan tossed me the bottle of rum and I just managed to catch it. 'Get some of that down you.'

I was scared enough to do as he suggested, knocking back an eye-watering glug of sweet, hot liquor. 'Is this normal?' I asked. 'Keystone sits on this coast, and I never saw a storm like this.'

Locan gave a shrug. 'Buggered if I know. But we're stuck between the shit and the stink. Dreadveil to port, rocks and reefs to starboard, storm overhead. I don't envy Huretio.'

In an ordinary storm, Huretio might have battened down the hatches, pulled down the canvas, and turned to face the waves, but the narrowness of our course made this impossible. If there was one thing any sane seafaring man would fear worse than a storm, it was to sail into the Dreadveil. I had survived my crossing of Midding and the attentions of the wraiths only by virtue of my immunity to magic.

'Guess you'd take Paleir over the Dreadveil?' I ventured.

'It won't come to that,' said Locan with a confidence I did not feel myself. 'Pirates like Huretio don't survive without knowing their business. He's spent thirty years dodging the emperor's patrols; if he can't find us a route through this, no one can.'

No one can. Not words you necessarily wish to hear while the floor is rolling up and down and the contents of your stomach are threatening to burst forth. Dodging Dominion patrols did not sound much to me like sailing through a storm. I caressed the hilt of my knife, taking comfort in its cold certainty.

Locan reached over to reclaim the bottle, and I took another swig before allowing him to take it. 'A bit of rain won't hurt us. Not next to what'll happen when we reach Rameon.' He took a long drink from the bottle then shoved the cork in it and rolled over in his hammock. 'I'm going to try and get some shut-eye, for all the good it will do me. Sleeping in this contraption leaves my back like a bent nail.'

I decided I would remain awake. If the waves claimed us, I wanted to be up and ready, not tangled up in my hammock while the water rose to drown us. Mercifully, the storm seemed to be abating, the beat of rain against the hull lessening slightly.

Huretio's warning about following Locan to Rameon had stayed with me. I knew nothing of the city. There were distant cousins I could seek out, but hosting Locan as well as me might be a hard imposition upon their hospitality. Guiltily, I wondered if we might be better to go our separate ways. Huretio had said we needed each other – but what if we only needed each other because together we encountered the sort of luck that had left us as two landsmen braving the fiercest storm that the *Red Fiend*'s crew could recall?

. . .

I was asleep when a violent collision bounced me half out of my hammock, smacking my head so hard against the low ceiling that I saw stars. The deck tilted, and I instinctively clung to my hammock to stop myself being thrown to the floor.

Outside, two claps of thunder sounded directly above us, followed by panicked shouts from the deck overhead. Another wave struck, and I scrambled out of my hammock before I could be tossed out, throwing my legs over and landing barefooted on the listing floor.

'Swear a horde of orcs could be banging on our door and you'd still sleep through it!' Locan bundled something into my hands, a hooded leather cloak, heavy and treated with oil. He had already donned his. I must have been asleep a while, because our lantern was almost out. Somewhere below, Morvolt was screaming, and the sound was like a dagger through my skull.

'I'm going to check on Morvolt,' I told Locan over the din of creaking timbers and the crashing waves. Another thundered into us, and I almost lost my balance.

'Your bloody horse is fine,' shouted Locan. 'Or at least no more scared than I am. I'm going to take a look up top, see if Huretio's got a plan to get us out of this mess.'

Locan raced for the deck, and I followed him – Morvolt would be better served if I could at least see what was going on. As we clambered towards the deck, the *Red Fiend* rolled violently under our feet, sending us careering around corners into walls and tripping us on the stairs.

As we approached the hatch, a sudden rush of wind blew it open with a crash of timber. The sky opened above us, and my breath caught in my throat. The clouds were bruised black and crimson, reflecting the Dreadveil's unnerving glow. The sky flashed, and the ship tilted, nearly knocking me back down the stairs as I scrambled up behind Locan.

Outside the protection of our cabin, the storm was worse than we had thought. And on deck, all was chaos.

Half the men were shouting, while the other half were working with grim-faced determination to keep the ship afloat – retying the cannons, battening down the hatch Locan and I had just emerged from. A sailor screamed bloody murder in our face for us to get back below deck where we belonged, but Locan shoved his way past and headed for the quarterdeck with me following in his wake.

The rain came down in sheets, soaking us from seemingly three directions at once. The rigging shook as if seized in the grip of a leviathan. A wave leapt over the port rail and sent a tide of icy saltwater over us. The *Red Fiend* was so close to the Dreadveil that misty tendrils of magic seemed to reach for us like grasping, blood-soaked fingers.

Locan took the stairs up to the quarterdeck three at a time. Huretio was lashed to the wheel, clinging to it with white knuckles while Stye-eyed Shiv screamed at him. Another wave of black water leapt from the depths, soaking us and nearly taking me off my feet as the deck tilted again.

'We should get below, Captain!' cried Shiv, wiping the water from his face. Both men were sodden from head-to-heel. 'Batten down the hatches, turn ourselves to beam wind, and trust ourselves to the Seamstress!'

'Do you suppose she's out in weather like this?' Huretio gave a manic laugh as if to beckon the storm on. 'I do believe we are past the point of prayer.'

'At least drop some canvas! If we lose a mast—'

'If we do as you suggest, we'll either founder on the rocks or be dragged into the Dreadveil!' That smog of its black magic was so close that I could almost smell it, sulphur and poison fire, feel its evil in the waves that rocked our portside and threatened to swallow us. Within the mist, faceless wraiths glided past, waiting for the wind to carry us to them. 'You can pry this wheel from my cold, dead hands!' Beyond the haze, dawn was rising, bathing the water in a red glow as if we sailed on a sea of blood.

Huretio looked up at my and Locan's approach, his usual gregarious face twisted in a livid grimace. 'Goblin-fucking lunatics! Do you want to drown? Get back below!'

'If we're going down, I'd sooner go down up here!' Locan replied.

Overhead, the mainmast creaked ominously. A man was clambering down from the crow's nest at a frenetic pace. The wind died for just a moment and then roared back to send a great wave surging across our bow. My eyes were fixed in horror on the groaning mainmast, but when the angry sky flashed again, the bolt of lightning that followed missed the mainsail and struck the ship's bow, and with a horrifying crack of timber the foremast *snapped*.

Screams filled the air as a tangle of canvas, rope, and wood plummeted over the side into the churning sea. The deck tilted, and I was slipping and then falling, while Huretio turned the air blue with curses as he fought against the wheel. My shoulder hit the deck hard just as the sail struck the water.

Huretio and Shiv were both shouting, 'Axes! Axes!' Already, men were rushing to the forecastle to chop away the ruined mast and sail before their weight in the water spun the *Red Fiend* off course or caused the ship to capsize. Already the ship was leaning and listing to port.

Shiv hauled me to my feet and thrust an axe into my shaking hand. 'Either get below or make yourself useful!' he screamed in my face. 'Help them!'

I had no chance to assist. To credit the crew of the *Red Fiend*, they knew their business. The ruined foremast tumbled over the side into the churning water to be left in our wake, and as swiftly as the ship had tilted, it crashed back to the horizontal with a heavy splash.

Huretio fought against the waves and the howling wind,

forcing the wheel to starboard to put us beyond the clutches of the Dreadveil. 'Get back below!' he shouted, turning his ire at the storm upon me and Locan. There was no trace of Huretio's usual cavalier spirit, for the whites of his eyes were bright with fear tending towards madness. He shoved me back towards the hatch.

We departed with Huretio still at the wheel, shaking his fist into the wind as if he meant to fight the weather and the Dreadveil both. 'Think you can take my ship?' he cried to the howling gale. '*My* ship? Come on, you—'

The second lightning bolt struck the mainmast with such unerring accuracy it was as if it had been flung from the heavens by a vengeful god. Locan and I were on the stairs back towards the main deck. There was a hideous crack, and we were both thrown from our feet, the unexpected tilt of the deck catapulting us down the stairs and sending us sliding across the boards to collide painfully with the rail. The deck shifted towards the vertical, and when Locan landed beside me I had to grab his wrist to stop him going overboard. There was a splash as something, or someone, went into the water.

The deck shifted again, and together we scrambled away from the rail. Those sailors who had managed to keep their feet were already rushing towards the mainmast to cut the sail loose where it was dragging in the water. Above the chaos and the deafening wind, I heard Huretio at the wheel still giving orders, fighting to keep our course. The collapsed mainmast was dragging the *Red Fiend*'s bow to starboard, leaving the Dreadveil to aft, and with the mizzenmast still caught in the storm's grasp we were plunging towards the coast of Paleir at a rate of knots.

Locan and I made it to our feet. He turned to say something but could not get the words out before the *Fiend* crested a great wave, and as it touched down again there came from below an awful ripping of timber as something tore into the keel, and once more we were flying through the air.

My head and hip struck the rail, and I landed in a pained, crumpled heap on the deck, soaked to my bones by the relentless waves and with my senses spinning.

Locan seized me by the collar and hauled me staggering to my feet. The tilt of the deck now seemed to be permanent. The *Red Fiend* was not so much sailing as it was a piece of driftwood caught at the mercy of the waves. The wind and rain had lessened, as if the storm was a cat that had crippled its prey and was now content to play with it.

'We're taking on water, Captain!' Edlin Eight-Fingers cried, straining to be heard over the roar of the waves. By our listless course and the rapidly steepening angle of the deck, the damage to our hull was serious. No sooner had the words left Edlin's mouth than there was another horrible crunch from below and the jolt sent him flying headfirst into the waiting maw of the North Water.

On the quarterdeck, Huretio still held the wheel in a white-knuckle grip. Whoever had been in the crow's nest had gone tumbling into the sea, and the captain was seemingly steering by feel and luck alone, trying to find a way through the reef around Paleir's coast that did the barest damage to his ship.

Locan pointed beyond the bow, to where the island's granite cliffs loomed against the stormy sky, so close now that I could make out a rugged beach of dark pebbles. 'We are, to coin a phrase, fucked eight ways to the Underrealm. Hope you can swim.'

In a lull of the wind, there came from the depths of the ship a high scream of fear and fury, and a sharper dread broke through my terror at the storm's merciless wrath. Morvolt was still down there somewhere. My horse would fight anything, but he could not fight the certainty of the water that was currently coursing its way through the *Red Fiend*'s lower decks.

With no thought for my own safety, I scrambled towards the hatch, but Locan seized my shoulder.

'Don't be such a giant-fucking *fool*,' he hissed. 'You want to drown with that horse? We need to get to the shore.'

But I would die myself before I left Morvolt to drown in the dark terror of belowdecks while the *Red Fiend* was dragged to the depths of the North Water. I shrugged Locan's hand away and raced for the hatch. I threw it open and practically leapt down the stairs.

All the lamps had gone out, plunging the deserted lower decks into bleak darkness. I felt my way along the corridors, finding my route by my vague memory of the ship's layout and Morvolt's increasingly desperate screams, the floor continuing to list and lean under my feet. When I reached the set of stairs that led to Morvolt's deck, there was, to my relief, still one lamp burning, but the deck itself was taking on water at a rapid rate. Before I could change my mind, I jumped down, and the freezing grasp of the seawater drove the breath from my body. It was as if I had been encased in ice from the thigh down.

I plunged onwards, battling against the overwhelming current, barely keeping my feet, the height of the water ebbing and flowing as I hauled my way through dark, mazy passages. The strength of Morvolt's cries drove me on, and as I stumbled around a corner, only narrowly keeping my feet where the corridor sloped steeply downwards, I gripped the open door-frame of the makeshift stable and threw myself inside.

Morvolt had retreated to the highest corner of the tilting room with his rump to the wall, keening in fury as he kicked and stamped and snarled against the rising water. Clinging to the wall, I hauled myself towards him, but when I reached out a hand to soothe him he snapped his teeth at me.

'I'm trying to help!' I protested. My heart was pounding, the mad foolishness of what I was doing beginning to set in. There was no prospect of me getting Morvolt out through the tight, twisting corridors of the *Red Fiend*, not when the route that had got me here was already half submerged and would only get more treacherous.

Worse still, the room's slant was worsening by the minute. Morvolt was already having to scramble against the slick deck to keep himself from plunging headfirst into the wall that was slowly becoming the floor. An ordinary horse might have already succumbed. Whatever I was going to do, I would have to work fast.

Without warning, Morvolt bucked and kicked his back hooves into the wall behind him, splintering the timber.

'Stop, you'll make it worse!' I cried out. If he punctured the keel, the sea would be rushing in from two directions and doom us.

But when I looked at where his hooves had connected with the wood, I realised that my fears were unfounded – the tilt of the ship had taken that section of the keel above the waterline. I could hear the waves crashing against the hull, but there was no water pouring in through the hole he had made.

Morvolt was readying himself for another kick, but I placed a firm hand on his back to stop him. 'Stop, let me.' I did not want Morvolt inadvertently toppling himself into the rising water. I still had the axe that Shiv had given me hooked into my belt. I moved to the wall and began to chop away at the hole Morvolt had made, sending chunks of wood flying as I tried to open it wide enough for our escape.

I had to work quickly – I needed to make a hole large enough for Morvolt, and the water was creeping inch by inch up the cabin. Morvolt continued to snarl and scrape his hooves against the floor in his effort to remain out of the water, but my presence seemed to calm him.

The waves sprayed saltwater into my face as I worked. The *Red Fiend* seemed to have slowed to a halt, bobbing like flotsam in the surf. The cabin continued to fill with water, more quickly now. With a floor that was approaching a forty-five-degree angle and with no room for a run-up, Morvolt might struggle to navigate his way out of the hole. We might need the water to float us free when the *Red Fiend* at last succumbed to the water it was taking on and began to slow and sink.

But as ever, Morvolt surprised me. I was just beginning to think that the hole might be large enough for him when he brayed a warning. Morvolt turned clumsily on the tilting deck, and I barely had time to duck out of the way as, with a fearsome kick of his back legs and a neigh that was equal parts terror, triumph, and fury, he leapt for the hole.

His hind legs caught on the lower edge, but I heard his front hooves skittering against the *Fiend*'s hull as he fought his way free. His right, rearmost leg narrowly missed my face as I foolishly tried to chop away more timber to get him free, and then he was gone, sliding down the hull and entering the water with a splash.

I leapt after him. The lower half of me was already soaked, and I was so relieved to be free of the ship that I threw myself gladly into the water.

My head went under. All I knew was cold, cold enough to shrink my lungs to the size of grapes as the air fled from them. I had not been prepared for how icy it would be. I gasped, flailed, and kicked against the sea's grip, went under again, swallowed half the North Water, then came up spluttering before going under once more. I tried to swim, but the roiling waves against the bulk of the *Red Fiend* made it impossible. Blinded by wind and churning sea, I could hardly tell up from down, just kicking my legs in utter panic and praying with each breath that it would not be my last.

The cold air I fought to draw down burnt in my lungs. Sharp raindrops pecked at my face. My legs were already tiring, but I had barely moved any distance at all from the hulk of the *Fiend*. If it went down, it would drag me down with it. Another wave rose over my head and submerged me, and then another.

My lips and tongue tasted of salt. Somewhere, someone was screaming. Overhead, gulls whirled and shrieked against the slate-grey sky. A flash of lightning and a roll of thunder. Another volley of water over my head.

I got my head up just enough to see the *Red Fiend* on its side with its rudder out of the water. Sailors were swimming free, making for the shore. I called to them, but my voice was drowned out by the roar of the waves. I was fading, exhausted, cold seeping into my bones while my heavy cloak continued to drag at me. Another high and heavy wave hit me, and I sank beneath the icy water.

There was something watching me. A silhouette, gliding through the icy depths on sleek black wings, circling beneath me. Waiting. The sea was eerily still, as if even the waves feared this creature of the deep. I was sinking, but it felt as if I was witnessing this scene from overhead, from a long, long way away, as if my soul had already given my body up for dead. Nevertheless, instinct took over, and I was gripped by panic. I tried to kick my way clear of it, but then I realised I was already moving, something dragging me through the waves in its jaws—

Something struck my chest and water plumed from my open mouth. Overhead, the sky was clear. I tried to take a breath and choked, then rolled my head to the side to cough up what felt like half the sea.

'Tough as bloody dragon scales!' came a proud exclamation. Locan was kneeling beside me, breathing hard, his hands clenched from where he had been pounding at my chest.

'Thank you.' It hurt my throat to speak. 'How—'

'Not you, the horse.'

A rough tongue lapped at my face, covering me in saliva.

'I'm awake! I'm awake!' I cried out as Morvolt nuzzled at my head.

'That beast is a bloody hero,' said Locan, hauling me to my feet even though standing was the very last thing I wanted to do. 'Thought you were dead as the dwarves. He must have dragged you all the way here in his mouth.'

My wits were swimming, which given how cold I might have been otherwise was probably to my benefit. I only then realised that Locan had stripped off all his wet clothes and was standing there in just a pair of filthy linen pants.

We had come ashore on an expanse of pools and craggy black rocks, with a wide beach of rough stones inshore from us, littered with what looked to be the debris of past shipwrecks. Looking around, I saw that several of the *Red Fiend*'s crew had also reached the shore at various points along the beach, though I could not see Huretio among them. Back out on the water, what remained of the *Red Fiend* was being carried towards the shore, now fully on its side with water pouring in through its many wounds.

'Is this Paleir?' I gasped, shivering in the cool air as my senses returned to me.

'Where else would it be?' said Locan. 'Starting to think you're bad luck.'

That seemed harsh – Locan had hardly been drowning in good fortune when I met him. 'Better than drowning.'

'Barely.' Locan spat into a rockpool.

Above the beach stood a high sea wall wrought from tarnished blue stone, its battlements topped by a long row of leaping dragon statues in various states of decay, their features, wings, and heads lost to time and sea. A shiver went through me, this one not from the cold. This could only be High Tulbar, the ancient capital of Paleir. From here, the Mórs of Tulbar and their dragon allies had once ruled the whole isle. I had never thought to see this place. Tulbar was a land of legend; no Harkken had set foot on these shores since before the coming of the Abomination King and the rise of the Dreadveil.

'Ah fuck, here comes the welcome party,' said Locan.

We were not alone – a crowd of locals was striding down the beach towards us. By their determined gaits and surly expressions, they were not here to give us blankets and welcome us to warm ourselves by their fire.

'What you doing on our beach?' called out their leader, a burly man perhaps a few years older than me with a wide fore-head. There were around ten of them, carrying a variety of weapons – mostly cudgels, hammers, and daggers in varying degrees of disrepair. Some way distant from the fearsome repu-tation of the dragon kings of Tulbar, but that had been over four hundred years ago. For all I knew, this mob was the present monarch and his courtiers.

'The big wooden thing behind me not enough of a clue?' said Locan, gesturing back towards the *Red Fiend*. Even naked and unarmed, if he was troubled by their number he gave no sign. In my weakened state with the taste of bile and saltwater still burning in my throat, I did not expect to be much use if it came to violence. 'You goblin-fuckers never seen a ship before?'

The burly man chuckled. The party behind him wore a mixture of black scowls and mean, hungry smirks. 'Got ourselves a wit here, boys. Who wants a funny slave with no clothes?'

'That'll ruin our fishing, that, Hobbo,' groused one of them, a short, sour-faced man with a rheumy eye that his long fringe did not quite cover, dressed in a rough leather coat belted at the waist by a fraying rope. 'Might as well give up on the day. Bloody waste. We should take them to the Mór.'

There was still a Mór in Tulbar, then, as the Palish called the rulers of the various petty kingdoms that made up the island. That suggested there was at least some trace of civilisation left here. Of course, the Mór might just be an ancient fisherman with hands like knotted rope.

'Blinky, nobody cares about your bloody fishing,' said Hobbo. He slapped his cudgel against his thigh. 'And how many times do I have to tell you that no one gives a shit about the Mór either? This beach belongs to Ulf, and that means you two do as well.' He pointed his cudgel towards Locan. 'It'll be the mines for you – too old to learn anything new, so they'll work you till your heart gives out.'

I looked for my sword, but it must have slipped from my scabbard during my escape from the ship. My axe was gone as well. Locan's knives were likely bundled up in the pile of wet clothes at his feet. These locals had us ten to two. The crew of the *Red Fiend* were not being troubled as we were, but they had come ashore in larger groups, leaving Locan and I looking like a pair of stragglers who could be easily intimidated. They may have also been drawn by the presence of Morvolt, who snapped his teeth as one of the men tried to approach and then cantered away across the rockpools, shaking the seawater from his coat.

'There are goods in the hold,' I said, gesturing towards the carcass of the *Red Fiend*. We did not know how long we might be stranded here for – it seemed better to try and reach a diplomatic solution. 'No doubt they'll wash up over the next few days. Please take them as recompense for any trouble.'

'*Please take them as recompense for any trouble*,' said a boy from the back, in a singsong cadence no doubt meant to mimic my speech, drawing a roar of laughter from his companions. The Palishmen spoke strangely to my ear, and clearly I did to theirs as well.

'Aye, we'll take those anyway,' said Hobbo. 'Anything washing up on this beach belongs to Ulf, which includes you.' He puffed out his chest. 'As deputy constable of High Tulbar, I'll be taking you in, and how gentle I am in doing it is up to you.

If you come quietly, I might even put in a good word for you, try to save you from the mines.'

If Hobbo was the measure of the law in this town, I did not fancy our chances of a fair hearing. He produced two sets of fetters and handed them to two of his companions. 'Take them.'

'It'll be a Rintish pillow-house for this one,' added a bearded older man with half an ear missing, leering at me as he stepped towards me. This drew another round of sniggering. 'Prettier than my first wife.'

'Not half as pretty as your daughter,' added a younger man, stepping out of the way as Half-ear tried to clip him round the ear while their companions laughed.

I was struggling to find the humour in the situation – I was half-naked, shivering and soaking on a foreign beach, and due to be beaten and dragged into bondage – but that did not stop Locan laughing along with them. Our would-be captors fell silent, but Locan continued to roar his amusement to the sky.

'That's the Palish for you,' he said, pretending to wipe a tear from beneath his eye. 'Whole island of goblin-pissing jesters. Too busy being funny to ever bother leaving this floating turd someone crapped off the edge of Karvved, so they just stay here drinking till they're blind and trading better men like cattle.' He held out his hands towards them with his wrists pressed together. 'Try and put those shackles on me and I'll show you something we can all laugh at.'

'Locan,' I hissed. Even naked and unarmed, he would rate his chances of taking them, but we would still be stuck on Paleir, and he could not fight a whole island. We did not need to cause more trouble for ourselves by fighting with the locals, no matter how keen on the idea they seemed to be. I held my hands up placatingly to the crowd of men. 'There's no need for this. Our companions are just along the beach.' Perhaps the presence of the *Red Fiend*'s crew would dissuade them.

'Could make a headless goblin giggle, this lot,' Locan

sneered, ignoring me. There was a mad glint in his eye – the kind that told me this encounter could end only in blood. 'Suppose you'd need a good sense of humour if your women looked like theirs. No wonder they like fishing – their catch will be better looking than their wives.'

Hobbo took a step forward, slapping his cudgel against his palm. His forehead had turned slightly pink. 'Is that right? We'll see how funny you feel after I've hit your pecker so hard it scrunches back up inside you and they chuck you down the mines.'

'Yeah, you've said,' said Locan. His face wore a shit-eating grin. I could see what he was doing – trying to goad Hobbo into making the first move. The other Palishmen were coming towards us as well, with their weapons ready. 'But if you want to try and scare me, you should have brought your mother down here. You ever caught an octopus with all your fishing? I bet your mum's twice as ugly and four times as handsy.'

With a wild yell, Hobbo raised his cudgel over his head and charged.

Locan stood with his hands still stretched out for the shackles as the weapon fell towards his skull, and at the last moment stepped out of the way. Hobbo struck only air, overbalanced, and Locan kicked him casually on the ankle to send him sprawling face first into a nearby rockpool as the cudgel spun away into the rising tide.

So much for my hope of a peaceful solution.

'Clumsy of you,' said Locan. 'Do you want to lick stone, or would you rather stay out of my way and get to keep all your teeth?'

Two of the fishermen, Blinky and Half-ear, rushed towards Locan's rear with their knives out. I was ready to cry out a warning, but as soon as they were within range, Locan pivoted, and a high, spinning kick snapped Blinky's jaw back with a vicious crack of bone and sent him spiralling to the ground. As the first man fell, Locan grabbed Half-ear's wrist, twisting the knife from his grip and using his momentum to flip him over onto his shoulder. Half-ear's back came down on the rocks with a sickening crunch that echoed along the beach.

That was too much for the rest of them. Together, they charged me and Locan.

I backed away towards the water, dodging a wild punch from a tall man with a missing front tooth and catching another assailant on the side of the head with my elbow almost by accident. Most of them had gone after Locan and were swiftly made to regret it. Hobbo had just come to his feet when Locan threw two men over his shoulder to leave the three of them in a crumpled, wet heap.

'Step away!' Just as the remaining assailants had been debating whether to fight or flee from Locan's fury, a commanding shout echoed down the beach. A woman was striding down the shore towards us. There was a sword at her belt, and she wore a surcoat marked with a pair of crossed blades on one side and a crest showing a black dragon in flight over a blue sky on the other.

Locan let out a snarl of frustration. 'Can't you dragonturds just leave us alone? Who the fuck are you?' He caught sight of her surcoat. 'You the constable or something?'

'Constable, bailiff, and reeve,' replied the woman. 'You name it, I do it.' She was in her middle years, tall with steel-and-soot hair cropped short, broad shoulders, and the ruddy complexion of someone who always has somewhere else they needed to be. I had the immediate sense of someone fearsomely competent and not to be trifled with. She gave Locan a hard stare. 'You finished now, or do I need to give you a proper challenge first?'

Locan snorted. 'I'm not finished, but I reckon this lot are. Hope they've learnt their lesson about what I do to slavers, but if any of them need a reminder they're welcome to it.' He turned and prodded the dazed Hobbo with his foot. 'This one said he was your deputy.'

The woman's face flashed with annoyance. She gave a sigh. 'No deputy, just an idiot given too much responsibility, so I might let you off for giving him a kicking. Seamstress knows he probably deserved it.' Deciding we were no immediate threat to her, she thrust out a hand for Locan and I to grasp. 'I'm Chatten.' She eyed us up and down. 'Do they not wear clothes where you're from?' She gestured in turn to two of the fishermen. 'Birch, Galen, give them your cloaks before I lose my breakfast.'

Birch acted swiftly to remove his cloak, but Galen was staring at the prone forms of Blinky and Half-ear, the two who Locan had dished out the most vicious treatment to. 'They ain't moving,' he whispered.

I looked down at them. Both men were where Locan had left them. Blinky's jaw hung to the side of his face like an unhinged door, and he had fallen awkwardly with his arms tangled beneath him. Half-ear looked no better. His sightless blue eyes stared up at the sky. The crack when Locan had thrown him to the ground had been hideous.

Chatten crouched beside each of them in turn, laying two fingers against the sides of their necks. 'Well,' she said, looking up at Locan. 'These two won't be needing any more lessons from you. They're dead.'

Locan gave a disbelieving laugh. 'Come on now. I didn't hit them that hard.'

I crouched down beside Chatten and checked for myself. There was no pulse to either of them, and their skin was cool, the warmth of life already fading away. My mouth fell open, and I felt the colour pale from my cheeks. I had seen Locan kill before, but there had been no need here. He could have quelled them both with a couple of broken bones at worst. 'She's right,' I said. 'They're dead.'

Hobbo was coming to his feet, his face puce with rage, a

reclaimed cudgel clutched in his fist. 'You can't let them get away with this!' he said, staring hotly at Locan as he addressed Chatten. 'You're meant to protect us!'

'Wouldn't have touched them if you lot had the sense to leave us the fuck alone,' said Locan.

'They belong to Ulf,' added Galen stubbornly.

Chatten massaged irritably at her brow. 'This job ain't worth what the Mór pays me,' she muttered. She stood up and jabbed a finger in turn at Hobbo and Galen. 'Let's get one thing straight, I don't work for Ulf, and last I checked it was the Mór who ruled in High Tulbar.' She stepped towards Hobbo and snatched the cudgel from his grasp. 'Who gave you this? Your dad? I'll be having words with him.'

'That old bastard killed them,' muttered Hobbo, jutting his lip out sulkily. 'We were only doing what we were told. Ain't right.'

'One more word out of you—' Chatten raised a hand as if to cuff Hobbo around the ear, and the young man flinched backwards. 'I know it ain't pissing right. That's why I'm taking them to the Mór.'

After the welcome we had received on the beach, being taken to Tulbar's ruler was something of a relief. If the Mór was the true authority here, we could arrange shelter for ourselves and the crew of the *Red Fiend*, and eventually passage to Rameon or anywhere else. My young life had not prepared me for much, but I believed myself well-equipped to approach the ruler of a foreign court. I only wished that we had not been doing it immediately after Locan had murdered two of his subjects.

'Exactly the man we were meaning to see,' said Locan. 'Lead the way.'

Chatten looked around and addressed our assailants. 'Stop causing trouble and get those bodies back to town. With all these new arrivals I've got enough to deal with.'

. . .

The new arrivals Chatten was referring to were Huretio and his surviving crew. They were at the top of the beach below the sea wall stairs, milling around in a daze and watching their ruined ship bobbing over the churning waves. They had not received anything like the welcome Locan and I had – that had just been our ill fortune.

Huretio was quick to jump on the appearance of Chatten. 'Woman!' He strode up to her, sodden hat in hand, dripping water from the hem of his sea coat. 'Finally, somebody who looks like they're in charge. A shipwright! Tell me your town has a shipwright!'

Chatten's brow creased in a thoughtful frown. 'Not much cause for shipwrights round here, but there's a boatbuilder by the name of Barron. You'll find him at the Inn of the Broken Wheel.'

'Then that is where we shall go,' said Huretio, pumping Chatten's hand enthusiastically. 'Thank you. Lead the way.'

'I've no time for that,' said Chatten. 'But I can give you directions.'

'You can't be thinking of fixing the *Fiend*?' said Locan to Huretio with a disbelieving laugh. When he saw the distressed look on his friend's face, he threw a supportive arm around his shoulder. 'Huretio, I'm sorry, but the *Fiend* is gone.'

Huretio gave a stubborn shake of his head. 'Not so long as I draw breath. I have seven sons that I know of, but my only daughter is the *Fiend*. I swear to you Locan, I have never known a storm like that. That was no storm – it was a tempest, the work of Dagin himself. I will not surrender to the villainous sorcery of the Underrealm, nor will I sit idle while the *Fiend* is dashed on the rocks like some ponderous hulk that cannot keep an even keel.'

It had seemed, at least to my inexpert eye, an unusually

violent storm, and the bolts of lightning had fallen upon the *Fiend*'s mast with the unfailing accuracy of a master bowman. I was not yet ready though to credit what had befallen us to sorcery or the act of a god, although the shape I had seen beneath the water did give me pause for thought. I had thought it only a drowning-induced hallucination, but these were uncharted waters – who knew what vengeful magic might haunt the coasts of Paleir?

Huretio pointed at the men who were coming up the beach behind Chatten while keeping their distance from Locan. 'You – some of you are fishermen, yes? I need your rowboats, now!' He stopped as he caught sight of the two corpses being awkwardly carried up the beach by their arms and legs. 'Ah, Locan – it appears you have been making friends again.'

Chatten gave Huretio directions to the Broken Wheel, and we left him directing his crew and the fishermen as to the recovery of the *Red Fiend*. It seemed like folly to me, but I knew little of ships, and Huretio seemed as undisturbed by our near drowning as anybody. Part of me wanted to never set foot on a deck again, and the other was eager to be away from Tulbar as soon as I could find some dry clothes, before we encountered any more unpleasantness.

I had been worried about Morvolt stranded out on the rockpools with the tide coming in and no way to scale the stony beach, but when I looked for him I saw he had found his way along the shore to where it met the sea wall.

I wanted to wait for him, but Chatten beckoned me up the sea wall stairs towards a rusted iron gate, with assurances that she would send somebody to collect and stable him. Being eager to get off the beach and away from the biting sea wind, I agreed.

'Best we just go,' Chatten said to us as she ushered us away from the scene. 'Before any of them think to try their luck again. My nephew is too stone-stupid to learn his lesson.' Back on the beach, Huretio and the fishermen were now involved in a heated debate as to the price for the use of a rowboat.

At the top of the stairs, I was able to get a proper look at the sea wall that lined the edge of the beach. It was a dark blue, but there were faded flecks of gold where someone had once gilded the stone before the carapace had been washed away by wind and waves. The ancient Tulban kings' fixation with making this city the Rameon of the North had extended even to an attempt to emulate the city's great golden wall.

Up close, the dragons that ran along the top were even less impressive than they had seemed from the shore. The mouths that might once have revealed painstakingly chiselled teeth bared in roars that mimicked the fury of their flesh-and-blood cousins were no more, jaws and tongues chipped away by the sea to leave only a pale mockery. Empty sockets stared out from where once bright jewels might have gleamed in place of their eyes. As I gazed on them, a sense of melancholy fell over me, knowing that I looked upon a lost past that could never be again. Not only the death of the dragons, but the fall of High Tulbar, the seat of the High Kings of Paleir reduced to small, angry men willing to fight shipwreck survivors for a few yards of beach.

'Do you get a lot of shipwrecks here?' I asked Chatten. I had seen driftwood on the beach, rotted planks and broken oars.

'More than we used to these last few years,' said Chatten. 'You're the first survivors we've had though. Usually we just get driftwood and bloated corpses washing in with the tide. That lunatic with the hat must be one heck of a captain. Since the Dreadveil started rolling back, ships keep trying to cheat their way down our coast instead of going the long way round and they get caught out by the reef. Doesn't stop folk speculating that it was a dragon protecting Tulbar from invaders of course.'

Locan gave a bark of laughter. 'A dragon? Thought we'd landed on the wrong island, not the wrong century.'

'Is it true?' I asked, trying and failing to contain my eagerness. 'A dragon?' Most of Paleir had been cut off from Guiland for centuries – perhaps the dragons had never truly gone. I would have sailed the North Water a hundred times if I believed I would see a dragon.

'Might be. Enough folk say they've seen one,' said Chatten, her neutral tone suggesting that she had no opinion one way or the other. 'You'll hear about it soon enough.'

Entering through the rusty gate, I gazed upon the city of High Tulbar for the first time. Like the stone dragons that patrolled its coast, the city was a place that made me feel I was looking through a window to the distant past. Cobbled streets that once might have sparkled with dizzyingly colourful mosaics were now shabby and broken, leaving unpaved patches where weeds were sprouting through the mud. Squat shacks with doors falling off their hinges crowded around the wide bases of towering pillars of chipped white marble. I craned my neck to stare up at them, wondering what purpose they could have served, what else of old High Tulbar had now crumbled to dust. To judge by their crumbling summits, these vast columns had once been even taller.

'Dragon roosts,' said Chatten, following my wide-eyed gaze. 'They used to have perches running between them. The last one collapsed when I was a girl.'

I could only stare in silent wonder at where once upon a time dragons had surfaced from the sea and descended from the clouds to commune with men. Here, in this grey city of ruins and derelict hovels.

The faded glamour of High Tulbar's ancient pillars and mosaic streets formed a sharp contrast to the shabby, sour-faced state of those who dwelled here. The townsfolk we passed eyed us warily, as if believing we were brigands here to steal what little remained of the city's wealth. A gang of scraggy stray cats watched us with hungry eyes from a ruined fountain that had long run dry. A woman outside a tumbledown shack opened a threadbare cloak as we passed to offer us her emaciated flesh, causing me to look away in embarrassment. A gang of shirtless boys raced across our path, their bare feet throwing up water from the cobbles and earning a curse from Chatten with a promise that she would set their mothers on them.

Tulbar reminded me in some ways of Poignmuda, the renascent town in Narlond we had briefly stayed in, if significantly larger. But if Poignmuda was like a warrior desperately trying to recapture the strength of his youth, Tulbar was a warrior who had given up on glory and put away his sword for good, refusing to claim it even when the wolves howled in the night and scratched at his door. All that held this city together was a memory, an echo of what it had once been.

The streets became better maintained as we got further from the sea, and the houses more upright, with only maybe one in every two looking to be abandoned. The town had woken with the dawn, and the first plumes of smoke were rising into the air. As we followed Chatten deeper into the settlement, we passed a young girl selling cockles from a squeaking wheelbarrow and a baker shouting the price of fresh bread. A woman poured a bucket of slop into the street from the first floor of an inn, narrowly missing us and receiving a tirade from Chatten in reply.

'That's where we're headed,' said Chatten as we walked on, pointing to a dark fortress set on a hill slightly above the settlement as it came into view between a tannery and a forge where the sharp strike of hammer on iron was already splitting the morning. 'Caradrahan Hall.'

A shiver of anticipation went through me. Caradrahan Hall. Where the High Kings of Paleir had once communed with dragons and used their mastery over sea and air to claim the whole island. High Tulbar might have faded, but that did not lessen the thrill of knowing that I might soon walk its halls.

But to my disappointment, Caradrahan Hall looked in no

finer state than the city it watched over. Of the keep's four turrets, two had crumbled to ruin. A third, somebody had tried to rebuild in a white stone that did not match the rest of the fortress's deep cobalt, before giving up halfway. Only the fourth still stood, together with the high central tower, stretching towards the clouds and topped by a stone dragon that was at least twice the size of those on the sea wall. The beast was perched as if about to soar into the sky, its wings nearly fully outstretched and its mouth open mid-roar. If I squinted my eyes, I could almost imagine it was real.

Just past a church to the Seamstress, far less grand than its equivalents in Guiland, we turned a corner and Chatten brought us abruptly to a halt. At a crossroads ahead, the street was swarming with people, crowding around some commotion we could not see.

'What's happening?' I asked Chatten, standing on tiptoes for a better view.

'New slaves,' said the constable flatly.

'I thought the slave markets were in Varned and Carnaway,' I said, meaning the two western kingdoms where the men of the northlands would sell their cargo on their way home. The slave markets of Paleir's eastern kingdoms had dried up with the rise of the Dreadveil.

'Folk still need potboys and prostitutes,' said Chatten. 'Tulbar's never lost its taste for slavery. Ulf probably bought this lot in Varned. Got the look of oarsmen.' She caught Locan's dark expression and added, 'Not how I'd like it to be, you understand, but the Mór don't pay me enough to worry about the rights and wrongs.'

Ahead, eight men connected by a long ankle chain were being forced through the street at spearpoint. They were shirtless, revealing lean, powerful torsos, which fitted with Chatten's summation. A tall, bearded man cracked a long whip through the air, leaving a bloody gash across a man's bare back.

'Bloody goblin-fuckers,' muttered Locan. He spat on the ground, drawing side-eyes and scowls from nearby Palishmen who were watching proceedings.

I moved closer in search of a better view, with Locan and Chatten following. A stout, black-garbed man looked to be having some disagreement with the crowd. A great golden medallion hung down over his ample stomach, and his black cloak was rich sable. 'Move!' he snarled. 'This lot aren't for sale.'

This led to some disappointed muttering, but the crowd began to back away, the spears of the burly guardsmen discouraging them from forcing the issue.

'That's Ulf,' said Chatten, indicating towards the man who'd spoken.

'Is it now?' said Locan, his dark eyes roving over Ulf, for whom a path through the throng was currently being cleared by his guardsmen. 'So he's the one who set those fool boys at the beach on us. Think I might go and introduce myself.'

'I'd suggest you don't,' said Chatten with a heavy hint of caution. 'Ulf's one of High Tulbar's Keykeepers, probably the most powerful man in the city.' She paused for a moment and then added as if it was an afterthought, 'Him and the Mór, of course.'

'He didn't need any provoking to send his little welcome party after me,' growled Locan. 'Maybe I'll deliver him the same treatment.'

'How has Tulbar survived so long since the dragons left?' I asked, hoping to distract Locan before he caused us any more trouble. I was fascinated to learn more of what had become of the city. Whenever news of here reached Guiland, it was via intermediaries from Varned, Carnaway, or Bastden, depending on which kingdoms were currently in the ascendancy, being divided among a Mór's multiple sons, or in the process of being conquered by a neighbour. There were currently six Palish kingdoms, I believed, but a few years earlier there had been five.

'And "survived" is all we've done,' said Chatten, rubbing her jaw. 'I don't know – I wasn't around four hundred years ago, old as I might look to you. But it's iron, I suppose. Carnaway and Varned get our iron and men like Ulf and the Keykeepers get their slaves to drag more of it out the ground. As the Dreadveil fades and the North Water opens up, the hope is that we can reopen the markets and start trading our own slaves again.'

'Four centuries to learn something new, and these people still can't wait to get back to the old ways,' said Locan. He spat forcefully against the broken mosaic under our feet. 'And what's Ulf planning for those wretched men exactly?'

Chatten pointed over the rooftops to a tall circular structure several streets over. It was honeycombed with high arches that might have been impressive in their day, but were now beginning to crumble. There were figures visible against the sky, leaning insouciantly against the disintegrating walls and talking to one another. Chatten flashed a dark smile, glinting with menace. 'Why don't we take a look? See what's waiting for you if you cause any more trouble.'

We entered the arena through a wide, sweeping archway. The walls had been carved to show scenes of battle, shirtless men with rugged torsos wielding spears locked in combat with an assortment of creatures: lions, great lizards, and what appeared to be human-sized crows with beaks full of tiny, triangular teeth. The carvings were crumbling now, the figures left faded and featureless by time. Just like the dragons and much of the rest of the city. I could scarcely turn my head without seeing signs of the glory of the former capital of Paleir, the little that was left after four centuries of decline.

'This is like the Dome in Rameon,' said Locan. 'The Dome if it was small and shit.'

'Are there gladiator fights here?' I asked, my interest piqued. I had long held dreams of visiting Rameon and attending an event at the Dome, and my parents' refusal to sanction it had only heightened that desire.

'Ulf keeps saying there will be,' said Chatten. 'He has a lot of ideas, does Ulf.'

We advanced through the tunnel into a vast empty circle of dirt and sprouting weeds, close to eighty yards in diameter surrounded by tiered stone seating. Curiously, several deep pits had been dug into the earth around the arena. As we approached one of them, there came a chorus of excited squawking, like a collection of caged birds.

'Take a look,' said Chatten.

Locan and I peered over the edge of the hole, and my eyes watered at the smell of filth that assailed my nostrils. I took a step back, wiping them and trying to focus on the writhing mass of flesh below.

'Dragon's piss,' said Locan. 'I knew you Palish were mad, but...'

He seemed to be lost for words. I wiped my eyes again and held my nose, forcing my vision to focus.

There were at least two dozen of them, writhing and climbing over one another like crabs in a bucket. Naked, hairless, their skin tinged sickly green. They stared up at us with beady black eyes that glistened like glass marbles over sharp, sickle-shaped noses, weak chins, and black teeth overbiting their bottom lip. Like us, they had four fingers on both hands, but their fingernails were long and dark, and they were without thumbs. I coughed as the scent of filth wriggled inside my nostrils again, and Chatten grabbed my shoulder as if she were worried I might fall.

'Goblins,' I gasped, pulling back from the edge, suddenly light-headed. 'Are those goblins?'

'Well, they ain't fucking elves, that's for sure,' said Locan. He looked at me. 'Thought your lot killed them all?'

Over the centuries, the Guilish had pushed the goblins out

of Karvved until they were isolated in the western hills of Midding. They had been on their way to extinction before the Abomination King's rise, when he had recruited them to his army with the promise of peace and land. It had been a promise broken. The Abomination King had turned his black arts upon the goblins, mixing their blood and seed with those of men in his experiments, and manipulating their minds until they were bound to obey him without question.

'You'd be surprised how well they can swim,' said Chatten. Her face remained expressionless, but I could tell she was relishing my discomfort. 'Used to wash up on the beach in twos and threes, blabbering, scared out of their minds. These are all those that have appeared since the Abomination King fell.' At the sound of their master's name, the goblins began to squeak excitedly, jumping and scrambling over one another to try and scale the walls.

'You should kill them and be done with it,' said Locan. 'What's the sense in this?'

Chatten pointed towards the far side of the arena. A twenty-strong group of men were training with wooden swords under the watchful eye of armed guards. Among them, I recognised some of those we had just seen being paraded through the street. Ulf was now standing on the first level of the amphitheatre with his thumbs jammed into his belt. He barked something to a guard who stepped forward and lashed out with a whip at one of the slaves' ankles.

Locan's lip curled in disgust. 'So, he's buying up strong slaves so he can have them fight the goblins and charge for the spectacle. You lot just love to dream up ways to torture each other, don't you?'

Chatten's face betrayed not an inkling of remorse. She had lured us in with her straightforward manner and obvious competence, but this was a woman not to be crossed lightly. 'And you just remember that. This is Tulbar – those that step out of line don't live to see the consequences. You killed two men, men that were meant to be under my protection. So when you meet the Mór, be sure you're on your best behaviour, or you can rest assured I'll give you to Ulf and he can do as he likes with you.

'We feed them on scraps – just watch what they'll do for a bite of man flesh.'

Chatten drew a knife from her belt then pressed it against her thumb, blood beading in the wound. The goblins began squeaking again, like ravenous baby birds, the larger ones shoving the others aside as they lifted their palms towards us. Chatten held her hand out over the pit, and squeezed to let a few drops fall.

One of the smaller goblins – a female or a youth, I supposed – took advantage of the press of bodies and jumped. The creature's leap took it clear of its fellows. Its fast hands plucked the drops of blood from their air, and before it had hit the ground again its black tongue had licked its palm clean.

The other goblins shrieked in rage. As the blood-drinker landed, a second goblin tackled it, driving it to the ground, and no sooner was it down than the rest of the hive descended in a swarm, nails tearing at the thief's stomach. Its black entrails sizzled as the skin split. The goblin shrieked desperately, until another ripped its tongue out and wolfed it down.

'Hope I've made myself clear,' said Chatten, already turning away. 'Shall we go to the castle?'

CHAPTER 5

We left the town and followed Chatten up the sloping road towards the gates of Caradrahan Hall.

'Goblins or not,' said Locan, 'I can cause a lot of trouble for you if you keep us here. Best your Mór puts us on the next ship south.' Tulbar's deep grey sky fully obscured the sun, so at present there was no hope of us escaping the city through Locan's shadow magic. Not that I particularly wanted to experience that again after my last brush with it in Narlond.

'You've already caused trouble,' Chatten replied. 'Thanks to you, there's two men dead. How are their families meant to feed themselves? Trust me, you'll want the Mór on your side – I'm the one keeping you out of the hands of men like Ulf, and my patience only lasts as long as the Mór's does.'

'Try me,' said Locan. 'I've put tougher folk than you in the ground. And I don't give a giant's piss about those dogs and their families – let Ulf pay off their families. They got what they deserved.'

'Could you stop?' I said, my irritation getting the better of me. Despite slaves and goblins, I felt Chatten had treated us fairly so far. 'We could have talked our way out of it at the beach. They just wanted to frighten us a bit until you started insulting them.'

'Bah.' Locan spat in the dirt. 'I didn't get this far in life by yielding to scared fishermen without a wit to rub between them.'

'And look where that's left you,' I shot back. Even if not for the welcome we got on the beach, it would have been only a matter of time before Locan started a fight with someone. 'When we meet the Mór, let me do the talking.'

The outer wall of Caradrahan Hall was forged from the same blue limestone as the sea wall. The portcullis was up, and the guards ushered the three of us inside. Chatten led us across the courtyard and up a set of stairs to a pair of tall double doors. The keep was strangely quiet – my mother's castle, Harkfall, was awash with servants and petitioners at every hour of the day, but aside from a smattering of guards and a lone groom mucking out the stables, Caradrahan Hall seemed deserted, as bare of life as much of the town over which it stood. Like the rest of Tulbar, the signs of its slow demise were everywhere – stairs in need of sweeping, dragon-faced gargoyles smeared with bird droppings, guards leaning against the wall and looking up at us with only a passing curiosity.

Chatten knocked for admission and from inside, a lone, bored-looking guard swung the door open. His mail was coloured with rust under his blue gambeson. We entered a square antechamber, occupied by a pair of burning braziers and a shield showing a black dragon on a blue field on both walls. Another set of double doors marked what I assumed was the entrance to the Mór's hall.

'Stay here,' said Chatten. 'And no running off,' she added. She opened one of the double doors and slipped into the hall.

With a groan, Locan collapsed onto a stone bench that ran along the wall. 'This place is dying,' he said, stretching out over the full length of it. 'I've known morgues with more cheer.

Hope those slaves enjoy getting eaten by goblins in front of five paying spectators.'

'Let me do the talking with the Mór,' I said again, taking a seat at the end of the bench and forcing Locan to move up. In lawless Narlond, Locan's skill with a blade had me at a disadvantage, but I was on more familiar ground here. The lifelessness of Caradrahan Hall put me of a mind that the Mór was equivalent to a minor lord in Guiland, the sort who might appear at Keystone once a year to petition for a temporary forbearance of taxes or for a contingent of the Queen's Guard to deal with a troublesome gang of outlaws. My royal lineage might serve us for once.

'Piss on that,' spat Locan. 'You think you're better to talk to him than me? Just look at the folk here – they bathe once a year on midsummer's eve and still think they smell of rose petals. Man in there's going to be a big, arrogant, goblin-fucking bastard who breaks his fast on raw meat and picks the gristle out of his teeth with a blunt axe – you think he's going to be impressed by some Guilish lordling?' He barked a laugh. 'Nah, not happening. I'll tell him those dead men are cretins who got what was coming to them, and that every slaver needs a long sleep at the end of a short rope. Then he can decide if he really wants the trouble of me shoving a sword up his arse. We'll be on a ship south by this time tomorrow. I'm not waiting around here while Huretio weeps over the *Fiend*.'

Before I could protest against Locan's ridiculous plan that would surely see us thrown in a dungeon, the doors to the hall burst open and three red-faced men marched out like ships under full sail with the wind at their backs. They were broad and bearded, wearing bright mail and rich cloaks that streamed in their wake. So intent were they upon their departure that they did not even glance at me and Locan. The guard moved quickly to open the outer door, but one of the men stopped abruptly and called back towards the hall, 'Your death, boy, I swear to you!' The man might have said more, but his two companions took him by the shoulders and ushered him out.

Locan got to his feet. 'Reckon that's our call to enter.' He headed straight for the hall and I hurried after him.

The hall was vast and draughty, the walls lined with empty hearths that looked not to have housed a fire in many a year. The room was not so stark as the antechamber, but there was not much in it. Whatever wealth there was in Tulbar's iron deposits, little seemed to have reached the Mór of Tulbar. Even the court of Chieftess Aala had shown more life. More dragon shields stared down at us, lit by wall sconces that only seemed to add to the room's gloom by the shadows they cast. A smattering of guards lined the edges, and a heavy carpet of white fur marked the way to a throne of austere wood, the only nod towards ostentation the armrests that had been carved into snarling dragon heads and the wings sprouting from the top rail. On the back wall hung a faded tapestry showing a richly dressed, red-headed man with a fierce beard standing proud and stern in the castle's courtyard, accepting homage from a bowing dragon while a crowd of onlookers stared on in wonder.

A man I presumed was the Mór was seated on the throne, watching us. Locan's prediction of the sort of lord who would greet us could have been wider of the mark, but not by much. The Mór of Tulbar looked little older than me, and the shadow of a beard that dusted his chin seemed only to add to his youth. His round, honest face dusted with pale freckles would have suited a stableboy better than a lord, and his chestnut-red hair had been cropped short above his ears, making him look slightly simple. He sat on the throne as if weighed down by the high-tipped silver crown that rested crookedly on his head, his shoulders slumped and his fingers tight against the armrests as if to hold himself upright, the grandness of his seat accentuating the softness of his body and the scrawniness of his arms. He looked less a lord and more a page who had taken the throne in jest when nobody was looking.

For all this though, when he looked up towards our entry he sat upright, and I saw tempestuous green eyes that glistened with a fierce intelligence, a slight smile playing around his pale lips.

Chatten was speaking in his ear. She looked up as we entered. 'It's these two, Lord. The rest I sent to find an inn.'

A neat, well-groomed older man in a garish burgundy doublet with silver buttons standing to the side of the throne coughed gently and announced to us, 'You stand before Mór Hosten Caradrahan, the heir of Clan Gál Tine, Mór of Tulbar and the true High King of Paleir, son of the late Mór Hardane, Guardian of—'

'That will do, Lenard,' said the Mór, flapping his hand to silence the man. 'If even my sworn lords are not impressed by my titles, why should strangers be?' His voice was slightly shrill, hinting at his anxiety, but it filled the hall well enough. He beckoned us forward, his mouth set in a stern line. It was an expression that would have suited an older, more seasoned lord, but it seemed only to accentuate Hosten's youth. 'Chatten tells me that you started a fight and killed two of my people.'

'They started it, I finished it,' said Locan, shoving his thumbs into the belt of his borrowed cloak as he stared arrogantly up at the Mór. 'You should tell your people that not everything they pull out of the sea is harmless. Hopefully the ones I left alive have learnt that now.'

'It was a misunderstanding,' I said, stepping in before Locan could say any more and get us thrown into a cell. 'An accident. Please accept our apologies, Lord.'

Hosten raised an eyebrow. 'One of you has some courtesy, at least.' I could see his nervousness – his fingers were gripping the armrests of the throne as if he feared somebody would take it from him. He could not have been the Mór for very long. 'I'll have your names.'

'Rig,' said Locan immediately. 'We were headed south from a trading mission with King Wexl of the Isles. We'll be on our way again as soon as we can find a ship going south.'

I let out an exasperated breath. The lie was obvious. Honest traders didn't murder men at the first sign of trouble. The truth would serve us better here. I squared my shoulders and looked Hosten in the eye. 'My name is Cetrik Harkken, a prince of Guiland, son to Queen Trelaina and Prince Paramount Navvius.'

'Bloody idiot,' muttered Locan.

At the side of the throne, Chatten wore a smirk. 'I told you he would lie, Lord,' she said, looking at Locan.

'Prince Cetrik Harkken,' the Mór repeated. 'Not only courteous, but also wise enough to tell the truth. And his companion, the famed Locan A'Shadow.'

I flashed a triumphant grin at Locan. The Mór had already known who we were.

'I heard your tale from a visitor who passed through here over winter,' the Mór explained. As our exchange went on, he seemed to be growing in confidence. 'He described you both in some detail.' He looked to the man over his shoulder who looked to be his steward. 'Lenard, you recall his name, I believe?'

'Seamster Bastane,' said Lenard. 'A most charming guest, with an interesting tale to tell.'

I remembered Seamster Bastane. A treacherous, conniving priest whose scheming had led to the near triumph of Solis Deadhand and the death of my brother. 'Whatever he said against us is a lie,' I said acidly, eyeing the guards lining the hall, who at some signal from their lord had placed their hands ready on the hilt of their swords.

'Fine,' said Locan, spreading his hands in false apology. 'You know who we are. Doesn't change a goblin's fart. Find us a ship, and we'll never darken the shores of this fair isle again.'

The Mór was unmoved. 'Seamster Bastane says that you turned a tribe against him and forced him to flee for his life. That you were part of a Guilish plot to steal Narlond from under the nose of the Aegis.' His eyes narrowed. 'And now you are here. At your mother's behest, I must assume. What tale will you tell if I let you leave here, that Tulbar is ripe for conquest?'

'The Guilish designs on Paleir go back centuries,' added Lenard sagely. 'Of course as soon as the Dreadveil begins to recede they would try again.'

The blatancy of Bastane's falsehood caused the blood to rush to my head. 'That's a pack of lies!' I exclaimed. This could not be happening again: I had faced the same absurd accusations of spying among the Bucani tribe.

'Nevertheless.' The Mór gestured to Chatten who took a step forward, hand ready on her sword. Behind us, I could sense the tread of approaching guards. At my side, Locan stiffened – he might have changed his cloak, but he would have at least one knife hidden somewhere about his person, more likely a pair of them. 'That is the tale I have heard. And you've already killed two of my subjects and one of you has tried to lie about who you are. I would not be much of a king if I did not question your presence.'

'By the look of you and the three big fuckers we saw leaving, you ain't much of a king already,' said Locan with a sneer. 'You're about as much a king as the boy is a spy. Would have to be a pretty shit spy to give you his real fucking name the first time you ask.' He glanced back at the guardsmen. 'First one of you to draw a sword gets it shoved where the shadows don't play.'

I felt the guards bristle at the threat, but to my surprise the Mór gave a doleful smile. 'A fair point, Master A'Shadow. And as to the state of my kingship, I fear you are not far wrong.' He ran a hand through his hair and slumped back in his seat. 'The men you saw leaving my hall were once my loyal lords.' He gave a bitter laugh. 'Danning, Ulleách, and Arcalen. For thirty years they served my father, but they will not serve me.' He was no longer looking at us, but morosely staring past us as if we were not there, his fingers steepled anxiously under his chin. He glanced back at his steward. 'I am sorry, Lenard. I am not cut from the right cloth for this farce. I expect honesty from my subjects. What sort of Mór am I if I cannot myself be honest?' He looked me in the eye. 'Bastane was a snake. That's why I sent him on his way. I am grateful for your honesty, Cetrik of House Harkken. It has been over four hundred years since a Caradrahan hosted a Harkken. I am sorry that we have not met in more fortunate circumstances.'

I flushed with relief. I had been preparing myself to be manhandled into the dungeons.

'Lenard,' continued the Mór. 'Victuals for our guests. We'll eat together in my dining chamber.'

'Is that wise, Lord?' asked Lenard, his expression clouding with confusion.

'Was it wisdom that led us here?' asked the Mór. 'If so, I am done with being wise.' He yanked the crown from his head and came to his feet, letting it clatter onto the throne behind him. 'No amount of wisdom could have stopped my lords from betraying me, nor allowed me to prevent my father's death.'

There was still a gloominess to Hosten, heightened by this empty, faded hall, but he hastened down the steps and shook my hand warmly, kissing me on the cheek in the royal style. 'Please accept my apology, Cetrik.' He offered his hand to Locan. 'Lenard and Chatten advise me well, but our current circumstances breed suspicion.' The steward had departed to prepare our refreshments. 'I knew as soon as I saw you that you were no spy, just as I knew my lords were false the moment they stepped within High Tulbar.'

'What of the men they killed?' said Chatten.

'I am that sick of Ulf and the rest of the Keykeepers that I find it difficult to care,' replied the Mór. 'Based on what you've told me, the blame lies with the men.' He threw an arm around my shoulder and steered me towards a door at the back of the hall, Locan following sullenly behind us. 'This way. It will be fish, I'm afraid. All we ever seem to have is fish.'

I found myself slightly thrown by the abrupt change in his demeanour – it was as if the young Mór could not quite decide what sort of ruler he wished to be, trying out different faces in the hope that one of them would fit. Mostly though, I was ravenously hungry, unsurprisingly given I had almost drowned that morning.

'I am sorry for the loss of your father, Lord,' I said, finding myself slipping back into the learnt courtesy of my mother's court. 'And to have darkened your hall at such a time.'

'Call me Hosten,' said the Mór. 'And I'll call you Cetrik, if it pleases you.'

Hosten's easy manner reminded me my younger brother Divvock, without the arrogance. He seemed genuinely eager that we should be friends. I had never found it easy to relate to my brothers, not until the final few weeks of Javvian's life, and my parents had long bemoaned my lack of comradeship with my cousins or any of the sons of their closest lords. Alone in this vast, crumbling fortress, I sensed that Hosten's childhood might have been just as solitary as my own.

'That would please me greatly, Hosten,' I replied, and we shared a knowing smile at the unnecessary formality of this situation, at our inability to escape the cold courtesies we had been forced to learn as children.

'How long's your da' been dead?' asked Locan, breaking the moment.

'A few months,' said Hosten, as flatly as if he had learnt this truth by rote. I thought briefly of mentioning the demise of my brother Javvian, but it seemed too soon, too much of an intrusion on Hosten's grief, no matter how he tried to hide it. He was young indeed to shoulder the problems of a city as troubled as High Tulbar appeared to be, the evident conflict with Ulf and the Keykeepers, and the demands of the fierce lords I had seen leaving his hall.

We passed through a set of high doors banded in gold and covered with etchings of dragons in flight into a dining chamber. The room was as gloomy as the hall, with small, dirty windows and too few lamps, and dominated by a long, uneven table that would have seated sixteen, but which had been set for three. The wood was a deep, marbled red, until with a start I realised that it was not carved from wood at all, but from polished dragon bone.

Though we had departed the hall only moments earlier, several servants were already serving dishes of fish, eels, and wild vegetables – Lenard was clearly a very capable administrator. I also felt an immediate shift in Locan's demeanour as he spotted the tankards of ale.

Locan and I sat down opposite Hosten, and before the Mór could even raise a toast, Locan downed half his mug, let out a satisfied belch, and signalled to a servant for more. 'Got anything stronger?' he asked. 'Nearly drowning works up a thirst.'

'Brandy for our guests,' said Hosten, signalling to a servant, clearly glad to play the welcoming host and willing to tolerate Locan's insolence. 'And for me.'

The servant returned with a bottle and served us each a cup of amber liquid with a sweet, tangy aroma that made my eyes water. Hosten lifted his cup towards us. 'To unexpected arrivals,' he said with a smile.

Together we drank. Plums and grapes exploded on my tongue, and unable to contain my hunger any longer, I took a slice of hard, black bread from the middle of the table and tore into it.

'So,' said Locan, signalling for more brandy. 'Who do you want me to kill?'

Hosten's eyebrows shot up. 'What do you mean?'

'You know who I am, and I know how this works,' said Locan, fixing him with a stare. 'I've sat at enough tables with enough big-balled nobles, and it's never been for the pleasure of my company. Sometimes it's a creditor – as if they think they'll be better off owing me coin than owing them – sometimes it's a cad who's seduced their wife – as if that ever solved a wayward woman – sometimes it's a troublesome family member, but what links them all is that they don't want to pay. You think that if you agree not to give me any grief about those dead men who got what they deserved, I'll get rid of your enemy and solve all your problems at the flash of a knife. For all I know you sent those men after us to try and give yourself some leverage. And if you knew the slightest thing about me other than whatever that turd of a priest told you, you'd know a pit of starving goblins ain't going to scare me.'

The idea that the confrontation on the beach was Hosten's doing was obviously absurd – there would have been no time for him to give such an order; he would not have even known who we were – but even so, the young Mór showed no sign of taking offence. 'My father would have liked you, Locan A'Shadow,' he said. 'He had no time for men who would dance around a point. Unfortunately for me, this approach trained his lords to be belligerent and demanding, hence the three you saw leaving my hall.'

'One of them then, is it?' asked Locan. By the Mór's response, Locan's judgement was not far wrong, so I decided to let this exchange play out and focus on filling my rumbling stomach. 'Or all three? I don't do discounts.'

'It's not those three that most vex me, actually,' said Hosten.

His manner grew more serious. 'It's the man they mean to declare for.'

'Mór Shanoch of Varned,' said Lenard from the doorway. I had not even noticed the stylish steward's reappearance. 'The late Mór's brother.'

'Half-brother,' corrected Hosten. 'My half-uncle.'

I felt a heavy pang of sympathy. Being from Guiland, I was no stranger to the hardships of a newly made lord, where it was not uncommon for a powerful uncle to seek to usurp his recently inherited nephew and to force my mother's intervention.

'Dead kings birth dark ambitions,' said Locan, repeating a familiar saying taken from the Seamstress's Creed. 'I take it those lords weren't here to deliver you your uncle's best wishes.'

'An ultimatum,' said Hosten. He had not touched his food, but I could not hold myself back from sampling the dishes before us. 'If I do not cede my throne to Shanoch, he will march an army across the Homeless Hills and take it from me. Before my father's corpse was even cold, he sought to seduce my lords and then turn them against me.' Hosten was gripping his eating knife so tightly that his knuckles had turned bright white. 'If my father were still here, he would not dare. I swear, if I could prove Shanoch had anything to do with my father's death—'

'How did he die?' asked Locan.

'A fever,' said Hosten. His voice was tight, as if he was struggling to hold his composure. 'The grey owl is what commonfolk call it. Arrives at dusk and carries you away by dawn.'

'And so it was,' said Lenard. 'He was in fine fettle when I saw him in his study that evening, but hours later when I rushed to his bedside he was so jumbled by fever he could not speak, only gesture for water, trying to quench an unquenchable thirst.' The steward's voice broke slightly as he blinked back tears. 'It is the same ague that took the late Móra, three years ago.'

'My mother,' said Hosten.

He was young to be without both parents, and my sympathy for Hosten only deepened. I thought again of Javvian, whose death had widened the estrangement between me and my parents even further. Hosten's position was much harder. Following my ill-tempered conversation with my father, I owed no dues to anybody, while Hosten bore the weight of a whole kingdom.

'Ask anyone in the keep or the town,' Hosten continued. 'You'll find no man with a bad word to say about her.' A livid red blush was blossoming on his cheeks. 'She spoke to beggars with the same courtesy as she spoke to lords. Used to drive my father wild, but she never changed. And my father hunted and hawked and was the finest sword in Paleir. He...' Hosten swallowed, holding back tears. 'He...' The young Mór turned away to compose himself, unable to get the words out.

I took a long drink of ale, hiding behind my tankard. I had forced myself never to think of Javvian among the crew of the *Red Fiend* to spare myself the embarrassment I knew Hosten was experiencing now. It had been bred into me from an early age that such displays were weakness, that emotions were to be crushed in the iron vice of one's mind until they were small enough to lie hidden forever. I only thought of Javvian and the loneliness of my estrangement when I was safely alone, either by myself in the chamber I had been given on Great Yex or exploring the island alone atop Morvolt.

'I do not want you to kill Shanoch,' said Hosten, composing himself. 'There has been enough grief in my family. It is my hope that war might still be avoided. No, I have another task in mind for you. A task that perhaps only the great Locan A'Shadow can accomplish. Ever since I heard Bastane's tale, it has been my distant hope that you might find your way to High Tulbar.'

A curious look passed between Hosten and Lenard. The

steward raised a questioning eyebrow, and Hosten replied with a wistful smile. Unexpectedly, he looked to me. 'Tell me, Cetrik. What do they say in Guiland of dragons? You know our history? What my forebears were in the days before the Dreadveil cut my kingdom off from the world?'

I nodded. 'Your ancestors mastered the strength of the sea dragons and rose to rule all Paleir.'

'No man may master a dragon,' said Lenard. 'Dragons are bound by magic, not oaths, and magic is a fickle mistress.'

'My ancestors were obsessed with dragons,' said Hosten. 'All the more so since they disappeared and the Caradrahan star faded. All through my childhood, there were dragons every-where. Carved atop our walls, etched into our doors, stitched into our tapestries.' He let out a short, mocking laugh. 'My fore-bears were remarkable people, but they were not the most imag-inative when it came to decoration.'

'Chatten mentioned that there have been sightings,' I said. 'Is it true?'

'Indeed,' said Lenard. 'Whether you believe them or not may depend on how much you and the witness have had to drink.'

'*Credible* sightings,' said Hosten. '*Multiple* sightings. Enough that I dare not dismiss these tales as idle, drunken ramblings. Taverners report wings beating over Dragonwing Point. Fishermen claim to see dark shapes in the water.'

My breath caught in my throat. There *had* been something in the water while Morvolt dragged me to shore, a sleek dark shape far below me that flowed through the current so effort-lessly it was as if the sea submitted to its command, hardly making a ripple. When I had woken on the beach, I had dismissed it as the panicked hallucination of someone who had come within a fingernail of death, but now I had to wonder if I had truly imagined it. Was it possible that I had glimpsed a dragon? An exclamation that I had seen something too almost burst out of me.

Locan was sniggering. As eyes flicked towards him, he knocked back another measure of brandy and wiped his mouth. 'Once in Rameon,' he began, 'people swore there was a panther prowling the rooftops. It became something of a legend, the Panther of the Old City. And we aren't talking about just anybody seeing it either – these were patricians of the old families. One claimed it had stolen his grandson, and another even saw it and apparently fell dead from the shock. They paid me a king's ransom to go looking for it – turned out to be a fat black tomcat. And I mean *fat* – nearly put my back out carrying it down off the roof.' Locan chuckled to himself at the memory. 'Think the wife of one of the senators adopted it in the end. Anyway, easiest money I ever made. Another time, I took a job out in Yelano tracking down a chimera – didn't even pay that well; I just wanted to see a chimera – but it was only a big goat with a fuzzy mane and a taste for flesh. I've still got the scar where it bit me.' He pulled back his sleeve and pointed to a patch on his forearm that looked no different to the rest.

'You've also killed wrorcs and vampyres,' I replied. 'We *know* that dragons existed. Why shouldn't they still?'

'Because there's no way an eighty-foot-long winged lizard is hiding for four hundred years.' Locan took another drink. 'Point is that one person sees something, then another person sees it after too many ales, and before you know it they're making manticores out of moles. Probably just a pigeon with black wings and bad breath.'

'You should hope the dragon is real, Master A'Shadow,' said Hosten. 'Because you are correct that I will require a favour in return for overlooking your brawl on the beach. Centuries ago, my ancestors used the scales of dragons to bind these creatures to their will and claim kingship over the whole of Paleir. It is my fervent hope that it will be so again. First though, I must defeat my uncle. I need you to find the dragon and bring me one of its scales.'

CHAPTER 6

As the Mór's request settled in our ears, a stunned silence fell over the dining room, and it was as if nobody wanted to be the first to shatter it. My knife lay still on my plate. Hosten and Lenard were so still they almost appeared to be trembling with the effort of it. Even the servants were sharing side-eyed looks between themselves.

It was Locan of course who broke the silence first. He let out a rough laugh. 'You're joking, aren't you?' he said. 'The dragons are gone, lad. Put these supposed witnesses to the question and they'll change their tale soon enough – they'll say, "Actually, now you mention it, it might have just been an oddly shaped fish."'

'I am deadly serious,' said Hosten, with steel in his voice. 'In return for my patience and protection, you must bring me a dragon scale so that I may defeat my uncle.'

Locan stared back at the Mór, tilting his head as if he were a puzzle to be solved. Hosten did not even have control over his own lords – did he really presume to command the fabled Locan A'Shadow? 'Those boys at the beach tried telling me what to do,' said Locan. 'Didn't end well for them.' His eyes narrowed, his lip curled with a vague promise of violence. 'What makes you think it'll end any better for you?'

'There's no harm in us looking,' I said, trying to placate Locan before Hosten took offence. Until we could find another ship that would bear us south or in the unlikely case that Huretio could fix the *Red Fiend*, we were trapped in High Tulbar, unless we decided to take our chances inland and seek passage from Bastden or Carnaway to the south. So far, Hosten had treated us fairly, and it seemed wise to keep it that way.

'Except that dragons don't fucking exist,' snarled Locan. 'How am I meant to keep my side of the bargain when there's no dragon?'

'The dragon is real,' said Hosten firmly. 'And if you will not help, I will let Ulf deal with you as he sees fit. The future of my reign and victory over my uncle rest on finding a dragon scale.'

'So if I just wait around, your uncle will turn up to take your throne and I won't have to hear any more about this lunacy?' Locan gave a bark of laughter. 'You can barely hold onto the kingdom you have, and you're thinking about claiming the whole island. Did you lose your wits along with your father?'

'Matters in Tulbar are admittedly... unstable,' said Lenard, moving to stand beside Hosten. 'The death of the old Mór has sown fear and confusion. Men like Ulf and the other Keykeepers put their own profit above loyalty to their Mór. The people—' He hesitated, looking to Hosten for permission.

'Continue,' said Hosten with a sad smile. 'I know what the people say of me. Since I came to the throne, I have made misstep after misstep. My father always said that if I did not find the steel in my heart, then my reign would be a short, miserable thing. Perhaps he was right.'

'It is not so, Lord,' said Lenard, placing a loyal hand on Hosten's shoulder. 'Your father made his own share of mistakes at your age. There is still time.'

'But not enough, I fear.' He closed his eyes, the strain of

ruling showing in every line of his face, his boyish face ageing decades in the space of a blink.

My sympathy for Hosten deepened further. I saw so much of myself in him – the disappointed father; the fierce desire to prove him wrong – but also much of my brother Javvian's resolve, his single-minded ambition. Whatever his father might have thought, and however unlikely Locan might consider his aspirations for Paleir, I saw the steel in Hosten. A man did not agonise over matters as he appeared to without some measure of fortitude. A weak ruler would have done as Locan suggested and put the claims of those who had seen the dragon to the test under sharp blades and hot pincers. A lesser man would have sought only to hold onto Tulbar and never spoken of reclaiming all Paleir. I decided then that while we were here, I would help Hosten any way I could.

'Go on, Lenard,' said Hosten. 'Tell me what my people say of me.'

'Your proposal to end slavery was noble, Lord,' said Lenard, hesitating only slightly. 'But it has turned the Keykeepers against you, and with them the rest of High Tulbar. They do not believe Shanoch would be any friend to them, but they miss your father, and you have not yet proven yourself to them.'

I glanced at Locan, expecting some reaction to Hosten's aversion to slavery, but my companion showed nothing. After what I had seen that day, I heartily concurred with Lenard that its abolition was a noble goal. A just lord could not allow his people to debase themselves and others with the sale of human flesh.

'The tale of the dragon has not helped matters,' Lenard went on. 'The Caradrahans of old were the dragons' chosen. The people hear that a dragon has been seen again, then they look at their dead Mór and his young heir and see only men of flesh and blood. They begin to wonder by what right the Caradrahans still hold power in Tulbar.'

'It would be hard enough if I only had to face my uncle Shanoch, but it seems I must also contend with my own lords and people,' said Hosten with a rueful shake of his head. He looked from me to Locan. 'You see my difficulty. If there is a dragon to be found, I must master it and restore my line to the glory of ancient Tulbar. Otherwise, whether at the hands of my uncle or my people, the line of the Caradrahans ends with me.'

To that moment, Locan had been listening attentively, but as Hosten finished he abruptly rose from his chair, pushing it back across the flagstones with a shriek. He strode to the servant who held the bottle of fruit brandy and poured a large measure into his cup. 'Well, quite a predicament you've got,' he said, not returning to his seat. 'Not much to do with us though.'

'It has something to do with you if you hope to live to leave High Tulbar,' said Lenard, his façade of calm crumbling slightly for the first time. 'I know the men Ulf sent after you, but they won't make the mistake of underestimating you again. The other Keykeepers may also look askance at you being allowed to go free after killing two men.' He addressed Hosten. 'Lord, have your guards take this man to the dungeon. That would win you favour with the city just as surely as a dragon would.'

Locan tensed, his hands open and ready to reach for his blades, but Hosten smiled and raised a placating hand to his guards. 'I will not throw the lives of my men away so cheaply. Locan, if you wish to leave Caradrahan Hall, I will not stop you. I ask only that you consider my proposal. Bring me a dragon scale, and you may sail with my blessing, as soon as your friend's ship is fixed. I'll even help with repairs.'

'Piss on your blessing.' Locan jutted out his jaw belligerently. 'Try stopping me leaving and see what happens. I don't need your help in finding a ship off this rock.'

'Very well,' said Hosten. Despite Locan's refusal, the young Mór was still smiling slightly. 'If I truly cannot change your mind, you may return to the city and go in search of a ship. I've arranged rooms for you both at an inn, the Dwarf and Dragon. I hope it's to your liking.'

'You had me at the word "inn",' replied Locan. 'Hopefully they serve something better than this piss-weak brandy.' He claimed the bottle from the tray and turned for the door. 'Coming, Cetrik?'

'I'll see you there,' I replied. I was intrigued to learn more of events in High Tulbar. And I had spent enough time with Locan the past few months. Speaking further with Hosten was undoubtedly preferable to another evening watching Locan drink until the early hours when he eventually passed out.

Locan looked for a moment as if he wanted to argue about it, but then he gave a shrug. 'Have it your way. Just watch out for dragons when you come down to the city.' He gave a contemptuous laugh and offered some final words to Hosten: 'No wonder those lords don't want you if you'll believe any old goblin-shit. Cetrik, I'll see you later, once I've found us a ship out of here.'

Locan marched from the room, letting the door slam shut behind him.

'Should I go after him?' I asked.

'Leave him,' said Hosten. 'Our harbour has been empty for four hundred years. He may laugh, but he is more likely to encounter a dragon than a ship. At least Bastane did not lie about one thing: he is quite belligerent.'

I sighed. 'Sorry.' I would have blamed Locan's mood on the prospect of being trapped in a strange land rather than sailing south for Rameon, but he would probably have been just as antagonistic either way, only now it was Hosten on the sharp end of his ire rather than me, as well as the two men he had killed. 'Will Ulf send men after him?'

'Not immediately,' said Hosten. 'He'll be more cautious now, and after what happened at the beach he may struggle to find anyone willing to trouble Locan again. Fortunately,

Roddin, who owns the inn you'll be staying in, is no friend to Ulf. He is a Keykeeper, but he prefers the taste of coin to the taste of blood.' Hosten wiped his eating knife clean against his trencher and shoved it into his belt. 'I am glad you decided to stay. Would you like to go up to the battlements? You can see the whole city from up there.'

I nodded my assent. I suspected that seeing High Tulbar from the ground did not do the old city justice.

I found myself warming more and more to Hosten. As we ascended to the walls, he asked probing questions about Guiland, and of the journey that had led me to Tulbar, expressing astonishment as I told him the whole tale from my crossing of Midding to Narlond and the final battle with Solis Deadhand.

'Seamstress and Swordsman,' he said with a low whistle as I finished my tale. 'I fear I have led quite a boring life by comparison. Did you truly meet an elfling? Was she very beautiful?'

'Beyond words,' I said, thinking of Urlissa, the enchanting elfling maiden who had so bewitched me and, as it turned out, Locan. My resentment over that affair had lessened in the months since.

'And your parents let you go?' asked Hosten.

I let out a low laugh. 'Not exactly.' I gave a brief explanation of my childhood and my recent estrangement.

When I was finished, Hosten threw an arm around my shoulder. 'Your father sounds a lot like mine,' he said, with a detectable undercurrent of bitterness. 'When I was a boy, I was more interested in stories and drawing than I was in the sword, so to toughen me up he forced me to fight against boys twice my age. It was almost a blessing when I broke my arm in two places.'

'That's awful,' I said.

'It was,' agreed Hosten. 'I miss him though. He would have sent Danning, Ulleách, and Arcalen running home with piss down their legs and thrown Shanoch back across the Homeless Hills.'

We reached the battlements, and High Tulbar spread out below us like a bruise, the white columns that Chatten had named the dragon roosts standing out above a maze of streets and the churning grey water. From here, I could see how the sea wall turned inland to embrace the whole city. Squinting through the gloom of the overcast sky, I believed I could see rowboats battling the waves as they sought to drag the carcass of the *Red Fiend* towards a harbour that jutted from the southern end of the town beneath the shadow of a towering cliff above an ascent thick with pine trees. There were no other ships to be seen. The harbour was deserted, save a few miniscule fishing skiffs.

'Dragonwing Point,' said Hosten, seeing my gaze linger on the bluff. He stood beside me with his hands locked behind his back. 'They used to lay the dragons to rest up on the cliff. My mother is buried up there too, and now my father as well.'

His wistful tone elicited in me a pang of sympathy. When Hosten spoke of missing his father, it was a matter of practicality. But I sensed it was his mother he truly missed.

'My father was a different man after she died,' said Hosten. 'Started tormenting himself instead of me. Could hardly keep him away from the Point.' His tone turned bitter. 'There is a family crypt, but the Keykeepers do not allow those who succumb to the grey owl to be buried in the city, lest their death vapours infect others.'

The cliff did look a lot like a dragon's wing, I decided, formed of several sharp outcroppings jutting precipitously from the main bluff, nothing but water below. A dark, desolate place. Not somewhere to bury a loved one.

'Why do the Keykeepers hold so much power?' I asked.

'It was the price my ancestors paid for holding onto their seat after the dragons left and we lost our grip on Paleir,' said

Hosten. 'Granting the leading citizens of High Tulbar more say over their own affairs. The Caradrahans handed the keys to the city over to them, and they became the Keykeepers. There are only six of them, but they own half of High Tulbar. I even had to negotiate with them to get access to my own treasury. They would never have dared try such a trick if my father was still alive.' He released a sigh, gripping the crenelation as if he feared that the Keykeepers would claim Caradrahan Hall from him next. His voice grew quiet, pensive. 'With a dragon, I would not have to fear either the Keykeepers or my uncle. In time, I might even restore my line to its former glory. The fate of Paleir depends on it. With the fading of the Dreadveil, the world is shrinking again. Across the continent, they are re-examining the edges of the map and remembering again that Paleir exists. If this island remains a squabbling patchwork of warlords and petty kings, it will fall.'

'And you're sure there is a dragon?' I asked. I had seen *something* in the water. I wanted to believe it had been a dragon, but what Locan had said of how false tales could convince those who heard them that they had seen the same thing still rang in my ears. The dragons had been gone for four hundred years – why would they have returned now?

'I have to be,' said Hosten simply. 'It is the only hope I have.' He looked at me with bright eyes. 'Does Locan listen to you, Cetrik? Will you help me?'

Having heard Hosten's tale, I felt compelled to. We were trapped in High Tulbar for the foreseeable future – I could not sit idly by while Hosten's nascent rule crumbled, crushed between the hammer of his grasping uncle and the anvil of the devious Keykeepers. And eventually, Ulf would come for me and Locan again – I had seen his beady eyes and the cold, callous way his gaze roved over the slaves he had marked for death in the arena – he would not allow us to simply walk away after killing two of his men.

'I will do my best,' I said finally, and at Hosten's questioning look I added, 'I'll talk to Locan.' Locan's stubbornness was just another side to his determination. Once he realised there was nothing for us to do in Tulbar until the *Red Fiend* was salvaged or another ship appeared, he would put his whole self to the task. Locan was also pragmatic, sometimes to a fault – he would see the sense in an arrangement that would keep Ulf off our backs for as long as we were marooned here.

'You will?' said Hosten brightly, as if he could not quite believe it. He extended his hand to me. 'Thank you, thank you.' At my agreement, the relief began to pour out of Hosten, and he gripped my hand tightly as he added, 'Honestly, I cannot thank you enough. If you do this for me...' I could see the desperation in his eyes. 'If this works, I hope you will forgive me if I am ever grateful that your ship was wrecked on my shores. Getting a dragon scale is everything, Cetrik, everything.'

Already, I felt a deep kinship with Tulbar's young Mór. In the face of odds that were stacked against him, he refused to allow himself to be cowed, even if it meant pursuing the impossible dream of taming a dragon and restoring the fearsome repute of the Caradrahans. Many would have laughed at him, dismissed his ambition as a childish fancy, just as they would have dismissed mine if I had told anyone that I meant to cross the broken land of Midding and find the legendary Locan A'Shadow. I knew also how deeply the desire would burn in Hosten to prove his father wrong.

'If there is a dragon,' I said, 'Locan and I will find it. I swear it.'

CHAPTER 7

I left Caradrahan Hall late in the afternoon. I had intended to leave sooner to track down Locan, until Hosten and I had fallen onto the subject of his library and he had been delighted to give me a tour.

While perusing the stacks, we discussed at length the theory and nature of monarchic authority. Hosten challenged me robustly on my view that my mother's queenship derived its legitimacy from the consent of her lords and subjects, arguing that the customs and morality of Guiland derived themselves from Harkken rule – our resistance to magic and our resulting authority over the wizards gave us power to set Guilish affairs as we saw fit, and therefore the consent of the governed could not be separated from the Harkkens' unique lineage – our rule a right of birth and blood, rather than permission.

It was the sort of verbal sparring and overthinking that would have seen me mocked by my family as better suited to life as a scribe with ink-stained fingers than a prince of the Harkkens – even if I was sure my mother must have privately contemplated the same question – so I was glad to find a worthy opponent in Hosten. Caradrahan Hall even held volumes that scholars in Guiland had believed lost or destroyed, and Hosten had insisted I was welcome to return and peruse them any time.

It also turned out that Hosten was an avid player of Pillars, and he proceeded to thrash me three games in a row before I made my excuses and retired. I might have stayed longer, but I did not trust Locan to behave himself in my absence, nor did I want him to get so drunk that our assailants from that morning might decide to make another attempt. And if I was to help Hosten, I first had to persuade Locan.

That evening, I sat in the Dwarf and Dragon with Locan, where Lenard had arranged for us to take rooms. The sign over the entrance showed a grinning dwarf standing triumphantly atop a dragon's head with a sword plunged through its skull. The interior was a low-ceilinged common room of dark beams and dull lamplight, every other table occupied by locals who either could not help staring or ignored us as completely as if we were not there. Word of Locan's true identity had already circulated the settlement, and for all the dark glares we received, it was apparent that no man cared enough for the lives of Blinky and Half-ear to take it up with Locan, at least not without another dozen men standing behind them.

We had claimed a table in the corner, where I was nursing my ale while Locan assembled a steadily growing graveyard of empty cups in front of him. As Hosten had predicted, Locan had had no luck searching out a ship – he had gone to the harbour and seen just as I had from the battlements of Caradrahan Hall: High Tulbar's crumbling port homed only a few fishing skiffs and the overturned hulk of the *Red Fiend*.

On my arrival, I had tried to speak to the proprietor, Roddin, but the innkeep was in no mood to talk. 'I already spoke to your friend over there,' he told me with a sneer. 'More than I owe you. The Mór's paying me to rent you a room, not to be your pal. And don't be causing any more trouble.' I had taken an immediate dislike to the man, a short, weak-chinned fellow with limp, greasy hair and a superior air, as if to run an inn made him practically a Mór himself.

'Yeah, he's a pompous prick,' said Locan when I told him of my exchange with Roddin. He spoke slightly too loudly, and I hastily urged him to lower his voice. 'I got chatting with one of the guards on my way out of the castle. He said the Keykeepers have been a pain in Hosten's backside the last two months. Wouldn't recognise him as Mór for two weeks after his father died.'

'They wouldn't even give him the keys to his treasury,' I said, casting a dark look towards Roddin.

'Don't reckon he'll give us any bother though,' said Locan. 'You should have heard him talk about Ulf. If he weren't such a miser, I reckon he'd have given me a couple of free drinks for killing those two men and screwing up Ulf's plans. Not that Roddin's any better, and probably not the rest of the Keykeepers either – you don't get rich somewhere like this without being as mean as a cytroll and as grasping as a Seamster-priest. Every slaver I've met had a heart cold as a tomb and a ringpiece like steel. They'd sell their own mothers into bondage if you paid them enough.' Locan shrugged. 'Not that I wouldn't be tempted, which you'd understand if you met my mother.'

Locan knocked back another mouthful of sweet-smelling brandy. Ale alone was never enough for him, and there was no whisky to be had in Tulbar. Locan made a face, as he had with every one of the previous measures he'd consumed. 'No wonder the Palish are all half-crazed drinking this bollocks.' Neverthe-less, he signalled to the bar for another. 'Other thing is, Roddin says he saw the dragon.'

I sat up in my seat, immediately alert. 'Really? Why didn't you say so?'

'Saying so now, ain't I? Says he saw it swoop down over Dragonwing Point the other month.' Locan pointed towards another man, hunched over the bar staring morosely into his ale.

'That's Darry. He says he saw it too, diving into the water a few hundred yards offshore. Heard me asking Roddin about it – reckon he thought there was a drink in it for him if he backed him up.'

That Locan had already been asking about the dragon increased my hope that he would be willing to help Hosten. 'Do you believe them?' I asked.

Locan snorted. 'Of course I don't.' He leant towards me slightly, his eyes crinkling in suspicion. 'Do you? Don't tell me you bought the Mór's little sob story.'

I hesitated. 'I saw something, when Morvolt was bringing me ashore—'

'Oh goblins' black bones, not you as well.' Locan put down his tankard with a thud. 'I saw you when you came ashore – you were in no state for seeing anything.' He shook his head, a scornful smile creeping across his face. 'This is what I was talking about – heard a load of sightings second hand and now you're seeing things as well.'

'There'd be no harm looking into it though,' I said. 'Means the Mór will keep Ulf and his men away from us.'

Locan snorted. 'Reckon I can do that myself.' He nodded to a table in the opposite corner close to the door. 'Those three have been eyeballing me for the last hour. Another drink or two and one of them might get bold enough to try something.'

'We don't want that,' I hissed. I glanced over my shoulder towards where Locan had indicated. One of the three men briefly raised his gaze to meet mine, his eyes glistening with menace. I looked away. 'We might be here for weeks – do you want to spend the whole time fighting people? This slaver, Ulf, won't be sending boys and fishermen after us next time.'

'He can send who he likes,' said Locan. 'Next time, I'll kill three of them.'

I took a steadying breath. For a man who had made a living serving the nest of vipers that was the court of Emperor

Vurash IV, Locan was somehow completely deaf to diplomacy. 'Please. What's the harm? Wouldn't you rather *not* deal with them? Hosten – the Mór – can warn them off.'

'And all we have to do in return is find a non-existent dragon and nick a couple of its scales,' scoffed Locan. 'If we agree to this, what do you think happens when we don't find anything? This new friend of yours will turn on us as well. If that's how it's going to be, I'd rather deal with it now. And even if I did believe there was a dragon, does *dragon* means the same thing where you're from as it does where I'm from? Big winged scaly thing with breath that can fry the skin from your bones?'

'Sea dragons breathe steam.'

'And that makes a difference, does it?' Locan barked a laugh. '"Actually you'll be lightly seared rather than set alight"? I'm an assassin, not a dragon-hunter.'

'So you do think it might be real?'

'Of course I bloody don't. And even if I did, I wouldn't be getting involved. What we need to do is start thinking about getting out of here.'

'There are no ships until the *Fiend* is fixed.'

'We can ride south to Bastden, I don't care. I didn't get out of Narlond just to be stuck in another damp, stinking shit-heap.'

I was in no hurry to do that. We did not know the land, there was no guarantee of us finding a ship in Bastden either, and by the time we did, the *Fiend* might even be seaworthy again, assuming Huretio's certainty that she could be repaired was not misplaced. Nor could we rely on Locan's shadow magic to get us there more quickly: based on my understanding of his ability, the permanently overcast sky currently made traversing great distances through shadow next to impossible, and there was little sign of Paleir's weather improving.

Locan spoke slightly too loudly, drawing glares from a nearby group of fishermen who heard him even over the clamour of the inn. Locan looked back at them. 'You heard me –

shit-heap,' he said with a sneer. 'What of it? Is one of you going to shut me up?'

One younger man made to rise, until his friend put a hand on his shoulder to keep him in his seat.

'Yeah, that's what I thought,' said Locan. He grabbed his cup of brandy, only to realise it was empty. He slammed it back down. 'Where's that damn innkeep?'

'Hosten believes there's a dragon,' I said, seeking to return our discussion to the matter at hand.

Locan snorted. 'Of course you put faith in his word. I bet you had a grand old time up at the castle with him, pretending you were back in Keystone with servants and hot food whenever you feel like and not surrounded by sweaty, stinking sailors every hour of the day. Let me tell you, kings and lordlings are just as capable of believing bollocks as everyone else. Look at Wexl – he was stupid enough to believe you had the balls to fuck his daughter under his own roof. I should have told him what a pathetic, cringing milksop you are.'

His gaze glittered with malice. He had seemed well-minded towards me until that moment, but after several hours of drinking, Locan's moods could be as changeable as a weathervane. I refused to rise to it – he was only trying to bait me to anger, or to get me to tell him that I *had* bedded Spindle, which of course I hadn't.

I found myself thinking again of what Huretio had told me. Did I need to stay with Locan? More importantly, did I *want* to stay with Locan? I had enjoyed Hosten's company far more than I could ever recall enjoying Locan's.

'This isn't one of those books you've read,' Locan went on when I stared back at him in silence rather than letting him provoke me to a reaction. 'Elves, dwarves, giants – all gone. Why would dragons be any different? I'm almost minded to look into it just to prove to you what a fool he is. Tulbar might be better off with this Shanoch fellow.'

'How can you say that?' I asked with rising indignation. 'Hosten wants to *stop* slavery. Why won't you help him?'

Locan snorted. 'That's how it starts. Young rulers with big ideas. I watched Vurash the Fifth grow up before my eyes, and while few would believe it now, he had grand plans for the Dominion as well.' He began ticking things off on his fingers. 'End slavery. Decentralisation. More rights for the common-folk.' He laughed. 'All came to nothing.' He slapped his other hand down on the table with a detectable anger. 'And as his dad gave him more and more power, all those dreams faded to dust, bit by bit by bit.' He lowered his fingers one by one as he spoke, his voice growing gradually more bitter. 'And now he's no different to the four other Vurashes that came before him. Because no good deed or grand gesture tastes as sweet as power. That'll never change, and that's why slavery won't either.'

'Hosten isn't like that!' I exclaimed. 'He's—'

I did not get a chance to explain any further, for at that moment Roddin appeared bearing a jug of brandy for Locan. 'You got any more questions?' he asked, pushing his limp hair back from his forehead. 'Nearly my time to clock off. Other inns to visit, make sure everything's shipshape.' He paused. '*Ship-shape*. Probably not a word you want to hear for a while, eh?' He let out a burst of abrasive laughter.

'Do you serve drinks yourself at all your inns?' I asked. It seemed odd that a man wealthy enough to be one of the city's Keykeepers would work at his own establishment.

Roddin scowled at me. 'What's that meant to mean? Of course I do – couldn't trust anyone else with it. It's all please-and-thank-you when you hire someone, and then you realise your takings are down and they start turning up to work with new ribbons in their hair. Problem with bar staff is, you want someone who's clever enough to count past their fingers, but not so clever they think they can rob you and get away with it.'

He gestured towards the bar, where a blonde-haired girl

with her back to us was rushing to serve mugs of ale to several different tables while the patrons hooted and hollered for her to hurry up. 'Got lucky with that one, so far, except she fancies herself a bard, which means all the more work for me when she's hen-pecked me into letting her perform.'

'My friend here says you saw the dragon,' I said, seeking to move this interaction on from Roddin complaining about his staff. I was not going to miss an opportunity to enquire about the dragon.

Roddin scowled at me as if I had the cheek to suggest he give us our drinks for free. 'What's it to you?'

'What did it look like?' I wanted to know if Roddin's sighting of the dragon matched what I had seen in the water.

Roddin's scowl deepened. 'You simple or something? Like a dragon. Big lizardy thing with wings.'

Locan looked up from studying his brandy. 'And how drunk were you at the time?'

'I was sober as a Seamster.' Roddin's cheeks coloured in indignation. 'I'll not be insulted in my own inn. If you—'

Locan raised his hands in apology. 'No insult intended. The boy's only curious. We'll let you get back to work.'

Roddin gave me a dirty look as he returned to the bar, where he exchanged some cross words with the barmaid which ended when she threw a rag at him.

Locan watched Roddin with an intrigued look on his face. 'Doesn't seem the sort to let anybody convince him of anything,' he mused. 'Either he really believes he saw something, or he's an exceptional liar.'

'You think he could be *lying* about the dragon?' I asked. It was not even something I had considered – Hosten and Lenard had suggested that there were dozens of witnesses who had seen it; surely they could not all be lying?

'More likely than there being a dragon, ain't it?' Locan snorted and took a glug of brandy. 'He weren't exactly desperate to talk about it, was he? There's others we can ask tomorrow – see if one of them breaks.'

'I thought you weren't interested?' It was typical of the way Locan's cynical mind worked that he would only be interested in proving that a dozen different people were all dishonest.

Locan shrugged. 'Fuck all else to do here.' He gave me a hard look across the table. 'To be clear, doesn't mean I'm buying this orc-shit. The dragons are gone, as much as you might want to believe otherwise. There's as much chance of this ending with us finding a dragon as there is of me giving up drinking.' He knocked back another mouthful of brandy.

When it came to me and dragons, he was admittedly not so far from the mark. What boy would not be fascinated by dragons? I was old enough that I had begun to accept they were gone, but the idea that they might still be alive had lit a fire of excitement in me. Still, if the hope of proving everybody either delusional or dishonest was what it took to spark Locan to action, I was not going to complain. And the more credulous I was, the more eager he would be to prove me wrong.

A smattering of lukewarm applause from the inn's other patrons saved me from having to reply to Locan. The barmaid who had been arguing with Roddin was ascending the small stage in the corner, grasping a lute, and immediately I forgot all about my disagreement with Locan. There had been music in both Narlond and Great Yex – the deep, rhythmic drumming of the Bucani tribe and an elderly skald in King Wexl's court who often fell asleep halfway through the epic he was reciting – but I sensed I would enjoy this performance far more than I had those. She was of an age with me, tall and willowy with a cascade of golden blonde hair. Beautiful too, with wide blue eyes that were at once both innocent and alluring, a smattering of freckles on her cheeks, a stub nose, and plump bow lips that immediately put me to wondering what it would be like to kiss her.

'Put your tongue back in your head,' muttered Locan as the applause died down.

Before I could think of anything to say in response, with no further introduction, the girl plucked a note on her lute and began to sing.

> *'Flowers for the healer*
> *Jewels for the queen*
> *Silver for the troubadour*
> *Who is just about to sing.'*

Singers often came to Harkfall seeking my mother's patronage. On the rare occasions I was able to venture into Keystone, performers could be found in most of the taverns. I had briefly been tutored in the harp, before my father decided my talent was too meagre a thing to justify such an unmanly pursuit. I was therefore no stranger to music, and the folk melody crafted by her fingerpicking was nothing I had not heard half-a-hundred times before, but she played it beautifully, the fingers of both her hands finding their marks clear and true, the notes rich and ringing and perfectly in time.

> *'Scales from a dragon*
> *Cool mist upon your skin*
> *Shackles for the bandit*
> *Who keeps prizes from his king.'*

Her playing was remarkable enough, though nothing to set her above any court-trained musician I had seen in Guiland. What lifted her from being merely talented to transcendent was her voice. It was an alloy, as clear as crystal and as durable as steel. It evoked an aura of both fragility and resilience, like the *Red Fiend*'s ill-fated last voyage through the storm that had nearly claimed our lives.

'Bloody dragon scales again,' muttered Locan. 'Whole country's obsessed.'

In truth, I had been so mesmerised by the soaring melodies crafted by this nameless woman's voice that the words she sang had barely registered with me. Already though, I wanted to discover all there was to know about her, to hear every secret veiled behind her melody. I would listen as if her words hid within them the last hope of a doomed world.

> *'If you should claim a fortune*
> *Measured not in gold and gems*
> *Give your treasure to the water*
> *To wake leviathans from the sea.'*

When she finished, she sang two more numbers: a tear-jerking ballad of two brothers who fell in love with the same girl and died upon one another's swords, after which their heartbroken beloved threw herself from a cliff, then ended with a rousing drinking song that had the whole inn clapping along, me included.

When she descended the stage, I applauded as loudly as anybody, and then with a smile and cheery wave she was gone, back to the bar towards a scowling Roddin. The Dwarf and Dragon's owner evidently did not care for music.

'Not bad,' said Locan. 'I've heard far worse. Wasted in a dive like this.'

Whether he meant High Tulbar or the Dwarf and Dragon was not clear, but immediately I leapt to the barmaid's defence. 'Not bad?' I said with a laugh. 'She's incredible.'

'Oh, here we go.' Locan's eyes rolled to the heavens. 'If she were a one-eyed crone with no teeth you wouldn't be the slightest bit arsed, and you know it.'

'Which makes me a fool,' I replied, seeing no reason not to

acknowledge that Locan was likely right, 'but that does not diminish the truth.'

Locan gave a bark of laughter. 'Spoken like a poet. You going to add singing to your endless list of talents? That might impress her. Something like "*I met a girl, I liked her timbre, her voice did something, to my—*"'

A throat-clearing cough interrupted Locan's attempt at verse. Given he had mispronounced *timbre* to rhyme it with *member*, I believed I knew where it was going. It was the barmaid, delivering fresh mugs of ale. 'These are on the house,' she said with a smile. 'Just don't tell Roddin. He's just left for the evening.'

The right side of her face had been slightly angled away from us when she was performing, but now for the first time I noticed she had been branded – a faded 'R' tattooed just under right eye. Roddin's barmaid was also his slave. She must have realised I was staring at her, for she smiled shyly and lowered her eyes.

'Thank you,' said Locan, immediately seizing one of the tankards and raising it in a toast to her.

I rifled through my mind for something to say, something that might make her stay a moment longer. I touched a finger to my face, mirroring the place where she had been branded. 'Does it hurt?'

I regretted my question immediately. I could have asked her about her performance. The last thing a slave wants is to be reminded of their circumstances, not that they could forget. Nevertheless, she smiled and looked down at me with those bright blue eyes big enough to drown in. 'It used to,' she said softly. 'But not everyone wears their scars on their face. At least I don't have to explain mine to anyone.'

I had never thought to hear such eloquence from a barmaid. That is to my fault – I have met foolish kings and gravediggers who wrote poetry that could make a goblin weep; learning and rank are no measures of how one might see to the heart of truth – but that is the age I was. I had never even spoken to a slave before.

'I'm sorry,' I said, too flustered by my own foolishness and too dazzled by her beauty to say anything more astute. 'That was rude of me. What I meant to say is that you sing and play exquisitely. I've never heard those songs before.'

'Think nothing of it,' she said. She glanced back towards the bar. 'Far less rude than what I have to tolerate most days. And I'm glad you enjoyed it. They're old songs my mother taught me. She was a bard as well.'

'They are beautiful,' I said. In a fit of confidence, I flashed what I hoped was my most charming smile. 'What's your name? I must know it, so that I may tell every man from here to Rameon the name of the fairest bard this side of the Red Water.'

She blushed slightly, but met my eye with a bold smile and a raise of her eyebrow. 'Just this side of the Red Water? Are your compliments always so modest?'

'In the world, then,' I said. 'But I fear I would first need to travel across the Red Water in order to attest the truth of my boast. It is a treacherous journey, but I am sure the name of such a fair maid would be just the inspiration I needed.'

Despite the clumsiness of my compliment – recall, if you will, my tender age – to my relief she laughed. 'My name is Shaliya,' she answered, smiling brightly at me.

I could feel my mind fogging with every moment our eyes held. 'I'm Cetrik,' I managed to say, nearly tripping over my own tongue.

I could have stared at her forever, but an impatient cry for ale sounded from another table, and with a last lingering smile, Shaliya turned and walked away.

'Well that was quite the display,' said Locan. 'Are you sure Spindle didn't wander into your bedchamber by mistake? I've met orcs with more charm.'

I barely heard a word Locan said. 'Sorry?' I asked, tearing my eyes away from the departing Shaliya.

'Doesn't matter,' said Locan. 'Just don't be doing that again. Elflings and king's daughters are bad enough, but mooning over another man's slave is liable to get you killed.'

'But you hate slavery!' This warning was rich coming from a man who had already done his best to get us both thrown in a cell.

'Aye, but slavery won't be stopped by you trying to flirt with one of them. More likely to end with you having a letter branded on your face. Remember we're stuck here – no upsetting the locals. Same thing you told me.'

I almost laughed at how absurd this was – not fifteen minutes earlier Locan had been threatening to kill anyone else that Ulf sent after us and trying to start a fight with the next table – and now he was telling *me* not to upset the locals?

I was about to defend myself when there came a commotion from by the bar. An angry shout of protest, a shriek, and then as I turned towards the disturbance a violent clang of pewter against wood.

Shaliya was back behind the bar, and a large, broad-shouldered man wearing a filthy apron was looming over her jabbing his finger. 'Say that again!' he yelled. 'Say that again and I swear you'll regret it!' His voice was thick with drink, and he was having to lean on the bar to support himself.

A few other men looked over, then returned their eyes to their drinks. Shaliya was trying to stand her ground. 'But Roddin said—'

'Piss on what Roddin said!' The man brought his fist down on the bar. 'I'll take it from him, but not from you, you pox-addled slave. Get me another, or I'll beat that pretty face of yours to mush.'

This was too much for me to ignore. The man was much larger than me, but Hosten had been kind enough to replace my lost sword, and unlike this man I was sober. I rose from our table and moved to the bar, one hand on the hilt of my blade. 'What's the problem here?'

The man turned on me, his eyes bleary and shot with blood. He swayed slightly. 'This... this *whore* says I owe her master money.'

'He does,' said Shaliya. She kept her voice steady, refusing to be cowed by the man's insults. 'Roddin said not to serve you any more this evening, Darry, not unless you've got the coin to pay for it.'

'Just give the man a drink!' called out a woman from a nearby table. 'Whatever he wants. It'll be him making weapons for our lads when the Varnans come across the Homeless Hills. You need to show him some respect.'

An armourer, then. That explained the apron and the size of him. I slapped a coin down on the bar. 'I'll buy you a drink, sir.'

'Much obliged.' Darry immediately reached for the coin, but I covered it with my hand. 'On two conditions. One, you'll make this drink your last. And two, you'll apologise to Shaliya.'

'What?' Darry squinted at me, struggling to focus. 'Apologise?'

'Apologise, have your drink, then go home.' I spoke carefully, hoping that some logic of what I was proposing would penetrate his drink-thick skull. I twisted to display the sword at my belt in case he'd missed it.

Darry's bloodshot eyes flashed with fury, his want for another drink warring against the impulse to hit me. After a long moment, the fight went out of him. 'All right.' He looked briefly to Shaliya. 'Sorry, Shaliya.'

I slid the coin towards her. 'Thank you,' she said with a pretty smile that made my gut lurch. She began to pour Darry another measure of brandy. The man had slumped back on the bar stool, our brief confrontation already forgotten, staring at the measure of spirit as if all the secrets of existence swirled in its depths.

I returned to our table, where Locan had been watching with interest. 'Hope you weren't expecting me to intervene if that turned ugly,' he said as I retook my stool.

'I knew you wouldn't need to,' I said taking a sip of ale. 'That man's a coward.' I had clocked that fact as soon as I'd seen him trying to bully a girl half his size, and learning that he was an armourer had only served to confirm it. 'Men that size who like fighting don't beat metal all day.' And of course, the drink I'd taken so far had made me bold. One did not have to keep up with Locan for that to happen.

Locan gave a grunt of laughter. 'Sounds like wee Cetrik is ready to make his own way in the world! Hope you had a plan for if he decided to fuck the drink off and punch you in the face. We're unpopular enough as it is.'

Before I could tell Locan that at least I wouldn't have killed him, Shaliya reappeared, bearing another round of brandies for us. 'This is to say thank you,' she said, beaming at me to display a row of spotless white teeth. 'Roddin swore he'd beat me if I let Darry keep drinking once he'd run out of money. He already owns half Darry's business with what's owed to him.'

'Don't mention it,' I said, smiling back at her, struggling to contain the candlemoths flittering in my stomach. 'You won't get in trouble for giving us free drinks, will you?'

Shaliya shrugged. 'Roddin's tight as a goblin's hole, but he won't notice the odd drink.'

I liked the blunt way she talked about her master. I would have thought less of anyone who held another person in bondage, and meeting Roddin had done nothing to change that opinion. I was not sure how long Shaliya had been enslaved, but I was glad that a fire of defiance still burnt in her. I could not help wondering how she had ended up in slavery.

'You're the two who arrived on the shipwreck, aren't you?' she asked. 'The ones that the Mór asked to find the dragon?

'Tulbar's a small place,' she added, seeing my look of surprise that this tale had already circulated. 'Or it is these days. Nothing stays secret here for long, and badmouthing the new Mór is one of their favourite hobbies.'

'He asked me, and I told him no,' said Locan, scowling in spite of the free drinks. 'Thanks for the brandy. We'll let you know if we need anything else.'

If Shaliya noted Locan's rudeness, she gave no sign of it. 'If you want to know where you might find the dragon,' she said, 'you should go and see Namma. She's a hedge witch. She knows all sorts. She lives up on the cliff, just past Dragonwing Point.'

Hedge witches were not common in Guiland – the dark reputation of the Harkkens' wizards meant few people were willing to put their trust in magic – but it stood to reason there would be hedge witches in Paleir. The magic in this land was wilder – the home of dragons and unicorns and Halagrim the Deathmistress, the Abomination King's chief acolyte.

Shaliya continued. 'When a boar was terrorising anyone who went into the forest, she did something that made it run away. When the fish dried up a few years ago, she put some-thing in the water that made them come back. She—'

'We'll be sure to consider it,' said Locan, interrupting Shaliya. He motioned towards the bar. 'We best be letting you get back. I think there's some folk over there needing some drinks.'

'You didn't have to be rude,' I said, after Shaliya had departed, not before dazzling me again with another bright-eyed smile and letting her hand linger on my shoulder in a way that made my insides leap.

'She'd never have left if I hadn't,' said Locan. He leant towards me over the table. 'Maybe all the blood's gathered in your nether regions and left you without the wits to hear a word I'm saying, but I'll try again: Stay. Away. From. That. Girl.'

'I'm only being nice,' I protested. That was a lie, of course. I was deeply aware of Shaliya's presence over by the bar. My neck was getting hot with a desire to turn and smile at her again.

'Just like you were only being nice to Wexl's daughter,' said Locan. 'I indulged it then. I'll not make the same mistake here.'

'What's it to do with you anyway?' I said, suddenly irritated. It was no business of his who I talked to. I had come with Locan so I could be free, not so he could take the place of my family by deciding how every hour of my day was spent. 'I'm not making *you* talk to her.'

'It'll be my business if Roddin gets you thrown in jail for interfering with his slaves,' Locan shot back. 'Palishmen take that sort of thing seriously. You got the money to pay for her? Pretty thing like that won't come cheap.'

'I would never own a slave,' I said hotly. 'Neither would you. After what you said earlier, you want to just go along with it?' He was maddening sometimes: his apparent burning dislike of slavery did not extend so far as helping a Mór who hoped to abolish it or even speaking pleasantly to the slave who served us drinks.

'It's not about slavery.' Locan jabbed me in the chest with his forefinger. 'It's about not doing anything that's going to get us in any more trouble.'

'Like killing two men.'

'Exactly like killing two men. Except Roddin cares more about his slave than Ulf cares about his hired goons, and unlike me you can't hide in the shadows to escape your problems when things go to shit.'

I had to admit that Locan was not wrong. Roddin was already quarrelsome, and it would be better not to upset our host any further, even if all I was doing was speaking to Shaliya. 'Fine,' I said. 'I'll try to keep my distance.' I did not feel good about it – I did not see why anyone could object to me being friendly with Shaliya. That was how all her customers should behave, not insulting and pawing at her. Slave or not, Roddin should not have tolerated customers like Darry abusing her.

'I already know you won't.' Locan shook his head. '"*Try*" he says. If you need something to distract you while we're stuck here, keep worrying about this mystery dragon. Once Huretio's sorted out the *Fiend*, we can be on our way, and you'll never think about the girl again.'

CHAPTER 8

Word from Huretio reached us the next morning. A note penned by the man himself, bearing ill news.

Cetrik. We have saved the Fiend. *Unfortunately, the closest thing to a shipwright in this Seamstress-forsaken town is a drunk layabout who does not know a bilge pump from his backside. I have taken over repairs myself. We will be here for at least two weeks. Stay safe and don't let Locan lead you astray. Huretio.*

I was confused for a moment as to why it had been addressed to me, until I recalled that Locan could not read. Nevertheless, he was looking at it over my shoulder. 'Has an angry look to it,' he said. 'That from Huretio?'

I nodded. 'They can fix the *Fiend*, but it will take at least two weeks.'

From the doorway to our shared room, Roddin gave an impatient cough. 'The runner with that note woke me up,' he groused. 'The Mór ain't paying me to be your errand boy.' He held out his palm for payment.

Locan shut the door in his face. 'Too early for that arsehole,' he muttered. 'So, where is it you want to start looking for this dragon?'

I started in surprise. 'Really? Because you said—'

'I know what I said. But seeing as we're stranded here and my only other choice is to spend the whole day here with Roddin moaning at me, I might as well join you. It's either that or I have to listen to you keep crying about it. Shall we start going door to door, or did you have a list of suspects? Some of this lot are ugly enough to be a dragon. Or maybe we start swimming and see how long it takes to decide we look like a decent meal.'

In truth, I was relieved. I had not favoured the prospect of exploring this strange new settlement by myself without Locan's protection. 'We could start with the woman Shaliya mentioned,' I suggested, trying to keep from sounding too eager. If we went to see Namma, I would have a reason to speak to Shaliya again.

Locan snorted. 'There's strange crones living out in the wilds all over the world, and every one of them's a fraud. Not worth the bother. Best you can hope for is a love potion that doesn't leave your intended shitting their breeches the next morning.'

'Are you speaking from experience?'

Locan gave a grunt of laughter. 'I'm a natural charmer. You wouldn't believe the things women have done to spend a night with me.'

An idea struck me. 'Who knows what else she brews out in the woods? She might have something to drink you like better than Roddin's brandy.'

Locan grunted. 'Suppose it's possible. Fuck it, no harm in taking a look, just as long as you leave that girl alone.'

After breaking our fast on fresh fish and seaweed porridge cooked for us by Shaliya – to keep Locan happy, I spoke with her only briefly to get directions to Namma's – we left the

Dwarf and Dragon and headed for the town's southern wall. Following the high outcropping of Dragonwing Point, we ought to have found our way easily, but we had not reckoned with the dilapidated state of High Tulbar. Locan insisted on a shortcut through an alley that led to a dead end of fallen masonry. Another street had collapsed into the soil and was now a lake of stagnant water filled with naked children learning to swim.

Eventually, we reached a postern gate, and after some negotiation to convince the two men guarding it that we were not spies for Shanoch, we were allowed to leave.

Beyond the walls, a meandering dirt path led up towards Dragonwing Point through a dense woodland of bare, twisted trees, some of them so bent it was as if they sought to escape back into the earth. In Narlond, the unnerving feel of the Marblewood had stemmed from the sense that there was always something watching you from the shadows, but the forest was a dead, desolate place. There was a misery to the way the wind whistled between the bent trunks of the trees. Like High Tulbar itself, this seemed a place that had fallen on hard times but might once have teemed with life.

Half a mile along the path, past where Dragonwing Point jutted out into the sea, the woods opened to a clearing overlooking the water. In the centre sat a ramshackle hut of dark pine, ruling over the forest like a bedridden matriarch. A brace of dead snakes hung over the battered door, and nearby, a scarecrow of rags and sticks wearing a dented helm with a red plume stood guard over a neat vegetable patch with nothing growing in it. On the roof, an ugly weathervane of dark iron topped by the silhouette of a dragon spun and creaked in the wind, while a lazy cloud of blue-grey smoke bloomed from the chimney.

'Do you think we can just go up and knock?' I wondered aloud. By themselves, any of the hut's features would have been no reason for alarm, but together they served to create in me a deep sense of foreboding.

'That's how it usually works,' said Locan dryly. 'Unless—'

Whatever Locan was going to say was interrupted by the hut's door swinging open. The figure who hobbled out was several fingers under five foot, draped in a shapeless cloak of black wool complete with a hood and a cowl that covered her mouth and jaw. All that was visible of her face was her eyes, cobwebbed with crow's feet and milky with cataracts. She clutched a gnarled stick to support herself, and her slow, shuffling gait caused the soles of her shoes to whisper against the hut's porch.

'I don't know you,' she called out, 'but you look like trouble.' There was no trace of infirmity in her voice, which though croaky, was powerful enough that it could have carried clearly over the woods. 'Away with you!'

'Shaliya sent us,' I said. 'Are you Namma?'

'*Who* sent you?' The woman cocked her head and squinted. Given the cloudiness of her eyes, I was surprised she could see anything at all. She made a disappointed noise in her throat. 'Too tall. No business a boy being so tall. A boy should be the height of Yellen and no bigger or smaller.'

'Who?' I asked. 'I'm sorry we disturbed you. We were wondering if—'

'He is, fool boy!' The woman gestured at the scarecrow, which stood at around five and a half foot, or six if he received credit for the grand feather in his helmet. She shook her head. 'I can't give Yellen your clothes. It would look ridiculous.'

Beside me, Locan was trying not to laugh.

'And you!' The woman raised a withered finger towards Locan. 'No use for you either. How is a man your age going to chop my wood for me? Your back's crookeder than a Dychan tinker, and I know a thing or two about Dychan tinkers, let me tell you!'

'I could chop your wood for you?' I suggested. 'And I believe my friend's clothes might fit Yellen.'

Namma tsked, shaking her head. 'You're not the sharpest knife, are you? Your mother should have drunk more wormbrew when her time was approaching. No, no, that won't do at all. You weren't made for the chopping of wood. No more than your friend was made for the removing of clothes.' She put her hands to her hips, tapping her foot impatiently as if we had somehow wronged her, then a moment later turned her back on us and retreated inside her hut, slamming the door behind her.

A hushed silence fell between me and Locan. 'Reminds me of my great-grandmother,' he said eventually. 'The one I liked.'

The door abruptly opened again and Namma stuck her head out. 'Are you two coming in or not? I'm not bringing your tea outside. You don't bring tea outside when there's hungry squirrels in these woods. Squirrels steal anything.'

The door closed again. Locan and I looked at one another in bemusement before advancing into the hut, ducking beneath the pair of dead snakes.

A scene of chaos greeted us. A woodwormed table strained under the weight of a vast water-filled cauldron with broken twigs floating in it, exuding a shadowy red vapour. Four chairs stood around it, but all bar one of them were occupied by creatures assembled from hundreds of different twigs: a fox, a bird, and a bear. Muttering under her breath, Namma hastened to cover the table and its cauldron with a large, moth-eaten cloth.

Something ran over my foot, and I looked down into the inquisitive gaze of a piebald rat that gave a squeak of disdain before disappearing into the pile of sticks and parchment under the table. A second scarecrow under construction stood in the corner, its limbs and shoulders draped in snakeskins of shimmering blue and yellow. Under the chimney, a second cauldron bubbled over a small fire, radiating heavy blue smoke. Cobwebs covered every corner, and from the crossed beams overhead hung an array of red, grey, and black squirrel carcasses.

'You don't like squirrels, do you?' said Namma, appearing

from the haze of smoke and thrusting a cracked clay cup of mud-coloured tea into my hand. Even inside, she wore her hood and cowl, leaving only her scowling eyes visible. The drink smelt of rotting wood and sharp citrus fruit.

'I am ambivalent to squirrels,' I said, taking the cup.

Namma made a disappointed noise in her throat as she handed a cup to Locan. 'There's no being ambivalent to squirrels, not in this house, but throwing around words like "ambivalent" I suppose means you've got greater concerns. That's young people for you, too busy wandering around with their head in the clouds to look down and see the squirrel that's stealing their shoelaces.'

I was beginning to wonder if Shaliya had sent us here for her own amusement. Unless there was some missing link between squirrels and dragons, Namma would be no help at all. I was half-minded to go straight to the Mór and suggest the woman be brought to Caradrahan Hall to protect her from herself.

She turned away and waddled towards the cauldron over the fire, breathing hard and teetering so precariously on her stick that for a moment I thought I would have to dive across the room to stop her falling. The rat that had run over my foot skittered across the floor and climbed Namma's cloak to take up residence on her shoulder. 'That's young people for you,' she muttered again. 'Anyway, I assume you're looking for a love potion.'

I had just taken a sip of the foul-tasting tea and almost spat the mouthful out in protest. 'What?' I exclaimed. 'No!' Beside me, Locan was sniggering.

'You can stop laughing,' said Namma sharply, turning and fixing him with a pointed black stare. 'I'd need the rest of my life to brew a potion that could make someone fall in love with you.'

'Probably longer,' said Locan, flashing her a devilish grin.

'So what is it then?' said Namma, addressing me again.

'Rival you want to poison? Some girl's father you want to put to sleep for an evening?'

'No, nothing like that,' I said. 'As I said, Shaliya sent me—'

'Ah, Shaliya! Well, why didn't you say so? Lovely girl, beautiful. Comes to see me sometimes and never fails to bring a dead squirrel with her. Darling girl. And you're sure it isn't a love potion you're wanting? No?' The old woman shook her head. 'That's the trouble with young folk these days, you're all so serious! Not seen a smile out of you since you arrived.'

'We wanted to ask about dragons,' I managed to say at last. 'For the Mór. There have been some sightings in the city. Shaliya said you might be able to help us.'

Namma's gaze sharpened slightly. 'Oh yes.' The old woman's stick began tapping excitedly against the floor. 'If it's a dragon you're wanting, you've come to the right place.'

'Do you have one hiding in here?' asked Locan, looking about the cluttered cabin.

'My grandmother's grandmother saw a dragon once.' Namma continued as if she had not heard him. 'Two hundred feet long and breath that could slough a man's skin from his bones. Carried off three of her sheep.' She squinted at us. 'What's the Mór want with a dragon? Looking to restore his family glory, I'll bet.' Namma gave a world-weary sigh. 'Always the same, these Caradrahans. The Mór's a foolish old man.' There seemed little point in correcting her on the identity of the current Mór. 'Wouldn't know a dragon if it crawled out of his privy and bit him on the backside. The Caradrahans lost their claim on the dragons long ago.' Her clouded eyes narrowed. 'You sure you know what you're doing? Bigger men than you have gone hunting dragons and never returned.'

'I thought the Caradrahans and the folk of Tulbar worshipped the dragons,' I said. There seemed little use in asking how her great-great-grandmother had seen a dragon when nobody had laid eyes upon one for four hundred years.

'Not all gods are made to be loved, boy,' said Namma. She seemed more lucid talking about the dragon, as if the prospect of one still being alive had instilled her with purpose. She paused, pondering, tapping her foot while the rat on her shoulder worried at the threads of her cloak. 'Mistbreath Cove,' she said finally. 'Less than a day's ride down the coast from here. The last known dragon nest in Tulbar.'

'How do you know that?' I asked. Not even Hosten had been able to volunteer that information, but Namma had known immediately, and I had seen little to convince me the hedge witch's knowledge went beyond murdering squirrels, brewing foul tea, and training rats.

'Because, boy, knowing things is my business.' Namma looked up into my face, and her milky eyes bored into me. Though I swear she must have been half blind, it was as if my own eyes were a window into my soul, and she was picking her way through it, pulling apart the threads of my mind.

'Most people thought the dragons dead.' Her voice had fallen to a whisper. The way she was scrutinising me was almost kindly. 'But you don't, do you? No, I see that now. And you'd be right. The signs of their return are there for those who know what to look for. I've been reading the leaves and watching the stars.' Beneath her cowl, I sensed that the old woman was smiling. 'A dragon has returned to Paleir. And if one dragon has returned, more will follow.' A draught from the door sent a chill through my bones. The old woman's eyes were like saucers. 'They are coming, and with their coming, all the world will bleed.'

CHAPTER 9

Locan and I thanked Namma for the tea, which we left undrunk, and departed with promises that we would return soon with some clothes for Yellen the scarecrow and a strapping young man who could chop her wood for her, although not one any taller than Yellen.

'What did you make of that?' I asked, though I believed I already knew what Locan's answer would be.

Locan gave a black laugh. 'Can't believe you cut into my drinking time for that. Told you, mad as a sack of polycats. And don't even think of sneaking back there for a love potion.'

'She seemed most lucid when talking about the dragon, though,' I said, refusing to rise to Locan's bait. More than lucid – Namma's prophecy of the return of the dragons had been positively convincing, compelling.

'You mean like when she claimed her great-great-grandmother had seen a dragon?' said Locan with a smirk. 'Yeah, completely lucid. There is no dragon. Don't start buying into this nonsense just because some mad old woman's put a fear up you.'

But Namma's prediction had had a powerful effect on me. It

would be a beautiful thing to see dragons in flight again. And, if we were successful in finding a scale, a wondrous thing for Hosten and the line of Caradrahans, and a terrible thing for his enemies. A deep sense of purpose rose in me – we had been in Tulbar slightly over a day and already we had a possible nest for our dragon. If we explored Mistbreath Cove the next day, Hosten might even have a dragon at his command by the time his uncle reached High Tulbar.

We returned to the Dwarf and Dragon where an unsmiling Roddin served us each a mug of ale with a measure of brandy for Locan. There had been no offer of liquor from Namma, only more disgusting tea.

'Heard that Shaliya gave you drinks on the house last night,' said Roddin with a scowl. 'You can pay for those as well. As good as stealing in my view.'

'She gave them to us,' I protested.

'Well it weren't her right to,' Roddin snapped back, his mean little eyes boring into me. 'And no sweet-talking her either. I heard it all from Darry, you two smiling and simpering at each other. I don't know how things are done in Guiland, but here, a fellow who messes with another man's slave isn't fit to call himself a man. Touch her and I'll bring you up before the law, but not before I've beaten you to a pulp.'

'We don't keep slaves in Guiland,' I said coldly, leaning my full height over the bar. Roddin's threats had got my blood up. 'And as for beating me to a pulp, just try it and see what happens.' Roddin was no weakling, but he was thirty years older than me, short with a gut that sagged over the top of his belt.

Before matters could go any further, Locan grabbed me by the collar and wrenched me away from the bar. 'The boy's sorry,' he said. 'It won't happen again.' I tried to pull away and Locan tightened his grip on me.

'He don't look sorry,' said Roddin, still scowling. 'Just because you've got the Mór paying your way don't give you the right to insult a man under his own roof. I'm a Keykeeper. Any more trouble from him and you'll both regret it.'

Locan nodded. 'Understood. We're just here to enjoy our drinks in peace. If he troubles your girl again, I'll batter him myself.'

'What is wrong with you?' I demanded as soon as we were both seated. Locan never acquiesced to threats, certainly not from fat little worms like Roddin. 'When did you turn into such a... such a...'

'Coward?' suggested Locan. 'Or perhaps you were going to say pacifist?'

'Bootlicker,' I shot back. The day before, Locan had said that slavery would never be abolished by rulers like Hosten and Vurash V, but he refused to take any action himself either. 'You said you hated slavery, but you won't lift a finger to change it.'

Locan was smirking, which only served to infuriate me further. 'First time I've been called a bootlicker by a prince. I'm not going to fix slavery in Paleir in a day. Or in a lifetime. I've tried that before, remember?' His voice heightened a notch. 'Tens of thousands of my countrymen fought and died to save Kerado from the yoke of the Dominion. After the Rameans won the Battle of Kintala, they offered the surrendering Free Union-ists a choice: lose your eyes, or lose your freedom, and I'm sure I don't need to tell you which of those they picked. Only thing that saved me from that same fate was this accursed shadow magic that runs in my veins.'

A cold fury brimmed in his dark eyes. 'For as long as the world has stood, there have been those forcing the shit out and those being forced to eat it. I can't change that and neither can you.'

I wanted to protest, but I could not seem to find the words. I sometimes forgot how far Locan had come from his home, his true home, now reduced to another servile province of the Ramean Dominion. He had fought against the forces of

Rameon, and he had fought for its established order, and now he fought only for himself.

But I would not accept what he said as written. I had seen the festival of human suffering for which Ulf intended his slaves, and I had seen how slavery eroded the souls of both Shaliya and Roddin. I could not stand idle and accept that this was the way of things. I would find a way to help Hosten, and I would find a way to free Shaliya.

'And don't pretend this is the slightest bit about some moral objection to slavery,' Locan went on. 'I've seen idealists and fanatics, and you ain't one of them. You just don't like that there's a pretty girl you're not allowed to moon over.' He leant forward, dropping his voice to a growl. 'Bet you hate the idea of that fat cunt Roddin's hands on her, don't you? Doesn't look to be married, not that that would stop him, not with a pretty young thing like that. He'll wait till the inn's all quiet, then he'll sneak downstairs while she's cleaning and—'

'Stop it,' I hissed, my blood rising. 'Just shut up.'

Locan shrugged. 'It ain't worth getting so upset over. But if you want to take your rage out on somebody, you can hit me. I'll even give you a free shot.' He turned to present his cheek to me. 'And then once I'm done beating the goblin-shit out of you, Roddin can throw us out, and we can ask the Mór to give us rooms at Caradrahan Hall or find another inn, preferably one not owned by Roddin. That's what's best anyway, I reckon, if you're too stupid to leave that girl alone.'

I was about ready to hit someone at this point. Hot blood was coursing through my veins, making my face burn. I was gripping the handle of my tankard so tight that it almost shook in my fist. I was tired of Locan's naysaying about the dragon that I so desperately wanted to be real, tired of him refusing to take my side in what I considered a matter of honour. If Shaliya wanted to speak to me, Roddin had no right to stop her. I didn't care about some barbaric law that said otherwise.

But it was not Locan I wanted to hit. It was Roddin. I turned towards the bar, and the innkeeper stared back, eyeballing me as he polished a mug with a filthy rag.

'Keep your eyes on me,' said Locan sharply. 'You going to cause trouble, or can we have a nice quiet drink and talk about how we're going to steal a scale from a non-existent dragon?'

Grudgingly, I acquiesced. There would be no point to it. Moving inns might have been the sensible thing to do, but the barriers between Shaliya and me perversely made me want to spend more time with her. I forced myself to relax, taking a slow sip of ale.

Had Shaliya been in the Dwarf and Dragon when we returned from Namma's, there is no force of men or gods that could have stopped me reaching over the bar and slamming Roddin's head into it. For when she appeared two hours later, she was sporting a nasty black bruise under her right eye.

I had calmed down significantly by then, avoiding the topic of slavery while Locan and I pored over a map, ate a bland fish stew, and plotted our route to Mistbreath Cove. But when we both caught sight of Shaliya at the same time, Locan had to reach out and dig his fingernails into my wrist to stop me getting to my feet and going after Roddin.

'You can't help her by hitting him,' he hissed. 'And even if you could, all his pals are here now.' The inn had filled up around us, including the loathsome armourer Darry, who had betrayed Shaliya, propping up the bar wearing a shit-eating leer as she served him. 'Have a crack at them if you want, but don't expect my help.'

Reluctantly I remained in my seat and took an angry sip of ale. Locan could have painted the inn's walls with Roddin and Darry's entrails if he wanted to.

'I'm going to check on Morvolt,' I said, downing my drink

and rising from the table. Chatten's assurance that somebody would claim Morvolt from the beach for me had been unneeded. My horse had shown his usual unnatural intuition – when I had arrived at the inn the previous evening, he had already been waiting for me.

'Smart,' said Locan. He belched and signalled towards Roddin at the bar for more drink.

I slipped out the back door, feeling the innkeep's eyes on me every step of the way. It was too late this evening, but if we were going to remain in Tulbar I reflected that it might be wiser to seek accommodation elsewhere. We had passed other inns in the town, the Marsh King and the Old Laughing Lady, both of which looked like they might be home to a comfy bed, or we might join the crew of the *Red Fiend* at the Broken Wheel.

I found Morvolt in a black temper. I moved to stroke his nose and he snapped his teeth and pushed my hand away. When I tried to get closer he tossed his head and stamped his feet performatively.

'I know,' I said with a sigh. His nature was not suited to being stabled. 'But it's better than the ship. We'll ride tomorrow, I promise.' This seemed to mollify him slightly, and I managed to feed him an apple from my pouch.

'I gave him some strawberries I picked in the woods,' came a voice from behind me, making me jump. 'He seemed to like them.'

I relaxed. I knew whose voice it was. 'It's dangerous for you to be here,' I said, not turning around. If I didn't look at Shaliya, Roddin could hardly accuse me of bothering her.

'Roddin's bark is worse than his bite,' she said. Her footsteps whispered against the straw as she approached.

'It wasn't his bark that put that bruise on your cheek.'

Shaliya gave a dismissive laugh. 'My father hit harder. Roddin's a coward. He climbed into my bed when he was drunk once. I twisted his balls and told him that if he ever touched me again, I would rip them off. He gave me two black eyes for that, but he's never appeared in my chamber again.'

That gave me some relief. 'Did your father sell you to Roddin?'

'In a way.' I had still not turned around, but I could feel Shaliya standing only a few paces behind me. 'Roddin runs a card game here three nights a week. My father's a bad drunk and an even worse gambler. He gave me to Roddin to pay off his debt.'

She was trying to sound calm, but I could hear the sorrow beneath her words. 'A man shouldn't be allowed to sell his own child into slavery,' I said, fighting to stop my voice from trembling with rage. 'That's monstrous.'

'Living with my father was no better.' She was so close behind me now that I could hear her breathing. 'I took work up at the castle washing the guards' clothes just to get me away from him. It'll be my sister Kelah next, once he runs out of credit. Then he'll have no one left to keep house for him and he'll drink himself to death.'

My own troubled family life paled in comparison. 'And your mother?'

'She died ten years ago. That was when my father started drinking. He's actually worse when he occasionally gets sober for a few days and finds religion. Starts ranting about how I'm bound for the Underrealm because I'm living under another man's roof unmarried.' She scowled. 'As if he wasn't the one who fucking put me here.'

'Is he one of the men inside?' Hitting Shaliya's father might stop me hitting Roddin.

'He drinks at home mostly.' Shaliya let out a wistful sigh. 'I think seeing me working here shames him.'

'As it should.'

'I am not the only child to be mistreated by their father, nor will I be the last.'

I could not help but admire Shaliya's serenity. But what did her courage say about me, who had run away from my comfortable home just because my parents wanted me to marry someone, as everyone in my family eventually must? As hard as my father had been on me, even he would never have sold one of his children into bondage.

'Did you go and see Namma?' Shaliya was standing beside me now, leaning against the half-door and stroking Morvolt's neck. He whickered pleasurably and leant into her, rubbing his face against her back. She stood barely a foot away from me, and despite the grim nature of what we had been discussing, the air between us seemed to crackle with possibility. Her hair hung in a blonde braid that fell over her shoulder, shining like gold, and I longed to reach out and stroke it.

'Yes,' I said, a dry croak in my voice as I tried to hold my composure. The illicit nature of us being alone together made that dull, earth-smelling stable seem like a place of wonder, and I was sure Shaliya felt it too. 'She was...' I struggled to explain. I did not want to be insulting. 'She said you go and see her sometimes. It's good of you. I think she appreciates the company.'

'She deserves every kindness,' said Shaliya. 'She delivered me and my sister and probably half the folk of Tulbar. I wish more people would visit her, but I think they're afraid.' She touched my arm and smiled. 'I think you were kind to her. You seem kind.'

Had I been kind to the old woman? Locan and I had not laughed at her, but we almost had. I had left her tea undrunk. We could have offered to help her somehow. 'I will go and see her again,' I said, silently swearing to myself that I would do it, and chop the wood for her fire whether she liked it or not. 'Why does she cover her face?'

'Two and a half years ago the goblins started appearing. They were filthy and diseased and feral, but Namma treated them when no one else would.' Shaliya swallowed. 'She caught something from one of them. She covers herself to stop infecting anyone else or her animals.' She touched my arm again, her eyes brightening with excitement. 'And what about the dragon? Did she tell you anything?'

I glanced nervously back towards the inn. Would Roddin and the others have noticed our absence?

'They just started a card game, and your friend has joined them,' said Shaliya. 'They all had full drinks when I left and they'll be busy arguing about the stakes, so I've got a bit longer yet.'

I relaxed slightly. 'She told us to go to Mistbreath Cove.'

Shaliya frowned slightly. 'That's all?'

I nodded. 'That's all.'

She looked at me as if I had just announced an intention to swim from Tulbar to Guiland. 'And what are you planning to do if you actually encounter a dragon?'

In the face of Locan's scepticism, I had perhaps not given that question the attention it deserved. Locan and I had made no preparation for that possibility at all. 'I'm not sure,' I admitted. I had assumed that we would work out whether it was real and then decide what to do. 'I've read a lot about dragons, but nothing on how to get one to give up their scales.' I gave what I hoped was a disarming smile. 'Maybe we'll just ask nicely.'

'Because it's lost knowledge,' said Shaliya. Her exasperated tone told me what she thought of my lack of planning. 'The Caradrahans were so scared of their secrets being discovered that they never wrote anything down about how they bound the dragons, but I'm sure the scales didn't just fall into their lap.' She looked furtively back towards the inn. 'Have you heard the tale of Jelic the Martyr?'

The name sparked a memory of something I had once read. 'He brought the Creed of the Seamstress to Paleir, didn't he? They burnt his limbs one by one to try and make him recant. It inspired the spread of the Creed across the island.' That had been close to a thousand years ago, before the Aegis had organised the Creed for their own ends.

'That's the version the Seamsters tell, but there's another.' Shaliya spoke quickly, her deep blue eyes staring intently into mine. 'To prove the truth of his faith, the people of Carnaway challenged Jelic to enter the lair of the dragon Hellamnabis. Hellamnabis caught him, and would have burnt Jelic alive. To save himself, Jelic recanted his faith and spent a year worshipping Hellamnabis.'

'Then what happened?' I asked. In all my reading, this was not a tale I had come across.

'When Jelic tried to escape and return to the faith of the Seamstress, Hellamnabis turned his breath on him and boiled him alive.' Shaliya's hand was tight around my arm. 'Dragons don't care for the affairs of men, but if you flatter them, worship them, they might spare you.' She looked back towards the inn again. 'I should go, but if you do encounter a dragon, remember that and it might save your life.'

Without warning, she stood on her tiptoes and briefly brushed her lips against mine, then turned and without looking back hurried towards the inn.

I left a reasonable amount of time between Shaliya's departure and returning myself, mostly spent touching my lip where the heat of her kiss still burnt and wavering between elation and anxiety. It was what I had wanted, but also exactly what Locan had ordered me to avoid, on pain of Roddin's extreme displeasure.

I hardly knew what to make of Shaliya. All I did know was that I was enthralled by her. She had endured an upbringing trapped between the two evils of Roddin and her father, and had survived through her own fierce stubbornness. Roddin might strike her on occasion, but he did not dare go further.

Others might have wilted under such hardship, but not Shaliya. Through all of it, she had endured, like the shoots of green that had persisted through the centuries to one day worm their way up through the cracked mosaic streets of High Tulbar. She had even learnt to read along the way, and studied obscure stories like that of Jelic the Martyr. The alternative tale she had shared seemed immediately more reliable than the version spread by the Aegis.

The taste of her kiss lingered on my lips, but eventually I shook off my lovesick stupor, said farewell to Morvolt, and returned to the inn. Shaliya was back behind the bar and wisely did not even look at me.

'You took your time,' said Locan as I retook my seat. A large measure of brandy sat in front of him.

'I was talking with Morvolt. He's furious with me.'

Locan snorted. 'When isn't he?' He pointed across the bar to where a half-dozen men including Roddin and Darry were settled around a table holding cards with a pile of coins in front of them. 'I played a few hands. Lost just enough of the Mór's money that they might look more favourably on us. Or on me anyway.' He grinned and lowered his voice. 'Learnt a fair bit as well. Our drunken armourer, Darry – he's the bastard brother of the old Mór. And the skinny man next to him is Thoan, your pretty barmaid's uncle.'

'Her name is Shaliya,' I reminded him. I tried not to let my temper get the better of me in front of Locan, but nevertheless I could not help staring daggers into the back of Thoan's head. How could a man sit there and watch his niece be treated like chattel by a brute like Roddin?

Before we left here, I would find a way to free Shaliya. I would smuggle her out in the *Red Fiend*'s hold if I had to. But not before I caved Roddin's face in.

CHAPTER 10

We rose early, ate quickly, and were out the door just as the sun was rising beyond the shadow of the Dreadveil. We turned the corner into the yard, and almost walked straight into an altercation.

Roddin was nose to nose with another, taller man wearing a studded jerkin and a great gold medallion, jabbing his finger against the other man's chest.

'...not my fault,' Roddin was saying. His face was flushed an agitated red. 'If you'd sent—'

The other man glanced up at the sight of us, stopping Roddin in his tracks. It took me a few moments to recognise him – it was Ulf.

I tensed, immediately expecting trouble, but though Roddin scowled at the sight of us, Ulf showed a wide smile of squat yellow teeth that never reached his eyes. 'I'll not bother with introductions,' he said. 'I know who you are and I'm sure you know by now who I am. No hard feelings about the other morning – my men should have shown more sense.' He eyed Locan up and down, taking in his wiry, weathered frame, the slight bend in his back, the bleary-eyed scowl that he always wore before his first drink of the day. 'So, you're the man they call Locan A'Shadow,' he said, practically purring with false charm. 'Not quite what I expected when I heard you had killed two of my men. How many would it have taken to bring you to heel, would you say?'

Locan spat in the dirt. 'Of men like them, a couple of hundred.'

Ulf raised an eyebrow. 'I would wager a few dozen. Care to put it to the test? You in the arena against twenty of my best fighters.' His arms spread as wide as his smile. 'The great Locan A'Shadow, only in the fighting pit of a resurgent High Tulbar. Once word gets out, they will come from across the continent to watch.'

'And there's enough dead men's families who'd love to see it that they could fill your arena ten times over,' said Locan. 'Be sure you remember that. And when I decide to kill someone, I don't worry about putting on a show.'

Ulf gave a hearty laugh. 'You are as fierce as your reputation, Master A'Shadow. I hope our paths cross again.' He clapped Roddin on the shoulder. 'Roddy, I have other business to attend to, so I'll leave you to see to your guests. We'll continue this conversation another time.'

Ulf departed towards the gate, with Roddin scowling after him. 'Bloody cheating crook,' he muttered. He looked at me and Locan. 'What are you staring at?' he barked. 'Get out of my way.' He pushed past us back towards the inn.

Locan looked at me and shrugged. 'Glad to see he's just an arsehole and it's nothing personal.'

I turned to watch Roddin stomp away. I had known from Hosten that he and Ulf did not like each other, but I had assumed as Keykeepers they would set those feelings aside to serve their mutual interests and maintain their position as High Tulbar's most prominent residents. Evidently something had gone awry.

'What do you suppose that was about?' I asked.

Locan shrugged again. 'Gold, slaves, or gold and slaves. Take your pick.'

There had been something strange about the way they had stopped speaking when they saw us, something in their expressions that said this was about more than a disagreement on matters of business, but Locan and I had more pressing matters to attend to. We claimed our horses from the stable.

Roddin was still in the yard when we departed. 'Mistbreath Cove, is it?' he asked as we steered our mounts out of the gate. 'Careful out there. Wouldn't want you getting lost. The cliffs are treacherous.' He followed this with a bark of mocking laughter that left clear how little he would miss us.

'Ignore him,' said Locan in a whisper as I glared back at the innkeep.

Under a sky of slate-grey clouds, there were no shadows for Locan to use, so we journeyed together, him on a raw-boned nag rented from the detestable Roddin and me atop Morvolt. My ill-tempered horse could not hide his excitement at the open ground, and once we were beyond the walls of Tulbar I flicked my reins and let him gallop off some of his pent-up energy before wheeling him round and returning to Locan.

'Careful not to tire him out,' he said with an ironic twist of his lip. 'He might have to run away from a dragon later.' I was only slightly more optimistic than Locan about the prospects of that happening, but I intended to make the most of the journey. At the very least, I would see where a dragon had once resided.

We followed the coast south. Out at sea, the Dreadveil billowed and swelled with the wind, a threatening black smog that I did not seem able to shake my attention from. Even when I fixed my gaze to the right over the marshy lowlands of Paleir, its ominous presence seemed to break against my consciousness like the whitecap waves against the cliffs.

We passed one of Tulbar's famed iron mines, where a group

of sullen men in rags were shuffling from a ramshackle collection of huts towards an enormous pit. They stopped and turned to stare at us, until the shout of an overseer and the crack of a whip set them walking again.

'I'd sooner die than go down there,' muttered Locan as we rode by.

The mine was where Shaliya's father might have ended up, if he had not traded his daughter to Roddin. A braver man would have accepted his fate. The thought spurred me on towards our destination. If we could help Hosten, he might one day be able to end the barbaric practice that yoked Shaliya to Roddin.

'I know what you're daydreaming about,' said Locan in that infuriating way he had of discerning where my mind was. 'And I can tell you Hosten has as much chance of outlawing slavery as he does of climbing aboard this invisible dragon.'

'You don't know that,' I said. Locan might be ready to dismiss the idea that rulers could ever be both capable and benevolent, but naysaying was meat and drink to Locan. I had heard the breadths of Hosten's ambition – if we could help him, Tulbar would prosper. 'Hosten might surprise you. He's got his whole life to do it in.'

'I'm too old for surprises,' said Locan. 'And your friend Hosten will make young bones. If his father had lived a few more years, he might have learnt some sense instead of gambling his rule on a fairy-tale.'

'So why are you helping then?' I asked, trying to hold back the vexed reaction I knew Locan was trying to provoke. 'Why aren't you back at the inn drinking yourself into a stupor again?'

Locan gave a grunt of laughter. 'I don't need to be in the tavern to drink myself into a stupor.' He produced a skin of brandy, and the liquid inside sloshed around as he shook it at me. 'The only reason I'm out here following you in this mad venture is to kill the time until Huretio gets the *Fiend* patched up. We need to be out of here before Hosten's uncle arrives and your new best friend gets his head stuck up on a spike. I'm not getting caught up in another war.'

For Hosten's sake, I refused to believe that High Tulbar would fall so easily. 'If Shanoch comes, I'll fight for Hosten,' I said, my temper creeping up a notch. I had spent a whole day with the Mór – Locan had not seen his resolve, his great plans to restore High Tulbar and Paleir. Hosten was wise too, and this Shanoch was probably no different to a hundred other dumb and brutish kings who would tolerate misery and enslavement as long as it kept them on a throne. Other than stealing her away on the *Fiend*, Hosten was my best hope of freeing Shaliya. 'The world needs more men like him.'

Locan gave a black bark of laughter. 'Did you learn nothing from Narlond? Were you not listening to me yesterday? What the world needs is rarely what the world gets. Nobody ever got to be king by being kind and gentle. It's all "father of my people" when things are going well, but when the shit splatters into the privy it's all blood and steel and "form a shield wall", at least if they want to keep being king. And if Hosten's so wise, why's he got me tailing after a dragon instead of out there killing his uncle?'

'Not everybody wants to solve every problem at the point of a knife,' I replied hotly. I had played Pillars with Hosten – he was clever, too clever to try and defeat his foes with a single uncertain thrust. He would secure his own defence, lead his uncle into a seemingly safe position, and then the moment Shanoch realised he had been fooled, the trap would close.

'And yet it's always the most obvious solution!' Locan gave a devilish grin. 'If killing someone weren't the best way of dealing with them, do you think people would have paid me so fucking much to do it?' Locan reached back into his cloak for his skin of brandy. 'And one other thing – never give your blade away for free. However much you might like him, Hosten ain't worth dying over. And it'll be me that has to drag you out of there when High Tulbar inevitably falls. Thought fighting the Tilaxi might have been enough for you.'

I bit back my reply. I did not wish to spend the whole ride arguing with Locan, especially when I knew he was at least in part right. I had been in Tulbar for only two days – it shouldn't have mattered to me in the slightest who ruled here. What I would never say aloud to Locan – although he had probably guessed – was how much of myself I saw in Hosten. An afternoon in his company had passed with more ease than it would have with any of my brothers, even Javvian, despite the heavy burden Hosten bore. My flight to Narlond had led to Javvian's death, but I could still help Hosten.

We stopped briefly after midday to refill our waterskins from a stream. We ate as we travelled, feasting on hardtack and stale bread Roddin had reluctantly provided to us. Locan was drinking of course, but he did not guzzle Palish brandy the way he had the Narlish whisky.

'Is that on the map?' asked Locan some hours later, pointing towards a steep-rising, snowcapped mountain some way inland of us.

I retrieved the map from my saddlebags. 'Jarlanth's Peak,' I said, tracing our path from Tulbar to where the hill was marked. Mistbreath Cove was close.

We continued along the cliff. A cloying mist rolled in from the sea as we ascended a rise, leaving the way we had come lost from view. The ground grew craggier, strewn with rocks that made me fear for Morvolt's footing.

Eventually, the mist hung so heavy that we could see no more than a few yards in any direction. I could feel its dampness seeping through my clothes and settling against my skin. I looked back the way we had come, and realised I was not even sure which direction the water was. 'Namma didn't say anything about how we'd know when we got there, did she?' I wondered aloud, repressing my alarm. We were lost, and the most troubling thing was I was not even sure how it had happened. The mist had crept up on us so slowly that it had escaped my attention.

'Nothing,' said Locan. He gave a guttural laugh. 'Thought we'd just keep going until a dragon hopped out of the sea and burnt our skin off.'

'We should stop and get our bearings.' I strained my ears, listening for the lap of waves against the cliff, and was relieved when I heard it off to our left. We were still heading the right way.

We dismounted. There was nowhere to hitch our horses. If Morvolt took it upon himself to wander off, I might never find him again, or worse, he might tumble over the cliff. He allowed me to hobble him, though not without much irritable snorting.

'She never mentioned a mist either,' I said, a slight panic rising in me. The haze seemed no more natural than the Dreadveil. Locan was only a few yards from me, but wisps of white vapour swirled around him as if threatening to drag him away.

'She did not,' replied Locan. 'Probably slipped her mind, the mad old bat. Suppose "Mistbreath Cove" ought to have given it away.'

I remembered Roddin's last words before we'd left. *'Wouldn't want you getting lost. The cliffs are treacherous.'* I cursed under my breath. Of course that orc-fucker had not warned us. If we were not back by evening, he would laugh himself hoarse with his friends at the two foreigners who had wandered off and got lost in the mist.

Becoming exasperated, I handed Locan Morvolt's bridle. 'I'm going to find the cliff and see if I can see anything.' It was called Mistbreath *Cove*; where else would our destination be but by the water? If I could find a path down to the waterside, the mist there might be thinner. I rummaged through a saddlebag and found a torch. 'Light this so I can find my way back.'

'Brave boy. Come back and get me if you find a dragon.' Locan took the torch and sat down with a sigh. 'If you get back and I'm a pile of charred bones I'm sure you can work out what's happened.'

'You might be a little more concerned,' I said, unable to keep the irritation out of my voice. 'Doesn't this mist seem the slightest bit odd to you? And your bones wouldn't be charred – I've told you, it's a sea dragon, it breathes steam.'

Locan waved a hand. 'Whatever. Weather is weather and this dragon's probably no more than a pile of bones itself. You going to go exploring or just stand there yapping like a Rintish wine merchant? If you fall off the edge, just scream so I know what's happened.' He raised his skin of brandy towards me in salute.

I stomped away, ignoring Morvolt's whickered protest. It ought to have been Locan doing this – he was the one who'd be using his shadow magic to obtain a scale, but he wasn't inter-ested in being the least bit useful, just in making his usual bitter japes. If this was to be my life with him, letting him naysay and boss me around while he got steadily drunker and meaner, perhaps Huretio was right. How much worse would it be going around Rameon with Locan, where half the city apparently wanted to kill him?

The mist closed behind me. Locan still had not troubled to light the torch, but I could hear him arguing with Morvolt as the horse's complaints became increasingly frenzied. My absence had never worried my horse before; the stubborn fog was clearly troubling him as much as it was me.

It is quite disconcerting to walk through a thick mist when you are searching for a precipice over a hundred-foot drop. I kept my steps small, but when I reached the edge the ground fell away so sharply that I still had to scramble back to stop myself sliding down over the cliff, sending rocks tumbling down the bluff as I backpedalled. I grasped hold of a rock formation shaped like a crooked, twisted chimney and clung to it with both hands.

I willed my heart to still. The blustery sea breeze that ought to have blown away the mist instead seemed to grasp at my cloak as if it meant to pull me over the edge. The fog hid the drop below from view, which in my slightly panicked state was perhaps a blessing.

It took me a few moments to calm myself. All I had to do was find a safe path down. But I still did not feel secure enough to let go of the rock. Instead, I edged my way round it, aiming to put its bulk between me and a tumble into the watery abyss before I released my grip.

I was preparing to let go when I took a step and the ground fell away beneath me. My legs kicked for footing that was not there. My hands slipped, and I cried out as my palms were scraped bloody against the jagged pillar. I was falling, screaming, my hands clawing at the air for non-existent purchase. My chin struck an outcropping, sending a blinding explosion of pain flashing through my skull.

I struck the water, and its icy touch gripped my chest and squeezed all the air from my lungs. I fought for breath, floundering hopelessly as the depths sought to pull me under.

Blind, I trod water and to my relief one of my flailing arms struck something solid. I lunged in that direction, and I hauled myself up onto a rocky ledge just above the waterline.

It took a few moments to calm myself before I was able to consider my surroundings. I had fallen down some sort of natural shaft in the cliff, the opening through which I had plummeted visible as a circle of swirling mist far above me. My jaw ached where it had hit the rock. Had I been knocked out rather than merely dazed, I would have drowned.

For the second time in a matter of days, I found myself shivering on the edge of the North Water. I was in a sort of closed lagoon, a dark crevasse in the cliff with an aperture somewhere that allowed the seawater in. I quickly removed my soaking wet clothes and looked back up towards the hole. There was no hope of climbing out that way – where I had fallen was high above me, and there was nothing to grasp onto but sheer, smooth rock.

'Hello?!' I called out. My voice echoed within the confined space. I cried out again, louder. No answer came.

I tried to remain calm, clenching my fists to fight against both my increasing panic and my bone-deep shivers. My best hope was for Locan to find me. With his shadow magic, he could come after me and transport me back above ground. Travelling through shadows would leave me sick, but it was better than freezing to death trapped between the ice-cold water and the unyielding rock.

I went to my hands and knees and stared into the depths, hoping the faint light from above would reveal an escape. The black water stared back at me silently, ominous with the promise of my death.

The water lapped at my fingers, before a rhythmic pulse of the water swelled across my ledge. I got to my feet, craned my neck back, and shouted up the shaft again. 'Locan! Morvolt!'

Hopeless. How long would Locan give it before he came searching for me? A few minutes? A few hours? Night would have fallen by then. Hopefully I would not freeze to death before then. Locan would not wait so long – he would come searching for me.

It did not take me long to realise I might not have that sort of time.

The tide was rising.

When I had climbed onto the ledge, it had been an inch above the water line. Now, the waves had fully submerged my feet and were creeping towards my ankles, drenching my legs in glacial cold.

I called up again, a note of panic creeping into my voice. 'Locan!'

The only reply was my own voice echoing back at me.

The tide was rising impossibly fast, as if the black water had been alerted to my presence and decided to drag me to its depths. It was approaching my knees now. When it lifted me off my ledge I could tread water for a while, but in the end the cold would claim me.

Through escalating horror, I tried to think. The water was coming from the sea, fast. There had to be an opening of some sort, and likely a large one, hopefully wide enough for me to swim out.

I began scanning the depths again, but the gloom made it impossible. If there was a way out, I would have to find it by touch. I steeled myself, searching for the courage to throw myself back into the water. But in the end, the tide made my decision for me. As a swell lapped against my thigh, I took a deep breath and plunged into the water.

The cold was all-encompassing, like a barrage of sharp needles assaulting every inch of my flesh. I battled against my instinct to retreat, knowing that if I turned back I was lost. My fingers grasped blindly against the rock, searching for an opening. I kicked hard, driving myself deeper.

By the time I found the hole, my lungs were burning. With a kick of my legs I propelled myself into it, trying not to think of the consequences if this was not an exit.

The gap was tight, but once my shoulders were through, I knew the rest of me would follow. Battling with my elbows, I struggled along the underwater tunnel, trying to ignore the growing pressure on my lungs, hoping that the channel would at some point begin to rise and lead me back above the water before I drowned.

But as best I could tell the tunnel seemed to only lead me down. Overcome with panic, I forced myself on. The water tightened around my chest like a vice. My lungs began to burn, but it was too late to go back. If I did that, I would drown for sure.

It was too dark to see. Visions swam before my eyes. Locan wandering across the cliff, calling my name for hours. Morvolt neighing, stamping the ground, furious at me for abandoning him. An apologetic letter to my family from Huretio. Locan couldn't write and wouldn't bother even if he could. My body, trapped in a tunnel nobody knew was here, my eyes and flesh claimed by fish as my body began to decay. The urge to open my mouth and let the water in became overwhelming. Terror gripped me, the scream that would seal my demise burgeoning in my throat—

The opening widened, and I tumbled over a waterfall. A brief scream escaped my lips before I landed in a pool of water. I righted myself, sucking down air with ecstatic, relieved abandon. I had been only seconds from a watery grave. I let out a whoop. The water here was not even cold, it was pleasantly warm, approaching the temperature of a good bath, and once I had my breath back I did a few jubilant front flips before rolling onto my back and letting myself float. It was another cavern, larger and higher than the first, and this one was filled with daylight. And more importantly, I was alive.

'Who... are... you?'

The voice came from behind me, a bass rumble that crashed against the walls and ceiling, scattering particles of stone into the water. Fear found my heart like a knife. Not the rational terror of freezing or drowning; something deeper, bestial, a dread so indomitable that it had echoed through generations of my ancestors, a collective memory of power beyond knowledge and understanding.

Against every screaming instinct in my head, I turned into the face of death.

Bright, almond-shaped eyes the size of cartwheels stared at me from across the cavern, sunbursts of colour radiating from high, slitted pupils as slender as a dagger. Steam emanated from its cavernous nostrils like vapours from a cauldron of sorcery. Scales rippled along its body, along its folded wings, an endless shimmering blue so brilliant that all the shades of sky and seas could be seen in their lustre. At the far wall of the vast cavern, a long, slender tail flickered back and forth like that of an irascible cat.

A dragon, sixty feet long or more, lying prone in a pool of water. My heart was hammering fit to burst from my chest.

Its great eyes gave a slow blink, and it spoke again, a deep bass that rolled from its vast maw of a mouth. 'Who... are... you?'

CHAPTER 11

The dragon yawned, and though I was still twenty yards from it I felt the steam flash against my face. The temperature of the water noticeably rose. If I did not answer, it would broil the flesh from my bones.

'My name is Cetrik,' I managed to say, my voice high and fearful.

'Cet...rik.' As hot as the pool was, I shivered. To hear your name in the mouth of a creature of myth, centuries' old long before you were born and with centuries to live after, is not only to recognise your own insignificance. It is to feel it, to know it in your bones, to regard your own life and see only its futility staring back at you. Had I fallen dead on the spot it would not have been a surprise.

The dragon's tail flickered. It sniffed the air, licking its forked tongue towards me and giving me a glimpse of the double rows of teeth within, each fang as long as a man's fore-arm. I shut my eyes, preparing myself for the agony of being boiled alive.

'Cet...rik.' It sniffed again. 'You're... pale... for a goblin.'

'I'm not... I'm not a goblin,' I stammered.

The beast growled deep in its throat. I lowered myself until everything below my eyes was underwater, for all the difference that would make if the dragon decided to unleash its superheated breath on me. 'No... You don't... *smell*... like a goblin.' Its speech was heavy and ponderous, as if it were struggling to recall the words. 'But... no magic... that is why I tried to drown you.' A deep, rolling noise that might have been laughter rumbled in its throat. 'Thought you were a goblin!' Her great eyes blinked, squinting at me. I had read somewhere that male dragons could be recognised by the horns on their brow, so I assumed this one was female. 'No... a... hu... hu...'

'Human?' I suggested.

'*Human!*' The dragon laughed deeply again. 'Yes, indeed.' She sniffed again. 'A young... *male* human! A boy. I can smell your... foolishness.' Her great head tilted slightly, a dog-like gesture that was oddly terrifying when adopted by a creature of such a size. 'I smell you... but I sense no magic.' She snorted, bathing me in another blast of warm breath. 'I have forgotten your name. To me, you are now... Boy-who-hides-from-magic.'

'As... as it pleases you,' I managed to say, light-headed with both fear and the soporific heat of the water. Humans did not give names to creatures they one day meant to kill. Perhaps dragons were the same. Deciding I was safe, for now, I pulled myself closer to the edge of the pool and rested my elbows on the side.

'Why... have you... come here?'

Its speech was quickening as it wakened. 'I... got lost,' I managed to say.

The dragon made a noise that might have been a sigh. 'Where are your...' She paused for several moments, regarding me like a botanist discovering a new breed of snail. 'The word... soft scales... not fur...'

'Clothes?' I ventured.

'Clothes!' I threw myself below the lip of the rockpool as the dragon's shout sent a waft of blistering breath over me. It laughed again. 'Yes, clothes... fur you shed. I recall now. Yes, where are your... *clothes*, Boy-who-hides-from-magic?'

As long as I kept her talking, I expected I was safe, but there was no telling how long it might be before the dragon got bored or steamed the flesh from my bones by accident. 'We remove our clothes to swim,' I said, deciding against a long explanation. 'I fell into some water.' I swallowed, deciding it was my turn to ask a question. 'If I am Boy-who-hides-from-magic, what do I call you?'

The dragon pondered this, her tail flicking back and forth all the while. 'I have known many names.' Her wings convulsed in what might have been a shrug. Her back leg stretched forward to scratch at her neck, a gesture I hoped indicated she was relaxed and did not regard me as a threat. '*Aydhenia*,' she offered eventually. 'Yes... *Aydhenia*... they called me Aydhenia. I have eaten... *many* fish since then. They are dead. Your kind... I would swim and by the time I returned... *gone*.' She gave a great sniff, as if dying was the height of rudeness.

If I was to die here, I would at least meet my demise while learning something of dragons. Until recently, I had believed that nobody had even *seen* a dragon in centuries, never mind spoken to one. 'Have you... Have you been hiding here for four hundred years?'

'Hiding? No...' Aydhenia hissed, her tongue flicking over her bottom jaw. 'I have been below. Far from that vile red mist that hides the sea from the heat of the sun. The dolphins and the whales fled from it long ago. I had to swim to the deepest depths to feed on...' She hissed again. 'I do not know their names in your tongue. The mist smelt wrong. No matter how high I flew, it was always there, whispering to me.'

'In the Dreadveil?' I asked. For the first time, I noticed the gills on the dragon's neck. Could she truly have been in the

North Water for four hundred years? 'Who was whispering to you?'

'Him.' Aydhenia hissed again, blowing a thick cloud of steam towards me, and I threw myself beneath the water. As I resurfaced, she lashed her tail against the cavern wall, dislodging several chunks of stone. 'You hide from magic. He swathed himself in it, until there was nothing else. The-one-who-wraps-himself-in-magic. Every time I left the water, the red mist was waiting for me, whispering his entreaties in my ear, promising me treasure chests overflowing with gold and gems if I would serve him.' The tip of her tail flickered angrily. 'He knew nothing of my kind. My barbarian kin who dwell in great mountains and fear the sea might place great store in shiny metal crafted by human hands, but not I.'

The chamber was only lightly lit from some unknown source, but as Aydhenia spoke, I realised that the shadow she cast on the cavern wall was moving. Not just her swaying tail, but the shape of a man, creeping slowly along her rump. Locan, skulking through the shadows. He had found his way down here as well. If Aydhenia sensed him, she might become enraged and unleash the full intensity of her steam breath on me. If we were to claim a scale without me being steamed alive, my best hope was to keep her talking.

'You were wise not to heed him,' I said. The idea of the Abomination King recruiting a dragon to serve him chilled me to my bones.

A threatening cloud of steam emanated from Aydhenia's nostrils. 'You know him?'

'No! My father slew him, The-one-who-wraps-himself-in-magic.'

Aydhenia made a contented noise deep in her throat. 'That is good. That is why I have returned. The great fog of misery and lies that you call the Dreadveil is waning. I may roam the skies again and dive for fish from above instead of chasing them through the water.

'My kin are gone, and so the hunting is good. All the creatures of the deep fear the jaws of dragon. Axehead sharks flee from me. Razorsquid descend into the darkness hoping that I will not follow. Even the great krakens that slumber on the seafloor slink into the valleys when they sense the course of the dragon.

'But now I may fly again. The birds are a different challenge, one I have enjoyed. I am faster than them, but they are nimble. Though they have little meat.' The leathery skin of Aydhenia's eyelids descended in a slow blink, and when she refixed her gaze on me her pupils were as slim as stiletto blades, her eyes like great molten pools of fire. 'Tell me, Boy-who-hides-from-magic, what do you suppose *you* taste like?'

I froze. Aydhenia's eyes seemed to increase in size until they were all I could see. Her lower jaw hung open, revealing a black maw of teeth, each one as sharp as castle-forged steel. I could see the steam churning at the back of her throat.

'It has been a long time since I tasted human,' Aydhenia continued, her voice like menacing thunder. 'They are tastier than goblins, but more trouble. Foolish men will hunt you if you kill a human. If you leave humans alone, they will bring you sheep and goats. My kind grew fat on their offerings.' Amusement swirled in Aydhenia's amber gaze. 'Are there foolish men who will hunt me if you die, Boy-who-hides-from-magic? What do you offer me for your life?'

I fought to remain calm, denying the instinct to dive beneath the water as steam bubbled in Aydhenia's mouth. If she turned the full heat of her breath upon the pool, I would be boiled alive. 'If you eat me...' A flash of inspiration struck me. 'If you eat me, I won't be able to tell my fellow humans of your glory.'

Shaliya had told me how the martyr Jelic had saved himself

by falling to his knees and worshipping the dragon Hellamnabis. It was time to test the truth of the tale. I kept going – perhaps as long as I kept talking, Aydhenia would not devour me. 'I must tell them of your wisdom and magnificence, how your lustrous scales shine like the sea in the summer, of your tail that is at once both powerful and elegant.'

Aydhenia dipped her head and rolled her snout against the damp rocks, making small growls of pleasure in her throat. 'Go on,' she said. 'I have forgotten the pleasure of conversation. This is how you ought to have been talking the moment you arrived.'

'If I were to die, I would never see the splendour of your wings in flight,' I went on, fervent in my devotion. 'The shadow that causes all the creatures of the ocean to flee. The graceful dive that cuts the water, from which they cannot escape. I could not go to my grave without spreading the glory of your name. *Aydhenia*. The whole world must know of it. *Aydhenia*.'

Aydhenia eagerly pushed herself up onto her claws. 'Indeed. Indeed. You must see. *Come*.'

With my heart in my mouth, I pulled myself from the pool. Aydhenia began to manoeuvre herself towards the exit, an ungainly turn that set powder falling from the stone ceiling where her great head brushed against it, until at last she faced the open vista of the North Water.

'Watch, Boy-who-hides-from-magic. Watch, and spread the tale among your people so that all may know that the dragons have returned.'

Aydhenia gave a powerful kick of her back legs, and in a single flap of her wings leapt free of the cave and glided away across the open water, her belly brushing against the surface like a skimmed stone, before, with a powerful beat of her wings, she soared away into the air. I stared open-mouthed as she stretched her wingspan to its fullest extent, forming an awe-inspiring silhouette against the sky. She held there for a moment, then plummeted towards the sea, seizing something from beneath the water in her jaws before spiralling away again. The dragon tossed her catch into the air, then unleashed upon it a cloud of steam before snatching it in her mouth in the same motion.

She soared away, weaving into the clouds, becoming a distant grey outline before she was lost from view.

The dragons never did return to the shores of Karvved and Paleir in large numbers. Some mornings though, I will go and sit on the cliffs, letting my feet dangle over the edge like a callow boy, watching the horizon on the off chance that my eyes fall upon a distant shadow fading in and out of view as it weaves through the clouds, before plummeting into the waves as it sights its prey. I have seen dragons in flight since, and I hope to again, but none could ever stir wonder in me as Aydhenia did that day. A myth that men had believed gone forever, plucked from the past and thrust into the present, right before my eyes.

CHAPTER 12

I escaped the cave onto a stony beach beneath a high granite cliff face with the rain lashing down and the surf thundering against the rocks. Evening was falling, and I was shivering with cold, but I hardly noticed. My mind was afire with what I had just experienced. I had walked into the lair of a dragon and survived to tell the tale. If not for Shaliya's advice I was sure Aydhenia would have eaten me out of boredom and curiosity, yet instead I had spoken to a dragon and watched her fly, perhaps the first Guilander to do that in centuries.

I could not wait to get back and tell Shaliya, but first I needed to find a way off this beach. The sheer rockface was unclimbable; I would have to walk along the beach in search of a route up. And I was still naked, with dark setting in and the tide rolling up the shore. The cold and rising water would kill me just as surely as dragon's breath.

'Ho!'

I looked towards the cry from the top of the cliff, and I was shocked to see Locan staring back at me holding a torch. He waved. 'I suppose you want me to save you?' he called down.

'I would be very much obliged,' I shouted, cupping my hands to my mouth.

'Suppose I owe it to you. Hang on. Catch.' Without any further warning, Locan threw his burning torch down towards me, and I barely caught it before it landed among the stones.

'Good lad. Now angle it so your shadow stretches up the cliff to meet me.'

It took me a few attempts, but eventually I was able to position it so my silhouette stretched the height of the cliff. A moment later there was a ripple of darkness and Locan appeared beside me.

'Better give you some clothes before a fish mistakes that pecker of yours for a worm,' he said, tossing me a bundle of spare clothes. I eagerly pulled them on, then wrapped a dry cloak around myself. Now the excitement of encountering Aydhenia had worn off, the cold was such that I could barely stop my teeth chattering. Locan must have realised as well, given how uncharacteristically charitable he was being.

'How do we get back up?' I asked. I assumed through Locan's magic, but that would require someone to hold the torch and aim the shadow.

'It ain't the first time I've had to do this,' said Locan. 'Start collecting stones.'

Working together, Locan and I made a pile of sea-smoothed rocks, until he was satisfied that it was high enough. The waves were lapping at our feet now. 'Quickly,' said Locan. 'After the next big wave, put that torch down there.'

I did as he said, and its flame cast the stones' shadow the full height of the cliff.

'Right, grab onto me,' said Locan. 'Quickly.'

I put my hand on his shoulder, then swiftly slammed my eyes shut as we entered the shadows, though not being able to see did little to dispel the awful, gut-churning feeling of being trapped outside of space and time while the world rushed past me. I was familiar with the sensation, but it was not something I would ever get used to.

I materialised atop the windswept cliff, light-headed, nauseous, and overcome with dizziness. I would have fallen sideways if Locan had not been there to support me. He eased me down to the ground. With an excited whinny, Morvolt cantered over and lowered his head to begin butting me with his nose in admonishment for daring to leave him.

'He's barely stopped complaining ever since you left,' said Locan. 'Was a job and a half to get him to leave me alone long enough that I could come after you.'

'I met the dragon,' I said, once I felt somewhat safe back in my own body. Even though I had been there, I could scarcely believe my own ears. 'Her name's Aydhenia.'

'I know,' said Locan. He let out an impressed whistle. 'How's something that size stayed hidden so long? I'll hold my hands up – thought the whole town was pulling our leg. Fair fucks to you for forcing me to do this, and for getting out of there alive – reckon most folk would have pissed their pants and got their skin scalded off when they ran away screaming.' He slapped me twice on the back. 'Come on, we should get back on the road before this mist gets any worse.'

I had to assume that Locan's route into Aydhenia's cave had been less troublesome than mine. He did not even appear to be wet. 'Did you get a scale?' I asked, hauling myself atop Morvolt as Locan retrieved his own mount.

'Four of them.' Locan reached into his cloak with a grin and held out his hand, revealing four scales each slightly smaller than his palm, vivid cobalt shimmering with greens and purples. Even in the low light, I could see my wide eyes reflected back in them.

'Found them lying on the ground underneath her,' said Locan. 'Was worried for a bit I'd have to pull them straight off her back.'

I could not help but feel strange as I stared down at the scales. Aydhenia was as close as I was ever likely to come to encountering a god, a living, breathing relic of a world beyond mortal memory. I had not even thought to ask how old she was, whether she had known elves and dwarves and giants, whether she had served the Caradrahans before.

The last of these possibilities troubled me. Before I had met Aydhenia, dragons had existed only in the abstract, but now I had to confront why we had sought her and what it meant. I did not know by what sorcery the Caradrahans had tamed the dragons, nor whether Hosten could recreate it, but to see a creature as ancient and magnificent as Aydhenia forced to serve at the whims of men whose lifespans to her were barely the length of a blink would be grotesque, a tragedy, so much so that I actually felt bile rising in my throat. To involve a borderline deity in the petty squabbles of kings was the height of hubris. Not to mention the cruelty of it; there was little to separate enslaving a dragon from the Abomination King's treatment of the men and goblins he experimented on, nor the human-on-human slavery that troubled Tulbar to this day.

'What do you want to do with them?' I asked Locan.

He looked at me as if I had taken leave of my senses. 'Thought I might shove them up my arse. What do you think we're going to do with them? We'll give them to your friend the Mór, then we can stop worrying about the likes of Ulf and drink ourselves blind until Huretio gets the *Fiend* fixed.'

That did not seem so different from what Locan would have done anyway, but I let the point slide.

'Does seem a cheap price for a dragon scale though,' mused Locan. 'Think we should ask for money?'

'Or perhaps we should just... throw them in the sea?' I suggested. I looked away from Locan, already sure he would laugh at me. 'Binding a dragon to do your bidding doesn't seem all that different to slavery.'

Locan blinked at me, then looked away shaking his head. 'Boy thinks he's made friends with a dragon,' he muttered. 'First it was the Bucani, then Hosten, then the barmaid, and now it's a bleeding dragon!' He spoke as if he was not sure whether to laugh at me or try to slap the stupidity out of me. 'Is there *anything* you won't decide would be well-served by the patronage and protection of Cetrik bleeding-heart Harkken?' Finally, he laughed, letting out a high, half-mad cackle. 'Goblins' bones, it's a dragon! It can take care of itself.'

'It just seems... *wrong*,' I said, struggling to explain myself in the face of his tirade. 'You heard her talking – Aydhenia is clever. She's not an ox to be yoked to a plough or a horse to be ridden.' Beneath me, Morvolt snorted indignantly.

Locan shook his head. 'Listen.' He thrust a finger at me. The mist was thinning now, revealing our cliffside path back north. 'I didn't come all the way out here and sneak into that beast's lair to just throw these into the sea like diseased fish. You and I have been trapped by an invasion before, and if this Mór Shanoch is coming to High Tulbar, I want to be gone before he gets there. While I don't believe anyone could stop me if they tried, I'd sooner not take the chance.' He looked at me strangely. 'This is what you wanted, Cetrik.'

'I know it was!' I protested. I still wanted to help Hosten, but the thought of doing it at the expense of Aydhenia's freedom, forcing that deadly, beautiful creature with the coat like hammered sapphires to bend to his bidding, made my skin crawl. 'I just... changed my mind,' I said weakly.

Locan shoved the scales back into his cloak, then with a peculiar look in his eye pulled two of them back out. 'Here.' He tossed them to me so quickly that I nearly dropped one of them. 'One for me, one for the Mór, two for you, seeing as you're the one who was almost roasted. Can't say fairer than that. We can talk more back at the inn when I've got a fresh drink in my hand.'

CHAPTER 13

It was deep night by the time we reached Tulbar, the settlement appearing as a blur of faint flames in the distance.

'Not a moment too soon,' said Locan. 'I could drink a whole gallon of that pisswater Roddin serves. Could do with a hot meal as well.'

'We'll be lucky to get anything,' I replied. 'He's probably locked us out and given our room away.'

Locan did not reply for a moment, instead touching a finger to his ear and lifting it to the air. 'Can you hear that?'

I listened, frowning. The pealing of a bell reached my ear, faint and frantic on the breeze.

The only bell we'd seen in High Tulbar had been at Caradrahan Hall, in the tower topped with the dragon statue that watched over the town. 'What does it mean?' I wondered. I looked out to sea, searching for a ship that was floundering as the *Red Fiend* had, then when I saw nothing, I turned my eyes west, scouring the black horizon for the bobbing torches of an invading army. There was nothing.

'Nothing good,' growled Locan. He shook his head irritably. 'Knew the dragon was too easy. I'd say trouble likes to follow us around, but more likely trouble's just the state of things.' He urged his horse forward. 'Come on.'

Our approach revealed no enemy soldiers, but the streets of Tulbar were in a frenzy as people responded to the ringing bell, all heading towards the castle. We went against the tide, making for the Dwarf and Dragon, but our approach was interrupted when we encountered Chatten alongside two of the Mór's guards, stationed atop a table that had been dragged into the street where she was handing out spears to passing men.

'Get yourselves to Caradrahan Hall!' she was shouting. 'Men over thirteen and willing women over sixteen, take a spear and get moving!'

'Chatten, what's happening?' I called to her.

The constable started at the sight of our approach. 'Shanoch's army's been seen crossing the Bronzewater River. The Mór's going to address everyone up at the castle.'

I recalled the map of Paleir I'd seen. 'The Bronzewater is miles away, isn't it?'

'That was two days ago.' She flashed an irritated look at me as she continued to hand out spears. 'You planning to take one? If not, move.'

We rode on towards the inn. 'They must still be days away,' I said to Locan. Based on the map I had seen, I could not envisage a force marching to High Tulbar from the Bronzewater in the space of two days.

Locan spat on the ground. 'First sign of trouble and the young Mór's shat his breeches. Hope he's got whatever wizardry he needs to summon a dragon ready.'

We stabled our horses, then entered the inn's common room to find it almost deserted. Roddin was gone, as were all his lackeys, but Shaliya was there, running a damp cloth over one of the tables. In the lamplight of the common room, her cheeks were flushed, her blue eyes sparkled, and her blonde hair shone like starlight reflecting in the black sea of a moonless night. My heart leapt at the sight of her. I could not wait to tell her about Aydhenia.

'You're back!' she exclaimed, turning at the sound of the door shutting behind us. She smiled at me and my stomach practically flipped over. 'Roddin said you'd be gone for days.'

'Your master failed to tell us about the mist,' said Locan. 'Arsehole probably expected us to get lost and take a tumble off the cliff. He's gone up to the castle, I take it?'

Shaliya nodded. 'They all have. They stayed here drinking at first, but Chatten came in and cursed them all for cowards. First time I've ever seen Roddin look ashamed. I'd have gone as well, but he said someone needed to stay and watch the inn.'

'More drink for me then,' said Locan, moving nimbly to the bar and claiming two cups of ale from the barrel and a bottle of brandy.

Shaliya followed Locan to the bar. She poured an ale for me and then one for herself. 'Here,' she said, smiling at me in a way that was trapped somewhere between brazen and shy. Our fingers brushed as she handed the mug to me.

'Thank you,' I said, taking a long, refreshing gulp, only narrowly avoiding missing my mouth because I was too occupied with staring at her. Back inside the warmth of the inn, and having been sustained to this point by the adrenaline of my encounter with Aydhenia, I was beginning to realise how tired I felt. 'Is there any food?' I asked. 'We've barely eaten all day.'

'There's still some stew in the pot,' said Shaliya. 'I'll warm it up for you.' She danced across the room to the low fire and began stoking it with a poker. I could hardly take my eyes off her.

'Would you like a pipe?' she asked Locan, who was already on his second ale and making a steady dent in the brandy. 'There's some kishweed Roddin keeps hidden. Goes well with ale, I'm told.'

Locan shook his head. 'I've not had good kish since I left

Rameon. Not going to sully my lungs with whatever cabbage Roddin's got.'

'He bought it from a Rintish trader last summer,' said Shaliya.

A slow smile spread across Locan's lips. 'Rintish, is it?' The best kish was said to be grown in Rintland, on the slopes of the Blacknose Mountains just north of the Red Water. I was surprised and slightly hurt that Shaliya was not offering any to me – did she think I would not be able to handle it? 'Wasted on the likes of Roddin then. Would be rude not to.'

Shaliya had already moved behind the bar. She ducked underneath it, rattled around, and produced a short, simple pipe. It was deep black in colour, carved from fireproof goblin bone. She padded some herbs into the bowl and handed it to Locan, who was eyeing it greedily. I'd never seen him so eager for something other than liquor. He claimed the pipe and lit it from a nearby candle.

Shaliya continued to bustle about the inn, eventually putting a bowl of stew down in front of me. I tore into it, burning the roof of my mouth but too hungry to care.

'Did you find the dragon?' asked Shaliya.

Locan spoke before I could finish my mouthful. 'We did.' A cloud of purple smoke wafted lazily from his mouth.

Shaliya looked at him with narrow-eyed suspicion, as if she wanted to believe him but was not sure whether she should. 'Truly?'

'As true as a Seamster-priest is crooked.' Locan nodded towards me. 'Cetrik even spoke to her.'

She looked at me, and an uncertain smile began to blossom across her face. 'You wouldn't lie to me, would you?'

For the sake of having Shaliya smile at me like that, I would have sworn never to tell a lie again. I was caught between my hunger for the stew in front of me and my desire to talk to her, and ended up somewhere halfway, trying to speak with my spoon still in my mouth and dribbling stew from my lips back into the bowl.

'Sorry,' I said, wiping at my mouth with the back of my hand. I could feel my cheeks flushing with embarrassment.

But Shaliya was laughing. 'Never knew my cooking was that good.' She sat down beside me, her eyes wide with curiosity. 'Tell me. Did you really meet a dragon? Really?'

I described how I had come to enter Aydhenia's lair, the awe-inducing size of her and the impossible shimmer of her scales, and summarised what the dragon and I had spoken of – how the Dreadveil had forced her into the sea, the whispered entreaties of the Abomination King, and eventually how I had narrowly escaped being devoured.

Shaliya's eyes grew even wider as I went on, until by the time I finished, they were like two huge dinner plates hewn from dazzlingly blue marble. 'Seamstress's tits,' she breathed. 'Were you scared?'

'Terrified.' At some point, her hand had come to rest atop mine. 'I only survived because of that story you told me about Jelic saving himself with flattery.' Fire was coursing through my veins, though whether this was because of the attentiveness with which Shaliya was staring at me or my growing disbelief that I had survived and lived to tell the tale of my encounter with Aydhenia I was not sure. 'My bones would be in her belly otherwise.'

Locan, I realised, had not said anything for several minutes, not even to interrupt me with one of his usual jibes. I had been too busy getting lost in Shaliya's eyes to notice. I looked up and discovered he was asleep at the bar, his head resting in the crook of his arm, the pipe still stuck in his mouth with lazy tendrils of smoke spiralling from it while his stew sat there untouched. His face was uncharacteristically peaceful.

Shaliya's eyes followed mine, and she gave a small, satisfied laugh. 'I slipped some dreamshade into the kish,' she said. 'He'll sleep there until morning.'

'You drugged him?' I exclaimed. Dreamshade was a powerful sedative; at a high enough dose it could even kill. I would have sprung to my feet in alarm if not for Shaliya's calming hand on my forearm.

'He'll be fine,' said Shaliya. 'Namma taught me years ago the right dose to send a man to sleep.' She shyly dropped her eyes, displaying her long dark lashes. 'Until Roddin gets back, you have me to yourself.'

My mouth was suddenly dry as dust. To think I had believed encountering a dragon would be the high point of my day. 'For what?' I could scarcely believe this was happening. I ought to have been furious with her for drugging Locan, but my reserves of outrage seemed to have run dry. Locan had the constitution of an ox; he would be fine.

Shaliya's eyes flashed at me, one perfect brow raised in invitation. 'What would you like to do?'

I swallowed. My heartbeat was a hastening rhythm of trepidation and desire. For all my complaints, I knew that Locan was right about the folly of becoming involved with another man's slave, but with hot blood coursing around every inch of my body I did not care. 'To kiss you?'

Shaliya's smile was all the answer I needed. 'Why stop there?'

Her question was swallowed by silence as I leant forward to press my lips to hers, and in the heat of her tongue all thought of Locan and dread that Roddin could return any moment vanished. There was only Shaliya and me, locked in an embrace, our desperation for one another laid plain by the steady beat of our hearts, how my hands seemed to wind their way through the thick mane of her golden hair of their own accord, the way we moved as one, pressing our bodies into one another as if daring somebody to part us.

Against every instinct I had, I broke away from her long enough to ask, 'Why?'

Shaliya laughed as if I had said something funny. 'What do you mean "Why?" Do you want to stop?'

'No! I just mean—' I was not sure what I meant – all the blood seemed to have rushed from my head. 'I mean – why me?' I had washed up in Tulbar by mistake and been immediately hosted by Shaliya's lord while she worked herself to the bone for Roddin. We were the same age, and though I was prone to bemoaning my circumstances, fate had blessed me in a way Shaliya could only dream of, with wealth and a famous name and the freedom to travel as I pleased. She could have hated me.

Shaliya raised a mocking eyebrow. 'Was knocking your friend out not compliment enough?'

It was my turn to laugh. 'No—I mean yes. What I meant was—'

Shaliya placed a finger to my lips. '"Does it hurt?" That was the first thing you said to me when you arrived two days ago.' She touched the branded 'R' under her right eye. 'Since my father sold me, do you know how many times men have asked me that?'

I shook my head.

'None. You were the first person to ever care.' My heart broke for her, but before I could give voice to this, she pressed her lips lightly against mine. 'And you're brave. You stood up to Darry. You spoke to a dragon. And you're kind and honest enough that I believed you about that. And your horse is the most beautiful creature I've ever laid eyes on.' She gave me a wicked smile. 'And I suppose you're not so hard on the eye yourself.'

We kissed again, and after that we did not speak again for some time.

I had known Shaliya for less than two days at this point, but when you are as foolish and mad with desire as we were, two days can be enough to leave the shape of the other person's fingertips imprinted on your heart. If that seems unlikely, recall how easy it seemed to fall in love when you were young. I lived through it, but I am old now, and writing these words to parchment feels as foreign to me as translating the dead tongue of the elvenfolk to Guilish. To be young and consumed with righteous love is a feeling that translates as poorly to ink on the page as the deepest, most elusive magic there is.

As we rose from the table together, our hands scouring the folds and openings of each other's clothing, it was if our two bodies were acting in mimicry of our entwined souls. The common room of the Dwarf and Dragon slipped away around us, my whole existence shrunk to the warmth of Shaliya's body and the hunger of her tongue.

I will spare you further clumsy attempts to describe what occurred between Shaliya and me that night. This is intended to be a recounting of my time with Locan A'Shadow, not a tawdry scroll one might find in a pleasure house. I have not the talent to describe it, but if you recall your own youthful fumblings, throw in that I had come within a few breaths of being eaten by a dragon earlier that day and my fear that Shaliya's master might return with his friends at any moment, you might capture a fraction of the fervour I felt that night. I was on fire, enflamed by Shaliya's beauty, her bravery, our deep yearning for one another.

While Locan slept, we found our way to Shaliya's chamber, and that is where I woke the next day, with Shaliya's hair tickling my face, our naked forms pressed tightly together, and my arm tingling from where her head lay in the crook of my elbow. She slept so peacefully beside me that I could not bear to move her.

When your life is marred by strife as mine had been, whether the conflict between myself and my family, my travails among the tribes of Narlond, or even just the endless back and forth between me and Locan, it is easy to forget how it feels to be content. In those few moments after I woke in Shaliya's bed, I remembered, and perhaps for the first time since my childhood I was able to briefly let go of my longing to escape. I had been driven to flee Guiland by a mixture of frustration and despair and the desire for something else, and that feeling had dogged every step of my journey. Lying in Shaliya's bed, with her rose-water and honey scent in my nostrils, it was as if it had never been there at all.

I would free her of Roddin. I had no other choice. And then we would leave Paleir forever.

The lock to Shaliya's room gave a metallic squeak, and the door crashed inward.

My eyes shot open. Roddin stood at the threshold, his hands curled into fists, his face fixed in a rictus of unbridled rage.

'*You little shit!*'

With a roar, Roddin charged towards me.

He did not have to go far. Shaliya's chamber was small, and I was on the side of the bed closest the door. I barely had time to get myself free of the bedsheets before he was on me, and then I could only cover my face while Roddin punched freely at my head. He aimed a fist for my groin, and I barely managed to twist out of the way.

He was a broad man, but neither strong nor accustomed to violence. I survived his first flurry, and when I was able to push him away he took a step back, wheezing, lining up a wind-milling punch at my head. My senses were ringing with the blows he'd already dealt me, but this would have been an oppor-tune moment to counterattack, had Shaliya not got there first. Naked, she threw herself onto Roddin's back with an arm wrapped around his throat. This gave me the chance to stand, but Roddin reached back to grab Shaliya by the hair and fuelled by rage threw her forward over his shoulder, sending us tumbling together over the narrow bed and landing in a tangle against the wall.

Roddin's eyes were wild, but he restrained himself from leaping after us. 'You're for it now,' he said, his nostrils flaring like an enraged bull's. 'You've had enough warnings. Now you'll get what's coming to you.' He stomped to the door and closed it behind himself with a click of the lock.

'Shit.' I rushed about gathering the clothes I had left strewn about the room, throwing Shaliya's to her as I found them. We dressed in a hurry. 'Is there another way out?' I asked.

'Not unless you can fit through the window.' The window in Shaliya's room was tiny, locked, and overlooked the street below.

There came the sound of heavy steps on the stairs. I untangled my scabbard from my breeches, and with my tunic askew and still wearing only one boot I pulled my sword free. 'Get behind me,' I told Shaliya. I would kill Roddin and take my chances if I had to. Hosten would understand, and if the Keykeepers came after me, Locan would deal with them.

But when Roddin reappeared he was not alone. The door clicked, and he entered flanked by two men in the blue livery of Hosten's guard, with Chatten bringing up the rear.

'He fucked my slave,' spat Roddin, flushed with rage and breathing hard from the run up and down the stairs. He was holding a spear, presumably one of those that Chatten had been handing out the night before. He thrust it towards my face. 'He interfered with my property.'

I could hardly deny it, standing there in Shaliya's bedroom with my clothing all askew. 'I'll buy her freedom,' I told him. 'My family has money.'

'Wouldn't matter if you were offering me all the gold in the Dominion,' spat Roddin. 'She's mine and you can't have her. How are you going to buy her when you're *dead*?'

'Leave him alone,' said Shaliya. She was standing beside me, clutching her eating knife, staring at Roddin as if she meant to skin him with it. 'And leave me alone. If you come near me again, I'll stab you in the cock.'

Roddin flinched as if she'd struck him. 'After all I've done for you.' There were actual tears glistening in his eyes. He seemed genuinely pained. 'I've housed and fed you, and as much as I wanted to, I've never touched you out of respect for your father. Swore to myself I'd wait until you saw what a waste this was and agreed to marry me. Well, that changes today, I promise you. All I've done for you, and you throw yourself at the first greasy, pretty Guilander who strolls through my door as if he owns the place. You're a fucking *slut*, Shaliya.'

I moved forward, ready to hack my sword across Roddin's wide, stupid face, and damn the consequences, but Chatten stepped between us. 'Roddin, just shut up for once and let me do my job.' The constable of High Tulbar spoke with weary calm. 'I'm too fucking tired for this.' She looked me in the eye. 'When you washed up here, I warned you to keep out of trouble. You're not the first boy to lose his head over a girl, but I expected more from you, Cetrik, I really did. Thought you had a good head on your shoulders. I can see why the Mór took to you, but he won't excuse this.'

I felt a flicker of shame, then crushed it. It was Roddin's behaviour that had caused this quarrel, not mine.

'I hate you, Roddin,' said Shaliya, spitting fury. 'I know what you want, that one day I'll get so tired of saying no to you that I'll give up and invite you into my bed, but it's never going to happen. *Never never never!*'

Roddin's mouth twisted. 'Is that right? By the time I'm done with you, you'll be begging me to take you. I'll have you in the stocks, and any man who wants a turn can—'

'That's enough, Roddin,' said Chatten. By the furious look she gave him, the innkeeper had taken it too far. 'If you're feeling brave, you can suggest that to the Mór and see what he thinks.'

'The Mór can say as he likes,' sneered Roddin. 'Won't change a fucking thing.' No doubt he expected the other Keykeepers to support him; they would not care how he sought to punish me and Shaliya.

'I hope you die when the Varnans get here,' spat Shaliya.

'*Enough*,' said Chatten. She rubbed her temples. 'Dragon's teats, don't you lot know there's a war on? I'm too pissing tired to be dealing with domestic disputes and love triangles. Roddin, go downstairs and make me some breakfast. I'll be here every morning from now on to make sure you're treating that girl right. Any bruises I'll pay you back in kind.'

'What?' demanded Roddin. 'What about—'

'I will *get* to them,' said Chatten through gritted teeth. 'See if you can wake up the Ramean as well, before the grain of your bar gets left imprinted on his face.

'And you can wipe that smirk off your mouth as well,' she added, giving me a hard stare as Roddin reluctantly departed. I had been unable to hide a premature sense of triumph. 'Shaliya, keep out of Roddin's way the rest of the day. Go visit your family and come back tomorrow morning. If he doesn't behave himself, he'll have me to answer to.'

I immediately felt relieved. I trusted Chatten to keep her word and keep Roddin in check, and that meant Shaliya was safe. 'What about me?' I asked.

The constable sighed. 'Like it or not, Cetrik, this is Paleir, and Shaliya belongs to Roddin. If the Mór doesn't make an example of you, next week there'll be other men doing just as you did. Not to mention that I warned you, and you spat it back in my face.' Her face hardened. 'The Mór can decide what's to be done with you, and I won't be recommending he show mercy. Unfortunately, dealing with your idiocy is at the bottom of a very long list of problems right now – somewhere after the small matter of making sure this entire settlement doesn't get murdered in our beds, and maybe just above clipping my toenails, though I'll find that more enjoyable – so it'll be a long wait in the dungeon if I get my way.' She looked at my sword, weighing up my grip, the balance of my feet, the close confines of the bedroom. 'So, are you going to come quietly, or are you going to behave like even more of a royal little prick? The answer determines the number of teeth you'll leave this inn with.'

The two guards pulled their swords free and took a step forward. If Locan had been there with me, I would have liked my chances, but I could only assume he was still passed out downstairs. Even if I could get past the two guards by myself, Chatten would be waiting for me, and she looked like she knew one end of a sword from the other. And in the confusion of battle, I could not guarantee Shaliya's safety. One stumble or misstep and she might end up at the wrong end of a blade. Better to take my chances with Hosten. He might have to make an example of me to appease Roddin and the Keykeepers, but privately he would support me, especially if Locan and I gave him the scale. I could handle a minor punishment.

'I'll come quietly,' I said, letting the point of my sword drop an inch. 'Once Shaliya has left the inn.'

Chatten rolled her eyes and let out an exasperated breath. 'I'll look after Shaliya. I don't have the time or the patience for you to play the gallant hero.' She gestured to the guards. 'Take him.'

I made it easy for them. I let go of my grip on Shaliya's hand and tossed my blade at Chatten's feet. One of the guards could not resist jabbing his pommel into my stomach, but otherwise they treated me fairly, one man searching me for weapons while the other bound my hands behind my back.

I looked over my shoulder at Shaliya. 'I'd do it again.'

Shaliya's smile was like the radiance of the first dawn. With her clothes askew and her hair a turbulent golden storm, she had never looked more beautiful. 'I would as well.'

Chatten made a retching sound. 'Seamstress spare me from star-fated lovers.'

A slow, shuffling tread came from the stairs, and everyone looked towards the door. It was Locan. He looked rough even by his standards, one eye half open and bloodshot and the other seemingly stuck closed. He staggered, and slumped against the doorway to narrowly avoid taking a tumble. 'What did I miss?' he croaked.

CHAPTER 14

Contrary to Chatten's hope, I was not taken to Caradrahan Hall's dungeon. By Hosten's mercy, I was locked away in a guest room until he had the time to decide what was to be done with me.

My prison's double windows overlooked the yard. I spent the morning watching Tulbar's recruits drill with spear and shield and be taught how to properly form a shield wall by Hosten's increasingly enraged marshal, a fierce old warrior by the name of Grenick. Supposedly, every man of Tulbar was required to train with weapons at least one day out of seven, not unlike in Guiland, but I saw scant evidence that many took it seriously. There was no sign of Roddin nor the various sullen drunks we had seen pass through the doors of his inn, nor Ulf the arena-master, but Hobbo and the rest of the mob we had encountered on the beach were there, sullenly going through the motions.

A servant eventually appeared with a ewer of weak ale, which I sipped slowly, reminiscing happily on the previous day and night. I was the first person in centuries to speak with a dragon, and on the same day I had lain with the woman I loved. Imprisonment was a small price to pay.

But as the day wore on, and I grew bored of watching Grenick's fruitless attempts at training his charges, my thoughts turned darker.

A braver man than I might have sought to escape the Dwarf and Dragon at the point of a sword, but I had seen enough of the world by now to know that it seldom resembles the stories. Fighting would not have stopped me being taken, except I might have been here with Shaliya's death on my conscience. What would happen to her now? I trusted Chatten to keep her word, but her attention would be on the impending conflict, not on keeping an eye on Roddin.

Locan would by now have recovered from being spiked, and while I was detained I could not stop him delivering Aydhenia's scale to Hosten. I was hopeful the Mór would look favourably on me, but it would not hurt to have some leverage. Locan might even deliver a scale and leave me to my fate. With Locan you could never be sure.

But it did not take long for my fears to be assuaged. I was still sitting at the table beside the window when several sets of footsteps sounded in the corridor, and the door opened to reveal Locan, upright and seemingly sober, with Hosten beside him and followed by Lenard and two of Hosten's guards.

Locan gave a discontented grunt at the sight of me. 'You could at least have clapped him in irons. Least he deserves for drugging me.'

'That was Shaliya,' I answered, coming to my feet.

'Well, you might have stopped her.' Locan gave a slow shake of his head. 'You're a goblin-fucking idiot. I warned you enough times to stay away from her.' He looked at Hosten. 'You sure I can't persuade you to find him a nice comfortable cell? Maybe with thumbscrews and a rack?'

Hosten looked as if he had several days' sleep to catch up

on, carrying even more strain than when I had last seen him. He was pale, with deep bags weighing heavily under his eyes, and the mail he wore was too big for him, making him look even slighter and less like a warrior than he had already. It was hardly a surprise to see him so drained in the circumstances. His father's corpse was barely cold, and he would now have to defend his inherited crown against his uncle.

Hosten gave a heavy sigh. 'Cetrik, I cannot excuse this.'

'The way Roddin treats Shaliya isn't right,' I said, my blood already rising. 'You know that.'

'Cetrik, I know.' Hosten sank into a chair, a fingertip massaging his temple. 'And you know my hopes for abolishing the shameful practice of slavery. But alienating men like Roddin will not aid me in that cause. My authority with the Keykeepers hangs by a thread – I cannot fight against both them and my uncle. There must be consequences, as much as it pains me. Fortunately, whatever you may think, Roddin is a reasonable man.' The edge of his mouth twitched. 'For the most part. For his loss—'

'*His loss?*' I had told myself that I would remain calm when I faced Hosten, but I could not contain my outrage. The only victim here was Shaliya. 'There's been no loss! Shaliya will be back working in his inn from tomorrow, serving his drinks and—'

Locan stepped forward and slapped me hard across the face. 'Goblins' black bones, are you so desperate to talk your way into a noose?' I stepped back cradling my cheek. It stung like the fires of Sevash had been unleashed on it. 'Stop pretending you're not fucking clever enough to understand this. Shaliya. Belongs. To Roddin.' Locan punctuated each word by jabbing his finger into my chest. 'Not everyone gets to grow up isolated from consequences, and here outside your fancy family, *you* have to face them as well. Just be glad your little girlfriend seems to have got away with it.'

I did not agree. Not at all. Shaliya would be returned to Roddin, and one day in a mad drunken rage I was sure he would kill her. It was Roddin who continued to evade justice for his crimes.

'I have sought assurances from Roddin that she will not be punished,' said Hosten. 'It is all I can do. Chatten will be looking out for her.' He rose from his chair and placed a hand on my shoulder. 'Give me five years, Cetrik.' His eyes were soft with sincerity. 'Five years, and I swear to you High Tulbar will be a different place.'

Faced with Hosten's open repentance, I felt the fight leak out of me. With his uncle Shanoch's army on its way, he had greater concerns than dealing with me and Shaliya. I felt a pang of guilt for adding to his troubles. Hosten could not end slavery with the click of his fingers, and by coming into conflict with Roddin I had likely hindered that aim rather than helped it. If Hosten's reign failed, then slaves like Shaliya would never be free.

But Shaliya did not have five years. Hosten could afford to be patient, but I could not. When the *Red Fiend* was fixed, I would take her far, far away from here.

I could not bring myself to apologise, for I was resolved that I had done nothing wrong, but I gave Hosten a silent nod of acquiescence.

'You've not even heard your punishment yet,' said Locan, who had sat down and was now helping himself to the dregs of my ale. 'You might find it's to your taste.'

'What I was going to say before you interrupted,' said Hosten, though he was smiling at me, 'is that Roddin has agreed that you may compensate him by fighting for Tulbar in his stead.'

Locan sniggered. 'Bet he has, the fat craven.'

I stared at Hosten. 'You mean, I'm to fight against Shanoch? And Roddin won't even have to lift a spear?' I glanced at Locan, who was smirking as if rather pleased with himself. No doubt he recalled my idle words the day before that I would gladly fight for Hosten in Tulbar's defence.

'Seem to recall you being quite open to that prospect when we spoke yesterday,' said Locan, leaning back in his chair. He was clearly taking great pleasure in my misfortune. 'Unless you're all talk and no balls?'

I had said I would fight, but that had been before I'd seen the pitiful state of Tulbar's defenders. Hosten had fewer than a hundred warriors worthy of the name.

Nevertheless, I would not let Hosten down now. He had done what he could for me and Shaliya, while having much else to occupy him. I owed him for that, and having seen the sincerity of his resolve when he spoke of ending slavery, I could not help but support him.

I straightened my back and pulled back my shoulders. 'I'd be honoured to fight with you,' I said, giving Hosten what I thought to be a stiff martial stare. I had not disgraced myself in Narlond, and my swordsmanship had come on by leaps and bounds over winter under the tutelage of Locan and the warriors of Great Yex.

'If only I had another five hundred men who would say the same,' said Hosten, with an embattled smile. 'Keep your head down today, and report tomorrow.'

'I have arranged new rooms for you at the Merry Whale,' said Lenard, speaking for the first time from where he hung back behind Hosten.

'Seeing as I doubt we'll be welcome back at the Dwarf and Dragon any time this century,' said Locan. 'Lenard assures me there's no slaves working there for you to fall in love with.' He began groping in his cloak for something. 'In all the excitement of being drugged, I almost forgot.' He pulled out one of the shimmering blue dragon scales and held it up to catch the weak sunlight that stretched through the window. 'Your dragon scale.'

Hosten's mouth fell open. He looked back and forth between the scale and Locan's face, seemingly trying to determine whether his eyes were somehow deceiving him. He gulped a few times, as if momentarily robbed of the power of reason. In that moment, he looked younger than ever, gazing upon the scale in wide-eyed wonder. 'Truly?' he whispered finally.

'See for yourself.' Locan threw the scale and Hosten barely managed to catch it. He turned it over and over between his fingers, seeing how its deep blue shimmered between the shades of sea and sky. 'This is...' His mouth widened in an astonished smile. He stared at it in wonderment – this single scale had the power to change the fate of his kingdom. 'Impossible,' he said finally. 'I never even imagined...'

'You were right,' I said, a smile spreading across my own face. In his palm, Hosten held the power to save his kingdom. Such was his bewildered delight that in that moment I no longer cared about what this meant for Aydhenia.

'How?' Hosten asked, still unable to hide his disbelief. Lenard had come forward to examine the scale, and like Hosten seemed to be lost for words.

As I had with Shaliya, I recounted to Hosten my encounter with Aydhenia. His eyes grew wide as I explained how I had almost drowned before finding her lair, and the conversation between us where I had always felt mere inches from having my skin steamed off, and by the time I told him of how Aydhenia had spent four centuries swimming beneath the Dreadveil, Hosten's eyes were like dinner plates.

'I... I hardly know what to say,' said Hosten. With bright eyes he looked at each of us in turn. 'Thank you. Thank you. With this, I might save Tulbar.'

'Not near as mad as I thought you were,' said Locan grudgingly. With a groan he came to his feet. 'I trust then that once our ship is repaired, you won't object to us leaving?'

At Locan's words, Hosten's smile fell slightly, and some of his astonishment at laying eyes upon a dragon scale seemed to fade. With great care, he unlaced the purse that hung from his belt, placed the scale inside, and closed it again. He glanced meaningfully at Lenard.

'Your friend's ship is still some way from being fixed,' said the steward, seeming to take great care over his words. 'Repairs continue day and night, but we are informed it will be at least another week before it is seaworthy again.'

'And then we're leaving,' said Locan. His eyes flickered dangerously. 'That was the deal.'

Lenard frowned slightly. 'I believe the agreement was that you would obtain for my lord a scale with which he could tame a dragon and defeat Mór Shanoch. As yet, only one of those conditions have been met.'

'So use the dragon scale and summon your dragon then,' said Locan impatiently, looking at Hosten. 'Our task is done.'

An uneasy glance passed between Hosten and Lenard. 'Shanoch has moved more quickly than we expected,' said Lenard. 'Matters have accelerated.'

'They don't know how,' I said, intuitively seeing the meaning in the look that passed between the two men. The guilty look Lenard gave me told that I was correct. 'Shaliya said the Caradrahans never wrote down how to bind a dragon.' I could have laughed. 'They don't know!'

Locan's expression darkened. 'Tell me he's joking.'

'Now we have a scale, the way forward will reveal itself,' said Hosten, regaining some of his poise. 'Dragons are in my blood.'

'And your blood will be all over these walls if you don't start being straight with us,' said Locan. He took a threatening step towards Hosten and Lenard which brought the guards forward to place themselves in front of their Mór. He looked between the two men. 'You never meant to hold up your end of the deal, did you?'

'I swear this is not what I wanted,' said Hosten. 'Shanoch has left us no choice.'

'But it is what we agreed,' added Lenard. The steward had edged away, placing himself directly behind Hosten's guards.

I tried to recall the exact terms of the agreement between me and Hosten. I had taken him to mean that we needed only to bring him a scale, but clearly Lenard and Hosten had heard something different.

'The matter is easily resolved,' said Lenard to Locan. 'Shanoch is on his way to High Tulbar. Killing him should be a simple matter for a man of your talents.'

'A simple matter if you pay me,' said Locan dangerously. 'So far the only thing of value that's changed hands is the scale.'

'You did kill two men,' said Hosten. 'Given the ease with which you obtained it, a dragon scale hardly seems sufficient payment for the trouble you've caused.'

The two guards standing between Locan and Hosten had placed their hands ready on the hilts of their swords. Locan gave them a scornful look up and down. 'Don't worry,' he sneered. 'I'm not going to hurt him.' He stared at Hosten with contempt written across his features. 'I'm glad in a way. Now Cetrik gets to see the true nature of kings. Stick a crown on someone's head, and they can always find a way to justify being a duplicitous sack of shit.'

I had not forgotten Locan's pronouncement on the nature of rulers: that once they got a taste of power, clinging onto it was more precious to them than any principle or noble aspiration. Was Hosten's willingness to go back on his word the first manifestation of that?

But I still believed Hosten's aims to be just and that it was worth helping him; if he could not summon a dragon in time, it would be an easy matter for Locan to get rid of Shanoch.

'It's no delay to us,' I said to Locan, hoping to find a peaceable solution. 'The *Fiend* is still two weeks from being ready to sail.'

Locan gave an acid laugh. 'Ain't the point, but trust you to side with him.' He held out his hand. 'Give me the scale back. You want it, you can send every man you have after me and we'll see how many are left by the time Shanoch arrives.'

'Out of the question,' said Hosten, placing a hand protectively over his purse. 'It's because I hoped you would find the dragon and obtain a scale that I warned Ulf and the Keykeepers to leave you alone. Now if you want to leave Tulbar, your next task is to kill Shanoch.'

'Yeah? Good luck stopping Huretio once the *Fiend* is finished,' spat Locan. 'He's sailed the Rintish Passage half-a-hundred times – sure he'll have no trouble fighting past a couple of your poxy guards. You've not even got any ships.'

'I won't need to,' said Hosten. I could not help but admire his calmness when faced with Locan's barely repressed fury. Given his reputation, many men would have backed down already. 'I can conscript the men working on the ship into my army and requisition the timber for bolstering our defences. I could have your friend's ship broken apart for kindling if I chose. The Keykeepers would not oppose me.'

'Dare you to try it,' said Locan. 'You won't like the consequences, I can promise you that.' His hand moved into the folds of his cloak, and in the space of a blink a dagger was spinning through the air. It flew between Lenard and Hosten's heads and embedded itself deep in the door behind them, its hilt quivering in the wood.

The two guards had not even had time to draw their swords.

Lenard was pale. 'You tried to kill him!'

'If I wanted him dead, he would be,' sneered Locan. He looked Hosten square in the eye. 'Betray me again or stop me leaving this shithole and that dagger flies six inches to the right.

Now if you'll excuse me, I'm leaving before I do something all of us regret.'

The two guards made to draw their swords as Locan moved to walk past them, but Hosten bid them to halt. 'Let him go,' he said.

Locan departed, slamming the door behind him and setting it rattling on its hinges.

To my surprise though, Hosten was smiling. 'His reputation is well earnt,' he said.

'It's not safe to have him out in the town unchecked,' said Lenard. 'There's no telling what trouble he might cause.'

'He'll come around,' said Hosten. He pulled the scale from his pouch and held it up to the light to admire it again. 'Remarkable,' he murmured. He looked at me apologetically. 'I'm sorry, Cetrik. I am grateful for what you and Locan have done for me, but Tulbar must come first.'

I could understand why Hosten had done as he did, but that did not make it any easier to stomach. It was not Tulbar that came first, but Hosten's rule over it. 'You lied to me,' I said. Or, he had at least misled me. I hated myself a little for not storming out with Locan, but it made no sense to make an enemy of Hosten. One of us had to keep regard for our own safety.

Hosten gave a heavy sigh. He gestured to Lenard and the guards. 'Leave us.'

'Lord,' said Lenard, unable to hide his alarm, 'are you—'

'I am sure that Cetrik means no harm,' said Hosten, more forcefully. 'Leave us.'

Somewhat reluctantly, Lenard departed, followed by the two guards.

Hosten sat down at the table and bid me to join him. He poured us each a cup of ale. He shook his head and stared out of the window. 'It was not my intent to lie to you,' he said. The stress he was under was written in every line of his face. 'I hoped I would have time to uncover the secrets of the dragon scale before I faced my uncle.' He gestured below to where the men of Tulbar were still drilling in the yard. 'It is said that Shanoch rides with ten thousand men. Not only men of Varned, but Altan mercenaries riding warhounds that can outrun a horse and reportedly leap over a wall in a single bound. How long do you suppose High Tulbar will hold out against such a force? If the city falls, all your efforts in obtaining the dragon scale will be for nothing. I agonised for hours over how else I might defeat my uncle, but Lenard has shown me that I have no choice.'

He looked at me. 'Do you know how slaves are treated in Varned, Cetrik?'

I shook my head.

'Tulban law curbs some of the basest instincts of slavers. It is a crime to excessively beat your slave, to enslave a child, to fail in providing slaves with food, water, and warmth. Do not look at me so – I know it is not enough. In Varned, there are no such protections. A man may kill his slave with impunity. In Tulbar, they would face a heavy fine or even imprisonment. My uncle has ruled Varned for twenty years, ever since my grandfather died and his kingdom was split in two at the Homeless Hills. Do you know what he has done to improve things in Varned?'

I hazarded a guess. 'Nothing?'

Hosten nodded. 'Nothing indeed. My father was far from perfect, but he was a bolder and brighter man than my uncle. Shanoch is simple and brutal. He will bend Tulbar until it breaks, and cruel men like Roddin will prosper. If Tulbar falls, Shaliya's life stands to get a lot worse.'

I knew I was being manipulated, but I could not shake from my mind images of what might become of Shaliya if Tulbar succumbed to Shanoch. Hulking, fur-clad warriors atop slavering beasts breaking down the door to the Dwarf and Dragon while the roof was claimed by an inferno; Roddin standing over Shaliya's bleeding corpse, his fists raw from the beating he had dealt her.

Hosten gave a sad smile. 'Your face tells me you understand. Cetrik, there is nothing I would not do to restore Paleir to its rightful glory, to make it a kingdom where all can prosper and not only the likes of Roddin and Ulf. If I have lied to you, I am sorry, but I do not for one moment regret it. And if I am to defeat Shanoch, I will need your help again.'

CHAPTER 15

I departed Caradrahan Hall that evening with Hosten's entreaty to help him again still ringing in my ears. That Hosten had arguably deceived us no longer troubled me – his high ambitions for Tulbar and Paleir had my unerring support, and I could not fault him for doing what was necessary to achieve them.

The difficulty would be persuading Locan, particularly when he was still furious with me for allowing Shaliya to dose him with dreamshade. I was no less fed up with Locan; his opposition to slavery extended to beating up Ulf's men in a rage but not to helping Hosten actually do something about it. He might have less faith in Hosten than I did, but there would be no harm in trying. Locan would grouse and complain about anything but would never lift a finger to improve matters. It was beginning to grate on me.

The Merry Whale was an even sorrier establishment than the Dwarf and Dragon. Half the roof was thatched, and half had been haphazardly tiled, with many of the slates already cracked or fallen. The repetitive clash of a blacksmith's hammer resounded from the other side of the building.

Entering the yard, I was relieved to see that Morvolt had already been retrieved from the Dwarf and Dragon. He was inside one of the stable stalls, hanging his head over the half-door. I spent a few minutes trying to soothe his irascible temper and refilling his bag of oats and then made my way inside.

I stepped through a low doorway into an empty common room. It was smaller than the Dwarf and Dragon, with stools in place of chairs and overturned barrels in place of tables. A slender, older man with eyeglasses and a shock of white hair was cleaning the bar.

'Ho!' he greeted me, rushing out from behind the bar. I immediately liked him more than Roddin. 'Albart. My name's Albart.' He shook my hand vigorously, and I could not help but return his open smile. 'The Mór's man told me what happened. I may not get Roddin's custom, but I more than make up for it with my hospitality.' He practically leapt back over the bar and began pouring me an ale. 'Your first ale's on the house, but seeing as the Mór is paying, I'll do you a brandy as well.'

'He doesn't do well on brandy,' came a grizzled voice from a corner table. 'Best give it to me.' It was Locan. He looked up at me with a scowl. 'My belly feels like someone's poured a barrel of fish into it. If you ever poison me again, I'll cut out your liver and boil it.'

'It was Shaliya,' I told him, again. 'I didn't know until I turned round and saw you'd fallen asleep at the bar.'

'You're lucky that Chatten was too busy arresting you for me to get near you. I'd have given you such a kicking that your own mother wouldn't recognise you.'

My mother had a difficult time recognising me anyway. With a thanks to Albart, I took my drinks and joined Locan at the table. I pushed the brandy across the table to him as a peace offering.

'Much obliged,' said Locan, grudgingly lifting the brandy towards me in a toast. I half-expected him to immediately pick up the quarrel from that morning at Caradrahan Hall, but promisingly he seemed to have calmed down. 'If I drink enough I might forget that awful noise.' The hammering from the smithy was even louder inside the common room.

'That's my wife, Kelsi,' said Albart with a ringing note of pride in his voice. 'Ruins the atmosphere, but she makes more from her trade than I do from mine!' He laughed jovially. 'She keeps telling me to retire, but if I stop at my age I might never get started again.'

'Your wife?' I queried. 'I thought Darry was the only smith in Tulbar?' Given Darry seemed to practically live at the Dwarf and Dragon, it would be a wonder if the swords he forged even came out straight.

'Darry is Kelsi's father,' said Albart. 'Used to be a hammer in his hand, day and night, but to pick one up now he'd have to let go of the tankard. I cut him off here – couldn't let my own father-in-law drink himself to ruin – so after throwing every curse under the sun at me he went off to Roddin's.' He gave a rueful shake of his head. 'Darry's got even worse since Mór Hardane died, poor man.'

I was momentarily confused by what Albart had said. I would have put him at least ten years older than Darry, too old to marry his daughter. The hammering abruptly stopped, and an instant later the back door swung open.

A woman, Kelsi presumably, tramped into the inn. 'Get the pot going, Alb, I'm starving.' She was thickset, with dark hair tied back from a solid, square face drenched in rivulets of sweat, wearing a leather apron spotted with tiny burn marks. A heavy belly protruded underneath it, and I realised she was pregnant. She threw a pair of padded gloves down onto the bar. Albart was already rushing to serve her an ale. She caught sight of us for the first time and turned to regard us, squinting suspiciously. 'I know you. You're the boy that's put that fat weasel Roddin in a rage. We'll have none of your nonsense under this roof. We don't go running off to the constable to deal with our problems here.' She tapped the heavy hammer hanging from her belt.

'If he does anything like that again, you can join the queue,' said Locan. He gave me a dark look. 'Hoping he's finally learnt his lesson.'

'Young men don't learn anything,' said Kelsi. 'That's why I didn't marry one.' She came to our table and extended a calloused hand for both of us to shake. 'Kelsi. You might have encountered my father. Probably crawling around the outhouse floor looking for coins.'

We introduced ourselves.

'Already told you I know you, didn't I?' said Kelsi, retaking her stool at the bar. 'Alb, where the pissing hell's my food?'

'Coming, sweetness.' Alb was bent over a fire stirring a pot.

'Well, hurry it along. I need to get back to work.' Kelsi took a long draught of her ale and gave a belch Locan would have been proud of. 'Got the Mór and his men on my back demanding swords, spears, arrowheads. I told them, I've only got two hands. Because I'm a woman they think they can shortchange me as well – they'd never have done that if my dad were still in charge, and my work's thrice as good as his. I told them that as well.' Locan and I might have said something, but conversing with Kelsi was like being trapped in a whirlwind. 'Anyway, I hear he's got you chasing this dragon of his. I know he's not the only one, but if Roddin says he saw it, it was probably only a blood buzzard carrying a lizard. If he told me it was raining, I'd still look outside to check.'

I shared a look with Locan. Other than Hosten, Lenard, and their guards, only Shaliya knew of our encounter with Aydhenia, and Hosten had asked us not to share the tale any further.

'He has,' said Locan. Despite his fury with Hosten, he said no more than that. Another promising sign that he might yet listen to reason. 'And as of this morning, Cetrik here will be joining you in defence of High Tulbar.'

'Not with us,' said Kelsi. 'I'm pregnant, in case your eyes aren't working properly.' She patted her swollen stomach. 'And Alb's too old, thank the Seamstress.'

'I'd like to fight,' said Albart, putting an overflowing trencher down in front of his wife. 'I went to war with Mór Ruihan back in the day, old Mór Hardane's father, and I've not forgotten which end of the spear to stick a man with. It was the Mór of Bastden causing trouble back then, though he ruled half of Carnaway as well. The Varnans were our allies in them days. They caught us in a valley just north of the River Carrow, but we—'

'You great liar,' interjected Kelsi with her fork halfway to her mouth. 'You told me you got the shits, ran off and hid, then emerged for the victory celebrations. Even cut yourself under your cheek so you could pretend you'd done some fighting. Just serve the drinks and stop trying to impress people.'

The mention of Mór Hardane sparked my memory. Locan had said back at the Dwarf and Dragon that Darry was Hardane's half-brother. That explained why Darry's drinking had got worse since the late Mór's death, though there was nothing to indicate they were close. I wondered if Hosten knew he had another uncle living right here in High Tulbar.

'Cetrik, don't get married. You'll never know a moment's peace ever again.' Another man might have taken offence at his wife cutting him down like that in front of guests, but Albart was smiling amiably. 'It's mighty good of you though to go to war for High Tulbar.'

'Didn't have much of a choice in the matter,' said Locan, unable or unwilling to keep the acid out of his voice.

Our hosts returned to their tasks, Albart cleaning the tables and sweeping the floor while Kelsi finished her meal and retreated to her forge. Now Locan and I had some privacy, I decided to simply come right out with it. I had talked Locan into going after the dragon; I could talk him into killing Shanoch.

'Are you really going to stay here drinking while I go to war?' I asked.

Locan shrugged. 'You fought the Tilaxi well enough without me, to a point. I'm too old to go marching around the countryside and standing in shield walls.'

'The Mór intends to wait and face Shanoch here at High Tulbar,' I said. I looked Locan in the eye. 'Of course, if you—'

'Forget it,' growled Locan. 'If Hosten wanted his uncle dead, he should have asked for that instead of sending us off hunting for a dragon. He lied to us.'

'He didn't mean to,' I said, wincing as I heard how weak this sounded. 'He argued with Lenard for hours—'

'Of course he fucking blamed his servant,' said Locan with a laugh. 'Listen, when someone serves you a mug of warm piss, you throw it in their face. You don't praise the vintage and ask for more. I was the sharpest blade of the fucking Emperor of Rameon – anyone trying to screw me like this back then would have got a dagger through their bowels. Only thing stopping me doing that now is that if I wait a few days, Shanoch will do it for me. The boy's out of his depth.'

'He's only just taken the crown,' I replied. 'He knows he's not got everything right, but he's got grand ambitions—'

Locan snorted. 'Can you still call them ambitions if they won't come true? Dreams is what I'd call them.'

'—grand ambitions for Tulbar,' I finished. 'For all of Paleir. If he wins, then in a few years there might not be slavery anywhere in Paleir. Just think of it. What would you have done to save your fellow Kerandans from slavery?'

The look Locan gave me could have curdled milk, and I realised that this had not been a wise thing to say. 'Nothing, because that's just what I did. I walked off into the sunset and tried to never think of them again.' He threw back his remaining brandy then gave a bitter laugh. 'When I first started working for the emperor, I sometimes wondered how many people I might have to kill for him to make me the Prefect of Kerado or even the Governor of Ceretis. It kept me going sometimes, when I was putting in the hard yards, traipsing from this place to that place in pursuit of some rogue general who didn't keep his army in one place for any more than a night at a time. If I could just get enough favour and influence, perhaps I could go back and undo some of the evil the Dominion had done to my people.

'It came to nothing, of course. By the time I was high enough in Vurash's esteem that I could have raised the matter, I had my own villa, a household full of servants, and the biggest bed you ever saw that I shared with the most beautiful woman in the city. Who would take being the governor of some back-water province at the far end of the Dominion over that?

'So I'll tell you this.' Locan looked me square in the eye, his dark eyes so fierce that I could not avert my gaze. 'Whatever Hosten thinks he wants, abolishing slavery is nothing compared to the allure of wealth and power. In five years' time, if Hosten survives, nothing on Paleir will have changed, except it will be him sitting at the top of a mountain of skulls instead of his uncle.'

'Hosten has principles,' I protested. 'He wants to make Paleir—'

'The same principles that caused him to lie to us?' demanded Locan. 'He threw our deal over like that.' He snapped his fingers. 'You ever noticed how people's so-called principles align with what's best for them? You'd never shown the slightest interest in the plight of slaves until you found one you wanted to bed, and your qualms about giving one of the scales to Hosten disappeared pretty quickly once you became more worried about Shaliya than that dragon.' It was infuriating how easily Locan could read me. 'The moment it suits Hosten to keep slavery,' Locan finished, 'he will.'

I felt a flood of righteous indignation, largely because Locan was cutting dangerously close to the bone. I had debated the merits of slavery with my tutors, arguing vehemently in favour of the freedom that Guiland allowed to all, but I had rarely thought about it outside the cut and thrust of intellectual debate. Shaliya was the first slave I'd ever spoken to. Nevertheless, I couldn't help but feel he was being unduly harsh on Hosten. 'It *would* suit Hosten to keep slavery,' I said. 'That would ensure he had the support of the Keykeepers.'

'Or it would suit him if the Keykeepers had their wings clipped a bit,' said Locan with a shrug. 'Appreciate you think that the sun shines out of his arse because you've found someone of your own rank that doesn't treat you like something they scraped off their shoe, but that's not my problem. There's nothing to separate Hosten from any of the five other petty kings on this turd of an island, except he's the only one who's lied to me.

'The answer's no, and it will always be no. Even if Hosten offered me all the gold in his treasury. You can face the consequences for leaping into bed with that girl, and he can face the consequences for not keeping his word.' He laughed. 'Besides, I want to see what happens when he tries to get Huretio to stop working on the *Fiend*. Between the Keykeepers, his uncle, and two dozen angry sailors, I'd say your friend's days are numbered. Hope he's got big plans for that scale, because based on the sense he's shown so far I'd say you and I have got a better chance of summoning a dragon.'

Without another word, Locan departed to the bar, leaving me to stew and ask myself what more I could do.

For sheer obstinacy, Locan was rivalled only by my father and my horse. I had been lucky before that he'd been sufficiently bored to go in search of the dragon with me, but I would not be so fortunate this time. The assassin was stubborn enough to let High Tulbar burn for the sake of taking vengeance against Hosten. He might act to protect those who could not save themselves, as he had when Poignmuda had been invaded by my father, but he would not lift a finger for the sake of Hosten's war against Shanoch.

In truth, he was not far wrong about the flexibility of my principles. I had sworn to help Hosten, but if there came an opportunity to escape Tulbar with Shaliya, I would take it.

It was also time to accept that, if we ever did leave Tulbar, I might be better served by parting from Locan. No doubt he thought his cynical contempt for everything and everyone around him made him wise, but all I saw was another form of cowardice. If you believe in nothing, then what else does life hold, except to go to your grave searching for the non-existent answers at the bottom of a skin of liquor? I was tired of it. Locan's volatility had put us in Hosten's debt, and Rameon would be all the more dangerous for him. I had fled Guiland in search of adventure, but also in search of something of more importance than the bitter power struggle that diseased every member of my family. I would not get that by acting as a glorified nursemaid to a has-been assassin who would eventually drag me down with him. The little I had written of Locan had been ruined when the *Red Fiend* went down, but in truth I had not picked up a quill in weeks. When I left Tulbar with Shaliya, Locan and I could go our separate ways.

CHAPTER 16

It was two days later when the army of Mór Shanoch was at last sighted on a hill outside Tulbar. The panicked edge that had been lingering over the town for days was at last honed to a razor-sharp point, not least because there had been no warning. The tales told by the steady stream of desperate refugees arriving from the countryside with all the possessions they could carry agreed on neither the size of Shanoch's army nor its movements. Since the first reports of the Varnans crossing the Bronzewater, no Tulban scouts had returned, and given the size of the force it was easy to see why.

I was among the first to spot them. Rain drizzled from an overcast sky, and the afternoon of their arrival found me atop Tulbar's north wall, wearing an ancient, rusted hauberk granted to me by Hosten's marshal and an open-faced helmet that had been too large for me until I had asked Kelsi to beat it into a more closely fitting shape.

West of the town, thousands of men swarmed like ants over the distant hillside, more than I would have believed the kingdom of Varned could hold. Certainly more than the number of fighting men within High Tulbar, even with the arrival of various lords sworn to Hosten. First came the Varnan lords, ahorse beneath bright pennants snapping in the bite of the east wind, tall men in mail and plate, trailed by outriders lightly armoured in leather. Most of the rest of their force was afoot, common folk bearing spears, halberds, and crossbows, but there were others who came after them that drew my eye, hulking men draped in furs, riding atop snarling beasts with dark striped fur that raced down the hill barking while their masters sought to direct them with short sharp whips to their sides.

I had read of the Altans, descended from the Odingr of the far north and who still clung to their reaving ways. I had known of the tusked warhounds on which they rode to battle, bareback and unbridled, but this was my first time seeing them in the flesh. My mouth went dry at the sight of them. It was said the force of their bite was strong enough to snap a horse's neck, perhaps why Shanoch's army looked to keep as much distance between the two breeds of creature as possible.

'Well, there they are,' said Chatten grimly. Even with her other duties, she had made time to take her share of guarding the walls. 'Shanoch must have emptied Varned of men to gather a force that size.' There was an exhausted note to her voice, no surprise given the little time she had to sleep with her various duties. I could only admire her diligence. 'I better get back to town and deal with anyone who tries to get out of the gate with all the silver they can carry. You all right by yourself for the next hour?'

I nodded, continuing to stare dumbly at the number of men arrayed against us. Hosten's instinct not to seek Shanoch in open battle had been correct. High Tulbar's walls compared poorly with the defences of my home city of Keystone, but they were stout and tall, and a man needed little training to be told to stab a spear at any foe trying to scale them.

As a part of Tulbar's army, I was expected to perform just

the same duties as the rest – drilling and patrolling the walls, for the most part. Otherwise, my time was occupied with trying to persuade Locan to accede to Hosten's request and help us deal with Shanoch. These efforts had met with deaf ears and Locan's inimitable variety of insults and curses, much to Hosten's frustration.

The Mór had not yet made good on his threat to halt repairs on the *Red Fiend*, and there was no sign of any trouble from Ulf, but it was surely only a matter of time before Hosten's patience ran dry. Locan remained in the Merry Whale, drinking until the early hours every night until Albart steered him upstairs, where I would be awoken by the sound of him staggering about our shared bedchamber. His drinking could usually be controlled by a limited supply or some purpose that required him to stay relatively lucid, but at this time neither of these was an obstacle.

The war and my efforts with Locan at least gave me something to think about other than Shaliya. Chatten said she was well and had returned to the Dwarf and Dragon, but that was all the word I had received of her. The constable had also, with some reluctance, agreed to deliver one of the dragon scales I had kept to Shaliya, as proof that I had not forgotten about her. I had conjured numerous and increasingly ludicrous scenarios in my head about how I might go to her without Roddin or anyone else realising, but as yet no opportunity had presented itself.

The arrival of the Varnan force soon attracted a crowd, armed men abandoning their duties mingling with women, children, and old men come from town for a closer look at the invaders. The lack of discipline gave me little hope for Tulbar's prospects; such a rabble should have found their path to the parapet barred by a force of Hosten's warriors.

There were cries of dismay at the force arrayed against the town. A grim-faced veteran pointed to where the Altan mercenaries were dismounting from their warhounds. 'Shanoch's brought the Altans with him. They'll sacrifice us to their cold god, if they don't sell us all into slavery first.'

If I were captured, I hoped that my name and parentage would be enough to spare me that fate, even if it meant writing a letter to my family begging them to pay the ransom. My parents would pay, but not without first determining how they would humiliate and punish me once I was again under their control.

I reminded myself that it was Hosten's hope that there would not be a battle – Locan would eventually come to his senses and assassinate Shanoch, and then the Varnan army would fall apart. I checked the sky, looking for any break in the blanket of miserable cloud. Locan might be more amenable to the idea if there were even a sliver of shadow for him to use, but the grim Palish weather offered none.

Hosten appeared a short time later, surrounded by his guards, who forced a path through the throng towards me. A coterie of lords and their sons followed him – some who had been summoned from their nearby lands, others who had arrived at the head of a train of refugees. These men had stayed loyal to High Tulbar, but mostly they lacked the fierce, martial nature of the lords Danning, Ulleách, and Arcalen who had gone over to Shanoch, either too narrow at the shoulder or with too much grey in their hair and beards. Between them they had added no more than a few hundred fighting men to our number.

More Varnans were cresting the hill every minute. Long spears that might have been tall enough to reach the battlements from the ground were being unloaded from carts. There were no cannons at least, but there were enough trees surrounding Tulbar that Shanoch would be able to build siege towers and mangonels if he had capable engineers.

I could not help but see Hosten's boyish face pale at the sight of the vast host arrayed against us. The strain he bore showed in the bags under his eyes and the wrinkles furrowing on his forehead, but he still did not look old enough to lead a kingdom in a time of war.

'We will ride out and meet my uncle under a peace banner,' said Hosten, steeling himself. 'Cetrik – fetch Locan A'Shadow.' He had become less courteous over the passing days, and with all the demands on his time, there had been no question of he and I sharing a jug of wine over a game of Pillars.

Murdering a man at a truce in Guiland would see your family's name blackened for centuries, but the Palish did not stand on such lofty pretensions. It was hard to find a Palish king of note who had not murdered a relative at some point. If Hosten did not move against Shanoch, he left himself open to an attempt on his own life before it came to battle.

It would be the same answer I had received each of the last three days. I might draw Locan's attention to the sheer size of the Varnan force and the lives he would save by removing Shanoch, but at this point Locan's stubbornness had set him beyond reason. 'It might go better if you went and asked him yourself,' I suggested.

'I send you in my stead,' said Hosten. 'You are a prince of Guiland, aren't you? And you'll ride out with me – a Guilish prince might give Shanoch reason to reconsider. We should have had a banner made for you.'

I pushed my way through the crowd and made for the Merry Whale. The arrival of Shanoch and the Varnans had sent the town into chaos. Troops of men were hastily donning their helmets as they were marched towards the wall, but kept having to stop or divert to avoid the panic of those who were too old, feeble, or female to be enlisted by force. A man with one leg was hobbling down the street on a crutch clutching a silver plate in the other hand, but his progress was blocked when a soldier broke rank from formation to give chase. He tackled the one-legged man to the ground, punched him twice in the nose, and grabbed the plate from him. I was left none the wiser as to its true owner.

I was so preoccupied watching this that I nearly walked straight into the middle of a fight taking place between three women, swerving at the last minute and receiving the follow-through of an off-target punch for my inattention.

'Watch where you're going!' one of them screeched at me.

'Yeah, watch it!' added another.

When they realised I was not Tulban, the three women seemed to decide together that they would rather fight me than fight each other, and I quickened my pace with their insults ringing in my ears.

There was more disorder, of course. I passed Chatten angrily brandishing her blade at two older men who looked to be arguing over a slave girl whose shift had been torn down the back. One of the larger houses was being looted, and a man who might have been its owner was sitting dazed in the street with blood trickling from his head, clutching his shoulder.

In a fit of gallantry, I challenged a man coming out of the front door with a large, decorated vase clutched in his arms. 'Put it back.' I shoved him against the doorway and pulled my sword free an inch. 'Now.'

The man was skinny, with two front teeth missing. 'Fuck off, you sack of piss Guilish goat-shagger.' He tried to shove me away.

'Get off him,' came a rough voice from the hallway. There were half-a-dozen others, all clutching loot. Men I had seen before – Ulf's thugs from that first day on the beach who had seemingly already deserted.

'You should be on the walls,' I told them, pulling my sword another inch from its scabbard.

'Well, we ain't,' sneered the first man. It was Hobbo, their leader, who had started the trouble at the beach. He hefted his cudgel towards me. 'Your foreign friend ain't here to protect you now, so get out of our way before I shove this sideways up your—'

There came the heavy tread of footsteps in the street behind me, and the gang shoved past me and ran.

Chatten appeared a moment later, red-faced and panting. 'Don't worry about those goblin-fuckers,' she said, 'I'll deal with them. Bloody Ulf needs to keep a handle on his ruffians. Get on with whatever you're meant to be doing, as long as it's not deserting.'

'Hosten told me to find Locan.'

'Well hurry up then! And when you see the Mór, tell him I need more men. No sense fighting the Varnans if our own people rip Tulbar down with their bare hands.' She wiped a sheen of sweat from her forehead. 'It could be worse. Caught two girls trying to let the goblins out. Fools seemed to think they might help us.'

I hurried on. Hosten's fears of opposition to him within High Tulbar as well as without seemed to have been proved true, and he seemingly lacked the men to deal with both.

The Merry Whale was mercifully untouched by the violence. I quickly checked that Morvolt was safe in his stall and, finding that the entrance to the inn was barred, I knocked for entry. Albart opened the door for me. The common room was empty, save for Locan hunched over a table playing a game of Pillars. Albart resumed his chair across the board from Locan.

'Well,' said Locan, 'the brave watchman returns! Hear it's like the last days of the First Rameon out there.'

'Chatten is dealing with it,' I replied. 'The Mór wants you. We're riding out to meet Shanoch.'

'Thought I made myself clear before.' Locan looked back to the board and placed a counter, as if to prove how little he cared. 'How's his plan to summon a dragon going? Badly, I hope. If the Mór wants me, he can come and find me himself, and then I'll tell him where he can stick that dragon scale.'

I rolled my eyes. I had given up on the possibility of a dragon coming to our aid. 'Please, Locan. What do you think happens if Shanoch wins?'

'A man's got to have his pride,' muttered Albart, placing his own counter. 'The old Mór understood that, even if the new one doesn't.'

'Well it's not the Mór asking,' I said. 'It's me.' That should have counted for something.

'Bah.' Locan put a thumb to his nostril and snorted, then took a drink and swilled the ale around his mouth. A half-empty bottle of whisky rested on the table.

'Where did the whisky come from?' I asked.

'Albart, my new best friend.' Locan raised his mug towards Albart. They knocked them together. 'Tell your pal Hosten I'll come when this bottle is finished.'

I took a deep calming breath. I had never imagined meeting someone I found more vexing than my own family. 'Shanoch has an army,' I said through gritted teeth. 'A big one.'

'When men want me to kill someone, they can come and ask me themselves,' said Locan, placing another counter. 'If Hosten can't look his uncle in the eye, he can at least look me in mine and give me an apology. Not that I'll do it, mind. It would just amuse me to see him beg. And besides' – he gestured to the window – 'have you seen the weather? I walk through shadows, Cetrik, not puddles.'

Talking about the conditions in which he would be able to kill Shanoch was at least a slight softening to Locan's position. 'Wouldn't you rather come to a parley instead of sitting here drinking and playing Pillars?' I asked.

'No.' Locan took a glug of ale and let out a long belch. 'Tell the Mór to shove his parley up his bumhole. He should learn the consequences of not keeping his word.' He gave a black laugh. 'Assuming his own people don't kill him before his uncle does.'

'And what are you planning to do if Tulbar falls?' I asked. 'Because unless you do something, we'll both be stuck here.'

Locan shrugged.

'Even if Hosten did say the *Red Fiend* could leave,' I went on, 'what difference would it make? Huretio said repairs are still at least a week away from being done.' We had received a note from Huretio the day before, with much grousing about the work ethic of his crew and the denizens of High Tulbar, along with the weather, the women, and the stiffness of the Broken Wheel's mattresses.

'Maybe you should go,' said Albart, addressing Locan. 'I know there's trouble between you and the young Mór, but' – he pointed towards the back, where even with the Varnans at the gates, Kelsi's hammer was still ringing out – 'I've got a pregnant wife out there. Our first child. I'd rather it wasn't the last. No harm to you in at least getting a look at Shanoch.' He picked up a counter. 'I've won anyway.'

Locan stared down at the board, disbelief rising in his expression. 'Goblin bollocks.' He lifted his tankard and found it empty. He looked towards the back door, towards the sound of Kelsi's hammer. He may not have cared about me or Hosten, but I knew Locan well enough to know he would not refuse Albart's earnest plea for the safety of his wife and unborn child. 'Fine. Fine. Goblin-fucking fine.' Locan replaced his mug on the table with a clatter. 'But when I get back, we're having a rematch.'

The town was calmer now. The Mór had granted Chatten additional men, who together seemed to have got the fighting and looting under control. A dozen of the worst offenders were being herded towards the jail as Locan and I rode our way to the wall.

'Took you long enough,' said Hosten when he spotted us.

He was surrounded by his lords, every man of them ahorse. Hosten detached himself from the group and came forward to meet us. 'My uncle Shanoch has agreed to our parley.' His eyes roved over Locan. 'You're here then. Finally.'

Seeing the black look on Locan's face, a pair of guards steered their horses after Hosten and moved to bar his path to their lord. Locan regarded them with disdain. 'Relax, boys. If I wanted to kill him, there's fuck all you could do to stop me.' A sneer stretched across his lips as he regarded Hosten. 'I'm just here to see your uncle make a tit out of you.'

Hosten's face darkened. 'I had hoped you might be in a more amenable mood by now. I've been as forbearing as I can, but with my uncle at my gates I can be no longer. Kill Shanoch, or I'll have your friend's ship destroyed plank by plank and give Ulf permission to send another gang after you.'

Locan snorted. 'I'm not *amenable* to those I regard as friends, never mind those foolish enough to cheat and threaten me. And from what I've seen, I don't reckon you've got that sort of authority. The Keykeepers don't give an orc's shit about you – if Ulf cared about me killing two of his men, he'd have done something about it whether you gave him permission or not.'

'Locan's going to ride out with us,' I said, hoping to reach a resolution that did not involve Locan killing Hosten before the war had even begun. This was not the amiable Hosten I had become familiar with – the size of his uncle's force seemed to have frayed the last measure of the young Mór's patience. If Shanoch was as callous and brutish as I expected a Palish ruler to be, it was my hope that after meeting him, Locan would regard killing the Mór of Varned as a lesser evil than keeping him alive, but I had no way of communicating that to Hosten.

'Lord, we don't have time for this,' said Lenard, bringing his horse up alongside Hosten's. 'If we delay, the Varnans might decide to attack while we are not prepared.'

Hosten looked as if he wanted to say something else to

Locan, but in the end managed to compose himself before he could give voice to anything he would regret, the repressed fury fading from his face. 'Well, you're both here, and for that I am grateful. Perhaps my uncle will take one look at the fierceness of my defences and lose his nerve.' He gave an ironic laugh. He looked from me to Locan. 'All I have done, I have done for the future of Tulbar and Paleir. I know you fault me for that, but I hope you can find some measure of understanding.'

I wanted to tell Hosten that I did understand and did not fault him. That I shared his hopes for what Paleir might become. That for as long as I remained in Tulbar, I would fight for his victory. But, before Locan could offer any caustic reply, Hosten brought his horse around towards the gate, his lords falling into formation behind him as the portcullis creaked open.

The Varnans rode out to meet us on horseback, surrounded by a formation of warriors bearing dragon shields five across and four deep. While the dragon banner of Caradrahan Hall and Tulbar showed a black dragon in flight against a blue sky, Shanoch had taken as his coat of arms a dragon standing on a green field, roaring towards the heavens. It was not difficult to identify Hosten's uncle – the Mór of Varned rode at the centre of them, a tall, broad-shouldered man in his middle years with wild auburn hair and drooping moustaches, fierce-faced beneath an open helmet topped by a pair of silver dragon wings. His armour was notched with scars, each a tale of a battle fought and won.

They came to a halt twenty yards apart from us. 'Nephew.' Shanoch raised a hand in Hosten's direction, a mocking smile playing about his lips. 'The last time we met, you came up to the height of my belt. I think I preferred you that way.'

Hosten returned the smile, though I could see the strain in

the tightness of his jaw. 'And I preferred you within your own lands across the Bronzewater, Uncle.'

Shanoch chuckled, making his moustaches wobble. 'And I would sooner have remained there.' His expression darkened. 'But what is a Mór to do when his people's crops blight and their children sicken and die in the cradle? Your father and I lived in harmony these past twenty years – did you suppose I would put it down to chance that this would occur within weeks of my brother's death? I suppose I should not be surprised. Your mother's dalliances with witchcraft were well-known. It must have shamed Hardane to have sired such a cringing, craven whelp.'

Even as a newcomer to Paleir, this seemed an outrageous lie. Hosten did not even have control over his own people, never mind the wherewithal to influence matters in Varned. Beside me, Locan gave a snort, and muttered, 'Goblin bollocks. Crops fail and children die in winter the world over.'

We were several rows behind the front line, but Locan voiced this thought a little too loudly. There was bristling from both groups of men that a stranger should speak, but Shanoch seemed untroubled. 'Grumble all you please, Locan A'Shadow,' he said. 'Just as long as you do it where I can see you.' He gave Hosten a contemptuous glare. 'It is brazen indeed to bring an assassin to a peace council.'

I glanced sideways at Locan. He showed no indication he was as surprised as I was. Perhaps I ought to have expected it – there was bound to be somebody within High Tulbar hostile enough to Hosten's rule that they would turn traitor for Shanoch.

'Yes, I know who you are,' said Shanoch scornfully. 'Just as I know the identity of the man next to you.' He nodded to me. 'Prince Cetrik Harkken. I know too how you come to be here. Ships foundering in my nephew's waters, whether by fair means or foul. One of a litany of his reign's failures, I am sure. Know that I have no wish for conflict with Guiland, but if you fight for my nephew, I will show you no quarter. Your family's power ends on the far side of the North Water.'

He next addressed Hosten's lords. His words rang with kingly authority, such that no man dared interrupt. 'My quarrel is with my nephew, not with any of you. You all served my brother loyally, as did several of the men arrayed behind me' – he gestured to his rear, where the three lords who Locan and I had seen hastening from Hosten's hall looked on – 'and some of you my father before him. Should you wish to join me, you will be welcomed with open arms, but if you choose to fight, I will understand your choice. I respect loyalty. When I take High Tulbar, you will be treated with all the respect and mercy your rank accords you, and I will confirm you to your lands in full. I ask only that you look at my nephew, and then look at me, and ask yourself which of us has the strength to protect Tulbar in the years to come. With the fall of the Abomination King, the world is changing. The Dreadveil that has protected Paleir's eastern shore for four hundred years is fading. Paleir must be united, or we will fall.'

I had heard Hosten express much the same sentiment. 'My terms are these, Nephew,' Shanoch continued. 'Abdicate and give over your crown to me. A ship will be arranged to take you to any land you choose, where you may live out the rest of your days in exile. But you must never return to Paleir.'

I could not help but be impressed by Shanoch's politicking. In one meeting, he had neutered Hosten's plot to use Locan, made generous entreaties to Tulbar's lords, and granted Hosten an honourable escape that would spare his life. If Hosten refused, Shanoch could not be faulted for responding severely, and some of Hosten's own lords might see his inclination to mercy as reason to turn Hosten over to Shanoch themselves. With his fierce speech, fine helmet, and battle-worn armour, Shanoch also looked more a king than the mild, boyish Hosten, and the lords of Tulbar could not fail to see that.

'If I set foot on a ship chartered by you, I would be food for the sharks before we were even a mile offshore,' said Hosten, lifting his chin in defiance. 'My own terms are these: return to Varned with all your men and I will not destroy you.'

Even to my ears, this sounded the idle boast of a boy. Knowing smiles and low laughter passed between Shanoch's followers. The traitor lords Danning, Ulleách, and Arcalen muttered to one another and shook their heads.

Shanoch's nod of acceptance was tinged with sadness, as if this was what he had expected. 'I am trying to spare you, Hosten. Do you expect your people to throw their lives away for the sake of your childish tantrum? Very well, my second offer: single combat, to the death. The victor claims the crowns of both our countries.'

'Agreed,' said Hosten without hesitation. 'I nominate Locan A'Shadow to be my champion.'

This pronouncement caused consternation among the lords on both sides. Even I winced, the regard I had for Hosten making this misstep all the more painful. These Palishmen were proud; they would not follow a king who appointed other men to fight in his stead.

Locan gave a loud snort. 'Well, that ain't happening. You think I reached this age by fighting fair and letting the other man see me coming?' He began to turn his horse around. 'I'll take my leave. No idea why I'm here in the first place.'

Hosten looked to me as if expecting I would persuade Locan to stay, but I knew any such effort would be futile. Getting him here had been hard enough. Perhaps it was the pressure telling upon Hosten once again, but naming a reluctant Locan as his champion was an error from which there was no sparing him.

Shanoch was smiling. 'It seems the last hope of your kingship wants nothing to do with you, Hosten.' Locan was already riding for High Tulbar. 'I'll fight any man you please, but it's usually wise to make sure they agree first.'

This drew laughter from all those on the Varnan side. I glanced around Hosten's lords and attendants. The three who looked the most like warriors had already defected to his uncle. Those who remained had seen too many battles or too few, and Shanoch looked a fierce fighter who would make short work of them. Chatten could handle herself in a fight, but she seemed better suited to breaking up back-alley brawls than meeting a warrior sword to sword.

'None of you?' said Shanoch. 'Disappointing.'

'Just kill them here,' growled Lord Danning, one of the defectors waiting behind Shanoch. 'The town will throw open its gates to us.'

Immediately, Hosten's lords and warriors moved to form a wall of flesh in front of their Mór. I readied my hand on the hilt of my sword, and between my legs Morvolt stirred, sensing the change in the mood and readying himself to charge. I gave a sharp tug on the reins before he could act.

'I will not sully my reign over Tulbar by beginning it with the slaughter of my kin and bannermen,' said Shanoch, in a tone of fierce certainty. 'This isle has seen too much drawing of familial blood.'

'As he did, you mean?' said Lord Danning, levelling Hosten with an accusatory stare. 'The men around you may be weak-minded enough to believe in tales of sudden fevers bringing down a man in his prime while sparing everyone else, but not I. You killed your father, boy. Every man here knows it.'

This accusation elicited gasps of dismay among the Tulban lords. I was about to leap to Hosten's defence – it was an absurd accusation; his reign over Tulbar had been fraught with diffi-culty from the beginning; if Hosten's father had not died, we would never have reached this point – but Shanoch got there first. 'A man who makes such an accusation in my presence had best bring proof,' he said, turning to glare at Lord Danning. 'Evidence your claims and I will slay my nephew where he stands.'

Danning met Shanoch's glare with a fierce stare of his own. 'There is no evidence,' he admitted grudgingly. 'You have levelled charges of witchcraft against your nephew without proof. Why should I not do the same?'

'Because I am the Mór, charged with the defence of the people of Varned, and you are not.' Shanoch addressed Hosten again. 'For all your faults, I will not believe you killed my brother. But the world is changing, and if Varned and Tulbar do not change with it, both our kingdoms will fall. If it will not be exile or single combat, it will be war. You have until dawn tomorrow to change your mind.'

Hosten seemed so stunned by Danning's accusation that he could muster no reply as the Varnans turned for their camp. The blood had drained from his face, and he spent several seconds staring blankly after the retreating Varnans.

'Lord?' said Lenard softly after the younger man had not spoken in several seconds.

Hosten blinked. 'Back to the city,' he said. 'With all haste.'

Locan was waiting for us back inside the gates, lounging against a wall and drinking from a skin. As soon as we were inside, Hosten leapt from his horse and stamped towards him.

'Did you think I invited you to that so you could sit there and look simple?' he raged. 'You coward!'

It was the first time I had seen the strain Hosten was under cause him to fully lose his temper. The encounter with Shanoch and the size of the force arrayed against us looked to have shaken him to his core. From experience, I knew it would not move Locan an inch.

'Was I not clear enough?' said Locan, still lounging against the wall. 'I never agreed to kill for you, and I certainly ain't going to die for you. No shadows, a dozen men around him, and he knew I was coming. I'm an assassin, not a fucking magician.'

'Very well,' said Hosten, his nostrils flaring as he tried to contain himself. Nearby, his lords watched on in concern, perhaps wondering whether anyone would stop them if they turned for the gate and raced towards the welcoming arms of Mór Shanoch. 'Tonight then. Kill him, or I swear you and your friends will never leave High Tulbar again.'

'I won't,' said Locan. He looked Hosten straight in the eye. 'You broke your word to me before. Why would I trust you again? Let that be a lesson in kingship. If you want your uncle dead, be a man and kill him yourself. Watching you get your arse spanked would at least be entertaining.'

With a contemptuous sneer, Locan turned and stalked away.

CHAPTER 17

For all Shanoch's talk, he did not begin an assault on High Tulbar that day, nor the next, instead using his men to encircle the city and probe for weaknesses. The Tulbans lacked the numbers to counterattack, but the city was well-suited to a siege. With the North Water at their back and men who knew how to fish, there was little chance of the settlement being starved out. The walls were not so high or thick as they might have been, but Mór Shanoch could not build siege weapons overnight, and there were enough Tulbans to see off the few Varnan attempts to scale the fortifications with long spears and pots of boiling water. The high cliffs and rugged terrain made it near impossible for the Varnans to come around the flanks in great numbers, and those who did find their way to the beach were swiftly dispatched by sorties from inside the sea wall. I fought in two of them myself, killing three men and wounding two more, receiving a nasty gash to my neck in return. Albart treated the wound for me with boiling wine, and I have never screamed so painfully loud. A few of Mór Shanoch's men scaled Drag- onwing Point to fire arrows down on the town, but the shafts were caught by the high winds, either blown out to sea or landing harmlessly in the streets.

Chatten had quelled the disorder in the town, and a half-dozen bodies now hung from the dragon roosts as a warning to others. On Chatten's advice, Hosten had ordered a gold piece be fastened between their teeth, the message being that those who rioted could keep their plunder, but it would serve them little in the Underrealm.

Tulbar's position was therefore not so hopeless as I had believed following the summit with Mór Shanoch. Even the troublesome Keykeepers united behind their Mór in opposition to Shanoch, perhaps having seen enough of Varned's Mór to know he was not a man who would be easily bent to their whims. The opposition to Hosten's rule within the walls was scattered and divided, and any man brave enough to repeat Lord Danning's allegation that Hosten had contrived his father's death was quietly dealt with.

When the dust of the parley between Tulbar and Varned had settled, the coming of Shanoch that many thought would mark the end of Hosten's brief reign seemed to have strengthened his position. I was sure Hosten would be a good Mór, if older, more cynical men would only give him the chance, and I was relieved that he would have the opportunity to prove it. My affinity with Hosten went beyond us both being born of a line of kings. I had been abandoned by my family; he was a recent orphan. The likes of Roddin and Shanoch scorned him as a weakling, as I had been scorned and underestimated by my own family. Locan A'Shadow was an infuriating distraction to both of us.

When my duties on the wall did not occupy me, I found myself spending less and less time at the Merry Whale with Locan – who in his eagerness to be gone from High Tulbar had also taken to wandering over to the Broken Wheel in search of updates from Huretio on when the *Red Fiend* would be seaworthy – and more time at Caradrahan Hall with Hosten. The Mór quizzed me on sieges of Guiland, and I did my best to recall the details I had read in books. We never spoke of the fate of the dragon scale – if Hosten was attempting to summon Aydhenia to serve him, he was keeping it remarkably close to his chest.

'There are three ways to lose a siege,' Hosten was saying. Following a tour of the walls to examine where the Varnans might seek to strike, we had retreated to his private chamber for a game of Pillars and a cup of wine. 'Starvation, mutiny, and siege weapons.'

'Tunnels,' I added, recalling the Siege of Barron that had ended the Tollhouse Rebellion in Guiland two centuries earlier.

'Our earth is rocky and rich in iron,' said Hosten. 'It would take the Varnans years to dig beneath our walls.' I had feared for him after the meeting with Shanoch and his explosion of temper against Locan, but he had mastered himself in the days since. He seemed to become more assured with each hour the siege went on. He sighed. 'It is the thought of siege weapons that keeps me awake at night.'

On the hill where they had made camp, Shanoch's men had begun to gather timber for the building of siege towers and mangonels. The incessant rain had hindered them at first, but though the sky remained overcast, the deluge had lessened to a drizzle, and they had taken to drying the wood they gathered by digging great firepits and laying the timber over the top, beyond the reach of the flames. Slow work, but the first of the war machines that would flatten Tulbar's walls was beginning to take shape.

Hosten bent forward, contemplating the Pillars board. 'I need you to speak to Locan again.'

I had lost count now of how many times I had tried to persuade Locan to assassinate Shanoch, and each time his posi-tion had only become more entrenched. The man was as foundry-forged steel. If I could convince Locan, that would be more valuable to Hosten than any number of spears atop High Tulbar's walls. I still believed I could talk him round. Hosten had not yet made good on his threat to stop the repairs to the *Red Fiend*, but when the time came that it was ready to leave he had it within his power to close the harbour. Should that happen, Locan would have to set aside his ego.

I nodded my agreement. 'I'll go now.' Locan's mood was most variable in the evening, ranging anywhere between merry to morose. His drunkenness had not yet made him more agreeable, but like a spurned suitor I could only try again.

'I'm sorry you've been dragged into this. And know that I don't feel proud of how I've treated you. I know what a weasel Roddin is.'

'I'll help any way I can.'

Hosten reached across the table to shake my hand. 'You are a true friend, Cetrik, and a most noble prince. One day, when you are Prince Paramount of Guiland and I am High King of Paleir and we bear responsibility for the fates of whole nations of people, we will look back on these simpler days and say that these were the good times, because even in the midst of a siege we had the time to drink wine and pass the hours with one another. We will ask ourselves why we ever wanted more than that.'

I prepared to laugh, and then by the thoughtful look in Hosten's eye I realised he was not joking. 'I... I will never be prince paramount,' I said slowly. I had dozens, maybe even hundreds of cousins who would claim the role before me.

'Do not say such things, Cetrik,' said Hosten, gripping my shoulder. 'If I can prevail against my uncle, why should you not prevail against your own family?'

But being prince paramount was not something I had ever wanted. That had been Javvian's dream. I shook my head, wishing to change the subject. 'When High Tulbar is secure, I will think of my future.' I was not sure I had the patience for another sea voyage with Locan and then to follow him around Rameon, while every utterance that left his mouth was to naysay and insult me. Shaliya and Hosten needed me more. Especially Shaliya. While I passed the hours in the relative comfort of Hosten's study, she lived every minute with the risk of Roddin's temper reaching its end and him turning his fists on her. I was meant to be fighting in the defence of Tulbar – it was me who should have been risking my life.

'Think on it, Cetrik,' said Hosten. 'Who would have backed the Abomination King to claim Midding and break Karvved into three kingdoms? You might surprise yourself.'

It was true that the Abomination King had risen from nothing and reshaped nations, but he was the last ruler I would ever seek to emulate. Over four centuries, he had been responsible for the death and mutilation of thousands upon thousands of my countrymen, several of my kin among them. Guiland would yet bear the scars of his reign for centuries hence. One had only to look out from Tulbar's coast to see the lingering evil of the Abomination King, the shroud of the Dreadveil and the wraiths that had patrolled it since his death.

'The Abomination King killed thousands, Hosten.' I spoke carefully, wishing to keep my rising outrage under control. 'Thousands upon thousands.'

'I do not deny it,' said Hosten. 'But if not for the presence of the Dreadveil, reavers would have continued to raid Karvved. His magic broke the slave trade and forced the Odingr to seek out new routes down Paleir's western coast. My own ancestors might have looked across the North Water and thought to use their dragons to claim your house's kingdom for themselves. Sometimes disagreeable deeds may achieve righteous ends.'

Hosten spoke so easily that I thought he must be making a poorly chosen jest, but his expression remained sincere. 'What the Abomination King did was not *disagreeable*,' I said hotly.

'Brightwater and all its citizens, lost. Children stolen from their beds. People mutilated and turned into monsters.' I knew of Guilishmen who had fallen upon their own swords because of the horrors they had seen at Sevash. That Hosten would find reasons to compliment the Abomination King sickened me. I swallowed the bile that rose in my throat. Perhaps in Paleir they were less aware of his crimes. 'I don't call that disagreeable. I call it *evil*. The Abomination King committed atrocities that were far worse than slavery.'

While I'd been speaking, Hosten's face had fallen. 'I'm sorry,' he said. 'Of course, the Abomination King was your family's enemy. Sometimes I read something in a book and I forget...' He shook his head, evidently irritated with himself. 'I should have spoken more carefully,' he said, more firmly. 'But they do not name Paleir the Land of a Hundred Kings for no reason – we are a quarrelsome people, and if I am to one day claim the whole country, I must find a way to be stronger than my forebears, even if that requires looking to kings who did not always rule justly.'

'It's fine,' I said quickly, biting down on my temper. Even that sentiment made me slightly uncomfortable – the Abomination King had been an enemy to the world, not only to my family. I stood up abruptly. 'I'd best go and see Locan. If I don't go soon, even if he agrees he'll be too drunk to recall our conversation.'

Hosten beamed. 'Would that I had known a friend as true at any time in my twenty years on this earth. Thank you, Cetrik. I'll not forget this. When we prevail against Shanoch, I will be sorry to see you leave.'

I nodded to Hosten and departed, still feeling discomforted by his ignorance. At a more appropriate time, I would explain to Tulbar's Mór the full litany of what the Abomination King had done to earn his name.

· · ·

I left Caradrahan Hall and made for the Merry Whale, but I was not prepared for what awaited me there. The inn that had previously been almost deserted was now awash with noise that could be heard from several houses away, with men's shadows spilling into the yard every time the door opened. I gave a brief greeting to Morvolt, who nuzzled into my neck before snorting and headbutting me away as if this display of affection had never happened, then stepped inside.

With the wall of noise and flesh that met me, it took me several minutes to locate Locan. Albart was so rushed off his feet serving drinks that Kelsi had joined him to assist, keeping up a constant stream of commands to her husband as she carried heavily laden trays from table to table. Most of the men here wore armour, fresh from their shift on the town's walls and now wishing to drink their fear and boredom away before they had to do it all over again tomorrow. A few greeted me as I passed, but most ignored me – I was still a stranger to them, and my closeness with their overlord marked me as even more of an outsider.

I found Locan at a back table, lounging in his seat surrounded by half-a-dozen soldiers, regaling them with some tale from his past.

'...and the empress replied, "I'm fine, it was just a little prick!"'

The delivery of this line by Locan set the whole table rolling in their chairs, while Locan sat there grinning. 'And I had to stand there with a straight face, if you can believe that!'

'Sorry to interrupt,' I said, drawing the eyes of the whole table. 'Locan, I need to talk to you.'

'Whatever it is, just tell me here!' Locan laughed thickly and seemed to be having some trouble focusing on me. 'Friends, here's the lad I was telling you about! He wants to write a book about me.' He cackled. 'Well, bugger his book. Who wants to read about a man when you can drink with him?' He shouted towards the bar, 'Another round, Albart!'

There were cheers from the table.

'I'd sooner we spoke privately,' I replied. I did not need to plead for Locan's help again in front of the whole inn.

'What for?' Locan's eyes narrowed aggressively. 'I know just what you're going to say.' His apparent mirth had disappeared as swiftly as the stars fleeing the dawn. 'The Mór's asking me to do his dirty work for him again.' He brought his fist down on the table. 'Well, my answer's not changed. I'm not one of your fucking subjects, *Prince* Cetrik.' He reached for his tankard, then when he found it empty shoved it aside and leant back to address the whole table. 'Goblin-fucking nobles telling me what to do again! Saved his life twenty times at least up in Narlond, and the thanks I get is him teaming up with another stone-stupid posh boy.' He gave a bitter laugh and squinted up at me with bloodshot eyes. 'If you want my blades, you can pull them off my stinking drunken corpse.' He cackled, and then as Albart appeared bearing a tray overflowing with yet more ales and brandies whooped his pleasure and stood up to help in distrib-uting them.

There was no sense speaking with Locan while he was like this. I retreated to the other end of the bar, as far away from him and his new friends as I could go. I would never feel comfort-able joking and jesting with strangers whose names I knew I would not remember the next day, certainly not when so much of Locan's behaviour seemed aimed towards humiliating me. There was no doubt that was what awaited me in Rameon if I stayed with him – watching his back and stomaching his insults while he drank and reminisced about the good old days and shared vague plans of getting his vengeance on the current emperor, just as soon as the next drink was finished.

'Your friend's become a bit of an attraction,' said Kelsi as I took a place at the bar. 'Never seen the Whale this busy.' She put a tankard down in front of me. 'Look like you could use a drink.'

'Thanks,' I mumbled. There was a roar of laughter from Locan's table. Clearly he preferred their company to mine. In truth, I did not blame him. This was his place, and I was more at home among the likes of Hosten, sharing ideas and history over a slow game of Pillars.

'Doesn't mean I like the man,' Kelsi added. 'Women can spot an arsehole.'

'He's not...' I was ready to leap to Locan's defence, but my heart was not in it. I took a drink instead.

'You don't have to stay with him, you know,' said Kelsi. 'See how long a man like that lasts in the world without you watching his back. Doesn't matter how good you are with a blade when you're passed out drunk.'

I did not tell Kelsi that her words almost perfectly echoed my own thoughts. There were many enemies waiting for Locan in Rameon. His death might be the small matter of a knife between the ribs in the early hours while he snored in a chair. When I had imagined Locan returning to Rameon before, it had always been with me at his side. Now, my presence there seemed to wax and wane. I had always hoped to one day gaze upon the golden walls of Rameon, but I wished for it to be on my terms, not as Locan's manservant, fated to be dragged along every time he decided the simplest way to solve a problem was to pull a knife, and somehow faced with even more difficulty when he decided not to.

My musings were interrupted when there sounded a distant rumble, followed by a cacophony of collapsing masonry, so loud it was as if the inn's walls were falling in. The floor was shaking, setting bar stools teetering and causing cries of alarm as customers gathered their drinks from atop shuddering tables.

The disturbance lasted for several seconds. 'What was that?' said Kelsi as it faded. The laughter and conversation of the inn had abruptly died, men looking around at one another in confusion.

And far away in a tower of Caradrahan Hall, a bell began to ring, high and frantic. The signal that the Varnans had breached High Tulbar's defences.

'To the walls!' cried a man. Stools tumbled to the floor and ale went flying as men leapt to their feet.

I rushed for the door and was one of the first outside. In the yard, the bell rang loud and clear. Morvolt seemed to sense the coming violence, kicking pugnaciously against his door in his desperation to be freed, and when I opened the stall he almost knocked me over in his haste to be outside. I hastily saddled him and we were away, Morvolt's hooves drumming against the cobbles.

Outside the Merry Whale's yard, men and women were rushing into the streets, peering into the night as if the Varnans might already be inside the walls. Before I could get my bearings and decide where the noise had come from, Morvolt nearly tossed me from the saddle as he reared up on his hind legs before breaking into a gallop towards the west gate, outside which the bulk of Shanoch's forces had congregated.

Others were running towards the disturbance as well, but they had to leap out of the way to avoid being mowed down by a rampaging Morvolt. I could only shout back in apology. I pulled my sword free. Given the magnitude of the blast, I half-expected to find Varnans already pouring into the town, but mercifully we reached the walls without encountering any.

To my relief, Tulbar's defences still stood, if only barely.

A ten-yard stretch of wall had been reduced to a pile of rubble barely half the height of what had been there before. Fur-clad Altan mercenaries were picking their way across the wreckage, bellowing wild screams of challenge while Tulban archers fired at them from the intact parapets either side. A handful of Tulbans waited in a makeshift shield wall, while their leader screamed for them to hold their position, but a pair of Altans cleared the ruined wall and cut down two men before they could blink. The defenders had numbers on their side, but instead of stepping in and spearing the invaders, they were backing off in the face of the fierce war cry of the Altans, allowing them to begin establishing their own shield wall as others rushed to join them, raising a lattice of shields over their heads to cover themselves against the falling arrow fire.

At the sight of an enemy, Morvolt vaulted forward with a wild snort of challenge, and as we reached the invaders I swung my sword in a clumsy backhand slash across the nearest Altan before he could add himself to their growing shield wall. I aimed for his neck, but he twisted away and instead my blade sliced through his ear. Before the man could raise his axe against me Morvolt rode him down.

Morvolt's instincts were as keen as those of a veteran warrior of one hundred battles. The shield wall was in its infancy, and instead of ploughing straight into it he veered around its edge, allowing us to assault their unprotected rear. Neither my experience of battle nor my training on Great Yex had prepared me for single-handedly attacking a mass of screaming warriors, and I gave a war cry that was equal parts bravado and terror as I brought my sword down, taking a man at the nape of his neck just below his tarnished iron helm. Such was the force of my blow that my sword was almost yanked from my grasp as its tip caught against his collarbone.

The Altans were turning towards me, ready to overwhelm me with the weight of their number. I brought my sword across barely in time to deflect an axe blow that would have separated my leg at the knee, then nearly lost my seat as Morvolt bucked and wheeled, kicking his rear legs as they began to surround us.

There were more than enough of them to cut me down, but Morvolt's mad charge had lent heart to the Tulban defenders. They rushed forward, and a storm of Tulban blades fell upon the flank of the Altans who had turned to engage me. More men were running to join the fray, summoned by the incessant chime of the bells, and those Altans who had come through the breach in our walls found themselves outnumbered. There were more rushing over the wreckage to join them, but the uneven stone made for slow going, while arrows continued to rain down from the walls.

A wild howl split the night, drawing my eye to where an Altan warrior was urging his huge warhound across the rubble with repeated lashes of a short whip across its haunches. The beast crossed half the width of the wall in a single bound, dodging a Tulban spear before sinking its teeth into the thigh of the man who wielded it. In an awesome display of strength, it flung the man against the wall, where he struck the stone with a sickening shattering of bone and crumpled to the ground like a rag doll.

I wanted to be nowhere near the beast, but across the chaos, my eyes met the blood-crazed stare of its rider as he spotted me atop Morvolt. The creature's broad shoulders were near the height of a man's chest, and though it was covered in a thick pelt of reds, blacks, and browns, I could see the dense muscle that rippled beneath its flesh. A mail hood covered its face and forechest, revealing only two eyes as hot and foreboding as pits of molten iron, and slavering jaws dripping with black blood, the longest of its teeth the length of a man's handspan. At the sight of Morvolt it froze, and I felt my steed stiffen beneath me before making a deep growl in his throat that I had never before heard from a horse.

Even a trained warhorse might have shied away or fled from such an infernal, merciless predator, but not Morvolt. I pulled at the reins, fearing what would happen if the warhound's jaws found their way to my horse's unprotected neck. But Morvolt was a prince of the *I'bruidhine*, a tribe of wild horses that roamed the far steppes of Ilssia. He did not see a predator, only a foe to be vanquished. He scraped his forehooves several times against the cobbles in challenge, and the two animals charged towards one another, as another blood-twisting howl escaped from the hound's black maw.

I managed to steer Morvolt to the warhound's left, allowing me to bring my shield to bear as the Altan's heavy axe swung up towards me. The blow sent chips of wood flying from my shield and numbed my arm up to the shoulder. As we passed, the hound leapt for Morvolt's withers, but had to twist away in mid-air as my horse bucked and tried to kick his rear hooves to shatter the creature's ribs.

As we swung around for another charge, my eyes locked again with the hound-rider. His lips stretched in a rictus smile, revealing yellowed teeth filed to hideously sharp points like a forest of spear heads. When his mount howled again, the Altan howled with him, an ear-splitting shriek that sent a tendril of fear straight to my heart. No training had prepared me for a joust to the death against a fur-clad lunatic descended from the clans of the pitiless Frost Isles.

For all the Altan's ferocity, I had two advantages. Morvolt gave me close to two feet in height on my enemy, and the Altan had no shield, his left hand holding the whip with which he had trained his fearsome beast to obedience.

All around us, chaos reigned as Tulbans and Altans clashed, but Morvolt and the warhound had eyes only for each other. They thundered towards one another once more, and this time, even over the thunder of battle, a plan formed in my mind.

With the shield protecting my left side, this time the Altan whipped his charge towards Morvolt's right, presumably hoping either to rake his axe down Morvolt's flank or up into my chest, relying on his strength and speed to get past my sword. Against all my instincts for self-preservation, I let him. As the animals galloped towards one another, I loosened my grip on the shield, and just as the Altan pulled his axe back I threw it towards him.

Against a man on horseback, riding at close to the same height as me, this would have been much less effective. The shield would have struck them somewhere around the hip, perhaps surprising or unbalancing them and little more. But the Altan rode lower to the ground than me, and with no shield of his own to parry with, the projectile struck him full in the face, disorientating him as I followed up with my sword.

Whether through luck or judgement, the tip of my blade caught him straight through his open mouth. The force of the Altan's charge drove it straight through the roof and up into his skull. As he fell, the sword was torn from my grasp, and I barely kept my seat as Morvolt twisted out of the way of the warhound's jaws before kicking out with his back legs again. I heard a brief squeal of pain, but then we were past, with Morvolt already swinging around for another attack, his horse-shoes screeching against the cobbles.

But there would be no further charge. The warhound was on the ground with its back legs twisted at a sickening angle, its pelvis shattered by Morvolt's hooves. It was barking and snapping its jaws, furiously trying to rise on its front legs and turn towards Morvolt, its eyes red with rage. Even in what must have been unbearable agony, its instinct to maim and kill could not be tamed.

I dismounted, and walked towards it. Most of the fighting had ceased now, save a few isolated pockets. A trickle of Altans were still stumbling over the rubble, but the Tulbar numbers on the wall and on the ground had swelled, and those mercenaries who wished to live to fight another day were slinking away. Had Shanoch committed more of his force, he might have overwhelmed us before we could bring our numbers to bear, but he appeared to have committed only his mercenaries.

The warhound was still slavering and growling when I reached it, but its efforts were weaker now, and I could see the shadow of its anguish written in the fading fire of its eyes. I have never been able to bear seeing an animal in pain. I reclaimed my sword from the mouth of the dead Altan, and drove the point through the beast's skull.

When the hound stopped moving, I remounted Morvolt, patting him appreciatively on the neck. 'You were incredible,' I whispered. 'Brave enough for both of us.' My praise did not stop him stubbornly ignoring my pulls on the reins in order to approach the dead warhound and nudge at its corpse with his nose as if checking it was dead. Once satisfied that the beast would not rise again, Morvolt snorted in triumph, then promptly turned around and emptied his bowels all over his vanquished foe.

With the fighting close to done, I approached the walls. I could see where the foundations had been compromised. A heavy divot had been quarried beneath the wall, collapsing it under its own weight. For an instant, I wondered if Hosten had been mistaken in his assertion that the Tulban earth was too solid to be tunnelled, but as I stared past the breach I realised there was one way to lose a siege we had not reckoned with.

In Guiland, wizards endure because of what they offer my family. In return for thirty years' service, they will receive the Harkkens' magic-resistant blood, and be freed from their curse. They are not common elsewhere. Far from it. The Rameans hunted them to near extinction across the continent, and Paleir is a land of beasts and barbarians, with scant and strange magic.

But there are always exceptions.

What I saw outside the walls I had witnessed only once before. Every precaution is taken when training nascent wizards who might one day serve the Harkken dynasty, but sometimes in their efforts to control one of the four elements of the Under-realm – wood, iron, fire, and shadow – they summon a demon that is beyond their ability to master.

I am told that this is most common among those whom the wizards call blue-mooners – those for whom Dagin's Bloom comes only rarely, perhaps once a fortnight, and erratically, making these events near impossible to predict, and so even harder for them to control. I had seen it before in the grounds of Harkfall, my parents' castle. The corpse of an apprentice wizard, her face frozen in terror, her flesh hideous, mottled with purple burns that wept blood, the sockets of her skull empty where her eyes had burst like overripe grapes. The vengeance of the demon she had brought into our world without the necessary strength to bind it to her will.

So it was here. By his garb, the man had been Varnan. There was a furrow of tunnelled earth running between him and the wall, presumably the path of the creature of the Underrealm that the wizard had infused into the iron hidden in the soil beneath Tulbar's walls. To the reprieve of Tulbar, this Varnan wizard had been unable to master its nature long enough to bring down the whole thing, and he had paid the price.

The demon had turned his flesh to stone. Iron ore had spread from the ground up the man's legs, slowly encasing him in a layer of metal. By the scream on his frozen face, he had lived until the raw iron had reached his mouth, at which point it had swept into his throat and choked the man to death.

Repressing a shiver, I tore my eyes away, giving thanks once again that I had not had the misfortune to be born a wizard. Perhaps it had been a relief for the man – without the patronage of the Harkken family, he would have been doomed to suffer Dagin's Bloom for life.

Shanoch's plan had failed. But respite for the Tulbans would be brief. The breach gave Shanoch a target, and if he sent the rest of his force against it tomorrow there was no certainty the town would hold. Hosten would also need to commit much of his strength here, and in doing so he might leave other parts of the wall vulnerable to a Varnan assault.

The last of the Altans turned and ran for the breach, provoking much cheering and shaking of swords and spears among the Tulban defenders. My blood was cooling now, and I felt a measure of pride. If I was any judge, Morvolt's charge had ensured the town would stand another night, and if not for the distraction we had posed to the warhound and its rider, the fearsome creature might have killed dozens of Tulbans, perhaps even enough to send the town's defenders fleeing in fear.

I only wished that my father had been there to see it. Or, better yet, Javvian.

'What happened?' came a voice from my rear. Hosten, wild-eyed and with hair streaming in the night wind, ahorse and accompanied by Lenard and his guards. He was staring at the breach in the wall as if he could not believe his own eyes.

I urged Morvolt towards him and filled Hosten in on events as swiftly as I could, including my theory about the wizard's gruesome death.

Hosten was pale by the time I had finished. 'Seamstress and Swordsman,' he breathed. He turned to Lenard. 'Can we fix that?'

Lenard's brow furrowed as he stared at the breach in the wall. 'I will ask the masons. Perhaps they can salvage something by morning.'

'Send every mason we have,' said Hosten. Despite our victory, his face was grim. 'If we cannot patch that wall, the city is doomed.'

Despite Tulbar's weakened prospects of withstanding the siege, I rode back to town feeling as proud of myself as I had in a long time. I had Morvolt to thank of course, but without our charge, the Altans might have lodged a foothold within Tulbar's walls for Shanoch to mount a full assault on the city.

With my blood still singing from the thrill of battle and elation that I was still alive, my immediate instinct was to go in search of Shaliya, Roddin be damned. Fortunately, sense won out over recklessness – if I felt bold enough later, I could creep into the Dwarf and Dragon after closing time – and I made my way back to the Merry Whale. I returned Morvolt to his stall with two large carrots that I stole from a nearby vegetable patch – it was dark, and I was sure its owners would not miss them – and promised to brush his coat in the morning. It was not necessary – he was no ordinary horse, and his raven-wing coat retained its sheen without intervention, but he always seemed to enjoy it in any case.

I strode into the Merry Whale with a spring in my step. Thanks to Morvolt, I would be the first man back from the walls. I might even have the chance to at last speak privately with Locan and beg again for his help.

The state of the common room stopped me in my tracks.

The inn was strewn with fallen chairs and overturned tables. Albart lay slumped across the bar with blood leaking from his skull, unconscious or dead. At the far booth, Locan was snoring softly with a jug still gripped in his fist.

And in the middle of the room, a man stalked towards a heavily pregnant Kelsi, a long knife tight in his fist. This was no fur-clad Altan mercenary – he was garbed lightly, in black breeches, shirt, and boots, dressed for skulking through the night.

'Get back!' Kelsi lashed out with the fire poker in her hand, and the man leapt lithely aside, closing the distance between them and forcing Kelsi to retreat clumsily behind a table as she came within the length of his blade.

The man could have killed her there and then, but instead sought to dodge around the table, forcing Kelsi to move the other way to block his path.

'Stay out of this!' The man kicked the table towards Kelsi's pregnant stomach, forcing her a clumsy step back, but when he sought to side-step away, she again moved to block him.

It was then I realised the stranger had no interest in Kelsi.

He was trying to reach Locan, passed out on the far side of the room.

Had I come to this fight cold, I might have hesitated, but my blood was still up from the night's slaughter. I pulled my sword free with a flourish and strode towards the man with murder in my heart. As vexing as Locan was, he was still my companion, and I would die before I let this man within a blade's length of him.

My approach trapped the man between me and Kelsi. His eyes flicked back and forth between us, and he backed away from Locan, trying to keep us both in his eyeline. I grabbed a chair with my spare hand and heaved it towards him.

With my wrong hand the throw was clumsy and fell short, but it clipped the edge of the table, forcing the man back and allowing Kelsi to move in towards him.

She swung the poker, and the man hissed as it connected with his wrist, but his reactions were whip-fast, a flick of his blade drawing a red line across the back of Kelsi's hand. She leapt away, dropping the poker and letting it clatter to the floor.

'Get back!' I shouted at Kelsi. I did not want her dying for the sake of Locan. The man was cornered. To reach Locan he would have to best two of us. I rushed forward with my sword raised, but the man kicked an overturned chair towards me, and as I leapt over it a length of cold steel flashed past my temple sending a spray of blood into my eyes. My clumsy sword swing found nothing but air, and had the man not already thrown his knife at me he could have stepped inside my guard and thrust it between my ribs.

Faced with two foes between him and his prey, the man circled away, not towards Locan but towards the door. With rare athleticism, he leapt atop a table and with long, lithe strides bounded across the inn towards the exit. I hurried after him, but the man was already through the door. I raced out into the yard and caught a glimpse of Locan's would-be assassin flashing away around the corner – I hurried after him, but when I reached the street he was gone, lost to the night's darkness.

I cursed, and in a rage thrust the point of my sword down into the mud. The side of my head stung where the man's knife had caught me, but I had been lucky – an inch to the left and I would have lost an eye.

I retreated to the inn, where I found Kelsi trying to revive Albart.

'He's alive,' she breathed. Albart groaned and with Kelsi's help got his head up from the bar. She scowled towards Locan. 'No thanks to that useless sack of pickled goblin-shit. Like I said, what's the use of being a world-famous assassin if you're too drunk to defend yourself?'

Assured that Albart had survived, I went in search of our would-be assassin's weapon. The knife was embedded in the wood of an overturned table. I pulled it free. The blade was the length of a man's forearm and sharp enough to shave with, but the hilt was plain, unadorned leather. It could have been made anywhere.

I went to check on Locan. I tapped lightly at his face a few times, and when he did not respond, pried the tankard from his grip and poured its contents over his head.

He woke up spluttering. 'What the piss was that for?'

'You just slept through your own murder.' I slammed the dagger's point down into the table. 'If Kelsi hadn't been here, you'd be dead.'

'Couldn't let you die with your tab unpaid,' said Kelsi. She was trying to help a woozy-looking Albart to a chair, and I rushed to help her lower him down into a seat. 'If you weren't such good business I'd have let him kill you.'

She was trying to put a brave face on it, but I could tell she was shaken. Who wouldn't be? Once Albart was safely seated she collapsed into a chair, cradling her swollen belly, and I rushed around the bar to get them each a brandy.

Another man might have responded with a string of desperate apologies to Kelsi and Albart, but not Locan. He blinked, wiped his bleary eyes, and bent his head to examine the dagger. 'He caught you with it,' he said, his eyes flicking to my temple.

I touched a finger to my wound and it came away bloody. 'Just a scratch.'

Locan grunted. 'Be quicker next time.' He picked the blade up by the hilt and held it to the light. To his credit, he had roused quickly. 'No poison on it, fortunately for you. Ugly work. And blunt. The smith who forged this must have been blind drunk. He'd have needed to saw through a few layers of scar tissue to hit anything important.' He tossed it down on the table. 'Bloody amateur, then. Did you catch him?'

I shook my head. 'Any chance of a thank you?'

Locan paused, and for an instant I thought he would refuse, but eventually he grunted, 'All right. Thanks, all of you. Did any of you see who it was?'

'He was Varnan,' breathed Albart. 'I heard his accent when he ordered a drink.' He touched his swelling forehead and winced. 'That's when he smashed my head against the bar.'

'I heard the commotion from outside,' said Kelsi. She wrapped her hand around Albart's and kissed his blossoming bruise. 'Lucky for you, you damned old fool.'

'Lucky for both of us.' Locan gave a forceful shake of his head, as if trying to dispel his drunkenness. 'Height of rudeness to kill a man while he's in a tavern. That might just be the last mistake Mór Shanoch ever makes.'

The mood of Tulbar's defenders when they returned to the Merry Whale was jubilant. Understandably so – they had repelled an assault by a battle-hardened cohort of Altan mercenaries, and the immediate question of repairing the wall was a problem for somebody else. Albart and Kelsi shook off their injuries to serve the necessary drinks, and as the tale of the attempted assassination was told, Locan, who was now very much awake, loudly proclaimed me, Kelsi, and Albart the heroes of the hour, and to much hooting and hollering swore to take his vengeance on Mór Shanoch.

My own excitement at our victory had diminished with the escape of the assassin. I did not like to think of a man who would kill someone while they slept being free to go about the night. But Locan would be more than safe surrounded by so many Tulbans who he had thrilled with free drinks and tales of Rameon. As exhaustion crept up on me, I headed to bed.

Unfortunately, when I lay on my mattress, sleep remained elusive. If not for the timely arrival of me and Morvolt, High Tulbar might have fallen this night. There would be more battles to come, more bloodthirsty Altans riding fearsome warhounds hungry for the flesh of men and horses, and still to come the Varnans that made up the bulk of Shanoch's army. He would not delay and allow the Tulbans a chance to repair their ruined defences. If Locan was to make good on his oath to take vengeance on Shanoch, he would have to do it soon.

Eventually, I must have slept, and the next thing I knew, the miserly light of a Palish dawn was streaming in through our dirty windows, and Locan was sitting on the edge of my bed watching me.

He put a finger to his lips. 'We need to talk,' he whispered. His face showed the signs of a heavy night – squinty eyes and wine-stained lips.

'Have you been to bed?' I asked blearily.

'A little.' He shrugged. 'Needed to make a show after that little assassination attempt. Someone worked hard to make it look legitimate.'

I blinked. 'Legitimate?'

'Keep your voice down, would you? And think quicker.' He flicked the cut in my temple, causing pain to flash across my forehead. 'That's for throwing a drink over me. The next time you want to wake me, try pouring it in my mouth.'

I pushed myself up in bed, trying to gather my thoughts. 'You said you would take vengeance against Shanoch,' I said slowly. 'You didn't mean it.'

Locan gave a black grin. 'Course not.' He held up the blade that would have taken his life. 'You met him. If Shanoch wanted someone dead, he wouldn't send an amateur with a blunt blade who runs at the sight of a pregnant woman and a lad that's skinny as a stream of piss.

'And what would be the point? Shanoch knows that Hosten and I don't see eye to eye. I might be the only man in Tulbar who *doesn't* want Shanoch dead.'

Locan's words began to permeate my waking mind, and though I could see the sense in his deduction, my instinct was to act as Locan would have in the reverse scenario – to disagree. 'But the attempt happened while everyone was at the wall,' I said. 'They made sure the inn was empty. Whoever arranged the assassin knew there would be an attack on the walls. Maybe Shanoch hoped his assassin would have more time.'

'I have my own suspicions,' said Locan. He fixed me with a dark gaze full of meaning. 'Hosten.'

That one word woke me as surely as if Locan had thrown a vat of icy water over me. 'No,' I said immediately. 'That's not possible.' Were Locan to die, Hosten would gain the least and lose the most. Now that there was a breach in the wall, persuading Locan to deal with Shanoch was one of the few paths to victory left to Tulbar. Hosten was not capable of such a thing. He was ambitious of course, but this war was Shanoch's doing, not his. 'You can't kill Shanoch if you're dead.'

'But the assassin didn't *want* me dead,' said Locan, his voice sharp and insistent. 'He made sure that Albart knew that he was Varnan. He fled at the first sign of trouble. He wasted time fighting Kelsi when he could have been killing me. What if he only wanted us to *think* that he was trying to kill me? The hope being that I would immediately assume it was Shanoch and would be immediately out for revenge. Hosten already betrayed me once – you really think he wouldn't betray me again?'

I shook my head stubbornly. 'He *didn't* betray you; he just didn't expect Shanoch's attack to come so soon.' Though I was still troubled by Hosten's failure to wholeheartedly condemn the Abomination King, I was perversely angry that Locan would accuse someone I considered a friend. Was he jealous that I preferred Hosten's company to his own? 'And Hosten wouldn't take a risk like that.' It was still his hope that I would talk Locan round – even after so many failed attempts, he had kept faith with me.

But asking me to try again with Locan had not been the only thing that Hosten had spoken to me of the previous evening. I had known of his ambition, but I had not reckoned on him speaking with admiration for the achievements of the Abomination King. If Hosten could find aspects to admire in the Abomination King, was sending an assassin after Locan truly beyond him? Of course it wasn't – he had sought to do the exact same thing to Shanoch.

'And you've still not answered my question,' I went on, scrambling for reasons it could not be Hosten. 'How would Hosten know when the Altan attack was coming?'

Locan rubbed at his unshaven jaw. 'I don't know.' He shook his head and made a frustrated noise. 'I don't know. Goblin bollocks, I'm not cut out for all this thinking. I can't even fucking read.' He got to his feet and began striding impatiently up and down the room. 'That's why I woke you up. Tell me you don't think there's even the slightest possibility that Hosten had something to do with it.'

'There's one other possibility,' I suggested. 'Ulf.'

Locan snorted. 'Ulf's had enough opportunities to come after us again. Why wait until now? And he wouldn't send one man – he'd send a whole gang of them.' He made an irritated noise in his throat. 'Ulf, Roddin, Hosten... This town's crookeder than a three-penny coin. Someone here is fucking with us, and unfortunately you're the only person I can trust. I know you still want me to kill Shanoch, but I'm not going near him until we work out what in the Underrealm is going on.'

I was oddly touched that Locan named me as the one person he could trust. It felt as if all our disagreements had been reversed and we were once again on the same side. All it had taken was me thwarting a possible attempt on his life while he slept – just the sort of task that might be expected of me if I continued with him to Rameon.

Three suspects – Shanoch, Ulf, and Hosten. As far as I was concerned, the obvious candidate was still Shanoch. The assassin had been Varnan. The assassination attempt had coincided perfectly with the assault on the walls. Perhaps he had determined he could not take the risk of Locan coming after him and decided to strike first.

'Also,' said Locan, 'has Hosten ever mentioned the dragon scale to you again?'

I shook my head. 'Not since we gave it to him.'

Locan made a face. 'Doesn't that strike you as a bit odd? We went through all that trouble for it, he makes a big song and dance, and now doesn't seem to give a shit. Why's he wasting his evenings with you playing Pillars and complaining about the hardship of growing up in lavish comfort or whatever it is you two do together if he's got a dragon he needs to work out how to summon?'

Setting aside Locan's insults, it did strike me as odd. Hosten was the only Caradrahan left, and they guarded their dragon magic jealously. If he wasn't trying to unravel that mystery, then nobody was.

We might have speculated further, if not for a creak of the chamber door, followed by a guttural curse from outside and the whisper of somebody's feet on the floorboards.

Locan was at the door in a flash, before I had even moved. In one motion, he lifted the latch and flung the door open, a knife having seemingly materialised in his hand from nowhere.

The man who had been crouched outside our door had the chance to let out a small scream before Locan clamped his arm around his neck with the blade of a knife pressed up under his jaw.

The eavesdropper flailed briefly, but stopped resisting as Locan dragged him over the threshold and slammed the door.

'Hear anything interesting, you fat drunken fuck?' Locan hissed. He threw the intruder to the floor and aimed a heavy kick into his gut, drawing a high grunt of pain. 'Who sent you?'

It took me a few moments to recognise Darry, the some-time armourer and acolyte of Roddin. His blotchy face was yet to take on the sheen of sweat that it would by evening, but that made him no less pitiable. His hair hung in greasy hanks, and without the bravery born of strong drink he seemed a diminished figure, particularly lying on his back holding his stomach. 'Nobody sent me,' he managed to say between breaths. 'I'm here because I heard you saved my little girl's life last night.'

'And I'm the fucking Dread King of the Muttalins,' growled Locan. 'What was the plan? Check if we were asleep and then murder us in our beds?'

Darry's eyes widened in fear. 'N-no! I've never killed anyone, I swear.'

Locan's lip curled in disdain. 'Now on that I believe you. You're a born coward. Nobody would be stupid enough to send you.'

This concession seemed to draw some of the fear from Darry's eyes. He gave a sad smile. 'I won't deny it. I'm a coward. Always have been. That's why I got into smithing. As long as I could pound metal, I'd never be expected to fight.' He looked at me. 'It was you, wasn't it? Kelsi said she'd be dead if it weren't for you.' There were tears glistening in his eyes, and they did not appear to be from fear alone. 'She's a good woman, no thanks to me. One decent thing I ever did. I had a good year once, about twelve years back. Her mother had run off by then. That was the year I taught her to smith, and when I fell back into the bottle she kept the business running.' He sniffed and wiped his eye. 'If anything happened to her, I'd throw myself off Dragonwing Point. So, thank you. And I'm sorry for giving you trouble before.'

'And I'm sure that's why you were listening at our door,' sneered Locan.

'It's true!' protested Darry. 'I was about to knock on your door, but then I heard you talking and it sounded interesting so I sort of... listened for a bit.' He held his hands up. 'Please don't kill me. I won't tell anyone.'

'Tell anyone what?' said Locan, brandishing his knife threateningly towards Darry. 'What did you hear?'

As Darry explained, it soon became clear that he had heard everything. All Locan's suspicion of Hosten and all the discussion that followed.

'I'm sorry,' he said again. He was snivelling with fear now. Locan's blade had not left his hand.

Locan sighed. 'I'm sorry too. Morning's no time to be killing someone. I've not even had a drink yet.'

He took a step towards Darry.

I leapt to my feet. 'Locan. His daughter is downstairs. You can't just kill him.'

'Can't let him go either,' said Locan. Darry was still on the floor but he had shunted himself as far away from Locan as he could until his back was pressed up against Locan's bed. 'He'll tell anyone who asks what we were talking about in return for a thimbleful of ale. You want the Mór's soldiers knocking down the door?' He took another step towards Darry who cringed away from him with a shriek. 'You want one death on your conscience or a couple of dozen?'

I stepped in front of Locan before he could do something we'd both regret. 'Locan, he'll scream. And what are we going to do with the body?'

'Hide it here until the *Red Fiend* is ready. Won't start smelling for a couple of days.'

'You don't have to,' said Darry. 'I know something you'll want to hear.'

Locan snorted. 'I'd sooner hear from my chamber pot.'

'It's about the Mór!' Darry was desperately eyeing the knife in Locan's hand. 'You'll want to hear it, I promise you.'

A sceptical look passed between me and Locan. I struggled to imagine what useful information Darry could have about Hosten. They hardly ran in the same circles.

'You know I'm his uncle?' Darry continued. 'Or half-uncle, at least.'

'Yeah we heard. Mór Ruihan was your father but his wife wasn't your mother,' said Locan impatiently. 'You here to explain how that works to us? Just get on with it so I can kill you.'

Darry sniffed. 'If I tell you, you have to let me go.'

'You're hardly in a place to be making demands.' Locan ran a finger down the blade. 'Tell us what you know and I'll decide whether it's worth your life.'

This seemed to be good enough for Darry. 'I knew the old Mór back when he was just Hardane,' he said. 'His brothers – *our* brothers – never cared a dragon's shit about me, but he was his dad's third son, and in our youth we ran wild together. Used to sneak in through the back door of the Dwarf and Dragon back when it was just called the Handsome Dwarf and drink our stolen ales down on the beach. Then the grey owl fever came down and carried his brothers off, and he became Mól Hardane, then a year later Mór Hardane, and we didn't speak much after that.'

'Touching,' sneered Locan. 'Why would we care?'

'Because I saw him the night he died!'

Locan and I looked at each other. This was intriguing, assuming Darry was telling the truth. 'Go on,' said Locan. He was still holding the knife.

Encouraged, Darry continued. 'About once a moon he'd show up at the Dwarf in disguise. Since his wife died. Always when it was busy so no one else recognised him. We'd have a quiet drink together and laugh about the old times.' He gave a sudden smile. 'There was this one night. We'd have been fifteen or sixteen. A man named Bilge owned the Dwarf back then. Used to—'

'Just get to the point,' said Locan. Darry was stalling, as if caught between his fear of Locan and the fear of whatever he thought he knew.

'Hardane was worried about his son, the night he died,' said Darry. He wiped at his weeping eyes. 'Don't know if he'd ever mentioned Hosten to me before, but something had him spooked. He had this look in his eye, the sort you usually only see in men being sent to the mines.'

Darry almost made it sound as if Hardane had feared Hosten. But nobody was afraid of Hosten. The Keykeepers did not respect him. His lords had betrayed him. His attempts to intimidate Locan and Shanoch had been met with ridicule.

'What did he say about Hosten?' I asked, my voice half a whisper.

Darry swallowed. 'He said he had a hard conversation coming. A hard conversation with his son.'

At Darry's revelation, all the air seemed to draw out of the room. Hosten had told me he lived in fear of his father. Hardane had not conversed with his son, he had issued commands.

'A hard conversation about what, Darry?' I asked.

'That's all I remember him saying. I was dead drunk. We both were.' A shadow passed over Darry's face. 'And the next morning, he was dead.'

I shared an uneasy glance with Locan, and I knew we had both picked up the same intimation: Darry was suggesting that Hardane had been murdered. By Hosten.

Locan gave a rough bark of laughter. 'I don't believe it. Not that bloodless sop.'

'I'm only telling you what Hardane said,' said Darry. 'I never made no accusation.' He now felt safe enough to get to his feet. 'Can I go now? I swear I won't tell anyone what I heard when I was at the door.'

'But why?' I asked. 'There must have been something else Hardane said to you.'

Darry shook his head vigorously. 'I swear, anything else he

said I've forgotten.' He put his hands together in supplication. 'Can I leave? Please don't kill me.'

Locan stepped towards Darry so fast that I did not even have time to cry out. I was sure that he was about to drive the knife up into the armourer's heart and let him bleed out on the floor, but he only grabbed him by the collar and pushed the tip of the blade up against his throat. 'One word of this escapes your lips, I'll cut you from ear to arse and hang you up by your toes to bleed out. You never heard anything, and you never told us anything. Understood?'

Darry nodded, whimpering as he stared down at the blade pressed against his flesh. 'I won't tell anyone.'

Locan shoved him towards the door. 'This is your lucky day. Against my better judgement, I'm going to let you live. Just stay downstairs where I can see you.'

Darry nodded frantically. 'I will. Thank you.'

Without another word, he ran to the door, wrenched it open, and fled down the stairs.

'Well,' said Locan. His grin when he turned to face me was as black as the mouth of a skull. 'How about that then? Still reckon your friend Hosten pisses gold?'

My mind was reeling. I could not believe Hosten was capable of what Darry had as good as accused him of. His father had died of a fever. Lenard had said the same. There had been no whisper of anything untoward. I had sought to help him because I believed in his vision of a brighter future for Paleir, one where slavery was outlawed and the whole island was united under his authority.

But there were other matters to consider. Hosten had reneged on our agreement, even if I had understood his reasons for doing so. He had held no qualms about seeking to have Shanoch assassinated. He had spoken of his admiration for the Abomination King. When I thought on it, given everything else, it was not such a stretch to believe that he would fake an assassination attempt to try and bring Locan to his side. But murdering his *father*?

I could not in good conscience hide from Locan what Hosten had said to me the previous evening. It was not only that I thought it could not be Hosten – it was that I could not face the possibility that it *had* been Hosten. If he had killed his father, that meant almost everything I had done during our time in Paleir had been based on a falsehood. Even if it had not been a genuine attempt on Locan's life, it could have ended far worse for Albart and Kelsi.

'There's... something else,' I said reluctantly. I quickly filled Locan in on what Hosten had revealed to me the previous night – his indifference to the deeds of the Abomination King and the apparent good his rise had done for Guiland and Paleir.

Locan was frowning by the time I finished. 'Warned you about lords and kings, didn't I? There's no principle a man who's had a nibble of power won't set aside to claim the whole feast.' He paused. 'Doesn't mean he murdered his father, of course. There were those in Rameon who saw no problem with the Abomination King – it was all so far away, and they didn't see any difference between him and the Harkkens of Guiland. There were some senators who advocated privately for an alliance and to cut Guiland in two – half for the Dominion, half for the Abomination King.'

'Really?' I asked, shocked at this revelation. 'Did news of what he did to the Guilanders he captured not reach as far as Rameon?' That seemed impossible – the Abomination King had reigned for four hundred years.

'Oh, it did,' said Locan. 'But there's always those willing to dismiss stories like that. Guilish embellishment designed to turn opinion against the Abomination King. No acolyte of the Abomination King ever sank Ramean ships or allied themselves with Unthian rebels.' He shrugged. 'Those who thought that way were in the minority, and you'd struggle to find anyone who'd admit to it now, but they were there.'

'So, what do we do?' I asked. A thought struck me. 'We could still walk away from this. If you kill Shanoch, the siege will end. The *Red Fiend* must almost be fixed by now.' We could settle matters with Hosten, leave him to his strange opinions and his wild ambition to restore Caradrahan rule over Paleir, and sail within a matter of days, ideally with Shaliya in tow before Roddin realised she was missing. We would never have to think again about how Hosten might have come into his crown.

'That's what I've wanted to do since we first arrived,' said Locan. 'But now someone's trying to piss in my flask and tell me it's whisky, and before we leave I'd at least like to know who it is. And if someone did genuinely want to kill me, they might try again.' His right hand worried inside his cloak for one of his hidden blades, as if checking it was within easy reach. 'And whether it was him or not, we can't trust Hosten.' He grimaced. 'Not that I trust Darry's word either. He's probably run straight off to Roddin to tell him how he saved his life with some goblin-crap story about the old Mór being murdered.'

Before I could reply, a bell began to peal, an insistent, clamorous succession of chimes that echoed back off the city wall. The high bell of Caradrahan Hall, calling the defenders of Tulbar to arms once more.

'I have to go,' I said to Locan. I was still sworn to defend High Tulbar, and if Shanoch threw the full weight of his force at the ruined section of wall, it might take every man in the city to throw him back. 'What do you want to do?'

'Just go,' said Locan. 'If the city falls, none of this will matter a goblin's fart.' He gave a rough laugh. 'At least then we won't have to worry about whatever Hosten's been doing.'

For all Locan and I had discussed, there were people I wanted to protect in Tulbar – Kelsi, Albart, and most importantly of all, Shaliya. And also, Hosten. What we knew and what he was accused of did not make him guilty of anything. If we could hold High Tulbar, he would have the chance to prove himself, to forge a Tulbar and a Paleir that I would one day be proud to say I played my part in creating. The word of a desperate drunk did not change that, at least not without proof. I dragged my armour on, thundered down the stairs, and left the inn at a run towards the west wall.

CHAPTER 19

The bell tolled insistently in my ears. I ran towards where I believed the attack would come, through a cloying, early morning fog that made it feel as if I was wading through icy swamp water.

The mist grew all the thicker as I approached the west wall, shrouding the world in white, reducing the scene that waited for me to a confusion of bobbing lights and shadowed figures. The torches belonged to the city's defenders atop the parapet, but the bewildered shouting and erratic arrow fire suggested they could see no better than I could. The sounds of battle at the site of the breach reached my ears, a cacophony of clashing swords and fearful shouting.

I moved towards the melee cautiously, peering through the gloom, searching for a familiar face, anybody who might be in charge. It was then that I sighted the massed ranks of Varnans, moving over the rubble at a slow march towards the Tulban defenders, the changeable ground making their shield wall a drunken, clumsy thing. In ordinary circumstances, such a disordered force might have been beaten back easily, but the mist gave them cover, hindering the defenders' response. Panicked

Tulbans were rushing their tangled formation in ones and twos and being dispatched easily. Arrows flew from the wall, but the archers could barely see their targets.

In battle, I have learnt that sometimes the weather has a way of conspiring to determine the outcome more so than any strategy or subterfuge. As heavy snow might have left the besieging Varnans to freeze in their camp, or blazing sun might have led them to dehydration and irritability, this unnatural mist might give them the victory that Shanoch craved.

Already, a steady stream of Tulban soldiers were fleeing the wall, whatever courage they had having already reached its limit. A limping man cradling one arm in the other passed within a few feet of me. I grasped him by the collar and he gave a cry of pain. 'Who leads?' I demanded.

'The Mór has gone,' rasped the man. 'He fled, the coward.'

I pushed him aside. I did not want to believe it. I had seen the depths of Hosten's resolve; his courage could not have failed him.

My sword still rested in its scabbard. I had sworn to defend High Tulbar, but my immediate reaction was to go to Shaliya. I had not seen her in days, and I feared what would happen to her if the city fell. In the fog, we might escape unseen and head south for Bastden. This was not my city, and I would not die for it when so many of those who dwelled here seemed not to care for its fate.

A commotion of heavy footsteps came from behind me, and I had to leap out of the way as Chatten thundered past. She had eschewed her usual garb for mail, and ran at the head of a group of reinforcements. They launched a forest of throwing spears and without waiting to see what they had struck, pulled their swords free and raced towards the breach.

Reckless courage won out over rational cowardice. I drew my own blade and hurried after them.

I believe I did my part in what followed. There is little that lives so briefly in the memory as battle, not least when you and your foes are swathed in dense fog, reducing enemies to faceless wraiths and making your sword seem slow and clumsy in your hand. I recall a wound I took to my wrist and the warm rush of blood of the man who dealt it to me, and I remember Chatten's valiant fury, tearing into the enemy line with a blade in each hand after she had thrown her shield into a Varnan's face before he could deliver a killing blow to one of our companions.

I recall also the moment that Chatten fell. She turned too slow, and the point of a spear caught her in the soft part of her throat. It was barely a moment later that a second Varnan line rushed to meet us, when the defenders of Tulbar lost heart and ran.

I fled with them. There was a time when that shamed me, but with a moment of cowardice I earnt my next fifty years of life, and spared myself the ignominy of dying for the sake of a foreign, long-fallen kingdom, no subject of which would have remembered my name.

I ran for the stairs up to the battlements, and with two men I did not know we together reached the decision that this was as good a place to die as any, and as one we turned with our shields raised. The few Varnans who came after us fell to arrow fire from above, our foe now so close that even in the fog the men arrayed atop the walls could not miss. The ground in front of the breach was a melee of churned mud and blood, all battle lines forgotten as more Varnans hurried over the rubble to engage and overwhelm the remaining defenders. In the mist, it was near impossible to tell friend from foe.

Through it all, I searched for Hosten. His subjects may have been divided in their opinion of his rule, but I do believe the sight of him sharing the same dangers they faced would have lent heart to them. I saw Tulbans throwing down their weapons and casting off their helmets and running for town, perhaps hoping to grab what wealth they could before they fled the city forever, men who might have stood if only someone had been there to lead them.

A figure caught my eye at the edge of the chaos. Slight, unarmoured, with a litheness that belied their limp and stooped back, moving with such poise that it was as if they were one with the mist. A dagger flashed, left, right, and two Varnans fell with their throats gaping open and blood gushing free in a torrent. I blinked, and the figure was gone, reappearing on the other side of the battle in two more swishes of steel that sent another pair of men tumbling to the ground.

I believe that I knew Locan would come. Not because of any great affection for me, but because of who he was. He might have claimed to be no hero, but that never prevented him acting like one, ever on the side of bold underdogs and the doomed dispossessed.

Recall, if you will, what I said of battle, the way the truth of it flows through your memory like water through your hands. Locan was ever an exception to this. He fought like a poet's hero, verse wrought in ink and parchment and transmuted to steel and flesh, stanzas that you read as a boy and find they are etched into your soul. He weaved through the fray, a symphony written in blood.

But Locan was only one man, and the Varnans were many, and the mist gave him no shadows in which to work his gore-soaked deeds. I saw him snarl as a wounded Tulban stumbled into him, throwing off target a thrust that would have severed a Varnan's neck, forcing Locan to let a knife fall from his grip as he seized the man's collar and pushed him onto a riposte that would have taken Locan in the chest. Before the Varnan could pull his blade free, Locan dragged the blade across the man's neck.

But he was down to one blade, and several Varnans at once seemed to have realised the threat this dark stranger posed. Locan leapt over a pike thrust, sliced through the head of a spear and kicked its wielder into a man drawing his sword back. A bowstring thrummed, and Locan ducked, letting the arrow fly harmlessly over him to take the man behind him through the eye, causing him to crumple shuddering to the ground.

And still more closed in. Too many Tulbans had fled, and many Varnans were pursuing them into the town, just as many were realising the threat in their midst and bringing their weapons to bear against Locan.

They would kill him, I saw then. Locan was unarmoured, one man with a knife surrounded by dozens. I looked around for a torch to cast a shadow, but those on the battlements were too far away.

I had already shamed myself by fleeing. I would not let that same weakness cause me to stand back and watch the death of my friend, or whatever Locan was to me. I leapt down the stairs, and with my sword raised, I barrelled into the fray with a howl of fury on my tongue.

I saw my death waiting for me. Massed ranks of Varnans who would end my charge before it began. Those nearest turned towards my cry with their weapons raised. Through the mass of armour and flesh I caught Locan's eye briefly before he was lost behind a sea of bodies. I picked a target, aiming to knock his blade aside and be inside his guard, and after that I would give my fate to the Seamstress and hope that Locan could save me.

I had only yards to spare when there came from the sky a high and terrible shriek, like the fury of a god or the crack of the sky being torn in two when the Seamstress returns to earth. The force of it sent me sprawling face first into the gore-soaked cobbles, and, whether through some force of magic or innate, immutable fear, the Varnans fell to the ground as well.

I lifted my face to the sky, my heart frozen with terror, and rapt with wonder, I could only stare.

High above the fog, a sight to strike fear into even the

boldest hero's heart flew on wings of shadow. It was little more than a speck against a distant sky, so small I could have covered the entirety of it by my thumb, and yet I believe even those who had not before seen such a creature could tell its enormity, could sense the sheer scale of it in the way its scream set their blood running cold and trails of fearful urine trickling down their leg.

Should my mind one day fail me, I still do not believe I will ever forget what I saw that fateful morning. The first time a dragon had been sighted over a Palish battlefield in hundreds of years.

Men came to their feet, staring dazed up at the sky, Varnan and Tulban alike. The thrum of bows and the screams of men fell silent, even the dying being glad they lived long enough to see such a thing as a dragon in the full majesty of flight. I could see Aydhenia's hypnotic beauty in my mind's eye, the cobalt shimmer of her scales and the swirling depths of her inscrutable gaze.

The day that the people of Tulbar had believed they might never see again had come to pass. Aydhenia flew to the kingdom's defence.

Or so we hoped.

With a shriek that could twist the black blood of an orc, Aydhenia dived, and men on both sides ran screaming in terror.

An Altan mercenary nearly knocked me over in his haste to escape, but I slipped round him and then I was running for Locan. He came to his feet from beneath a pile of bodies just as I reached him, and then we were fleeing with the rest, throwing ourselves behind an outcropping of stone in the wall and cowering as Aydhenia plummeted towards the battlefield.

Her trajectory took her east to west, bursting from the far-off sun of grim morning in a blaze of fervid blue. Varnans who had pushed into the town were running from her, making for the breach, but it was clear they would not be quick enough.

The dragon's mouth opened to a black maw, and a wave of blistering heat burst forth. Not a blaze of fire, but an eruption of steam, fired to boiling and beyond in the bowels of the beast and unleashed upon the defenceless mass of Varnan invaders.

It is said that the flames of a fire dragon of the south burn so hot that men are incinerated in an instant. It is no pretty way to die, but if you are fortunate enough to take the hottest part of the flame instead of being winged by it, it will be quick.

Not so the searing steam of a sea dragon. Their breath is as hot as fire, but it does not burn. It scalds.

Aydhenia swept overhead in a flash of scorching steam, and those men still out in the open writhed and screamed for mercy as their exposed skin turned from white to red, searing and blistering and cracking. They tore wildly at their armour, then screamed again as their palms blistered where they touched the superheated metal.

They danced like death-worshippers at the end of the world, leaping and pirouetting in a hopeless effort to evade the inescapable agony. Those with skins of water or liquor reached for them and poured them over their faces, and their screams became wails as the liquid boiled against their flesh, scalding them all the worse. Some had been blinded, turning towards the dragon Aydhenia as her mouth erupted, leaving their eyes bloodshot and milky and sightless.

It was horror the likes of which I have never again seen. Men in their hundreds, still alive and yet begging for death, falling to the dirt and screaming for their mother or the Seamstress or even the dragon herself to end their torment.

Aydhenia's breath blazed so hot that even the air itself seemed half on fire. The mist had melted away, leaving behind the acrid smell of burning ether ripe in my nostrils.

Locan recovered first, but as he came to his feet, his skin was several shades paler than it had been only a few seconds ago. For once, he even seemed to be lost for words.

I looked to the sky, tracking the path of Aydhenia. Across the field, the Varnan reserve waited, Shanoch atop his horse and visible by his streaming red hair.

With another ear-piercing screech, Aydhenia dived, and the Varnans ran. As the mist cleared, I was able to see her more plainly. With astonishment, I noted that a tiny figure clung to the dragon's neck, impossible to identify at this distance, but unmistakable.

I grabbed Locan by the shoulder, pointing frantically. 'There's someone on her back!'

'What?' Locan squinted. 'Nah.'

I couldn't make out the figure either now, but I was sure of what I had seen. There had been something familiar about them. I was about to insist that Locan look again, when there came a battle cry and a thunder of feet from behind us.

We turned. Hosten, resplendent in gleaming plate armour and a helmet topped by a pair of gilded dragon wings, was running towards us from the city, backed by hundreds of Tulban reinforcements.

They fell upon the dying Varnans. It was not battle. It might have even been called mercy, if not for the bloodlust of the Tulbans. Swords and knives were drawn across Varnan throats in their hundreds, the Tulbans moving so fast through the dying that they were upon the next before the first man's head had even fallen.

'Leave half-a-dozen alive!' cried Hosten, shoving aside a wailing Varnan whose whole face had been flayed by Aydhenia's breath. He had never seemed a warrior, but his eyes were bright, fervent with victory.

Locan looked on wearing an expression of distaste. 'Bloody savages, the lot of them,' he muttered. He uncorked a skin, drank long, and offered it to me.

It was hard to disagree, but war makes beasts of all men, whether they choose to fight or are driven to flee. It was no worse than what the Varnans would have done to the Tulbans, I told myself. They just did not have a dragon.

A screech from the sky drew the eyes of the Tulbans away from their bloody work. Far overhead, Aydhenia glided, steering her way through the sea wind with lazy flaps of her wings. A trail of seabirds followed her path as if on instinct, and when she roared again the Tulbans raised their weapons in salute.

'*A dragon! A dragon!*' they roared together, until as Hosten leapt atop the walls to address them their cry became, '*Caradrahan! Caradrahan!*', cheering the name of Hosten's ancient line.

A wild-eyed Tulban grabbed Locan and I by the shoulders and gave us a vigorous shake. 'The young Mór prayed for a dragon to save us, and she came! Hail to the Mór! Hail Hosten!'

Before Locan could stop him, the man seized the wineskin from his fist and stumbled on, drinking deep as the victorious Tulbans saluted their Mór.

'Suppose I can let him have that,' said Locan. 'Thirsty work, victory.'

'You came,' I said, unable to think what else to say.

Locan grunted. 'Thought someone ought to save this shit-heap.'

Over the sea, I watched the distant shadow of Aydhenia bank into the clouds. I squinted through the fog. The figure was still there, hunched over the dragon's neck, a tiny black flea against the grey sky. As I stared after them, their head turned to look back towards the city. No hair streamed from their crown, but a dark cloak flapped in the high breeze, and a shadowy cowl obscured their face.

And as the Tulban celebrations went on around me, I realised where I had seen the dragon rider before. I had met only one person in Tulbar who dressed in black and covered their face.

It was Namma.

CHAPTER 20

The great chamber of Caradrahan Hall was considerably livelier than when Locan and I had last set foot inside on our first day in High Tulbar. Gaudy dragon tapestries adorned the walls. A fire blazed in every hearth, but with the press of people in the hall the warmth was such that they were hardly needed, for everyone in the city had been invited inside the Mór's fortress to celebrate the victory. A band played a jaunty tune, drowned out by the sound of so much lively conversation and frequent toasts to victory, Hosten, and of course the return of the dragons.

The Varnan besiegers had been vanquished, their unfinished siege weapons burnt to cinders. It was believed that Mór Shanoch had escaped Aydhenia's searing breath, but of the three traitor lords, Lord Danning was dead, Lord Ulleách had been so badly burnt by dragon breath that he could hardly speak for the agony, and Lord Arcalen had been found hiding in a tree. The latter two had joined the ranks of caged men decorating the city's western gate, their wounds and wails a warning to any Varnans who might still be in the vicinity. There had been no talk of mercy. The rules of war as applied in Guiland did not apply in Paleir. This was a land built on slavery and the scalding breath of dragons, too brutal for a Mór to be anything other than brutal in return.

Locan and I had retreated to a corner of the hall to watch proceedings. Perhaps in a measure of our mood, Locan was, by his standards, drinking moderately, limiting himself to ale.

'They've all changed their tunes,' said Locan, eyeing the dais where Hosten was receiving the effusive congratulations of his previously hesitant lords. 'Suppose that'll happen when your overlord has a dragon ready to burn your skin off.'

The mystery of Namma clinging to the dragon's back had plagued me ever since that morning. Those who had seen Aydhenia spoke of her only in tones of giddy wonder that they had lived to see the dragons return to Paleir, with no mention of any rider, Namma or otherwise. Meanwhile, the tale of Hosten leading the charge while Aydhenia spread chaos among the Varnan ranks had spread like wildfire, and nobody saw reason to doubt the obvious conclusion. The dragons had returned to serve the Caradrahans, and Hosten was the saviour of High Tulbar. Several of the repeated toasts to his rule had named him the future High King of Paleir, fated to conquer the isle and be the first man to hold the title in centuries.

'Are you sure you didn't see anyone on the dragon's back?' I asked Locan.

'For the third time, no,' growled Locan. 'Not Namma, not anybody.' He held himself like a tightly coiled spring, just one misplaced word away from violence. The war was over but the mystery of what had occurred in High Tulbar continued to occupy both of us. Through all the hardships he faced, Hosten had prevailed, but was the man who now stood to rule Tulbar unopposed and claim Paleir a marvel or a monster?

I could not believe I was the only person in the room who had seen the figure on Aydhenia's back. Could it really have been something I'd imagined in the heat and confusion of battle? None of the texts I had read mentioned anything about the Caradrahans actually riding the beasts. I might have asked Chatten, the closest person Locan and I had to an ally in the town, but the constable was dead.

The only other person in Tulbar I trusted was Shaliya. Not for the first time, I looked across the hall for a glimpse of her blonde hair, but she was not there. My gaze lingered on Roddin, wondering if Shaliya was currently locked up in the basement of the Dwarf and Dragon. He must have sensed my scrutiny, for across the room he turned to meet my eye with a black glare and I looked away. Slightly beyond him, I saw Ulf, surrounded by sycophants and wearing a smile that failed to reach his eyes. There was already word that he was planning to celebrate Tulbar's victory by finally hosting an event in the disused arena, perhaps even as soon as the following day.

'My friends!' A jovial voice greeted us, and Locan and I turned to see Huretio bearing down on us. He had lost a remarkable amount of weight, but otherwise was the same flamboyant figure he had always been.

He locked both of us in a bear hug and drew back wearing a grin as wide as the North Water. 'You are a sight for sore eyes, both of you!' He clamped his hands on my cheeks and kissed me wetly on the mouth, and then gave Locan the same treatment. His breath stank of brandy. 'Where have you been, eh?' he asked, his voice falling in mock reproach. 'Since we washed up here, I have been working every hour the Seamstress sends to restore the *Red Fiend* to seaworthiness, and neither of you have even offered to lend a hand!' He grabbed his chest as if he had been stabbed. 'It wounds me terribly. I was starting to think we might never see you aboard the *Red Fiend* again. She is better than ever. You could scour all the Endless Water and not find a ship so swift.'

I forced myself to return Huretio's smile, though I was still too preoccupied with the mystery of the dragon rider to fully embrace his good cheer.

'We've had troubles of our own,' said Locan. 'Did you miss that there's a war on?'

'Missed it? I have been working my hands raw to try and escape it!' Huretio displayed his palms, which were indeed covered in blisters. 'Do not tell me of your troubles, Locan A'Shadow – I know you have spent every hour drunk, while I have spent every hour worrying about what should become of us if the city fell.' Huretio puffed out his cheeks. 'Thank the Seamstress for dragons. I will have to find the Mór and give him my congratulations. The good news is that the *Fiend* is ready to sail with the morning tide, an hour before dawn.'

Locan and I caught each other's eye, and I knew we shared the same dilemma. We could escape High Tulbar and never think again of what had occurred here, and I sensed we were both ready to leave. But my certainty that I had seen a rider on Aydhenia's back, if only for a moment, had only added to my questions about Hosten's true nature. Was he my friend, with great hopes that would improve Paleir for the better, or was he a coldly pragmatic liar who had murdered his own father, an opportunist with no right to the acclaim he was now receiving from the people of High Tulbar? We might leave Paleir never knowing for sure.

'Do not both thank me at once,' said Huretio, though despite our lack of enthusiasm he was still smiling. 'We will be in Rameon within the turn of the moon, and I am sure you would rather be there than here – better weather, finer company, more beautiful women!' He slapped me hard between the shoulder blades. 'You will love it, Cetrik! Do not fear the sea – I swear on my mother's memory that this time no sorcerous storm will keep us from reaching Rameon.'

I offered him a weak smile. 'We'll be there in the morning.' I had still not worked out how I would get Shaliya aboard. If I went to the Dwarf and Dragon before dawn and brought her to the *Red Fiend* I did not think Huretio would refuse me. And I did not care where we went, just as long as Shaliya was with me. Huretio could drop us at the first friendly port we encountered, even Keystone.

'Be sure that you are,' said Huretio. 'The crew are that desperate to leave this place that I am not sure I will be able to persuade them to wait for you. The inns here are full of mites and I have not once seen a woman I wished to speak with. We will be glad to have a deck under our feet again.' He squeezed my shoulder and shook Locan's hand. 'I must find the Mór and then see about some supplies.' He wagged a warning finger at us as he departed. 'Do not be late.'

'Suppose that's that then,' I said to Locan as Huretio disappeared into the crowd. 'We're leaving.'

'Not before time.' Locan's face remained fixed in a scowl. He shook his head as if trying to dislodge something. He dropped his voice to a murmur. 'How sure are you that you saw a rider on the dragon?'

'Certain,' I said without thinking about it. 'Or at least, nearly certain.' After all that had occurred, I could not be certain of anything any more. Not a single other person had seen Namma atop Aydhenia.

Locan nodded. 'Remember when I walked away from you in Narlond?'

I glared at him, wondering why he would bring that up now. 'When you handed me over to my father and fled?' The months had only slightly dimmed my rage at Locan for that. If he had stayed, Javvian might still be alive.

Locan grunted. 'All right, stupid question. But what I was going to say is that I made a mistake. I shouldn't have done that, and I'm sorry.' By the lack of mockery in his voice he actually meant it. 'Well, I don't want to do the same thing here. I never believed you about the dragon, but you were right about that. So before we go, I want to know for sure what happened here.' He looked over the throng to where Hosten was in deep discussion with his lords. 'I don't like being fooled. And something here ain't right.'

I was torn. Part of me wanted to walk away with my illusion of Hosten intact. But I could not shake from my mind all I had discovered. Nobody had gained more from the dragon's arrival than Hosten, and he had not hesitated to claim the credit. Had he made a deal with Namma? How was it possible that the decrepit, confused hedge witch we had met had been able to master the dragon? All the breadcrumbs would lead somewhere if only I could pick up their path. 'What are you proposing?' I asked.

Locan stroked his chin thoughtfully. He seemed to have been thinking about this for some time. 'Would be bad for my reputation not to at least try and find out what's gone on. How's that going to look when you eventually write all this down? My first thought was to dig up the old Mór's body and see how he died.' He saw the look I shot him and immediately corrected himself. 'Until I realised what a shit idea that was. I could tell you whether a man had been murdered with a stiletto blade or a throwing knife, but I don't know the first thing about figuring out whether he died from fever or poison.'

'Not something I'd like to be caught doing either,' I said. Graverobbing was, and remains, one of the basest crimes in existence, a mockery of the Seamstress herself and with the risk of rousing a creature from the Underrealm.

'Agreed.' Locan's gaze was still fixed upon Hosten. 'Don't reckon there's anything more we can get out of Darry. Can't trace the assassin. I'm about ready to give up, get on the *Red Fiend*, and never think about this again.' He gave a wry smile. 'But, what if you're right?'

'Namma was riding Aydhenia,' I said again, as if I could make my accusation true simply by repeating it.

'Then the way I see it, the one thing we can do is go back to that shack in the woods. If that old crone really was up on that dragon, that's the only place we'll find an answer. Worst thing that can happen is we wake her up and frighten the life out of her.'

'Is that really the worst thing that could happen?' I said. 'What if she sets a dragon on us?'

Locan shrugged. 'Then at least we'll know.'

Namma's cottage was outside the walls. There had been no word about her fate in the aftermath of the Varnan invasion. I swallowed, relying on my curiosity to overcome my fear. It was the only lead we had. 'Tonight then?'

'Last chance, isn't it?' Locan dropped his voice. 'We should leave it a bit though. Don't want anyone wondering what we're up to creeping about the walls in the dead of night. Give it a few hours, once they're all too blind drunk to miss us.'

Across the room, Hosten said something, and the crowd around him burst into gales of laughter. 'We'll go at the hour of ghosts,' said Locan. 'That's when the lightweights will have rolled their way into bed and the diehards will just be getting started. Should mean we can sneak off without anyone noticing. Until then, let's enjoy ourselves, or at least pretend to.'

'And you'll be sober enough for this?' I asked.

'On this pisswater?' He hefted his tankard. 'I'll be the soberest man in Paleir.' He cackled. 'Best we circulate. Separately. Already looks like we're plotting something. Talk to Hosten; maybe he'll get drunk and say something incriminating. Meet later at the south gate.'

With no further ado, he wandered off into the crowd, hailing some men I recognised from the Merry Whale and claiming a fresh tankard from one of them.

Despite his insolence and unpredictable bursts of aggression, Locan never seemed to have too much difficulty making friends when he made the effort, particularly among sots, courtesans, and general ne'er-do-wells, not to mention all those who were dazzled by his reputation. I had never relished mass gatherings – I would sooner have sought out Hosten's library to see if there were any texts on dragons I'd not read. But given our friendship, it would look suspicious if I did not spend at least some time speaking with Hosten, though I did not relish the prospect. I set out across the room towards him.

I was briefly waylaid by Albart and Kelsi, full of the joys of victory.

'We can't thank you and Locan enough,' said a rosy-cheeked Albart, pumping my hand forcefully. 'You being here has brought the Whale back to life. I may even change the name – *the Merry Shadow*.' He laughed heartily. 'I'll be telling my grandchildren that Locan A'Shadow once drank in my inn!'

'And you can also tell them how he almost got killed while you slept on the bar and left your wife to defend him,' said Kelsi, though she was smiling as she said it, with one hand locked in Albart's while the other rested on her pregnant belly.

I spoke with them for a time, but embarrassed by their gratitude and with my mind still whirling with thoughts of Namma and Aydhenia, I soon made my excuses and began again to navigate my way through the press of bodies, narrowly avoiding a heavily inebriated Darry, who was being practically carried towards the doors by a pair of burly guards.

Two cousins I knew from defending the walls, Samm and Jeamon, beckoned me to join them and thrust a skin of something foul-smelling into my fist, which I only pretended to drink. I needed to have my wits about me.

'To the dragon!' exclaimed Samm, who was tall and thin, throwing his arm drunkenly around my shoulder. 'Our vigilant protector! My dad always said they would return!'

'Never thought I'd be so glad to see men broiled alive,' laughed Jeamon, leaping onto his taller cousin's back and planting a wet kiss on his cheek. 'To the dragon and Hosten fucking Caradrahan! Always knew he'd be a great Mór.'

Through the hall, the topic on every person's lips was how Hosten had succeeded where so many of his forebears had failed, completing the ritual that had invoked the dragon to fly to Tulbar's aid. Presumably, nobody had seen this magic first hand, but I imagined Lenard had done a decent job of spreading the tale.

By the time I reached Hosten, there was no opportunity to speak with him. His lords bellowed for silence as Tulbar's victorious Mór climbed atop a table, red-faced and smiling, and gradually the clamour of the hall faded enough for him to be heard. His success in battle had invigorated him. He stood taller, broader, and the sword at his belt now seemed to belong to him rather than having been given to him by mistake. There was an easiness to his smile that I could never recall seeing before. For all his ambition, this was the first time he appeared to believe that he was Tulbar's Mór, rather than a boy dreaming of the day that somebody would hand it to him.

Hosten raised a hand for silence. 'I mean to be brief—'

'As brief as Shanoch's invasion of Tulbar!' cried someone from the back, to much hooting and hollering.

Hosten grinned broadly, his face shining under the heat of so many lamps and hearths. He gave a soft cough, suddenly serious, and raised his tankard in a toast. 'To the dead.'

'*To the dead!*' came the reply. Thinking of Chatten, I joined the cry.

'It is on their sacrifice that this joyous evening is built, and I count my father among that number,' Hosten continued. 'I grieved his death, still do, and always will. I did not expect to become Mór for many years, perhaps decades, and it seemed at first a cruel unfairness that I should inherit in such circumstances.' The hall was deathly still, the only sound the crack and crackle of so many fires. Hosten pitched his voice a tone higher.

'But I see now the Seamstress's plan. Our prayers for deliverance were answered. If it was necessary that my father should die, then I will bear that sacrifice with grace, just as he would wish.'

Spontaneous applause and hollering broke across the hall like a rush of water through a dam. I searched Hosten's face. Did he speak from the heart, or were these the false words of a poisoner?

'Let the return of the dragon Aydhenia stand as a first monument to my rule!' cried Hosten over the tumult. 'A new age of victory and prosperity for all, made possible by the grace and glory of the dragon Aydhenia. To Aydhenia!'

'*To Aydhenia!*' came the reply. I half-heartedly joined in with the cry. I knew what I had seen. Namma, riding atop the dragon, contrary to every tale and every text.

'Aydhenia serves as a willing guardian to our kingdom,' continued Hosten. 'Let her favour be a boon to all of you, to every man, woman, and child in Tulbar. Know that you, *you*, embody this great realm just as richly as I do.' He punched his right fist against his left palm. 'One people, one kingdom, one island.' He lifted his tankard. 'My friends, I drink most of all to you! To Tulbar! To Paleir!'

'*To Tulbar! To Paleir!*' the crowd replied as one, and I joined them, drinking deep and finishing my ale. Better not to draw attention to myself by refusing to join the cry. Reclaiming the whole island seemed a life's work, but I had seen enough to know the wisdom of not underestimating Hosten. He had turned circumstances to his own ends, however little it may have been down to him. His ancestors had used their mastery over dragons to claim the whole island of Paleir, so why not him?

As the cheering died down, I continued to watch Hosten as he descended from the table. He had a vision for Paleir, but was it to be a place of peace where slavery was only a memory, or did his admiration for the Abomination King speak of a deeper, darker version?

Through the crowd, Lenard appeared at my elbow. 'Hosten wants to see you.'

As I had hoped. I followed Lenard through the press of people, and Hosten pulled me into a giddy embrace. 'My fellow prince.' He kissed me forcefully on the cheek and laughed merrily. 'You are a credit to your family, to your line.'

In spite of everything, the smile I gave him was genuine. No one had ever said that of me before. 'As are you, Lord.'

'Please keep calling me Hosten. Nobody else does.' He drew me closer and steered me away from the crowd towards the rear of the dais. Lenard and a pair of guards tried to follow, but he waved them to stay where they were, leading me to an alcove behind a dragon statue beneath one of the many tapestries. 'Will you return to Guiland?' he asked. 'It would suit me well to have a friend across the North Water. The Dreadveil recedes a little every month – it is my hope that we will have trade between our countries within just a few years.'

I hesitated. If I did not follow Locan, where else was there for me and Shaliya to go? 'Perhaps,' I said, noncommittally. Being surrounded by so many people celebrating the ascendancy of their realm had stirred a twinge of homesickness in me. But even if I returned to Guiland, I would never have what Hosten had here. 'I do not know what the future holds.'

Hosten gave a weary smile. 'None of us do. I am sorry for your troubles. I am familiar with the trials of family. Whatever you decide to do, you have my gratitude.' He extended his hand to me. 'You gave more than I should ever have asked from you. If not for your efforts when the wall collapsed, High Tulbar would have fallen. I'll not forget it.'

I shook his hand, blinking back faint tears. Nobody had ever thought to thank me as graciously as Hosten had. It was more appreciation than I had received from my family my entire life.

I hated that I could not shake my suspicion of him. 'It was nothing,' I said, with what I hoped was a modest smile.

'It was far from nothing, Cetrik.' Hosten gripped me by the shoulder. 'And whatever you may think, you would make a fine prince paramount. Once matters are settled in Paleir, you need only ask and you will have my support.'

I looked at Hosten, trying to detect what he meant by that. Unless I was mistaken, he was offering me military support to claim the position of prince paramount. Nobody had taken the crown by force in over six hundred years, not since the rise of Edrick Forgefound. Such a thing was impossible. Whatever I might think of my family, I would never raise an army against them. This was the other side of Hosten, the part of him that left me wondering whether he truly had murdered his own father to usurp the throne. He spoke of war against Guiland as if it were nothing.

I could not speak of it further. 'Congratulations on summoning Aydhenia,' I said, wishing to move the topic on as swiftly as possible. 'How did you do it?'

'I may be drunk, Cetrik, but I am not drunk enough to tell you that.' Hosten laughed. 'But be assured that I will use the power that has been granted to me to restore Paleir to the glory it should always have had. There will come a time when no man or woman or child on the island of Paleir may be owned by another, and that day has only been hastened by all you have done for me.' He threw an arm around my neck and pulled me close to whisper in my ear. 'You still hope to free Shaliya?'

I nodded. 'More than anything.'

'Then go to her. Go now.' My eyes followed Hosten's as he scanned the room. Across the hall, a red-faced Roddin was sculling from a horn of ale while an assembly of men cheered him on. Hosten looked to me with a glint in his eye. 'I'd say you have at least a few hours before he even thinks of turning for home. You have a passage arranged for tomorrow?'

I nodded. 'Huretio means to sail with the tide, an hour before dawn.'

Hosten's voice dropped a notch further. 'Then take her with you.' His eyes shone with conspiracy. 'I will square matters with Roddin. He will not like it, but he will suffer it.' He winked. 'He can hardly do otherwise after today.'

I looked at him, astonished. 'You're sure?' My heart sang a song of hope.

'Go now, before I sober up and change my mind!' Hosten laughed as he shoved me towards the door. 'My spirit is so light this night that I may give away half my kingdom before morning! Go!'

Before I could thank him properly, Hosten disappeared into the crowd.

I watched him leave, trapped somewhere between elation and confusion. Hosten was a man I would have been proud to call my brother, but there was a darkness in him. His easy praise of the Abomination King and the nonchalance with which he had suggested we go to war against my own family had chilled me to my core. As much as it pained me, I did believe he was capable of murdering his own father, and much else.

I looked briefly for Locan, wanting to make sure that he did not see me leaving. If I told him that Shaliya was coming with us, he would be so dead set against the idea that he might even tell Roddin. There would be difficulties, I knew – Huretio might be funny about a woman aboard the *Fiend*. But Shaliya would be free of Roddin, and she and I would be together.

To my relief, Locan was very much distracted, holding forth about some great adventure of years past to a gaggle of admirers. I would meet him later, but in that moment all I could think of was Shaliya. Despite my certainty that I had seen Namma atop Aydhenia, it was my fervent hope that our investigation of her shack would turn up nothing. Then we could leave and never think of Paleir again.

I slipped out of the door as a pair of men were returning from the privy, and raced across the courtyard and out of the gate towards the deserted town, making for the Dwarf and Dragon as if pursued by all the fires of the Underrealm.

I was out of breath by the time I arrived. I found a horse trough, dipped my face in and washed it thoroughly, ran my fingers through my hair a few times, straightened my tunic, then with a deep breath I stepped into the inn.

It was empty, of course, except for a willowy figure with her back to me. The sight of her caused the breath to catch in my throat. Her blonde hair was like a river of gold. Her figure like a goddess of desire.

Shaliya turned. The delight in her smile could have made me weep.

We did not say a word to one another. We raced across the inn and our bodies met like two clashing shield walls, in a heady embrace of craving and relief.

'I thought I might never see you again,' she said as we broke away. There were tears streaming down her cheeks. 'I thought you were going to leave without saying goodbye.'

'Never,' I replied. 'I'm leaving in the morning, and you're coming with me.'

She blinked. 'What do you mean?'

'Hosten said I should take you with me. I would have done it anyway; I've been planning it all along. I might have to square it with Huretio, but it will be fine.' The words were tumbling out of me in a rush. 'By the time Roddin finds out, we'll be far away from here. Hosten's said he'll settle matters with him once we're gone. It's all arranged!'

Shaliya stared at me with wide eyes, so close to me I could see my spellbound face reflected in them. 'Truly?'

'Truly!'

A slow smile began to creep across her face, so bright and blissful that it dazzled me. I was enraptured, my heart bursting with pride to be the man who would get to take her away from Tulbar and from Roddin. My mind spiralled with possibilities. What could Hosten think I would want with Guiland when I had Shaliya? We could go to Rintland and make love under the olive trees. We could go east to Ilssia where the sun glows red and the moon never fades from the sky.

'But we need to leave in the morning.' I held tight to her, afraid she would bolt at the prospect of such boundless freedom. 'Do you want to say goodbye to your father and sister first? We can go to them now?'

Shaliya pulled away to look at me, chewing her lip, and for a moment I thought she would balk. But then the smile returned, and she embraced me again, locking her lips against mine.

She pulled away. 'My dad can rot, but I should tell my sister – she'll worry otherwise, and she'll want to meet you. I'll tell her she needs to get away as well. We can go now, while everyone's at the castle.'

I was about to agree, until I recalled my and Locan's plan. I was so giddy I had almost forgotten. 'What hour is it?' I asked.

Shaliya turned to check the notched candle burning at the bar. 'Half gone the hour of graves. Why?'

I cursed under my breath. The night had passed faster than I thought. 'You'll have to go without me. There's something else I need to do.'

Shaliya looked at me doubtfully. 'Are there other girls you're planning on bringing with you?'

I panicked slightly at her tone, but then by her smile I realised she was teasing me. 'No.' I laughed. 'No, nothing like that.'

'What then?' Her eyes narrowed in suspicion. 'You're not being false with me, are you? The Mór has really given you permission?'

I nodded. 'I swear. It's just something I need to do.'

At the doubtful look on Shaliya's face, I broke. I told her

everything. My concerns about Hosten's admiration for the Abomination King. The attempt on Locan's life which he had blamed on Hosten. Darry's suspicion about Hosten's father. How I had seen Namma on the back of the dragon.

It was this fourth element that caused Shaliya to break her silence. She gave an incredulous laugh. 'Namma? You've met her, haven't you? She can barely climb her front step. Not even the Caradrahans have ever ridden a dragon.'

'I know,' I said. Dragons were not horses to be ridden. It was a truth known the world over. 'But I also know what I saw. That's why we're going to Namma's tonight to look around. We probably won't find anything, but—'

'You'll only scare the poor woman half to death,' said Shaliya. She frowned. 'Can't you just leave her be? She's been through enough.'

The look on Shaliya's face caused me to doubt the wisdom of our plan. The Namma I'd met had not been a well woman – who knew what distress we might cause her creeping around her home at night?

But I knew what I had seen. If there was any answer to be had before we left Paleir forever, I needed to have it. 'We won't wake her,' I said. 'She probably sleeps like a log.' I tried to make my voice sound reassuring. 'I know it's mad. I just need to be sure. What would you think if you'd seen an old woman riding a dragon?'

'I'd think I'd lost my mind,' said Shaliya. She folded her arms and glared at me. 'I'm not about to run away with a madman, am I?'

'I know how it sounds,' I said. 'Look, maybe it was just the pressure of battle. It was foggy. Maybe my mind was playing tricks on me.' I looked at her imploringly. 'I just... need to know? I swear after tonight I'll never mention it again.'

Shaliya shook her head. 'And the Mór wouldn't kill his father either. Darry's a drunk and a bloody liar. I never saw the old Mór in here, not once. I'd have told you that if you'd asked me.'

'It's only Locan who thinks that about Hosten,' I said. It was half true. 'Look, just meet me at the ship, please? Then we can sail away and never think about this place again.'

For a moment, I thought Shaliya was about to refuse me, but after a few doubtful seconds her face slowly began to brighten. 'All right,' she said, with some reluctance. 'Just don't give Namma a scare.' She stood on her tiptoes to kiss me. 'And don't make me regret this.'

CHAPTER 21

I left the Dwarf and Dragon with my feet feeling as if they were made of clouds. I had only to get through one likely fruitless task, and then Shaliya and I could be together. It was tempting to tell Locan that we should forget about it purely to please Shaliya, but I could not help my curiosity. I had to know how Namma had come to be atop that dragon.

I found Locan at the south gate. He looked no worse the wear for many hours more of drinking, and certainly in a better state than many of those returning from Caradrahan Hall I had passed on my way.

'Didn't see you in the hall,' he said by way of greeting. 'Thought I might find you puking your guts up somewhere from too much ale.'

'Just some last-minute nerves,' I said. 'Let's do this before I change my mind.'

Locan barked a laugh. 'Hiding somewhere shitting yourself, were you? It's just looking at an old witch-woman's hovel. Nothing to get your breeches in a twist over.'

The postern gate we left by was unguarded, the sentries presumably having abandoned their posts to join the celebration at Caradrahan Hall. Locan bent to the lock with a pair of knives, and in no time at all the door creaked open.

'I'd have made an outstanding thief,' he said, admiring his work. 'Been accused of it enough times.'

We walked away from the city, up through the woods towards Dragonwing Point. The night was still, and through the trees the low-hanging moon reflected off the glass-flat sea in a trail of light. Above the horizon, the Dreadveil waited, an ominous crimson glow against the charcoal clouds. It was certainly retreating though. It might take one hundred years, but one day the North Water would be open again.

The woods leading up to Dragonwing Point took on a different character by night. The darkness made it harder to navigate, slowing our pace as we watched our step to avoid hidden obstacles. Still no creature stirred in its depths, but this left the darkness open for the trees to come alive. Their bare boughs became arms reaching down to claim us, their gnarled, knotted trunks the faces of bent-backed watchmen, staring down in judgement at these strangers in their midst. A sea wind blew from the east, prickling the hairs on my skin and rustling the branches, setting my nerves on edge.

'Let's hurry this along,' said Locan, quickening his pace. 'Before you chicken out. You're shaking like a shitting dog.'

'It's cold,' I hissed. 'And keep your voice down.'

After ascending the slope, we emerged through the trees into the clearing over the cliff. Namma's ramshackle hut waited for us, ensconced in shadow like a cutthroat lying in wait. Its dragon weathervane spun in the ill wind, creaking ominously with every change in the breeze. Otherwise, all was still. Had we come upon the hut for the first time, I would have assumed it abandoned.

The light changed as a cloud passed across the moon, briefly bathing the shack in a cold glow. Something caught my eye before the sky shifted again and the darkness returned. I could see the gaunt silhouette of Namma's scarecrow guardian with the dented iron helm, but there had been something strange about how the light had caught the vegetable patch. Without a word to Locan, I crept from the path towards it.

'Where are you going?' he hissed. When I gave no reply, he followed.

I was halfway when the moon emerged again from behind a cloud, revealing what had become of Namma's vegetable patch.

Where there had once been a square of barren earth, there was now a vast hole, perhaps thirty yards in diameter and near the same again deep, surrounded by a barrier of dislodged earth. I stifled a gasp. A pit, as deep and ominous as the darkest dungeon. It was as if the fist of a god had broken from the heavens and sought to smite this patch of land from the world.

I hurried up the mound with Locan following me, any attempt at going unseen forgotten. We stared together into the depths, and Locan gave a low whistle. 'Someone's been busy.'

My hope that this would be an uneventful walk in the woods swiftly evaporated.

There was no possibility that Namma could have done this alone, but as I stared down into the pit, I realised that no hands of man could have dug such a chasm. The sides were uneven. The mounds of dirt were powdery, scattered, and uncertain beneath our feet. There were no shovels, no footprints, no sign of any human involvement at all. It did not seem as if something had dug down into the earth, but as if something had sponta-neously *burst* from the ground.

Locan pointed to the far side. 'Look.' He spoke as if at war against his senses, as if to acknowledge what he saw was to give it weight, to invite it into a world where it had no business in being.

Across the pit, a gulley split the heaped earth in two, leaving the ground so muddied and confused it was as if it had been trampled by a whole herd of horses. But there were no hoof prints, only deep gouges dug in the earth, with yet more forming a ladder that reached up the side of the hole. From where we stood, they almost looked like claw marks.

I turned to Locan, my mouth hanging open in disbelief. 'You don't think...?'

He pointed down into the hole. 'There's more.'

I had to squint into the darkness, but as the moon again appeared from behind a cloud I saw what Locan was referring to. At the very nadir of the pit lay a tangle of dead snakes. Hundreds of them.

'It's not possible,' I whispered, as if by saying it aloud I could make it so. This was Dragonwing Point, where Hosten had told us the Caradrahans had once buried their dragons. Deep claw marks up the side of the hole and dead reptiles at the bottom of it. One did not have to be adept in magic to deduce what creature had crawled out of this pit.

'I'd say it very much is,' said Locan. He sounded as sober as I'd ever heard him. 'I'm guessing whatever magic the Caradrahans of old used to summon dragons didn't involve batty old women living in the woods and holes in the ground. Did Hosten ever mention using Namma to summon the dragon?'

I shook my head. The Caradrahans of old had summoned living dragons. The sight before us was as if one had crawled out of a grave. 'Never.'

'Aye. Didn't think so. Guessing those dragons didn't slither out of the earth either.'

'It still saved High Tulbar though,' I pointed out. Perhaps it did not matter how the dragon had been summoned. 'And Hosten might not even know. He might have thought his ritual worked.'

Locan snorted. 'So she's just saved the city then flown off to let Hosten take the credit? You're smarter than that.' He peered down into the pit and sniffed. 'Bad smell to this.' He was right – the hole reeked of death, rank and wrong, cloying pungently in my nostrils. 'Let's take a look in the hut. Wherever Namma is now, I don't think she's inside.'

But Namma could not have done this. Elderly hedge witches who served foul-tasting tea and brewed love potions that did not work did not summon dragons from the bowels of the earth.

As if to correct me of my doubts, the first thing I realised about Namma's cottage was that the snakes that had previously hung above the door were gone. The interior was unchanged, the same haphazard jumble of wicker animals, rusted cauldrons, and dead squirrels hanging from the ceiling.

As if he already knew what he was looking for, Locan stepped to the table and whipped back the cloth from the cauldron that sat atop it. I was struck by a faint memory from our last visit – Namma moving uncharacteristically quickly to hide its contents from our eyes.

The interior was filled with water, with small shards of wood floating on the surface. Locan reached inside to claim a piece of timber dripping with water. Unmistakably, it had been carved in the shape of a ship's bow, complete with a miniature rail. Three tiny scraps of canvas swirled among the debris, like ruined sails floating amidst the ruins of a ship.

My heart dropped into the pit of my bowels. 'Namma... Namma caused the storm,' I whispered. This was magic beyond my understanding, beyond the capabilities of the wizards of Guiland, perhaps even beyond the blood sorcery of Solis Deadhand. We had washed up on the shore of High Tulbar because Namma had summoned us here. Whatever she was, she was no simple hedge witch. 'How?'

Locan's face was grim, gaunt with shadow from the moonlight that crept in through the hut's bare window. He did not speak for several moments. 'If I could tell you how, I wouldn't have wasted my time as an assassin. A better question might be "Why?"' In a fit of fury, he shoved the cauldron off the table, sending a cascade of water surging across the floor. He moved to the bed of blankets in the corner and flung them back, as if Namma might still be hiding there. A hundred instincts and emotions seemed to play across his face at once. 'We should leave,' he said finally. 'She's not here, and there's fuck all else we can do.'

'What about the dragon?' I asked. 'What about Hosten?' I was busy examining the construction of Namma's second scarecrow, but it offered no clues. The piebald rat from our last visit scurried atop its head and was now considering me with its dark, glassy eyes, its small pink nose twitching as it sniffed at me.

'Doesn't matter,' said Locan. He was already reaching for the door. 'We need to get to the *Red Fiend* and tell Huretio to start throwing up every bit of canvas. Whatever purpose Namma brought us here for, I don't reckon she's done with us yet.'

Before I could offer any disagreement, Locan opened the door. But we were both stopped in our tracks by the sight that met us outside.

A crowd of a men waited for us, cloaked and hooded against the night's chill. There were more than a dozen of them, many of them holding blazing torches against the dark.

My instinct was to remain where we were, but though Locan might fear Namma and her dragon, he had never been a man to retreat from a fight. He stepped out into the night. 'Who are you lot then? Been following us?' His lips twisted in a black grin. 'Thought you'd want to be enjoying your celebration. How about you just let us go and there'll be no trouble?'

A figure stepped forward from the group. He was slighter than the rest, of average height. He drew back his hood, and my heart immediately sank into my stomach.

'Hosten.' I greeted him, too shocked to think of anything more to say.

Whatever Locan and I had discovered, a part of me still refused to believe Hosten could have known anything about it. Hosten's eyes roved over the pit of dirt that had once been Namma's vegetable patch, but his face betrayed nothing. He met my eye with a peculiar expression, as if he were at once both proud and disappointed. 'Well,' he said with a slight smile, 'now you know.'

But I did not know. Not really. My mind was burning with questions, too many for me to give voice to. Who was this man who I had believed my friend? What dark bargain had he made to save his city?

'We know fuck all,' said Locan. 'Just that there's a big dragon-shaped hole out here and a cauldron full of model ship debris in there.' He pulled a knife from his cloak. 'Either you start explaining or I start slitting throats.'

Hosten gave a small laugh. 'Always so belligerent.' He was eerily calm, as if he had been expecting this meeting from the moment we arrived. 'There's really no need to be. I will gladly explain.'

I felt a rush of righteous anger. How could Hosten remain so irritatingly calm in the face of what we had learnt? If Namma had brought a dragon forth at Hosten's command, did that mean she had caused our ship to founder on the rocks at his command as well? I had fought for Tulbar because I believed in Hosten. How had he sat and played Pillars with me for so many hours while hiding this from me? He had betrayed me. There was no other explanation. 'You never summoned the dragon,' I said. 'Namma did.'

Hosten gave a small laugh. 'Cetrik, what does it matter? The dragon will serve me. How it came to pass is irrelevant.'

'What about the storm?' I countered. 'We nearly drowned! Was that you as well?'

I was expecting a denial, but Hosten gave a regretful nod. 'I'm sorry. Namma and I agreed that we needed you in Tulbar.

She said she could achieve this, but my mind was elsewhere and I never thought to ask how.' He put his hand over his heart. 'It was never, *never*, my intention for either of you to be harmed. Please accept my apology.'

I watched him carefully. There was no trace of a lie.

'Is there any need for this, Lord?' asked one of the men, pulling back his hood. It was Ulf, the thuggish slave-master. His dark eyes glittering with malice as they roved over me and Locan. 'Let's just take them and be done with it.'

Beside me, I felt Locan tense. I readied myself to reach for my sword.

'No,' said Hosten. His stern tone brooked no argument. It was a measure of his new standing among the Tulbans that none complained. 'It began when Bastane arrived in High Tulbar.'

Of course. I recalled Hosten's words the first time we met. '*Ever since I heard Bastane's tale, it has been my distant hope that you might find your way to High Tulbar.*'

The realisation hit me like a gut punch. 'You needed us to get the dragon scale,' I said.

Hosten beamed. His manner was as if none of this mattered, as if it had all been a simple misunderstanding that he would now correct. 'Indeed. I knew the moment we met that you had a mind to be reckoned with, Cetrik. I needed somebody who could creep into the dragon's lair and claim a scale without being detected.' He glanced at Locan. 'And perhaps the only man alive capable of such a feat is standing in front of me. And thanks to Bastane I knew he would be sailing south, past High Tulbar.'

He was trying to flatter me – and Locan. Our arrival in Tulbar could not have been more convenient for Hosten. I cursed myself for not putting together the pieces sooner. 'And you always knew where it could be found.' This was a guess, but there seemed no other conclusion – there had been an agreement between Hosten and Namma from the beginning. 'Why the deception?'

'Because if I had told you I knew where to find the scale, the natural question would have been why I did not send one of my own men to claim it. Whereas if I recruited you to find it for me...' Hosten shrugged. 'I could not take any chances. Once again, I apologise – there was no time; such deceptions were necessary.'

'Piss on your apologies.' Locan spat. It landed several feet short of Hosten, but the message was clear. 'The fight on the beach. That was your doing as well.' His eyes flicked to where Ulf was standing. 'This supposed conflict between you and the Keykeepers. Load of goblin-shit.'

With a jolt, I recalled the agitated conversation between Ulf and Roddin we had come across outside the Dwarf and Dragon. The conspiracy had been staring us in the face, and I had been too blind to see it.

The satisfied smile Hosten wore told me that Locan had found the mark. The noble image I had crafted of our host was coming apart at the seams.

'I needed leverage,' said Hosten. 'The Keykeepers and I came to an understanding. I had not reckoned with your... obstinacy. Fortunately, Cetrik was eager to help me.'

I could see the other reason Hosten had crafted that particular lie – the desperation of his plight had moved me. Without that, I might never have talked Locan into helping him. How many other things had he lied to me about?

'You killed your father.' The words tumbled out of me before I could stop myself. 'You poisoned him and made it look like a fever.' When Danning had made the same accusation, Hosten's face had blanched as if he had seen a ghost. How I had I not realised then?

Hosten's smile faltered. 'A lie,' he said unconvincingly. 'I loved my father.'

Locan gave a bark of laughter. 'For a dishonest, devious sack of goblin-shit you're a lousy liar. Was never sure about that until just now.'

But Locan was wrong of course. Hosten was far from a lousy liar. From the moment of our arrival, he had played us both for fools. Even when there had been so many reasons to doubt him, I had never imagined the scale of his deception.

Hosten's eyes flashed with fury. 'How would you know? Who told you?'

Uneasy glances passed between the men accompanying him. The moon had reappeared from behind a cloud, revealing their features. Some of the guards I knew, and Grenick the marshal, and to my surprise Roddin was at the rear, watching me with sneering hatred. There was someone else with him, and as the light shifted I realised that a sack had been dropped over their head and their hands were bound behind their back.

'Is it true?' asked Grenick. His shock seemed genuine. The grizzled marshal would have once been the old Mór's ally.

'It doesn't matter,' said Hosten. His voice was harsher now, cruel in a way I had not heard before. He glowered at Locan. 'If you accuse me of such again, I will have both of you cut down where you stand.'

Locan's lip curled in a black grin. His knife flashed quick as silver through his fingers. 'Try it.'

Hosten's smile was as sharp and curved as a sickle blade. 'I had hoped we might resolve this peaceably. You are still free to leave High Tulbar with the tide, if that is what you wish, but I ask you to refrain from any further accusations.'

'The assassin was your doing as well,' said Locan.

Hosten gave an untroubled shrug. 'I admit it. As soon as the Varnan attack came, I sent him after you. Rash of me, but there was no question of him actually harming you. I hoped it might motivate you to remove Shanoch for me. I was not certain whether the scale would work.'

'How did you know we were here anyway?' asked Locan. 'Have you been following us?'

I had been wondering the same thing. Until Hosten's surprise that we knew about the fate of his father, I had assumed Darry had informed on us. The figure Roddin was restraining tried to break away from him, then reacted with a squeal as the innkeeper drove his fist into their stomach. I froze. Wrought with pain though it was, I recognised that voice.

Hosten raised an eyebrow. 'I have been watching you both ever since you came to High Tulbar. It grew more difficult when you managed to get yourself thrown out of the Dwarf and Dragon, but there are always willing men.' His cold smile sent a spike of dread through me. 'Willing men, and unwilling women. Cetrik, you should be more careful with whom you share your secrets.'

He gestured behind himself. The men parted, and Roddin stepped forward, roughly pulling the sack from the head of his struggling captive.

Shaliya, shivering from the cold in the same thin dress and apron she had worn at the inn. There were tears in her eyes, but as soon as the hood came off she defiantly spat in Roddin's face. He flushed red with anger, then pulled his hand back and slapped Shaliya across the face.

My sword was halfway out of my scabbard when Locan stepped behind me and grasped me around the throat. 'You goblin-fucking idiot,' he hissed. 'You've screwed things up enough already. Don't go getting yourself killed over her as well.'

Reluctantly, I let my blade slide back into its scabbard. I would free Shaliya, but I could not help her if I was dead. She looked at me, and my fist clenched as I realised what they had done to her. There were bruises under both eyes, and a fresh, weeping burn where they had branded her other cheek with a slave mark, and several more around her neck. Her hair was wet where they had thrown a pail of water over her when she fainted. She had not given up my plans easily, but in the end she had succumbed.

'Why, Hosten?' I asked, hating how weak I sounded. 'What could be worth this?'

'*What could be worth this?*' Hosten gave a bitter laugh. 'Cetrik, I may have deceived you, but I have never made any secret to you of my goals. What lengths would I not go to for the sake of my kingdom?' His green eyes glittered like two cold shards of jade. 'My father would speak long into the night of the days when our family ruled Paleir as high kings, but he had not the strength to reclaim those days for himself. The words of a man who was half-dead himself, lingering in life but without the will to use it. If he had stayed another year in power, it would have been as good as if this city had fallen into the sea. Our land has been dying ever since the day dragons departed, a carcass to be picked clean by the lesser beasts. It was only our name – Caradrahan – that men still respected, just enough fear still left in it to hold our kingdom together.'

Hosten had spoken to me of his wild ambitions, but there was something new now, an unsettling fervour in his gaze and the way his whole being seemed to tremor with excitement. I recalled his words to me in defence of the Abomination King: '*Sometimes disagreeable deeds may achieve righteous ends.*' This was where that credo led: the torture of Shaliya, the murder of his father, whatever dark bargain he had made for the sake of having a dragon, all necessary sins justified by the greater goal of reclaiming Paleir.

Hosten spoke on. 'I saw the seeds of trouble stirring, but my father was blind to them. After my mother died, he lost himself in drink. I knew Shanoch would move against us eventually. It kept me awake at night – would there still be a Tulbar left for me to rule one day? There were too few of us, with too little loyalty to the Caradrahan line and too little will to defend ourselves. Until three years ago, when from the depths of my despair sprung hope.'

A skin-flaying shriek lit up the night, sending seabirds nesting on the cliff scattering into the air. All eyes turned to the sky as a shadow passed overhead, flapping its great wings, and a powerful downdraught of cold air nearly swept me off my feet.

Hosten's satisfied smile sent a chill through me. 'Ah. Dragons have the most excellent timing.'

CHAPTER 22

Men stepped back as the dragon Aydhenia descended to the bluff, her scales as blue and beautiful as a sky of summer. Her golden eyes watched Locan and I with slow regard, her flaring nostrils bathing us in warm air.

But this beast was not Aydhenia. Aydhenia's eyes had swirled with intelligence and cold menace, eyes that a man would have willingly become lost in even as her scalding breath tore the skin from his bones. These eyes merely glowed, and as I watched, fireflies were drawn dancing towards their light. The scales shone blue, but they were not cobalt nor sapphire nor summer skies. Only blue, a blue a man might buy in any dyer's shop between here and Rameon. In patches, the scales were pale, new skin regrown over dead flesh and old bones. The air surrounding Aydhenia had swum with the heat of her presence, but the aura of this dragon was cold, almost corpselike. Even the way it was standing was wrong, its two feet wide and clumsy, its wings opening and closing awkwardly.

And from its back, a figure slipped to the ground. A figure I knew.

Namma shuffled towards us, swathed in the same black cloak she had worn when Locan and I had met her last.

Her mouth opened beneath her cowl, and I did not recognise the voice that came out. Even at her most cranky and confused, Namma's had been tinged with well-meaning warmth. This voice tasted like cold earth and maggots. The rasping voice of the grave.

'Boy.' She addressed Hosten. 'What is going on?'

'I came upon them exploring your cottage,' said Hosten. 'They know everything. Or almost everything.'

Namma's black beady eyes roved over me. She made a rough, rasping noise in her throat, somewhere between appreciation and irritation. 'Of course. That damnable Harkken blood of yours. You saw through my glamour and sighted me atop my creation, which led you here.'

'Who are you?' asked Shaliya, her brow knitting in confusion. I could hardly bring myself to look at her. I had believed we were going to flee Paleir together, but all I had brought her was agony and despair. 'Namma—'

'Namma was a helpless worm,' spat the woman. She had still not removed her cowl, but she was standing straighter, the stoop in her back all but gone. 'She wept when I took her magic away from her, what little she had. I buried the wretch beneath the floorboards. Three years, three long years putting on a show for the halfwits who came seeking pills and potions, rambling about reading the tea leaves and hunting squirrels and watching the heavens. I fed them tinctures of boiled piss and rotten vegetables and they thanked me for it.'

Locan had been quietly staring at Namma and her dragon ever since they had landed. The creature's presence was unsettling, like looking into a mirror and seeing someone else's face looking back at you. He was still holding his knives, but he was no longer twirling them through his grip. 'Who are you then, witch? Which piss-riddled hole of the Underrealm did you crawl out of?'

'She is my ally,' said Hosten, not troubling to hide his pride. 'That is all you need to know. With her dragon, I will make myself High King of Paleir.'

Whatever deal Hosten had made with this woman, it would be his ruin. This nameless witch was as dangerous as a nest of vipers.

'Is that what she told you?' sneered Locan. His pupils were small and focused, like those of a predator waiting to strike. 'Who are you, sorceress? Quite a performance you put on, with all your potions and creatures and awful tea.'

'Men see what they expect to see.' The woman's voice ought to have been muffled by her cowl, but her speech was rich and clear as a bell. 'At last, the indignity of that pretence is at an end.'

'You said you wore the cowl because the fever left you scarred,' whispered Shaliya. All the colour had drained from her face. 'I believed you, and all the time you were—'

'I was the most astonishing thing that ever happened in your miserable life.' The woman's voice cut across her like a flaying knife. 'If you knew who I was, you would fall to your knees in worship, instead of weeping over that stupid, decrepit woman.'

'So tell us then,' said Locan. 'Take off that cowl so Hosten can see the creature he's made his deal with.'

'A deal for the sake of Paleir,' said Hosten. For the first time, he appeared uncertain. 'She will support my claim.'

The woman laughed, a high screech like steel scraped on granite that sent a tendril of pain between my ears. 'Yes, you will have your claim. I could drag this island to the deepest fathoms of the North Water, but as you have served me well I will let you have your pitiful ambition.'

Her heavily wrapped hands began to slowly unwrap the cowl, foot upon foot of black wool unwinding to the floor.

'I am the thirteenth daughter of a thirteenth daughter, born under a black star with the fingers of an ill wind grasping at my swaddling. My parents were farmers, scratching a living from the thin soil of the Homeless Hills. Always pregnant and always starving. I watched eight of my siblings fall to fever and famine and raiding parties. When I was three, my father forced me to drown a sack of kittens, and when they rose from the water hale and healthy, he tried to drown me instead. They found him face down in a horse trough with a black goat horn shoved through one eye and out the other.

'I ran away when I was nine, searching for answers, for somebody like me. I brought a girl back to life in Arinton, and instead of thanking me her kin chased me from their village. Even before I opened my mouth, folk seemed to intuit what I was and cringe away from me in fear.'

Lengths of black fabric continued to unspool. A patch of mottled skin the colour of curdled milk briefly appeared beneath the cloth as the woman spoke on. Hot breath emanated from the huge nostrils of her dragon servant.

'When I was thirteen, my master came for me. He claimed me as a daughter, took me away from this island to somewhere my gifts would be celebrated rather than feared, a kingdom to be made in our own image where we could turn our talents to defeating the last enemy: death itself. We became lovers, our essences tangled together in a wondrous storm of magic, mortality, and eternal life. We took our knowledge past the edge of existence, to the Underrealm and beyond. We built a kingdom of learning, a paradise outside the misery of peasants and the petty squabbles of kings.

'Until they took it from us.' The woman's voice cracked with bitterness. Cloth continued to unfurl, so much of it pooling on the ground that it barely seemed real. There was a face beneath it, pale as death and with eyes like pits of fire. A burning white eye forced me to meet her gaze and I nearly recoiled at the hatred that blazed within. 'Men like you, who stole my master from me. Jealous lords who believe all the earth belongs to them and yet dare to name my master *Abomination*.'

The last of the cloth fell away. The woman's face was cadaverous, bones threatening to burst through pale, vein-webbed skin. Cheekbones so hollow that shadows pooled within them, hair like brittle brown grass, and flesh that drooped from a skeletal jaw like lumps of sour milk.

And at last, I knew who this woman was.

'You are Halagrim,' I said, as a mixture of wonder and terror coursed through my veins. 'The Deathmistress. The Necromancer of Sevash. The first disciple of the Abomination King.'

Her cracked lips stretched in a hideous smile. '*More* than a disciple. His closest confidante, his staunchest ally, the nearest he knew to an equal in all the world, our fates so tied together that when he fell, my magic fell with him. I had barely the strength to return across the North Water to the land of my birth, where just enough remained of what I had been to claim Namma's identity for my own.

'And for almost three years, I have been waiting, preparing for the day when I would rise again and restore myself to the throne of Sevash at the side of my master.' Her lips peeled back in triumph, revealing two rows of yellow teeth filed to sharp points and a tongue forked like a lizard's. 'With blood and toil, snakes and dragon scales, I am strong enough to ride across the water on wings of shadow, and with my army of the dead I will tear down my master's cairn and bring him back from death, and once more our fires will burn in the towers of Sevash.'

'A touching tale,' said Locan, pretending to stifle a yawn. The weight of his feet shifted, so imperceptible that had I not been standing beside him I might not have noticed. 'Drags a bit though. That's the thing about magickers. You're all so damn dramatic.'

Two daggers flew from his hands, half-a-second apart, and

came within a handspan of Halagrim's face before they fell from the air, their blades bent and buckled. The dragon's nostrils flared with steam, hot enough to melt steel, staring at Locan with its lifeless eyes as if daring him to try again.

'And you, Locan A'Shadow, you delivered the scales to me,' said Halagrim with a black laugh. 'I would have claimed them myself, once I was strong enough, but Hosten's quick thinking saved me the trouble.'

'I knew Shaliya would send you to Namma,' said Hosten, looking at Halagrim like a child in search of a mother's approval. 'Halagrim and I have agreed an alliance. She will claim Midding, and with the aid of the dragon I will claim Paleir.'

'You're mad,' I said, my voice shaking. I had known of Hosten's ambition, understood it, but I had never imagined the depths to which he would sink. 'Hosten, the Abomination King does not have *allies*.' Panic raced in my bloodstream. If Halagrim succeeded, the Abomination King would rise again. Because of what Locan and I had done. 'Do you know what she is? The things she has done?'

'I would have been mad *not* to do it,' said Hosten. 'Cetrik, these are the quarrels of another age. You do not need to cling to the grudges of your ancestors.' Bizarrely, he was smiling. 'Remember what I said? Help me take Paleir, and then Guiland can be yours. We can bring about a golden age, you, me, and the Abomination King.'

'Never,' I spat. The promises of Halagrim were poison. 'I'd sooner die.' I looked to the Tulbans assembled behind Hosten. 'Is this what you want?' I asked them. They were simply standing there, unmoved. 'Is this the man you want as your lord? You would ally with the Abomination King?'

'No man of Midding ever gave me trouble like you have,' said Roddin with a sneer. 'Guiland or Midding, it makes no difference to us, as long you both stay on your side of the water.'

'These are difficult times,' said Lenard. A distasteful look came over his face as his gaze flickered past Halagrim. 'And a resurgent Guiland able to reclaim the breadth of old Karvved would be dangerous to Paleir. I support Hosten's decision.'

Ulf was nodding. 'Hear, hear. The Dreadveil is fading. We've already had you and that priest passing through here. How long before there are more?'

I could only stare at these men in disgust. They knew nothing of what a resurgent Midding might mean for Paleir. It was only the vigilance and sacrifice of my countrymen, over hundreds of years, that had confined the Abomination King's ambitions to Midding.

Locan pulled his silver blades from behind his back so fast that I barely saw him move. The knives whistled through the air, and stuck in the side of the dragon's face with a violent hiss. It had thrown its head in front of its mistress. The wounds shrieked and steamed, but the beast made not a sound. Black blood oozed like oil from its wounds, pooling on the ground and bubbling as the grass began to melt.

Locan had already pulled a third set of knives free, and was now running towards Halagrim.

'Enough,' said Halagrim.

The necromancer produced something from her pocket, then took it between her finger and thumb, and with a crack and a scream Locan fell to the ground, his leg bent horribly at the knee.

With dark amusement, Halagrim held up the object in her hand so we could see. A small grey figure made of clay, with several strands of dark hair pinned to its scalp and one of its legs bent between Halagrim's fingers. 'I had my rodent friend claim some of your hair when you first visited my cottage,' she said. 'Cheap folk magic, but in the right hands...'

She was leaning against the dragon's neck for support. Though she was not as infirm as she had pretended, even this small show of magic seemed to cost her. Perhaps realising this, Locan dived into the shadow cast by the Tulbans' torches.

He appeared behind Halagrim with another knife raised and ready to open her throat, but as the silver blade descended, the necromancer jerked the poppet again, and Locan's wrists snapped like twigs, his knives falling uselessly to the ground as he overbalanced on his one good leg, his face twisted in a grimace of agony.

'Even in Sevash, your legend reached our ears, Locan A'Shadow.' Halagrim bent down and pocketed the dagger into her cloak. 'Cruel how time can ravage even the most talented killer.'

'You've got nothing left,' he hissed, gritting his teeth against the pain. 'You can hardly even hold onto that poppet you're carrying. Cetrik, gut her.'

Locan's words shook me to action, and I pulled my sword free. But within a few purposeful strides towards Halagrim, her resurrected dragon turned its neck and stared down at me with its nostrils flaring, daring me to take another step. I halted, fixed in place by the blistering steam emanating from the beast's snout.

'Wise of you,' said Halagrim. 'As you have shown more sense than the forebears who sought to challenge my master, I will allow you to remain in Tulbar.'

'You can't win,' hissed Locan, still on the ground cradling his shattered wrists. 'The Abomination King is *dead*. As dead as the dragons. Buried under a thousand tons of stone.'

Halagrim's smile was terrifying. 'But the dragons are not dead, Locan A'Shadow. And that which dies does not always stay dead, as you will soon learn.'

Halagrim reached into Locan's cloak and pulled free one of the remaining dragon scales, small and shiny and blue. Wordlessly, she held it up to the sky, turning it over and over between her fingers, letting the pale gleam of the moonlight reflect in its cobalt depths. She crushed it in her fist, scattered the particles to the air, and blew them down the hill towards Tulbar. We watched as they withered on the breeze, their light blinking out over the city like a cloud of dying fireflies.

There had been no opportunity yet to bury the dead. They had been piled haphazardly against the walls, Varnan and Tulban alike, two divided peoples united in death. So many had perished in the breath of Halagrim's dragon that these piles of corpses became hillocks, in some places half the height of the wall. And as we stared down the hill, they rose.

They came with intestines leaking from their wounded bellies and with hideous burns where the dragon's steam had touched them, limping on shattered legs and shambling on bare feet from which scavengers had claimed their boots. Thousands and thousands of them, shadows in the night, streaming up the hill towards Dragonwing Point like believers summoned to worship. They crashed and stomped through the trees, a nightmarish collection of pale limbs and scalded flesh.

I looked for Hosten's reaction. The Mór of Tulbar's smile was fixed in place, becoming more of a grimace with every passing moment.

Atop Dragonwing Point, the dead halted, waiting, their grime-streaked hair flapping around their blank faces in the breeze. Some were so badly burnt that they were barely recognisable as human, just effigies of puckered misshapen flesh.

I had heard from veterans of Sevash the horrors the Abomination King had sent against them, wrorcs and winged goblins and other hideous half-breeds, but this was worse, a horrifying mockery of life. Weakened though she claimed to be, with a single dragon scale Halagrim had turned back death itself.

'The army that will rebuild Sevash,' said Halagrim. I recalled Shanoch's words, the allusions to blighted crops and dying children that had plagued Varned. Yet more of Halagrim's fell sorcery, the curses that had coaxed Shanoch to march his army across Paleir to where the witch could turn his dead to her own dark purposes. Her pale eyes were alive, filled with reverence at her own power. She pointed eastward, towards the haze of the Dreadveil and the broken towers of her master's capital. As if drawn by a single string, her dead army began to move.

In their hundreds, without fear, they ran to throw themselves from the cliff. Pale, lifeless flesh splashed into the black water like a storm of hailstones, throwing up spray and turning the sea into a raging tempest. I watched in horror as the dead surfaced, and, thrashing their senseless limbs, began to swim.

Nobody spoke a word. The only sound was the hot, steady breath of the dragon. Hosten was pale with shock, frozen in horror at what he had unleashed on the world.

Halagrim was struggling to pull herself up onto the back of her dragon. Her show at Namma's infirmity had been no act, and her stiff feet kept tangling in her robes.

'Old woman,' groaned Locan from where he lay helplessly on the earth. Pain was etched across his face. 'Crone! I need to tell you something.'

Halagrim turned. 'What?'

Locan worked his one good leg to manoeuvre himself to one knee. He should have passed out from the pain. All that kept him conscious was his sheer, bull-headed obstinacy, his refusal to let anybody else have the final word. 'I'll have to whisper it to you. It's about your master.'

Halagrim hesitated, but after a moment she retreated from the dragon and knelt beside Locan, a scowl fixed upon her ruined face.

He looked up at her, baring his teeth somewhere between a grimace and a smile. He grasped her cloak and pulled himself up to speak in her ear, then said loud enough for everyone to hear, 'Just wanted to see you try and get those old knees to bend.' He spat a thick glob of blood and phlegm in her eye.

With a screech of rage, the necromancer struck him in the

face and got creakily to her feet, while he lay on the ground laughing through his pain.

'There were others like you who came to Sevash,' said Halagrim, 'full of courage and useless pride, but they learnt their place in the end. Clearly that is something I will have to teach you as well.'

She returned to her dragon, and with a groan of effort she hauled herself up onto its back. The necromancer steered its great head towards Locan, and for a moment I thought she was going to order it to unleash its breath upon him, until the beast bent its neck and picked Locan up in its jaws.

At a whispered order from Halagrim, the dragon kicked its legs and pushed off from the ground. It hovered some twenty feet above the earth, the downdraught of its wings forcing men to cover their faces as they stared up at this monstrosity of dark magic.

Halagrim called down to Hosten. 'You should come with me, to Sevash.' The cold callousness in her voice would have caused most to refuse her without hesitation, but Hosten was staring up at her and the dragon in rapt wonder, dreaming perhaps of the day when he might strike such fear into the hearts of men. 'See the rebirth of my master with your own eyes. You will have much to discuss.'

Hosten's eyes shone with desire. 'Do you suppose?'

Halagrim showed a bone-chilling smile of sharpened teeth. 'A meeting between two rulers to discuss a formal alliance. What could be more proper? And you should be suitably rewarded for your assistance.'

Hosten walked towards the dragon as if in a trance. I almost called out to him, but by his dazed expression I saw it would do no good. For four centuries, no man who walked into Sevash had left there as he had entered. Hosten would learn the price of his ignorance the hard way. The dragon lowered its neck, and

Hosten scrambled up onto its back, taking a place behind Halagrim.

He waved to his followers. 'I will be gone no longer than necessary. Make whatever preparations are required in my absence. When I return, we ride to war, to reclaim all that was taken from us.'

Lenard called up to him. 'Lord, what do you want done with these two?' He gestured to me and Shaliya, still bruised and bloodied at Roddin's feet. At the sight of her, my heart broke all over again. We had missed our chance to leave High Tulbar, and now we would pay the price.

Hosten looked down at me, something like sadness in his eyes. 'Cetrik, this was our chance to build something better than what came before. Just remember that it was your choice, not mine.'

Sometimes, I wonder what might have happened if I had realised sooner what Hosten intended, how far he was willing to go. There are countless tales I could have told him of the Abomination King that might have made him reconsider his foolish infatuation, maybe even inspired him to cast Halagrim aside.

But in my heart, I know it could never have been so. Lords beyond counting have dreamt of greatness, of writing their names across the history books in letters bold as blood. There are scant few among that number who have realised their wild ambition without succumbing to the pervading temptations of corruption and avarice. Hosten had been lost the moment he dreamt of becoming the High King of Paleir.

I could have called out to him with all the multitude of reasons that he was making a mistake, or with a final plea that Halagrim needed to be stopped, but I saved my breath. It was too late.

'Shaliya is Roddin's to deal with,' Hosten went on. Even his objection to slavery had been false. He had told me what he knew I wanted to hear. He looked to Ulf. 'You will need more fighters for the games tomorrow. You may have Cetrik.'

So, Hosten was gifting me to Ulf. Evidence enough as to how little our supposed friendship had meant to him. I could not be sure what awaited me in the arena, but I could make a fair prediction. I recalled the pit of goblins and how it had teemed with bloodlust and hunger. A dozen of them would tear the skin from my bones in seconds.

'Fly,' said Halagrim, and with furious wingbeats and a sky-rending shriek the dragon launched itself into the air, bound for Midding, for Sevash and the tomb of the Abomination King.

CHAPTER 23

As soon as Halagrim's resurrected dragon had soared into the night, Hosten's men descended upon me. My blade was pulled from my grasp, and the weight of their numbers forced me to the ground. All I could do was cover my head and groin as they laid into me with their heavy boots. Roddin, of course, could not resist the opportunity to get in a few kicks of his own.

By the time they had bound my hands and set about dragging me back to High Tulbar, I was bruised and battered out of my wits. Shaliya cried out for me, but when I tried to call back to her I merely coughed up a mouthful of blood.

'Put him in one of the pits,' I heard Ulf say from somewhere.

At these words, I truly believed I was being carried to my doom. I had seen the deep hollows in which the Tulbans held their captured goblins, with their grasping fingernails and ugly, hairless features. I had smelt the eye-watering filth, witnessed the way that they broke into a frenzy when a piece of meat was dangled above them, kicking and gouging at one another to be the first to sink their piercing yellow teeth into the flesh. That was to be me, a pile of bones, the rest of me sitting in a goblin's belly, my heart and organs ripped apart.

I craned my neck to see the crumbling walls of the arena rise up before me, and broke out in a cold sweat. Goblins hate men, particularly our hair, for they have none of their own. I had seen beggars in Keystone who had survived being scalped, with only the back and sides of their hair remaining, the rest ripped away to display the pale, scarred skin underneath. Given the hunger of those I had seen, at least they might feed quickly and the agony would perhaps be brief. If not, the four-fingered folk would start by plucking out every one of my hairs, and only then would they begin to feed. They would begin with the legs and arms, allowing me to watch myself be devoured.

As we crossed the dry dirt of the arena towards the goblin pits, I thrashed against my bindings and let my feet drag in the dirt, but the four men restraining me paid my struggles no heed. They held me over a pit, and I screwed my eyes shut so I would not see the horrific end that waited for me.

I hit the ground hard, the impact bouncing my head off the clay and knocking the wind out of me. Above, the guards were laughing. 'This one's empty!' called down one of them as his fellows hooted. 'Don't worry, you'll be goblin gunk soon enough.'

I was in an empty pit, though the ground was littered with bones, both human and goblin, all covered in hundreds of tiny bite marks.

My captors departed, their laughter ringing in my ears. As soon as they were gone, I began an attempt to scrabble out of the pit, but my feet could gain no purchase on the steep sides, and my body ached from the beating I had taken at the hands of Hosten's men.

Realising my efforts would be in vain, I sank down against the wall, cradling my aching head. They had not even left me any water. But why would they waste water on a dead man? Tomorrow, I would be given to the goblins for the amusement of the people of High Tulbar, people who only the day before I had fought to save.

Hosten had no idea of the forces he was meddling with. The children of Paleir did not lie awake at night like the children of Guiland, afraid that the fell creatures of Sevash might pour across the border and eat them in their sleep. If he entered Sevash, he would likely never see High Tulbar again.

But if Hosten was naïve, what was I? Since my arrival in Tulbar, I had hardly put a foot right. I had trusted Hosten, admired his quiet conviction. He had been my friend. With Locan's help, I had delivered the scale with which Halagrim had summoned her revenant dragon. I had even involved Shaliya, and that mistake had left Locan and I trapped when we might have run. I did not even know what would become of Shaliya. Nor of Morvolt – perhaps the only friend left to me in Tulbar. Even when my folly had become clear, I had merely stood and watched while Locan had almost killed himself in his efforts to stop Halagrim.

The thought of what might become of him in Sevash filled me with horror. I pressed my knuckle into the bridge of my nose until I saw stars, consumed with self-loathing, savouring the pain that distracted me from the hopelessness of where I stood now.

My only hope was to reach Huretio, assuming the *Red Fiend* had not already fled High Tulbar. I would sail south with all haste and raise Guiland before Halagrim could resurrect the Abomination King and bring ruin down upon my family and my country.

Would Huretio wait on me and Locan? Would word of our fate reach him? I had a sudden vision of the *Red Fiend*'s captain bursting into the arena at the head of his crew, rattling his cutlass and demanding my release.

But this was no more than a daydream. If I was to escape High Tulbar, it would be on the sharpness of my wits and the strength of my sword arm. Wits that had failed me when the truth had been staring me in the face the whole time. A sword arm that tomorrow would be consumed by a horde of goblins.

That was when I heard them. Goblins are nocturnal by nature, and from the other pits their cries reached me, a mixture of guttural hisses and high whooping that chilled me to my core. Cries of hunger at the scent of a human in their midst.

All night I lay awake, listening to their shrieks and yelps, wracking my head for some plan that would see me go free. What I had learnt of goblins had not prepared me for the possibility of fighting them. A man will overpower a solitary goblin, perhaps two or three, but they would not come at me in ones and twos. They would overwhelm me with raw numbers. I tried to swallow my fear, but my mouth had turned as dry as the desiccated bones at my feet.

It is moments like this, when one's life balances on a precipice, that make a man realise how little the sum of his learning is worth. No book nor any clever argument will save your life. As High Tulbar had subdued the goblins, so the goblins would subdue me. Only they would not settle for confining me to a pit.

The little patch of sky I could see was turning from indigo to pink when I received my first visitors. Through bleary, sleep-deprived eyes, I stared up into the smug features of Ulf and Roddin.

'Not so proud now, are you?' sneered Roddin. 'This is what should have happened to you the moment you arrived.'

'Is Shaliya all right?' I asked. I had to know what had become of her.

'Oh, she's fine,' said Roddin with a mocking smile. 'We are to be wed. The girl's finally learnt what's best for her.'

I snorted. He was only trying to torment me. 'Liar.'

'Lying, am I?' The glee in his voice was enough to make me doubt myself. 'We'll see if I'm lying this afternoon when we get to see you get your insides torn out by those ugly little savages. Ulf's been starving them, so they're extra hungry.' I stared back at him defiantly, hiding my fear behind my hatred. 'Shaliya will attend the spectacle with me, and you can be sure she'll be watching. I've told her what will happen if she doesn't.'

'Where is she?' I asked. I pictured Shaliya chained in Roddin's cellar, her face blue and swollen from the beating it must have taken to get her to agree to wed him.

'She's bathing down on the beach. The wedding's straight after the games, and she said she wanted to be all clean for me. Took a walk down there on our way here just to see what's waiting for me.' Roddin's face contorted in a leer, sending a shudder of revulsion through me. 'All mine.'

He turned to Ulf. 'You sure we have to give it to him?'

'It would be a poor show otherwise,' said Ulf, studying me dispassionately as if I were a cut of beef. 'Not much meat on those bones. Perhaps the goblins will save him for last.'

Roddin laughed. 'I hope so. Then he gets to watch what happens to the rest of them first.'

Ulf threw down a wooden sword, and it clattered to a rest on the other side of the pit.

I picked it up. It felt flimsy in my hand, likely to snap in two the first time I swung it in anger. Not that I rated my chances against a horde of goblins anyway, but I had hoped I might kill a few of them before I died.

What I needed was time. 'My family is rich. They will ransom me.'

Ulf gave a thin smile. 'In ordinary times, I might have taken you up on that, but the Mór's orders were clear.'

'But I have seen the error of my ways,' I said, earnestly putting my palms together. 'Free me from this pit, and send word across the North Water to Hosten that I am ready to serve him.'

Roddin scowled. 'Shameless, cowardly sack of goblin-shit.

There'll be no weaselling your way out this time. The Mór's done with you.'

It had been worth a try. Hosten had exhausted all the value I could offer him. The last task I would do for him would be to die. I ought to have felt afraid, but strangely I felt calm. I had survived Narlond, in spite of all the myriad of ways I ought to have met my death. This tale could not end with my nameless bones resting at the bottom of a goblin pit.

But deep within myself, I knew what awaited me. Locan, Huretio, Shaliya. Of all those who might have cared, none of them were coming to save me, and wits and a wooden sword alone would not be enough.

When I refused to give them the satisfaction of watching me beg, Roddin and Ulf left me alone. I passed my remaining hours pacing the circumference of my pit and practising with my wooden blade, holding back so as not to shatter the flimsy weapon by mistake.

As the sun rose overhead, the chatter of the goblins that I had managed to banish from my consciousness began to be replaced by the excited chatter of arriving crowds. When I had pictured the Dome in Rameon, I had always imagined myself among the audience. My first experience would be rather differ-ent, trapped on the wrong side of the continent, on the wrong side of the barrier.

As the crowd grew louder, eventually the guards who had thrown me into the pit reappeared and lowered a ladder down. 'Don't think you can hide down there,' said one of them with a laugh. 'The biters'll have you either way.'

Steeling myself, I ascended the ladder.

The roar that met me when I reached the top was deafen-ing. The depths of the pit had insulated me; I had not been prepared for how crowded the rows of stone seats that surrounded the arena had become, every square foot occupied by a resident of Tulbar.

And of course, they were baying for my blood.

I scoured the arena for Shaliya, but with the distance and the heat of my pumping blood it was impossible to identify individuals among the swelling crowd. I gave a silent prayer to the Seamstress that I would have the courage to die well, but it seemed I had spent any reserve of grace she had spared for me, if she had ever been listening at all.

But at least I would not die alone. Other men were emerging from the pits, looking around in bewilderment and hefting their wooden swords. A mixture of shirtless slaves, trained by Ulf for just this purpose, and Varnan prisoners stripped of their armour.

The guards had now reached the last and largest of the pits, where by the chorus of high-pitched yips they had moved all of the goblins ready for this spectacle. The guards were readying a long rope to be lowered, but none of them wanted to be the man who had to stand at the edge and throw it down. I imagined the creatures' eager, ravenous faces, their black mouths of pointed teeth, their grasping, four-fingered hands.

The murmur of the crowd was growing louder with anticipation. I looked for familiar faces, but only the featureless visage of the baying mob stared back at me. Then, at the highest level of the arena, I caught sight of the squat figure of Roddin. I had thought he might wish to sit further down to better witness my demise, but of course he was too much of a coward to come so close.

For one bittersweet moment I caught a flash of Shaliya's blonde hair, but then her face was lost behind the press of the crowd as they came to their feet with a roar as the rope was cast down into the great pit that housed the goblins.

I gripped my wooden sword, willing my breath to remain steady. The guards were fleeing, but the man who had been closest to the edge was not quick enough. As he turned to run, a wrinkled, sickly green claw shot up from the pit and grasped his ankle.

The man was sucked under by a tide of goblin flesh. He shrieked in high-pitched terror, but none of his fellows turned to help him, already throwing themselves through the portcullis before it fell closed behind them. A few were too late, and instead ran to the wall, desperately pleading for somebody to take their hand and haul them from this madness.

And as the guard who had drawn the short straw was ripped apart, his hideous screams were drowned out by the arena erupting in thunderous approval.

I averted my eyes from the scene before me, looking about the amphitheatre with contempt. Men like that guard had fought for these people, thrown their lives down for them, and as he died in agony, the people of Tulbar were laughing.

For the first time, I saw what had eluded me through all my time in High Tulbar. It was not only the city that was decaying. It was its people. I had encountered kindness in the city, good folk like Albart and Kelsi. But there had been precious little of it. Tulbar was Ulf, Roddin, and Hosten. Tulbar was where the lives of men, women, and children could be measured in gold, where debtors claimed their dues not in coin but in flesh. The Rameon of the North, the poets had once named it. Perhaps when Hosten's ambition to restore the kingdom to glory had first blossomed, there had been some hope for it, but no longer. Hosten was the most corrupted of all of them. This was not the Rameon of the North, but one day, the Sevash of the West.

In that moment, I could have slain any citizen of Tulbar and never shed a tear. Better that Halagrim had remained here, better that she had bent the whole kingdom to her dark will instead, rather than turning her evil against my homeland.

The shout of one of the Varnans brought me to my senses. 'To me!' he was calling, and I realised that the other prisoners had allied, uniting to form a single cohort. They were scarcely more than a dozen and armed only with wooden swords, but I raced to join them.

None of them spoke as I fell into line. The guard's screams had fallen silent. We watched in horror as the goblins tore the man's clothes and scalp off and began to feed. More poured from the pit every minute, climbing over one another in their eagerness to claim a morsel of man flesh.

The prisoner beside me bent forward and heaved up a trickle of yellow bile. Fighting over the meat, the goblins' shrieks had become louder than ever. In their hunger, the goblins began to fight one another, and several of them were thrown back into the pit.

Then one of those closest to us sniffed the air, and at some signal the whole tribe of them fell silent. My heart dropped into the pit of my stomach as together they turned to face us, even those still gnawing on the guard swivelling their deep-set, devilish eyes towards us.

'Do not run,' said a tall man at the back of the group. 'They are fast.'

A goblin is barely two-thirds the height of a full-grown man. Armed or unarmed, a human warrior will have the edge against a goblin, our greater strength more than making up for the goblin's advantage in speed. But goblins are born in litters of thirteen, and it is said the females can give birth three times a year. My family claim that if not for Harkken rule, our queendom would have been overwhelmed by goblins decades ago. What they lack in size and strength, they more than make up for in sheer weight of numbers.

This host of goblins was at least one hundred strong, perhaps closer to two hundred. And they were hungry. Ravenous. Starved in a pit for years and forced to fight for their food. To them, this pitiful collection of men clutching wooden swords must have seemed a delicious mirage, a banquet upon which all their boundless hunger could be sated.

Black tongues lolled over their serrated teeth, their mouths drawing back towards their pointed ears voraciously in a way that was almost a smile. Their voices drew together to form a single, hideous note, a shriek that emanated deep in their throats with an undercurrent of sharp hissing. The crowd had fallen silent, whether in fear of these creatures or with shame that they had willingly unleashed them upon their fellow humans. Given my experience of the Tulbans, I suspect the former. It might have been easy to consider the goblins as of no consequence while they fought among themselves at the bottom of a filthy hole, but free from their imprisonment they were a different proposition.

Their war cry reached a frequency beyond the range of my hearing. A trickle of warm piss began to flow down my leg. In a storm of gnashing teeth and keen-edged claws, the goblins charged.

A man beside me who had been quaking with fear turned and ran, and it cost him his life. A mass of goblins pursued him like a storm of arrows, and in a matter of seconds they overwhelmed him, driving him to the ground under their weight. The air was shrill with his screams as they tore him apart.

'Stay together!' shouted the tall man.

After seeing the fate of the man who fled, I doubted any of us would be so foolish. We crouched together, forming a circle with our wooden blades facing outwards, each of us silently knowing it would not be enough. I glanced up again towards the top of the arena. Even at such a distance, I am sure I saw Shaliya cover her face with her hands.

I would like to tell you that in what I believed were my final moments my thoughts turned to the fate of Guiland, of all those young men who had died at Sevash to bring about the Abomination King's fall, and all the many more who would die at his rebirth. Of the furious vengeance he would take upon my country, depleted and defenceless from the grand sacrifice they had made to defeat him the first time. Of Locan, a hostage of Halagrim, beaten and bloodied and forced to watch as she resurrected her master. Even of Hosten, and the dark fate that surely awaited him in Sevash. Of my repeated failures to change from the course that had led us all to the precipice.

But when faced with certain death, I thought no further than the next moment, the next defiant breath that burnt hot in my lungs. One day, word would reach my family of my demise, and I did not wish it to be said that I had not fought, that I had let my mind float away and allowed the goblins to claim my flesh. I would bleed them for every inch of skin.

They were well into their second victim now, tearing through him like locusts, licking at his exposed carcass. A few turned and ran for us, perhaps hoping for the choicest pieces of their next victim. I jabbed at the face of the first one to come for me, as hard as I dared without breaking my sword. It fell to the dirt then rolled back to its feet, hissing angrily. The rest came more slowly now, stalking us, perhaps fearful of our swords.

A Varnan to the side of me lurched out of our circle, and in an instant the goblins were on him. Half-a-dozen dived for his ankles, and he toppled like a felled tree, windmilling his arms in a futile effort to stay upright. As soon as he hit the ground, a whole host of them leapt atop him. He swiped wildly with his sword, but dropped it with a scream as a goblin sank its teeth into his elbow. His shrieks were soon swallowed by the weight of his assailants, so many that his body disappeared from view. Up close, the sounds of their feeding were even more repugnant.

We tightened our circle.

'We should run,' said one man. 'They can't get all of us!'

But he was wrong. They would chase us down before we

came within five yards of the high walls that divided us from the spectators.

Beyond the chaos of the feasting goblins, I had a vague sense that the reaction from the crowd was more uncertain than before, some still cheering while others voiced their disgust or turned away. None of them had been at Sevash or heard tales from the men who had. This distraction almost cost me my place in the circle – a goblin leapt for my knees and I barely got my sword down in time to knock it to the ground.

Eventually, there would be too many. A shadow passed across the sun, ensconcing us in darkness, a premonition of what would shortly become of us, but I was too intent upon the goblins to take notice of it. Some, though, were lifting their eyes to the sky, men and goblins both, their mouths falling open in wonder.

An earth-shattering roar burst from the heavens. A roar that echoed through the ages, filling hearts with dread and awe alike, a collective ancestral memory that there are things greater than men and goblins and sorcery. That we are insignificant, living for barely a breath as the years and centuries roll past, that there are still some things in this world before which we can only fall to our knees in wonder.

Her skin shimmered, all the blues and boundlessness of the sea, dulling the sky to pallid grey by comparison. Wings so wide they seemed to stretch the whole breadth of Tulbar, sending seawater cascading like rain as she glided across the ether, the heat of her body warming it so that it fell on us like faded sparks of fire. Her great mouth distended, and as she roared, a plume of steam burst forth.

Aydhenia on the wing, the great sea dragon of Tulbar, and one of the most wonderous sights I had ever seen. How could anyone have placed their faith in Halagrim's forgery? It was to compare a candle to the incandescence of the sun. The whole arena stared open-mouthed at the sky, even the goblins struck dumb by this impossibility.

For centuries, it is said that the dragons unerringly served the Caradrahans of Tulbar. That leads some to deduce that they are dumb beasts, as capable of being turned to the violent desires of men as an ox is capable of being trained to plough a field. But whatever sorcery the Caradrahans practised, it did not dull the dragons' instincts, nor their keen, savage intelligence, nor the wisdom of men to fear them.

As unearthly silence fell over High Tulbar, the dragon tucked her wings against her lithe, long torso, and dived for earth. And everywhere men and goblins ran screaming.

Everyone, it seemed, except me. The wise thing would have been to flee with the rest, but this was no time for wisdom. When the odds are against you, sometimes you just have to close your eyes and gamble on the one way out still left to you.

I could not defeat Halagrim alone. Even supposing I escaped High Tulbar with my life, I could not cross the North Water. But Aydhenia could.

I dropped my sword and ran towards her as she began to pull up from her dive, waving my arms furiously. 'Aydhenia! Aydhenia!'

She swept past me, fifty feet overhead, and the heat of her downdraught knocked me to the ground. As she banked around the edge of the arena I was already back on my feet, running towards her, screaming again, 'Aydhenia! Aydhenia!'

She did not heed me. Everywhere, the people of Tulbar were fleeing in terror, pushing one another out of the way to be the first down the stairs. The dragon was a symbol of their city, but they had seen what happened to those who were caught in its steaming breath.

All except one. In the highest reaches of the arena, Shaliya waited with her hand outstretched towards the descending dragon, shouting something into the sky.

With the grace of a dancer, Aydhenia curved her dive directly towards Shaliya, like a falcon summoned to the glove of its master.

I turned my attention from the dragon to Shaliya. What was she doing? I waved my arms frantically over my head. 'Shaliya! Get down!'

Over the screaming of the fleeing crowd there was no prospect she had heard me.

The men I had stood with moments earlier were hauling themselves up the wall of the arena and making for the exits. The goblins were doing the same, working in teams to drag their fellows up. There would be hundreds of them loose in High Tulbar this night, but that was no less than the city deserved.

I had eyes only for Shaliya.

I threw myself over the wall and raced up the stairs. Aydhenia hung in the air above Shaliya, flapping her immense wings to control her descent, until her claws gripped the edge of the arena's top wall. Freed from the confines of her cave, she seemed somehow even larger, so vast that I feared the whole edifice would collapse under her weight.

'Shaliya!' I cried. She gave no sign she had heard me. She was gazing up at Aydhenia in rapt wonder, her hair fanning wildly in the downdraught of the dragon's wings.

I skidded to a stop and stepped in front of Shaliya to place myself between her and Aydhenia's searing breath.

'*You.*' Aydhenia bent her neck to study me with her molten amber eyes. 'I know you.' The dragon sniffed at the air with her cavernous nostrils. 'Boy-who-hides-from-magic.' Even after sending an entire arena of people and goblins fleeing in terror, she still spoke in the same childlike cadence she had in the cave. 'Did you summon me?'

'*I* summoned you.'

Shaliya stepped forward, and my head jerked in shock as I turned to stare at her. '*You* summoned her?'

'I did as the song says,' replied Shaliya, her eyes never leaving the dragon. She met Aydhenia's gaze like a warrior-queen, her chin raised in defiance, refusing to be cowed by this awesome creature, the breath of which could have sloughed the skin from our bones. She broke into the verses of the first song I had heard her sing in the Dwarf and Dragon:

> *'Flowers for the healer*
> *Jewels for the queen*
> *Silver for the troubadour*
> *Who is just about to sing*
>
> *Scales from a dragon*
> *Cool mist upon your skin*
> *Shackles for the bandit*
> *Who keeps prizes from his king*
>
> *If you should claim a fortune*
> *Measured not in gold and gems*
> *Give your treasure to the water*
> *To wake leviathans from the sea.'*

I have made many mistakes in my life, but this moment only served to confirm that falling in love with Shaliya had not been one of them. It is hard to say of whom I felt more in awe – Aydhenia, or Shaliya. I had intended the dragon scale to be only a keepsake in case I should fall – I had never considered that the answer might have been hidden in the first song I had heard Shaliya sing. She had saved my life, not with steel and fury, but with a rare faith in the power of song to reveal the truth and a daring that had seen her trick Roddin to allow her to wade into the sea.

'Goblin's black bones,' I whispered, still staring at her in amazement.

Shaliya grasped me by the collar and dragged me into a fierce embrace. 'And don't forget it,' she said, with a wild grin. 'When you sent me a dragon scale, you didn't just expect me to sit around staring at how pretty it was, did you?'

'You summoned me?' Aydhenia's gaze swirled like two whirlpools deep enough to swallow the world. I stepped again between the dragon and Shaliya, for there was anger in the beast's huge eyes, an anger that had been brewing for centuries. She gave an evil hiss, and steam billowed between her teeth. 'No human has dared... not for centuries. They cheated us, stole our scales, used our own magic against us to force us to do their bidding.'

Of course. There had never been any accord between men and dragons. The Caradrahans had done as the Tulbans had always done – bent others to their will with threats and coercion.

'That was not my intention,' said Shaliya. She took a bold step forward, putting herself in front of me again. My heart was racing. Every instinct told me to grab Shaliya and run, but my feet had turned to lead weights. 'I only wanted to see if you would come. To save Cetrik.'

Aydhenia hissed. 'That is how it always starts. But the greed of men is boundless.' She sniffed inquisitively at Shaliya, and her eyes softened. 'That song... I remember it. It is from before the men here began stealing our scales, when the people who lived here would summon us only to offer us food and seek our wisdom. I would swim in the sea with the children. They would climb up my neck onto my head and leap into the water. And you are very beautiful. And I suppose I am glad to have saved Boy-who-hides-from-magic.' Aydhenia leant back, flapping her wings in what might have been delight. The dragon's mood could turn in an instant. 'I missed you after you left, Boy-who-hides-from-magic. I did not realise it, but I have missed being around people, with your hair and your little legs and your funny little wings that don't even look like wings.' She snorted appreciatively. 'Well, Girl-whose-hair-is-like-gold, seeing as you are so very pretty and you've been so clever in remembering that old song' – Aydhenia hummed the melody, her vibrato setting the whole arena rumbling as if it was about to collapse beneath us – 'I will grant you a boon. Name the service you shall have of me, and if it is within my power, I will make it so.' Her eyes darkened. 'Thereafter, you shall forget you ever heard that song. Let every note and lyric of it be lost. If anyone should sing it in your presence, you will silence them.'

I felt a pang of sadness. Aydhenia might desire human companionship, but humans could not be trusted with the fellowship of dragons. There had been no golden age for Tulbar and Paleir. The glory of the Caradrahans had been built on a lie, on the coercion of dragons and the misery of slaves. Was it any wonder that Hosten had become what he was, given the history of his people?

Aydhenia lowered her head towards Shaliya with her neck flat, almost a signal of submission, and my breath caught as Shaliya reached out her palm to place it upon the snout.

It was one of the most wondrous things I had ever seen. The woman I loved, a slave, accepting the homage of a dragon, a moment so pure and perfect it was as if it had been long ago ordained. The clouds parted, bathing the scene in sunlight, catching on Aydhenia's scales with a sheen that was almost blinding. Shaliya's golden hair shone like a crown. Not a slave. A queen.

From a deep well of despair, there bloomed in me an inkling of hope for Tulbar. If such an accursed, corrupted city could produce somebody like Shaliya, a rose sprouted from a field sown with salt, there might yet be hope.

'What will you have of me, Girl-whose-hair-is-like-gold?' asked Aydhenia.

'I...' Shaliya glanced back at me. She might have asked for

anything, but she said, 'You need to help Cetrik. We need to stop that witch, Halagrim.'

By this point, the arena was empty. The crowds had fled and the goblins had spilled out onto the streets, where the Tulbans fought for their lives. A fair payment for Ulf's hubris, believing that goblins were like animals to be tamed and turned to a profit, and not a race every bit as violent and vicious as the race of men.

But there was one man still left in the arena. Coward that he was, I had never even thought to look for him. But as Shaliya communed with Aydhenia, there was a flash of movement behind me. Roddin had hidden in the shadow of one of the rows of staired seating, and now he emerged, a knife clutched in his sweaty, grasping fist.

There was a time when I could barely speak of what happened next. I locked it away in the deepest part of myself, where not even my broken heart could find it. Folk would ask me of my time in Tulbar, and I would shake my head and walk straight past them. As I have aged, it is a moment that has lost the power to shock me, but still it hurts. It is said that weapons forged in the furnace of Sevash will leave a wound to last for a hundred years, but some wounds are not dealt by steel. Some wounds are dealt by memories, by matters left unsaid and undone.

I should have expected him, known he would never be content to let anybody else have her. I should have been faster. I should have never let him within ten feet of her.

My hands grasped Roddin's shoulder just as his knife pierced the flesh of Shaliya's abdomen. Too late. Her mouth curved to a silent, shocked 'O' as she collapsed with the blade buried in her stomach.

I was on Roddin only a split second behind the moment his blade touched Shaliya. Blinded by rage and tears I barrelled into him. His knife flew harmlessly away, and I pinned him to the ground under my weight.

I might have rushed to Shaliya, but I had seen enough of battle by now to recognise a mortal wound when I saw one. No healer in any corner of the world could have pulled her back from death. I turned my grief and anger upon Roddin.

Even now, so many years hence, that choice still haunts me. I might have comforted Shaliya, shared some final, quiet words with her, let her tell me where she wished to be buried. Instead, I spent my love's final moments taking out my anguish upon the man who had stolen her from me.

Fate offered me a choice between love and rage. And I chose rage. I might condemn Hosten, and all the rest of Tulbar, but I am barely better than them. I do not even know where Shaliya is laid to rest, some mass grave with all the other victims of the Goblin Riot of High Tulbar.

I do not well recall what happened, but when it was over, my face was streaked with tears, and my knuckles were raw. Roddin's face was a patchwork of purple bruises. His eyeballs had burst in his skull, and my thumbs were dripping with blood and viscera. The beating I dealt him did not kill him. It was my hands around his neck that had done that. I sat there strangling him for a long time after he breathed his last. If I stopped, I would have to look away, and then I would see Shaliya. As long as I did not look, she might still live. She would rise and place a hand on my shoulder and tell me it was going to be okay.

It was Aydhenia who brought me to my senses. She butted my shoulder with her snout. 'I think he's dead,' she said. My grip on Roddin's throat relented. 'I think Girl-whose-hair-is-like-gold is dead too. I liked her.'

Aydhenia spoke with the cool detachment of a creature that has lived through centuries, to whom our own short lives are of no greater significance than a well-remembered meal. A god among mortals. An island of detachment among my all-consuming grief.

Wordlessly, I rose, and through tears stared down at what was left of Shaliya. Blood was still pooling beneath her, dripping steadily down the arena stairs. She had tried to move. There were bloody hand marks on the steps where she had tried to push herself up.

The wound was not even deep. She had still been alive while I beat and strangled Hosten to death. I could have held her hand while she passed, given worthless assurances that it was going to be all right. I wiped my eyes with my sleeve, and it came away stained with Roddin's blood.

'Did she say anything before she... went?' I asked Aydhenia.

The dragon seemed to think for a moment. 'Maybe. I don't remember. Humans talk a lot. I can't be expected to recall every word.'

I suppose she couldn't. Any more than I could recall the light of a firefly blinking out for the last time. Perhaps that was for the best – with her last breath, Shaliya would surely have scorned me. I knelt and laid a hand against her still warm cheek. Even in death, her face seemed to glow with compassion and forgiveness I did not deserve. Her eyes were closed, as if at any moment she might wake and ask how long she had been asleep for. 'I'm sorry,' I whispered. 'I'm so sorry.'

Aydhenia's snout nudged me again, her breath wet and warm against my face. Perhaps her way of comforting me. 'Was she your mate?' she asked. 'I had a mate once, I think.'

'She was.'

'And she called you Cetrik,' said Aydhenia. 'I won't remember that. I will keep calling you Boy-who-hides-from-magic.'

She was a perplexing creature. All the wisdom of the ages, yet at times as simple and tactless as a child. I wondered sometimes if so many centuries alone had robbed her of her wits.

I stared down at Shaliya, committing her face to memory, willing back the tears that threatened to fall. There was to be no future for us. What a mistake she had made, to hold faith that someone as incapable and foolish as me might somehow free her.

With the span of years, I sometimes ask myself if Shaliya truly felt as I did, or whether she saw me only as a means by which she might escape Roddin and High Tulbar. Time has a way of turning the earnestness of youth to folly. And yet, even as old and cynical as I am now, my heart still chooses to believe that what we shared was real. I still dream of her sometimes. In my dreams, she is old, as old as I am now, with grey hair and laughter lines, and we are surrounded by the happy sons, daughters, and grandchildren that might have been ours if we had only escaped High Tulbar when we had the chance. If I had only reached Roddin a second sooner.

Aydhenia sniffed. 'Disappointing. I wonder what she would have asked of me.'

Shaliya's last wish had been for Aydhenia to help me. Of course it had. Shaliya had offered me loyalty and affection to which I had no right. She might have asked anything of Aydhenia. She could have asked her to steam Roddin and her father and the rest of them alive, but instead she had thought only of me.

'She wanted you to help me,' I said. 'You heard her.'

Aydhenia tilted her head quizzically. 'Did she? Are you sure?'

I bit back my anger. 'You heard her. Do not pretend you have forgotten. I need you to carry me to Sevash.' I had no choice. Locan was counting on me. Guiland and the world were counting on me. Whatever I could do, I must. And if I turned myself to thwarting Halagrim, I would not have to think about Shaliya. 'I need you to fly me into the Dreadveil.'

A low growl emanated deep in Aydhenia's throat. '*Fly you?*'

Steam billowed from her vast nostrils, and for a moment I feared she would bathe me in her blistering breath. 'There were once dragons who allowed lesser creatures to ride on their backs. We fought a war to end that shameful practice. A dragon who would bend their neck so far as to allow such is no dragon.'

'You could carry me in your mouth?' I suggested, regretting the words as soon as they escaped my lips.

Aydhenia considered for a moment. 'That would not be wise,' she said carefully. 'It would be an easy thing to forget you are there and eat you on instinct. I have not tasted the flesh of men in many centuries.' She lifted her eyes, staring across the water to the crimson horizon of the Dreadveil. 'And I did not spend so long avoiding the poison air so that I might fly into it the first time a human asks me.' She gave a petulant beat of her wings. 'Girl-whose-hair-is-gold is dead. I will return to the water. Farewell, Boy-who-hides-from-magic.'

No. I had not endured so much to be thwarted now. Let Aydhenia blast me to the Underrealm if she wished, but if she left, I was doomed anyway. A swift death bathed in blisteringly hot steam might be preferable to the slow, excruciating suffering that awaited me in Sevash. I fumbled in my pocket, hoping that it had not fallen out somewhere along the way. My fingers came to rest on the warm smoothness of the final dragon scale, and before sense could rob me of my foolhardiness, I pulled it out and held it up towards Aydhenia. 'Fly me to Sevash.' I held it up higher so that Aydhenia could not fail to see what I had in my possession. 'Fly me to Sevash, or I swear I will force you to.'

I had no clue how, of course. The magic that had allowed the Caradrahans of old to bind the dragons to their will was lost to the ages. A final, desperate gamble, that would likely see me dead one way or another.

Aydhenia stared down at me with undisguised hatred, infernal fire roasting in the depths of her eyes, her long face half obscured behind the great clouds of wrathful steam that were pouring from her mouth and nostrils.

The next few seconds seemed to stretch into eternity. Every breath I expected to be my last, to feel the sudden, scalding agony of my skin being broiled from my bones and to awaken before Heoloran, the First Martyr, weighing the worth of my deeds for the fate of my soul before the entrance to the Seamstress's Golden Kingdom, or to know only the endless, empty silence of the void that a small, unspoken part of me believed waited beyond.

But though Aydhenia's steaming breath continued to surge and swell, something gave her pause. Emboldened, I began to sing:

> *'Flowers for the healer*
> *Jewels for the queen*
> *Silver for the troubadour*
> *Who is just about to sing*
>
> *Scales from a dragon—'*

'*Stop.*' Aydhenia's voice shook with fury. 'Songs will not save you, Boy-who-hides-from-magic. I should kill you where you stand, claim your stolen scale, then feast on your flesh.'

She was still talking to me. That meant I was not yet dead. 'We have to stop them,' I said. 'Halagrim and Hosten, they're flying to Sevash to resurrect—'

'*Flying?*' Aydhenia's tail flicked irritably. 'You lie, Boy-who-hides-from-magic. Men may walk on land and sail upon the water, but the skies belong to the dragons.'

I cursed myself for not seeing it sooner. 'Halagrim had one of your scales,' I told her, my voice becoming heightened with excitement. I explained, as quickly as I could, what Locan and I had seen at the necromancer's shack: the enormous hole from which the reborn dragon had hauled itself, its dead, sightless eyes and steaming breath, how it had bent to Halagrim's will.

Aydhenia was deathly silent when I had finished, such that I could clearly hear the ongoing chaos outside the arena walls. The tip of her tail was flicking back and forth incessantly, the gills on her neck rippling with repressed fury. 'A vile mockery,' she growled, her voice so deep that I could feel it vibrating through the stone under my feet. The whole structure shook as she stamped one enormous foot. 'If you are lying to me, Boy-who-hides-from-magic, I will carry you into the Endless Water. I will drop you there and let the flesh-eating fish claim you. They will start with your toes, then your feet, then the rest of you. I will watch, and when you are on the verge of death or drowning, I will pluck you from the water and leave what remains of you on the beach for the crabs. Flesh that is corrupted with such vile deceit deserves not the honour of a dragon's stomach.'

Her words sent a chill through me. An echo of Aydhenia's ancient viciousness, a reminder of the fearsome nature that prowled beneath her simplistic, almost naïve speech. 'It's true,' I said, willing that my voice did not tremble with fear. 'I will swear on anything you ask me to, on my own life and on the memory of Girl-whose-hair-is-like-gold, that I speak the truth.'

Aydhenia watched me, her eyes so deep and terrible that they seemed to pick through the very essence of me. After several long moments, her flickering tail fell still, and the steam that had been pouring in a thick torrent from her mouth lessened to a plume. 'Such foulness cannot be allowed to live,' she growled. She snapped her jaws and stretched her long neck to blow an angry breath of steam into the sky. 'Only a magicker would stoop to such blasphemy. I will hunt her false dragon to the ends of the earth and drag it to the bottom of the sea.' She lowered her head until it was flat against the stone, stretching out her long neck down the arena stairs. It took me several moments to realise that she was inviting me to clamber onto her back. 'Boy-who-hides-from-magic. You will show me where to find this creature.'

CHAPTER 24

I had been sitting at the base of Aydhenia's neck for only an instant when the dragon leapt into the sky, and when I did not immediately plummet to my death I became the first person in many hundreds of years to ride atop the back of a true dragon.

I barely had time to contemplate the momentousness of this. As we rose high above Tulbar and Aydhenia's powerful wings bore us out to sea, the howling wind in my face drowned out my screams. The air rushed past, threatening to push me from Aydhenia's back and send me tumbling into the depths of the North Water below. I was so small to the dragon that I doubt she would even have noticed. I stayed low against her neck, clinging on with my knees as best I could, my fingers locked tight to the gaps between her overlapping scales.

In a matter of seconds, we were miles from land and many hundreds of feet above the sea, above the clouds, where the wind screamed and the force of the gale sent tears trailing down my face, the air so cold that it turned them to ice. If not for the heat of Aydhenia beneath me, I might have frozen solid.

I lifted my eyes to the wind. The Dreadveil loomed before us, a cloud of black and crimson so thick and vast that it blotted out the sky, stretching from the sea into the heavens. It had not been possible to appreciate its true scale from the deck of the *Red Fiend*. Within its depths, the wraiths the Abomination King had left behind were still visible. I had passed them on my journey to Midding, but here they were even more frightening, their bodies stretching and distending, shapeless in the thin air. Long, slender arms reached out for nothingness as the creatures faded in and out from behind the haze. I tried to swallow my fear. They could not touch me, and they had never bothered Morvolt on my journey north, so Aydhenia ought to be fine as well.

Without warning, Aydhenia let out a long, angry blast of blistering air, the force nearly causing me to lose my grip on her scales. A portion of the Dreadveil retreated, but only for a matter of seconds, the smoke spreading and multiplying until it was as if the barrier had never moved.

Aydhenia hissed her fury. 'More vile sorcery.'

She wheeled around for another pass, and this time when the haze returned, Aydhenia roared and kept going. I gritted my teeth, and for the second time in my life I crossed the threshold of the Dreadveil.

The change was instant. The air became soupy, warm, so thick that every breath felt as if I might drown on it. No matter which way I looked, the scarlet haze obscured everything, rendering both the sea and the sky invisible. A faceless, formless wraith swept past me, and though I knew it could not touch me, I ducked on instinct.

'Hold on tight, Boy-who-hides-from-magic,' rumbled Aydhenia. I felt her words as much as I heard them, for the wailing wind and the deathly hum of the Dreadveil together combined to render me deaf.

Aydhenia's swiftness put the *Red Fiend* to shame, swallowing up the miles. When we had been flying for some time, with great care, I shifted my weight forward to look below. We were still over the water, but such was Aydhenia's speed, I predicted we would soon hit the coast of Midding, and when we did, Sevash would not be far away. I scoured the earth for the shore, but through the Dreadveil I could see nothing.

'We need to go lower!' I shouted.

My stomach lurched and my legs briefly lost their grip on Aydhenia's neck as she dived. I screamed in terror, the dragon spinning and suddenly banking upwards again, as if she meant to dislodge me.

'Slower!' I cried. Aydhenia did not heed me, immediately twisting her left wing to make an impossibly tight turn that nearly caused my stomach to overspill and threatened to send me careering into the air.

'What are you doing?' I shouted, for all the difference it would make. Then a shadow passed overhead, blotting out the distant light of the sun, and I realised what Aydhenia had seen.

Halagrim had sent her resurrected dragon to watch the coast. It screeched, and a gust of warm air rustled my hair as Aydhenia banked again to avoid our foe's searing breath. Her long neck turned back on itself and she sent a return burst of scalding air, but the creature flew straight through it and Aydhenia dived to avoid another attack.

She hissed her fury. I could feel her searingly hot scales burning through my breeches, but all I could do was cling on. I screamed and nearly lost my grip as Aydhenia banked to a sudden stop, protecting me by presenting her stomach to our foe and releasing another burst of superheated steam as Halagrim's creature flew straight for us.

It troubled the cold-eyed beast not at all. The false dragon flew past, and lashed out with its tail to strike Aydhenia across the chest. The blow set both of us spinning, and my hands slipped from Aydhenia's scales. I knew a brief moment of weightlessness before her body slammed into me again and I managed to grab hold of her. I was now several feet down

Aydhenia's broad back. I tried to pull myself up towards her neck again but she banked into another tight turn, and it was all I could do not to tumble into the air.

Aydhenia snarled, bucking and spinning as if trying to dislodge me, and this time my grip failed. My left hand and legs both went, leaving me upside down, screaming into the red haze.

My remaining hand slipped, and then I was falling, tumbling helplessly through the stifling atmosphere of the Dreadveil. I could see neither the earth nor the sky. I was accelerating towards the ground, with no way of knowing how far I had to fall. Formless wraiths swirled around me, their empty features mocking me, watching the boy they could not reach plummet to his certain death. Something hurtled past me, a twisting mass of dark limbs, but I barely saw it, shutting my eyes against the rushing air as the invisible ground hurtled to meet me. The Dreadveil thinned enough for me to make out the coast, still hundreds of yards below. My body would be dashed upon the cliffs of Midding, a meal for whatever creations of the Abomination King still stalked this land. Over the howling wind, I could not even hear my own screams.

Something grasped me from above, long talons tearing through the back of my cloak, and I let out a cry of relief as I looked up into Aydhenia's underside. There were long gashes in her pale blue belly, dripping oily, green-tinted blood, but she seemed none the weaker for it. The ground was still speeding towards us, but Aydhenia spread her wings wide to slow our descent. She released me a few feet above the ground, and I rolled to a clumsy stop only yards from the cliff edge.

I lay there, sucking down breaths, hardly able to believe how close I had come to my bones being shattered against the bluff. Wraiths crowded around me, their auras red and angry, but they did not trouble me. I was alive, and somehow unhurt save for some blistered skin where Aydhenia's scales had burnt away my breeches.

Aydhenia stalked towards me, as ungainly on land as she was graceful in the air, and sniffed at my body. 'Oh, you're alive,' she said. 'I am hungry, and there does not appear to be anything else to eat here.' She raised her snout to the air. 'This land is dead. It is no place for dragons.'

'You threw me off,' I said. It was all I could think to say in that moment. After my fall, neither my mind nor my body seemed wholly my own.

'If I had not, you would have been burnt to death by that creature's breath,' said Aydhenia. 'I could not fight that thing and protect you at the same time. You should be glad it was not a real dragon – I would let you die before I allowed myself to be seen carrying a human like a common land beast.'

I realised there was no sign of Halagrim's resurrected dragon. 'Where is it?' I said, looking around in alarm.

Aydhenia gestured towards the cliffs. I rose and walked tentatively to the edge. Below, the dragon's body tumbled in the rolling surf, repeatedly being dashed upon the rocks. Gallons of green blood were leaking into the water from the wound in its neck, where Aydhenia looked to have bitten the creature's head clean off. It was very much dead. Again. I breathed a sigh of relief. With the reborn dragon dead, with Aydhenia's help, I might stand a chance of slaying Halagrim before she raised the Abomination King.

'A kinder end than it deserved,' said Aydhenia. 'And now I will leave. Travel safely, Boy-who-hides-from-magic.'

'What?' I asked, aghast. 'You can't leave now!' Sevash was several days' walk away. Without Aydhenia I did not stand a chance. I had no provisions, nor Morvolt to bear me there. 'We need to go after Halagrim!'

The dragon was not even looking at me. She was gazing west. 'That mockery of my race is dead. I have borne you where you wished to be.' Aydhenia reared up on her back legs, revealing the softer scales of her underbelly, where the resurrected dragon's breath had charred her flesh and its claws had raked deep gashes. 'I go now to hunt, and to lick my wounds. If you wish to return to the Misty Isle, I will bear you there once more, but that is all you shall have of me. Your quarrel with the sorceress is your own concern.' Her eyes flashed at me. 'Now, my scale.'

'But she's the one who made the false dragon!' I exploded. 'You can't—'

I leapt backwards as Aydhenia sent forth a jet of steam, narrowly missing me. I yelped and fell as the vapour rushed past my feet, sending a hot sting of pain up my leg where it scalded me.

'*The scale.*'

Staring into Aydhenia's eyes was like staring into the deepest hell of the Underrealm. I was left in no doubt that if I refused again, Aydhenia would boil me alive. The dragon and I had forged a brief alliance, but she was no friend to me. With shaking fingers, I reached into my cloak and grabbed the scale, relieved to find it was still there and I had not lost it somewhere over the North Water.

I held it up towards her, and flinched as Aydhenia's forked tongue slipped from her mouth and wrapped around the scale. There was an audible gulp as Aydhenia took it in her mouth and swallowed it.

Aydhenia gave a grunt of appreciation. 'Farewell, Boy-who-hides-from-magic. And good luck. Travel swiftly and carefully. This is not a land in which any creature with blood in its veins should linger.' She gave an irritable flap of her wings. 'This is what men do. They work their own destruction, and when they are finished, they flee, and it is always the land that pays. If dragons acted as men do, the sea and the sky would burn so hot that the world would choke.'

Without another word, she pushed off from the ground and leapt into the sky. Within a few flaps of her wings, she disappeared behind the haze of the Dreadveil. I watched her until she was a dark speck, and then until she flew beyond the distance I could see. I wished to commit every beat of her wings and every twist of her sinewy neck to memory. I was not likely to see the like again, nor live long enough to write of it.

I collapsed back onto my rear, my thighs aching as if I had just run twenty miles from my futile efforts to remain aboard Aydhenia. I had known of her capriciousness, but I had not expected her to abandon me here. What was the use of killing Halagrim's dragon without killing Halagrim herself?

The grass beneath me was dead, like the rest of Midding. The dirt that remained was stained red, tainted by the Dreadveil and centuries of dark magic. Even the sea seemed lifeless, its grey water no more than a shadowy reflection of what a sea ought to look like. No fish dwelled in those waters. No crabs nor lobsters scuttled in the rockpools on the shore.

I had not even a crumb of food. All I had been able to take in my rush to leave Tulbar was a sword I had claimed from Roddin's corpse, the blade that had stolen Shaliya from me. I touched the hilt and a shiver of revulsion went through me. If I'd had any other weapon on my person, I would have gladly tossed the sword into the sea.

Reluctantly, I got to my feet. Guiland and Locan were counting on me. I had crossed the whole of Midding once before. I could walk to Sevash. If I walked east, eventually I would see the great plumes of corruption that still emanated from the razed tower, where the Dreadveil had been forged, the source from which it continued to radiate. A place of wickedness and malevolence seen only in my imagination, and in the dark tales of the Guilanders who had almost surrendered their lives and their sanity to end the dread rule of the Abomination King.

. . .

I was only a few miles into my journey when I began to lose heart. The wraiths that continued to swarm around me could not touch me, but with every breath I seemed to inhale some of the misery that hung over Midding. With neither food to sustain me nor Morvolt's presence to comfort me, a black shadow settled obdurately in my chest.

All of this was my fault, I knew. The dragon scales that had set the world onto this path had come from Locan's hand, but it had been my actions that had allowed him to claim them. Had we never set foot in Paleir, Halagrim would have been forced to remain disguised and powerless, and Shaliya would still be alive. High Tulbar would have fallen to Shanoch, and all Hosten's scheming would have counted for nothing. The only redemption would be if I could somehow thwart Halagrim. That was the cause that propelled me forward, as lost and hopeless as that aim might be.

I will spare you the details of the many days' walk it took me to reach Sevash. Suffice to say that it took every ounce of fortitude in my heart to keep going. And I had no choice. There was no way back to Paleir, and the rivers at which Midding bordered Narlond and Guiland were many more days of hard trekking away.

Every step, the wraiths followed me. Shadows of silent mockery, waiting for me to fall so they could stand over my corpse. They kept their distance usually, but occasionally one would swim directly past my vision, like a funeral shroud caught by the non-existent breeze.

Time stretched, though I did not hunger as I had expected to. The barren landscape and the constant weight of the Dreadveil were too strange and unsettling to experience something so human as hunger. I had not appreciated before how much I had relied on Morvolt's company to keep myself sane when I first journeyed through Midding. I tried to whistle a tune, a reminder that there was still a world beyond this one, but in the stifling air my lips could not give form to sound.

To sustain myself, I found ancient root vegetables, preserved by Midding's arid soil amidst ancient tumbledown villages. I followed the path of a dry stream for a time, falling to my knees every few miles to suckle at the scant moisture that could still be found on its silt bed, drinking down the dirty water as if it were the finest Rintish wine.

Following the stream also ensured I did not get turned back on myself. But there was little chance of that. With every step east I took, the hum of the Dreadveil seemed to grow louder. Those who had survived Sevash said that when they broke the final wall and reached the tower, the buzz had been so loud they could not even hear their own thoughts.

When I sighted a silhouette of ruined walls against the dusky horizon, I turned north. Towards Sevash. Towards my doom.

CHAPTER 25

Where Sevash now stands was once the city of Brightwater. The jewel in the Harkken crown, the brightest rose in the garden that was the great kingdom of Karvved. A city of elegant waterways and sleek turrets, where the cobbles were so small and closely fitted that the carts seemed to fly through the streets. The lords Mancellin had ruled there for generations, first as kings and later as the most powerful vassals of the Harkkens, renowned throughout the kingdom for their wisdom and justice. Under their stewardship, Midding flourished, the breadbasket of Karvved. For centuries, Guiland and Midding survived and thrived together, the Harkkens holding back those who would claim the island for themselves while the Mancellins' shrewd administration kept the country fed.

Accounts from the time mourn the loss of Brightwater nearly as much as they lament the rise of the Abomination King. It is said that when he claimed the city for his seat, a great portal opened beneath Cellinfast, the grand fortress of the Mancellins. Half the city toppled into the Underrealm, and with it every member of the Mancellin family. Only one survived – a nephew of the twenty-seventh Lord Mancellin who had been taken as a ward by the Harkkens. He died in a jousting accident two years later, bringing the ancient line of the Mancellins to an end.

Where Cellinfast had once stood, the Abomination King raised the dark tower of Sevash. Some claim that this means 'the fortress that heralds the fall' in the black tongue of the Under-realm, but this is an embellishment too far for my tastes. What was left of Brightwater, he levelled, and in the city's place he built thirteen walls behind which to practise his black arts. Those who had failed to flee Brightwater's end were seized and taken for the Abomination King's experiments in dark magic. On a clear day, those who lived on the south bank of the Gulmid, the river that divides Guiland from Midding, claimed that you could hear the screams of those trapped in Sevash's uppermost chamber. When the Abomination King ran out of subjects, it was towards those river settlements he turned, sending fell creatures raiding across the Gulmid to claim men, women, and children for his research. Even in the last days of his reign, when my father and his vast force of Guilanders laid siege to the thirteen walls and claimed them one by one, the Abomination King's experimentations endured. Many Guilish soldiers were captured from behind their siege lines and borne by his dark servants to the tower of Sevash.

At the end of the war, Sevash was toppled by my father. He might have hoped this would spell the end of the Dreadveil, but the stain of the Abomination King's magic was not so easily expunged. My father left the walls where they stood. There would have been no point felling them, he said – it would be many centuries before what had once been Brightwater would be fit again for human habitation.

The outermost of these walls seemed to rise from the barren plains like a malevolent ghost, sheer black granite a hundred feet high, crumbling in places where the Guilish cannonballs had found their mark. There was no gate, just monolithic rock stretching into the fire-stained heavens. My heartbeat rose as I stared up at it, awestruck at its immensity, my sense of dread growing with every step closer I came. The battlements were deserted, but there was a hum of evil in this place, a low murmur of the shades of all those who had perished here. I touched the wall with a curious hand, and recoiled in fear at the vision that flashed in my mind's eye. A tall, narrow figure, draped in armour of black adamantium, wearing a crown topped with sharpened, uneven spikes and with crimson eyes that seemed to burn through my flesh and leave my very soul exposed.

A shudder went through me. It was only an echo. If Hala-grim had already succeeded in her air of restoring her master to life, there would surely be some sign of it here. At least, that was what I told myself to temper my fear.

The outermost wall was many miles in circumference. I knew that the first breach during the siege had come to the south, so I walked anti-clockwise, keeping the wall on my left. It took me long enough to find it that several times I wondered if I had perhaps made a mistake and ought to double back. The remains of the Guilish siege effort were everywhere – broken swords and shattered shields, horses' ribcages, abandoned tents flapping in the ill wind. I swapped the blade I had taken from Roddin's corpse for another, and claimed a shield so battered that its heraldry could no longer be identified, then a sturdy iron helmet with the nose guard broken off. Every object I found was a reminder that I walked in the footsteps of those who had laid down their lives to put down the same evil I now sought to thwart.

The breach revealed the wall's sturdiness, twenty feet of solid granite. After their cannonballs had failed to penetrate it, the Guilish had tunnelled underneath. The skirmishes fought in the barren, lightless depths below Sevash were said to have been some of the most terrifying of the whole siege, men battling goblins and bloodworms in the dark, knowing that the earth might collapse in on them at any moment. Their reward had been a thirty-foot gash torn into the first line of the Abomination King's defences.

The vast pile of rubble they had left in its place was itself still an indomitable obstacle, but at least I would not have to cross it under a barrage of slings and arrows like those who had gone before me.

I picked my way across, navigating the capricious, debris-strewn ground as best I could, throwing regular glances up towards the ramparts. When I reached the other side, I threw myself against the wall, both relieved to have made it within the first wall and apprehensive of what was to come.

Twelve more times I would have to do this, and at the end, the true test awaited me. Halagrim and her army of the dead. Hosten as well – though in what state I would find him I did not know. I ought to have hated him, but mostly I feared for what might have become of him. He might need saving just as much as Locan did.

And, if I was too late, the Abomination King himself. The sword in my hand felt of little more use than the wooden one I had wielded in Tulbar's arena, but I held it tighter all the same.

Fifty yards of open ground divided me from where the Guilish had breached the next wall. Fear bristled up the back of my neck as I crossed towards it, the towering battlements creating the inescapable sensation that I was being watched. More relics of the siege littered the ground, black iron axes built for goblin hands, the tattered remains of a Harkken banner trodden into the dirt, the black bones of a creature with six arms and two heads. The Abomination King's experiments had yielded more error than success, and beyond his great force of goblins these failures had made up the bulk of his army. The successes, if you could call them that, were rarer, and no less horrifying – wrorcs, men whose own blood had been drained and replaced with that of an orc; harpies, goblins given the wings of bats so they could take to the skies and rain arrows down from above the Guilish lines; cynocs, humans transformed to slavering hounds, blessed with the obedience and ravenous instincts of dogs and the wits and speech of men.

If the Abomination King returned, such beasts would once again roam in the lands of Midding. Monsters would again steal across the Gulmid, snatching children from their beds to become subjects for his infernal research. And this time, there was not the strength in Guiland to stand against him.

It could not be allowed to happen, no matter if it cost me my life. It had been a source of great angst that my father had not taken me to Sevash with him. At last, I had the opportunity to prove that he had been wrong. There was no fault in my courage. I was here, alone, and with mortal weapons would have to find a way to slay one of the greatest sorcerers of our age, the woman who had stood at the Abomination King's right hand, bringing his prisoners back to life when the agony of his experiments caused their hearts to fail.

These were the thoughts that followed me as I made my way through the broken walls of Sevash. If my courage failed, then all else would fall with it. The wraiths that had stalked me ever since I entered the Dreadveil continued to swirl around me, the press of them growing thicker with every step, as if drawn by my fear. A force of men one hundred thousand strong had fallen upon this fortress, and still Halagrim had endured. What hope did I have? Locan would have been better suited to this trial, but Locan was lost to me, battered and broken somewhere within these walls, subjected to the infernal torments of the Deathmistress.

Before the twelfth, penultimate wall, I stopped. I had encountered no foe yet, but if Halagrim were vigilant, this seemed just the place she might station sentries, assuming enough of her dead followers' minds remained that they could follow such a command.

But the walls still appeared to be deserted. The breach here had created a route of haphazard stone up to the battlements, albeit a treacherous one that might crumble under my feet. For the sake of a look at what awaited me, I would have to risk it.

My long legs and lithe frame made me well suited for climbing, even if my fraying nerves and pounding heart did not agree. I reached the top and, keeping myself as low as possible, crept to the parapet.

The air was clearer up here, and the drone of the Dreadveil that had lodged itself in my ears lessened. A different noise reached my ears, and it was a sound that filled me with dread.

The scrape and thump of masonry. The steady sound of hundreds upon hundreds of bricks being cleared away.

The ruins of Sevash were hidden by the height of the thirteenth wall, but that noise told its own story. Halagrim's army was digging. Searching for the entombed body of the Abomination King.

Darkness fell, though with the haze of the Dreadveil it made little difference whether it was day or night. I carefully descended the way I had come and crept my way across the open ground to the thirteenth wall.

The breach here was thinner than the rest, no more than five feet across, where a cadre of wizards had worked together to pull apart the edifice at its foundations. It was said that the ferocity of the Abomination King's defence had made all else impossible, with every servant and every mote of his black arts turned in a last desperate attempt to throw back the Guilanders. The day they at last broke through was said to have been the deadliest of the siege, thousands of men funnelled through this narrow aperture while goblins and worse cast down rocks and boiling oil upon them. The marks of battle were everywhere:

discarded shields; black and broken goblin skulls; helmets melted and disfigured by sorcery.

I stood on hallowed ground, blessed by the blood of my countrymen. How many of them had given their lives for each inch of the ground on which I set my feet? Their only reward had been an unmarked grave in this broken, barren land. For a long time, I had believed that my father had denied me something in leaving me behind when he marched on Sevash. But he had spared me something as well.

I paused on the far side, ducking behind a section of broken wall. This had been the Abomination King's inner sanctum and last bastion, but I had not been prepared for the destruction I would see.

When men speak of the evil he wrought, they always mention the tower. I have never seen it as it was, but they say that a purple fire burnt in it every hour of the day for over four hundred years. This was where his wickedest deeds had taken place, where men were turned, where from his dark throne the Abomination King communed with the blackest forces of the Underrealm.

They scarcely mention what he did below.

Just beyond the thirteenth wall, the ground fell away into a great quarry. A maze of criss-crossing bridges covered it, granting access to the ruins of the tower via a series of precarious plateaus. But all else had been quarried away.

Filled with a mix of awe and terror, I crept to the edge and gazed down. The excavation was many hundreds of feet deep, a yawning chasm plunging so far into the earth that the fires below were visible. Magma churned and bubbled and plumes of lava leapt into the air, billowing torrents of hot, pungent smoke that forced me to cover my mouth with my sleeve.

It stank of iron and sulphur. Iron, sulphur, and death, the corruption that had given form to the Dreadveil and made barren the once fertile soil of Brightwater. I squinted into the smog, making out the fetters and manacles that decorated the sheer sides, some still containing deformed skeletons with misshapen skulls and uneven wings sprouting from their shoulder blades.

If any of these captives had still lived when the Guilanders breached the final wall, it would have been beyond the means of my countrymen to grant these wretched victims the gift of mercy. They would have died slowly, succumbing to the smoke and heat as the moisture bled out of them.

The depths seemed to stare back at me, the agonised screams of hundreds of ghosts beckoning me to go deeper. The wraiths swarmed around me like flies around a corpse, drawn either to this well of human misery or my own horror as I contemplated how many victims had their humanity stripped from them in this great inferno.

There might be worse yet to come, I knew.

Across a succession of rickety walkways, the ruined tower of Sevash waited for me, a carcass of black stone being picked apart by Halagrim's sightless, sleepless army. Great lumps of masonry were being dragged away from the ruins and cast into the fire below, sending up jets of lava hundreds of feet into the air. With a violent hiss, a plume of magma splattered across a wooden bridge, disintegrating ropes and sending planks of burning timber falling into the depths.

There was no sign of Halagrim herself, and that worried me. I scoured the battlements, but the only creatures watching me were the persistent spectral figures of the wraiths. Their movements were angrier now, as if they knew I was there to ensure their master remained buried. Clearly they did not perceive how little threat I posed. The only thing preventing the undead from tearing me apart was that I was still too far away for them to notice me.

A shadow passed overhead and I threw myself to the ground. It flew with a chorus of ghastly screeching, and when I looked to the sky, I saw that it was not one creature, but many. A flock of ravens wrought from coal-black goblin bones soared past, their wings shrieking in protest as bone rubbed against bone, and the cargo they carried chilled my blood to ice.

Halagrim descended from the violent red sky on the wings of her deathly servants, six sets of talons clutching each side of her cloak. Mercifully, she did not appear to have seen me, for they deposited her on the island that housed the broken tower, at the very top of the wreckage.

She stepped free of their grasp like a queen descending from her throne. I was too far away to see her well, and despite my pounding heart I suspected I was beyond the measure of her eyesight as well, but something in the way she stood told me that she was displeased.

'Hosten!' she barked. Her voice cut through the muggy air like honed steel through parchment. 'Attend me!'

I searched for Hosten, but did not see him among the undead. Then a figure began to shamble up the side of the ruins. It moved differently to the dead men, more lively, despite the awkwardness of its gait. It came on all fours, one of its back legs dragging lamely behind it, and as I realised what I was seeing, my stomach fell into the pit of my bowels.

The dream of any tyrant is the absolute obedience of their subjects. And for the Abomination King, not even the cringing, fearful submission of the men forced to do his bidding had been enough. Nor, it seemed, for Halagrim.

Nothing of the man I had known in Tulbar remained now. If Halagrim had not called him by name, I doubt I would have recognised him. Hosten's shoulders stood twice the width of his hideously tapered waist, as if his torso had been crushed and shaped by some torturous corset. His clothes were gone, revealing a body burnt and blackened to a leathery hide. His ears had been stretched hideously, the tops of them protruding above his head like a dog's. Even his limbs seemed to have offended Halagrim – in place of Hosten's scribe-like hands were now the three-fingered claws of a vast owl, and of his feet one had been replaced with the hoof of a bull and the other a dog's padded paw.

Of the dark bargain he had struck with Halagrim, Hosten had learnt the ultimate price, the reason why every Guilander spoke of Sevash in fearful whispers. My opinion of the Mór of Tulbar had been wavering ever since Locan had first voiced his suspicions, between seeing him as the clever, kindred spirit I had recognised when I first arrived in Tulbar and the devious, duplicitous creature he had since shown himself to be. But in that moment, my heart broke for him. All his dreams for Paleir were shattered, destroyed by his own hubris and the black arts of Sevash.

I searched his features for some flicker of regret, of shame, but his face betrayed nothing. His nose and jaw had been stretched to resemble the snout of a hunting hound, and his sharp green eyes had turned a sickly, jaundiced yellow.

It had been only a few days ago that Hosten and I had laughed together in the throne room of Caradrahan Hall. Locan had been right to warn me that a king's lust for power would eventually always triumph over their desire to do right. But he had not told me that sometimes, it was not their subjects who suffered the consequences, but themselves.

'Yes, mistress?' slobbered Hosten as he approached Halagrim. His tongue lolled out of the side of his canine mouth, his speech blighted by the unfamiliarity of his new form.

Halagrim gave a guttural laugh. 'I do prefer you this way.' A whip appeared in her hand, and she laid it threateningly against Hosten's snout. 'How can this be taking so long?' Her eyes fell upon the ruin she had made of his hands and feet. 'Perhaps another lesson in obedience is required?'

'Apologies, mistress.' The creature that had once been

Hosten cringed back from her, covering his face with one of his misshapen hands. 'If I had more men, stronger men—'

Halagrim lashed the whip against Hosten's snout, sending him cowering away in fear. 'We all wish for better servants, Hosten. You would not have been my first choice, but I have made do with the tools available to me.' She gestured towards his mismatched legs. 'Clear the wreckage by morning, and perhaps I will refine some of my... adjustments. Fail, however...' Her eyebrow arched. 'And the master will not be pleased. He is not so forgiving as I.'

At the mention of the word 'master', Hosten's ears pricked up. 'I will serve you and the master loyally,' he said, practically falling over himself in his desire to please her. 'But... my legs... my hands... please...' He fell to his knees, pressing his mismatched hands together in supplication. 'I swear, I've tried... just give me them back... I swear I will haul every stone...' He broke down in a cacophony of wracking sobs.

Halagrim's back was to me. I was still several hundred yards and several rope bridges away from her, but with Hosten's sobbing and the steady din of the stones being shunted away perhaps she might not hear my approach. She was not yet so powerful enough to survive a sword being driven up into her heart, at least I hoped. I crept towards one of the bridges.

Halagrim was now stroking between Hosten's ears with a pale finger, while his mottled purple tongue licked at her palm. A shudder of revulsion went through me. 'I know,' she said softly. 'I know you wish to see the master as badly as I do. But there must be consequences for failure. You will impress upon our workforce the need for urgency.' She held out the whip, and Hosten claimed it in his jaws. 'Dead they may be, but my servants will still feel the taste of the lash.' She turned away. 'I have other matters to attend to – our guest must be made ready. When I next appear, if there is a single pebble left uncleared, I will reclaim the feet I was merciful enough to grant you.'

The guest she had spoken of could only be Locan. He was still alive. If I saw where Halagrim went, I might follow her straight to him. As battered and broken as he might be at Halagrim's hands, I surely had a better hope of putting an end to the necromancer with Locan beside me.

The necromancer lifted her hands to the air, and her bone-ravens descended as if on strings. 'One more thing,' she added as she was lifted into the air. 'Where is my dragon?'

'I... Mistress...' Hosten was trembling. 'It has not returned.'

A flash of rage shuddered across Halagrim's ruined face. 'Our master's enemies gather. They may be close. Remain vigilant. I am sure I have sufficiently impressed upon you the consequences should we fail.'

I was waiting in anticipation for her to ascend. But to my dismay, Halagrim remained where she was. She contemplated her fingers, turning them over under her gaze as if they were the most remarkable things she had ever seen.

'I had forgotten,' she whispered. 'Even with our master fallen into shadow, simply being here, in his sanctuary, my magic begins to restore itself.' She let out a creaking cackle. 'And they thought him *dead*. Even *death* flees before the power of the Abomination King.'

Halagrim gave a lazy twirl of her hand. For several seconds, nothing happened, but then the earth shuddered, setting the bridge I had just ventured onto shaking violently, and from the fiery depths below hundreds of bones soared into the air, goblin and human and many more creatures besides. Halagrim manipulated her fingers with the dexterity of a tailor, and the shuddering flight of the bones became elegant, almost beautiful, spinning towards one another like partners in a dance.

When the necromancer was done, a dozen more of her bone-ravens patrolled the sky, staring down at their mistress with their empty eye sockets, waiting for their instructions.

'Sentries,' she said to Hosten. 'Should they find any intruders, you will send them to the depths.'

As Halagrim ascended into the air, her new creations took flight with her, but instead of bearing her with the rest they began sweeping across the sky. One glided right over the top of me, and I threw myself to the ground.

I watched as Halagrim was borne away on wings of death, leaving me trapped in the heart of Sevash, under the watchful eyes of her undead servants.

CHAPTER 26

To my rare good fortune, the plateau I had been watching from hid a small alcove just below the bridge. When I was sure it was safe, I carefully lowered myself down and swung inside.

My hiding place gave me a good vantage on where the excavation of the tower continued. Halagrim's shambling undead had redoubled their efforts. Hosten growled and shouted at those he perceived to be dawdling, taking the whip in one of his claws and lashing out at any who repeated the offence, cleaving dead flesh from bone.

If not for the patrolling bone-ravens, I might have been able to evade the dead, but until the winged creatures turned their attention elsewhere, I was trapped. Hunks of stone continued to be hauled into the pit, throwing up plumes of flame when they struck the lava. One came within mere feet of me, so close that I could feel its blistering heat against my face.

When dark fully fell, I would have no choice but to move. It could only be a matter of time before my luck ran out and my body was charred down to the bones. Halagrim's flight had taken her up to a section of the thirteenth wall's battlements. If I could find a way up there, I could put an end to her before she returned to raise her master.

Yet with each piece of rubble that was cast into the fire, I felt a deepening sense of despair. Aydhenia could have swept down upon Sevash and steamed Halagrim alive, but all I could do was watch as stone by stone, inch by inch, the necromancer's army came closer to liberating the body of her master.

Let him be dust, I thought to myself, mouthing the words as a silent mantra lest Halagrim's creatures hear me. *Let his body be crushed and beyond saving.* But I had felt the echo of his presence in the cool touch of the infernal walls he had raised, felt the cold malevolence that waited beneath that pile of stones. If I failed, the Abomination King would rise.

My only hope was to slay Halagrim. Without her ritual, the Abomination King's soul would remain trapped in the deepest circle of the Underrealm. I would cast his cold corpse into the fire, so that there could be no future Halagrims who sought to raise their sleeping master.

When I was sure it would become no darker, I moved, throwing my leg over the ledge above me and levering myself back onto the plateau. Across the columns of stone that teetered above the lava, torches had ignited seemingly by themselves, but it was my hope their brightness would give me a place to hide. Dead things feared the fire – even the wraiths that had been my constant companion through Midding shrank away as I crouched beneath the glow of the first flame I found.

I made it safely to the next plateau. I waited a few seconds for a caw of alarm from the sky, but none came, and I readied myself to cross the next bridge, the first of many that would lead me towards where Halagrim had disappeared. Even if the patrolling ravens saw me, they were only bones and black magic. One swing of my sword would knock them out of the sky. And I was quicker than the dead.

My foot was on the bridge when a shrill cry went up from the broken tower, chilling me to the depths of my soul.

'*Mistress!*' came Hosten's dutiful cry. '*Mistress!*'

I threw myself behind a torch. From the shadow of the thirteenth wall, a black silhouette rose into a sky of bleeding smoke. The wings of her sinister bone-ravens clacked against each other as, once more, Halagrim descended towards the broken tower of Sevash.

But this time, she had not come alone.

A second cloud of bone-ravens followed their mistress, their talons locked around a large, cumbersome cage. They struggled to control its weight, squawking in alarm to one another as it shook and staggered through the air.

As it passed overhead, I caught a brief glimpse of a figure through the bars. Locan. I claimed the torch and thought briefly of throwing it into the sky to cast the shadows with which he could work his escape, but as the ravens descended, I was able to discern more closely the cage's contents. It was Locan, but he was not sitting or standing in the cage as an ordinary man might have done. He was suspended in the air, thrashing with his legs as if to free himself from whatever invisible force bound him, his neck bent back towards the heavens.

The ravens flew on with their cargo. Halagrim was already down, sweeping towards the broken tower as her shrieking creations pulled away her cloak. She was naked underneath, her body as gaunt and pale as a shimmering crescent moon. I would get no other chance. As fast as I dared, I set out across the rope bridge that would lead me towards the excavation site.

Hosten approached Halagrim and went down on all fours in supplication. 'Mistress, it is done.'

'And not a moment too soon.' I caught the corner of Halagrim's cold smile. All the eyes of the dead were on her, and I hurried on while their attention was diverted.

'Pardon my question, mistress, but what is that?' Hosten indicated towards something in Halagrim's hand.

'This?' Halagrim held the object aloft, and I saw for the first time that it was a simple clay cup. She tipped it slightly, and a trickle of water fell to splatter against the ground.

From his cage, Locan gave a cry of alarm, and I was forced to throw myself flat against the bridge as all eyes turned towards him.

The necromancer let out a peal of laughter. 'A prison of my own devising. If you displease me, you may find yourself in there as well.' She tipped it back the other way, and again Locan cried out as his body suddenly lurched sideways.

I realised then how Halagrim was keeping Locan in the cage. The poppet she had manipulated to shatter Locan's arms and legs was in that cup. That was why Locan was kicking so hard – to save himself from drowning in the empty air.

'Men are much easier to control when they are this size,' said Halagrim. 'And so much quieter. Why, I've barely heard a sound from him since we reached Midding.'

The necromancer put her hand over the top of the vessel and spun it upside down, flipping Locan head over heels in mid-air. She turned the cup again, and Locan spun upright, thrashing desperately as he coughed and spluttered on invisible water.

Halagrim turned away and began ascending the ruined tower, while Hosten loyally dogged her steps.

Haste was more important than caution now. I raced over the last few bridges and skidded to a stop alongside Locan's cage.

'Locan,' I hissed through the bars.

His eyes flickered over his shoulder towards me, wide and blinking against the surf of the waves I could not see. He tried to speak, but his words were half lost to the water. He coughed several times. 'The fuck you... doing here?' he rasped. His voice was as frayed as a piece of old rope. I could see the crooks in his arms and his leg where Halagrim had broken them. The pain must have been agonising – it was a measure of Locan's stubbornness that he had not let himself sink to the bottom and drown. 'If you're... that desperate... to die... empty that... fucking cup...'

From the shadow of the cage, I watched as the dead advanced to the edges of the tower, gazing at their mistress. Their excavation had formed a pit in the centre of the rubble, and I lost sight of Halagrim as she reached the top of the slope and descended towards it. There was a sense of feverish anticipation – the muggy air felt warmer, the movements of the wraiths becoming more agitated. If I was going to act, it would have to be now. The Dreadveil hummed oppressively in my ears. In my mind's eye, I saw the tower of Sevash rising again, greater, taller, the fires of the Abomination King stretching into the crimson clouds, the screams of his victims echoing against the atmosphere.

My heart was thundering. My hand was resting on my sword hilt, rivers of sweat running past the cross guard and down the blade.

Locan's treading of the air was becoming more frantic. If I reached through the bars, I could try and pull him free, but that risked revealing myself to Halagrim.

Locan turned his head towards me, the cords of his neck standing out with the effort it cost him. 'Goblin-shitting coward... Get on with it.'

Locan's insult stirred me to action. I pulled my sword free, and barrelled towards the tower.

At the sound of my steps, Halagrim's undead servants sluggishly turned towards me. Some reached for me as I ran past, grasping at my cloak with their cold, dead fingers. I swished my torch in a wild arc, and they drew back, the flames reflecting in the whites of their fearful dead eyes.

A few tried to pursue me, but my feet were quicker than those of the undead. I scrabbled up a pile of broken stone, using the tip of my sword for balance, slowing so that Halagrim would not hear my approach. As I reached the top, I threw the torch behind me, scattering the persistent undead. The hum was reaching towards a crescendo now, so loud I could no longer hear the beating of blood in my ears.

At the top of the pile, the stones veered sharply downwards. Below, Halagrim stood at the base of a vast pit, where the rubble had been cleared away enough to reveal a floor of black, hexagonal flagstones bound with red mortar. Ruined pillars that had once held up the tower teetered ominously, threatening to fall. Halagrim was still clutching the cup of water, but her focus was intent upon the ground, and as I realised why, I swear I nearly cried out in terror.

They had buried him in his armour. Thousands of interlocking plates of black adamantium, like devilish snakeskin. A grilled helmet covered his face, wrought with jagged spikes, like a bloated, poisonous black fruit. Miniature blades stretched down the vambraces and up the greaves, sharp enough to gut a man if they were skilled or lucky enough to get past the huge morningstar that was still gripped in a gauntleted fist.

I stood in sight of the Abomination King, in all the glory of his war gear. It was his sorcery that had made him infamous, but my father still bore a wound dealt by that wickedly spiked morningstar. The air caught in my throat, now so thick that it hurt to breathe. Even in death, being within his presence was as if I had been submerged in hot, viscous soup. I fell to a knee, unable to stop myself. An army of wraiths flew back and forth over his open grave, too many to count, their spectral bodies fluttering with anticipation.

Hosten, too, had dropped to his knees, prostrating himself before the Abomination King's corpse, heavy tears dropping onto the flagstone.

'Get up,' snapped Halagrim. She pushed Hosten aside and knelt before her master.

This would have been the ideal moment to attack her. To rush down and bathe my blade in the witch's blood before she even knew I was there. The idea took form, but my body refused to obey me. A great weight seemed to press down on me from the heavens. My arm battled against the heft of my sword. Even the wraiths looked heavier, more corporeal, their ghostly forms solidifying in the cloying air.

'Master.' Halagrim laid her hands upon the chest piece of his armour, stark white against the black. 'Our realm calls out for the return of its true king. We beseech Dagin, the Lord of the Underrealm, to release you. We offer this soul' – she claimed the cup containing the poppet from where she had placed it on the ground – 'in exchange for our lord's freedom.' She balanced it on the corpse's chest. 'A soul whose weight might be measured in the souls of those who he condemned to your eternal torment. An artist of death, a worthy servant of your noble kingdom.'

I was stunned. She meant to exchange Locan's life for that of the Abomination King. Already, tendrils of black smoke were emanating from the poppet, like a wizard in the throes of Dagin's Bloom. Stirred from my stupor, I raced down towards them, ready to break this ritual by burying my sword in Hala-grim's black heart.

I was only yards away from her when something hit me from the side. Hosten's weight pinned me to the ground. I tried to bring my sword to bear, but the transformation wrought by Halagrim had imbued his twisted limbs with infernal strength. I cried out in agony as his slobbering jaws clenched around my elbow, causing the blade to fall from my fingers.

He straddled me, his mismatched claws pinning my arms against the flagstones, dark saliva dripping into my face as I struggled. He growled deep in his throat, then gnashed his teeth so close to me that I thought he meant to bite my nose off. 'Welcome, Cetrik.' His yellow eyes were bright with reverence. 'We will serve him together.'

A silver dagger had appeared in Halagrim's hand, the same blade she had stolen from Locan. The poppet was gone, disappeared in a diffusion of dark magic. With a cry somewhere between agony and ecstasy, she flashed the blade across her palm. She squeezed her fist over the corpse's head, and a course of black blood flowed through the open grille of the helmet. She stood, and trailed her hand in a circle, leaving a ring of blood on the flagstones. Immediately, it began to steam. 'We offer this blood as payment for his passage across the River Lechytus. Blood whose potency might be measured in the sorcerous mastery with which it radiates. Offered freely by one with the power to grant a second life to fallen souls, a humble servant before her master.'

If I understood this ritual, Locan was surely dead, but I could still stop Halagrim. I struggled against Hosten's weight, but his grip held firm, his claws tearing the skin of my wrists. Blood was leaking from where his teeth had sunk into my arm, a warm pool spreading beneath me, soaking my clothes.

The wraiths were a swirling storm, so thick in the air that I could hardly see Halagrim's naked form. Her pale flesh was withering, her breath coming low and laboured. She tilted her head back and squeezed some of her own blood into her mouth. 'Hosten.' She beckoned to her servant. 'Come. The wraiths will deal with him.'

The weight of Hosten's canine body against my chest relented. I grabbed for the blade that had been knocked from my grasp. In her rush to complete the ritual, Halagrim had forgotten my Harkken blood – the wraiths swarmed thickly but their spectral hands passed through me. I hefted my sword in my gore-soaked hand and flew through the ring of ghosts towards the necromancer and her dead master.

I swept towards Halagrim, bringing my sword back, willing all my remaining strength into a blow that would cleave the sorceress's head from her shoulders. She turned towards me, her eyes wide with fear, before a flight of bone-ravens bore her to the ground and my strike passed harmlessly overhead. A second flock came at my face in a cacophony of skeletal black wings. I swung blindly, knocking the infernal creatures out of the air, but there were too many. The wraiths were shrieking, sending sharp pain through my skull.

Halagrim was on her hands and knees, panting. 'We offer this body as the vessel by which our master will return!' she screamed over the din. Hosten had claimed the sword. He stood over the corpse, grasping the blade awkwardly in his owl claw and holding it out towards Halagrim. His back legs were shaking. 'A body forged from iron and sulphur by our master's hand!'

I screamed as Halagrim claimed the blade and in a spurt of black blood plunged it into Hosten's torso. He howled to the sky as she dragged it down his abdomen, his skin splitting like parchment as a tide of gore and viscera spilled onto the body of the Abomination King. His crooked legs buckled underneath him, and his body collapsed onto the corpse of his master.

The wraiths fell silent. The last of the bone-ravens clattered to the ground as I bludgeoned it from my path. Halagrim was still on the floor, trembling as if she did not have the strength to rise again, staring at the two entwined corpses. The circle of blood she had trailed around the corpse had disappeared.

For a time, nothing happened. The wraiths faded to nothingness, as if they had been no more than a fearful imagining. Even the constant hum of the Dreadveil seemed to have fallen still.

Then horrifyingly, Hosten's ruined corpse began to rise.

It turned towards us, with the slowness of long sleep, limbs struggling to move under their unfamiliar weight. Hosten stood as hale as he had moments earlier. The hideous wound down his torso had sewn shut, even as his blood continued to creep across the flagstones. His sickly yellow eyes blazed, bright and beastly.

'*Halagrim.*' His voice was a whisper. A sickle-sharp talon traced in the air in experimentation.

'*Master.*' Halagrim struggled to her feet. There were tears in her eyes. She glided towards him on steps light as air, reaching out a hand to take the beast's claw in hers in a gesture that shone with devotion. 'You have returned.'

The creature that had been Hosten withdrew its claw from her touch. 'And this... *vessel.* You believed I would welcome this?' Its voice crackled with contempt. 'The body of a petty king who believed himself my equal? This twisted corpse?'

Halagrim faltered. 'I... I worked with the tools I had, Master. The assassin's soul for your freedom, my blood for your passage, the boy's body—'

'The tools you had?' Hosten's brow rose, his muzzle distending in what might have been a smile. 'You always said you would do anything for me, didn't you, Halagrim?'

'*Anything,*' Halagrim gushed. 'You found me, raised me from nothing, showed me what my power—'

Hosten cut her off with a raised paw. 'Then you're going to have to die for me.'

I had only a moment to register the shock on Halagrim's face before Hosten's great jaws lunged forward and engulfed her head. She did not even cry out. There was a hideous crack of bone as those powerful teeth severed her spine at the neck, and with a great tearing of flesh, Halagrim's skull was wrenched from her body.

The necromancer collapsed forward, a fountain of blood spurting from her neck, as black and violent as burning pitch. It bathed the body of the Abomination King, seeped hungrily into his armour, the corpse soaking up every drop.

Watching Halagrim's fall stirred me from my inertia. All

around me, bones were falling from the sky as Halagrim's devilish ravens breathed their last. My sword still lay at the feet of the resurrected Hosten as he looked down upon the body of his master. I claimed it from the ground and drove the blade up between his ribs to where I hoped his heart would be.

He fell without a struggle, and for the second time that night the beast who had been my friend lay still.

I stared down at the Abomination King's corpse, too terrified to move. *Stay down*, I willed. *Stay down.* I whispered it to myself like a prayer.

And just as I dared myself to believe that the Abomination King's sacrifice of his closest acolyte had failed, the gauntleted fingers of his right hand began to twitch. And behind the grille of the helmet, I felt a pair of vengeful eyes flicker, then find me, fixing me with a black gaze that held me in place.

Metal scraped against stone, and, inexorably, the body began to rise.

I still held my sword, but for all the gold you could offer me, in that moment I would never have dared bring it to bear. I was frozen with fear, too scared even to blink.

The Abomination King had risen.

CHAPTER 27

He was not so tall as I had supposed. Even armoured, he was shorter than me by a finger. His helmet was dented at the temple, and as he reached a hand up towards it, he revealed the place where the supple mail under his arm had been pierced by the simple steel blade of my father. For a moment, I thought of stepping forward and burying my own weapon in the same place, but the sword in my hand was as heavy and immovable as death.

Slowly, the Abomination King removed his helm, every movement as deliberate as if he were making it for the first time. My heart was beating as if it meant to escape my chest.

For over four hundred years, the Abomination King had dabbled in the most corrupting magics of our and any realm, putrefying his own flesh with every sorcerous experiment. I could only wait, steeling myself for the horror that lurked beneath the black iron.

But as he placed the helmet under his arm, it was a man who stared back at me. Grey eyes like plumes of mist, silver-streaked black hair that hung loose to his shoulders, a long jaw with a jutting chin, and a mouth that sat as still and level as a moonlit pool. Just a man. I might have walked past him in any tavern in the world and never looked twice. He was a contradiction, a riddle where a monster ought to have stood.

Then he spoke, and my blood ran to ice. His voice was like rich honey poured over steel. 'Cetrik.' He gave a flat smile. 'So good of you to join me. I do hate to be alone. When the story of my resurrection is told and retold, you will be there to swear that it was so.'

I could not speak. My tongue was a dead worm, my legs like treacle. If I had taken a step I would have fallen flat on my face. My sword was on the ground. I had not even felt it slip from my grasp.

The Abomination King prodded at Halagrim's headless corpse with a toe. 'She knew it would end like this,' he said. His voice mirrored the timbre of regret, but I caught no hint of grief behind his cold eyes. 'She was always so fierce, so ruthless. Had she been the first to rise above the common magicker, she would have cut me down before I could grow strong enough to threaten her. But I was so young then. I believed that to succeed I must collaborate, that only by pooling our talents and learning from each other could we together build a new world. Halagrim the Deathmistress, Bannacus of the Boar's Head, Juniper Daginsbane, and a dozen others whose names escape me. My companions. My acolytes. All dead at my hand, and deservedly so. But Halagrim was the best of them. The only one who could have found the means to free me.'

He bent down to pick up the remains of one of her bone-ravens. 'Fine work. All she must have done to see me rise, and all with less than a sliver of her magic. It was centuries ago that she and I chose to bind ourselves to one another. We believed it would place us beyond the clutches of the Underrealm, but as in so much else, we were wrong. I fell, and her magic fell with me. There is a lesson there, Cetrik. Hold tight to what is yours.

Giving away even a sliver of yourself might one day spell your doom.'

He stepped towards me and kicked my sword aside.

'I suppose you are wondering how I know your name.' He was so close to me that even with my Harkken blood I could feel the heady miasma of magic radiating from his being. 'The wraiths were the little I could leave behind in this realm. I watched you every step of the way from Guiland to Narlond, you and that magnificent horse. I even spoke to you. The first time I have spoken through my wraiths without driving the listener to madness and despair. You heard none of it of course, but to you I have uttered every horror of the Underrealm, every daydream of what I would do when I escaped, even every word that passed between me and Dagin.'

My head was spinning. He was speaking of Dagin, the ancient god who had forged the Underrealm, whose rotting corpse still swelled there, radiating its foulness. It was impossible.

'Yes, it's true. I broke bread with Dagin.' For the first time, the Abomination King laughed, a discordant melody of broken bells. 'He lives, after a sense. Quite, quite mad, of course. He longs to claim this realm as well, to wreak vengeance upon the living, but five thousand years of stewing over it and still he is trapped. His rage when he learns I have escaped will be never-ending.'

The Abomination King's grey eyes glittered hungrily. 'But my time in the Underrealm has revealed to me what I always hoped for: the means to conquer death. Did your family ever wonder why I never sought to claim lands beyond the borders of Midding?'

'You feared them,' I croaked. My voice was as dry as the old bones that littered the ground. 'You feared us.'

The Abomination King's mirthful laughter was so vast that it seemed to shake the burning sky. 'Of course. The inherited arrogance of the Harkkens. How I could have used such pride in my youth.

'I learnt the folly of war when my kingdom was but a seed waiting to flower. In my haste to master death, I looked north, seeking the secrets of the elves. Narlond threw me back, as it eventually will every invader. Instead, I was forced to look inwards.' A malicious anger flashed in his eyes. 'And when I was but a few years away from my goal, your father tore down all that I had achieved. It cannot be helped – it is in the nature of humans to destroy. The elves, the giants, the goblins – all brought down for simply having the temerity to live, and so it was with me.' He gave a wry chuckle. 'I have known them all. The elves earnt their pride. They built great monuments while men were still scrabbling in the dirt in search of warmth. The giants in their wisdom understood their time was ending, and when they sought to withdraw and leave the world to the race of men, they were hunted down to the last infant. The goblins know their place – they are naturally subservient to those of greater stock – and though they pose no threat, men still see only foes where they might see servants.

'No. I never sought conflict with Guiland because there was nothing I could learn from you. You needed only to leave me in peace, and when the time came I would have shared my discoveries with you. Victory over Dagin and the Underrealm was at hand.'

He was mad, truly. He spoke of defeating death as if it were simply another land to be conquered, another magic to be discovered. As if his theories and experiments had not condemned thousands upon thousands of people to hideous, agonising ends, screaming for mercy. 'And what of the men, women, and children you stole from Guiland?' I said, gesturing to the remains that littered the ground, the pitch of my voice rising with my anger. 'What of their bones? Over the last four hundred years, who has been a greater servant to the Under-realm than *you*?'

'For the greater good, Cetrik!' The Abomination King flew at me, seizing me by the collar to stop me falling over in my haste to escape. Storm clouds thundered in his cool grey eyes. 'Surely you can understand that! When I found a way to give eternal life and end the stalking terror of the Underrealm, who would have complained? The lives of men are short, miserable things. The brothers and sisters of the dead would have known only the bounty of life. I would never have kept such a gift for myself. It could all have been yours!'

A shadow fell across his face. 'Shall I tell you of the Under-realm? All I have done pales in comparison to the horror. Dagin's hatred for men burns as bright as the day the Swordsman doomed him to the torment of his own infernal domain. Would you condemn yourself to that? Would you condemn your *children* to that?'

I refused to meet his gaze, unable to face the madness that swirled within. Even if his aims were true, what he sought was impossible. He had brought agony and terror upon thousands for a dream that was no more real than a glint in the eye, than a whisper on the wind.

With an angry sneer, the Abomination King thrust me aside. 'Such remarkable mediocrity. So wrapped up in fear and false morality that you refuse to even comprehend the signifi-cance of what I am telling you.'

He was right: I was afraid. The bubbling terror that had been on the cusp of overwhelming me ever since I had witnessed the beginning of Halagrim's ritual at last overcame me. The Abomination King was alive, and death had not improved him. Sevash would rise again. Its walls would be rebuilt. And south of the Gulmid, fires of torture and death would once again be seen reflected against the clouds over the northern horizon.

Seeing my dread, the Abomination King smiled. He backed away to claim his adamantium morningstar, its chain the length of three men, its spiked head a black promise of death. 'Your father was a worthy foe. Even as the last wall fell, I did not believe that any man of flesh and blood could best me. This time, he shall not be so lucky. I know how many men died here, how few capable of taking up a sword must remain. When I enter Guiland with a force of goblins and my improved creations at my back, they will be too few to oppose me.

'And you. You will be the first of them.' His voice was as cold as an open grave. 'With your Harkken blood, I will forge something never even contemplated, and once we have together crushed Guiland, all the secrets of death shall be mine.'

Without warning, he spun his morningstar and lashed it towards my legs, with speed and force enough to shatter my kneecaps to dust. I lurched backwards, and the tip of one of the spikes flashed past me, drawing a thin line of blood across my thigh.

I leapt for my sword, but a crashing blow of the morningstar forced me to roll away, shattering the flagstones where I had stood only a moment before. I turned to run, but made it only a few yards before the morningstar's chain wrapped around my legs and brought me down hard against the rubble.

'You do not have to try so hard.' The Abomination King stalked towards me like a waking nightmare, slowly, deliberately, a man with all the time in the world. I tried to free myself, but he yanked at the chain, pulling it tighter. He reached out his hand, offering it to me. 'In all the time I have spent here perfecting my work, I have not once hosted a prince of the Harkkens.' His eyes glittered, following the trail of blood still leaking from where Hosten's teeth had pierced my wrist. 'The subjects I had were weak, their bodies frail and too receptive to magic. You, though. Cetrik, you do not understand your own strength.' The red sky flashed with the lightning of a distant storm. The Abomination King's face was tight with hunger. 'It was never my wish to create monsters – I only wanted to improve, to *perfect*. Give yourself to me, and together we can banish the forces of the Underrealm *forever*. Everyone you know, everyone you love, will be saved from that torment. You want this, I know you do.'

I stared at his hand. Was Shaliya now trapped in the Underrealm, subject to an eternity of torture? It could not be so. Shaliya's goodness had shone from every aspect of her being. She would have been claimed by the Seamstress, her deeds weighed by Heoloran the Scale-taker and found worthy of entrance to her Golden Kingdom.

But nobody could know for sure. Except perhaps the man standing before me.

But as fresh and raw as the death of Shaliya was, however much I yearned to know what awaited her in the life beyond this one, I had seen only a fraction of the horror the Abomination King had inflicted on his victims, and that had been enough. The half-mad veterans begging in Keystone, consumed with the whispered entreaties of the Abomination King's wraiths. Half-Helm, the wrorc I had encountered in Narlond, who Locan and I had slain to deliver him from his torment. The goblins of Tulbar, enslaved under the Abomination King's whip, who had fled with his fall and found only torment and starvation across the North Water. Every discarded bone that littered the ground belonged to one of the victims of Sevash. Even Hosten, so reckless with ambition that he had allowed himself to be mutilated and slain in the Abomination King's name.

The wizards of Tulbar are known for their melancholy. The misery that Dagin's Bloom forces upon them reduces their waking life to a series of distractions – whatever allows them for a few sweet minutes to forget the horrors they must endure when the forces of the Underrealm rise and claim them. For thirty years' service to the Harkkens, they are promised deliverance from their curse – the blood of Guiland's queen to deaden them to magic and allow them to enjoy what remains of their life free from the torment of Dagin's Bloom. The Blood Price. All they have suffered in the Harkkens' name traded and forgiven for a single mouthful of my family's birthright.

Any Harkken discovered granting a wizard their blood without their queen's leave will learn soon enough that their birth is no protection from her wrath. My sister Leanie learnt this the hard way, but that is a tale for another time. The Harkken dynasty is built on their pact with the wizards – it is why we guard our line so fearfully, ensuring that no child of our stock is born without the knowledge of the queen and those who serve her.

But for the Abomination King, I hoped that my mother would make an exception. I wiped my fingers against the stinging bite wound that Hosten had left in my arm.

I took the Abomination King's offered hand. A surprised, satisfied smile flashed across his face, and I thrust the blood-stained fingers of my other hand towards his mouth. Just a smear across his tongue to end his reign. He would kill me in his wrath, but Sevash would remain in ruins, and never again would he maim and torture in the name of his doomed, unholy experiments.

But something must have shown in my face. A flicker of triumph in my eyes, or the tremor of my hand as our palms met. My fingers were an inch from his face when he recoiled from me, my fingers leaving only a bloody smear from the edge of his mouth to his ear.

My other hand was still locked in his. With impossible strength, he lifted me and slammed me against the flagstones. I felt something inside me crack, and the whip-like motion almost yanked my arm from its socket.

My pained cry heightened as my lung brushed against the sharp edge of a broken rib. Above me, the Abomination King touched a finger to the bloody stain I had left across his cheek, fear and anger warring in his eyes. 'Do you suppose that is the first time a Harkken has tried that?' His voice trembled with fury. 'There was a time when you sent envoys, bearing false gifts laced with blood. Assassins sneaking into my chamber to spike my wine.' He set his steel-shod foot upon my neck and pressed down on my windpipe. 'So be it. You are as foolish as the rest. By the time I am finished, not even your own parents will recognise you. Whatever I remove from you, I will send them as a gift.'

I wanted to tell him there would be no surer way to my parents' good graces, but with his foot on my throat I could not get the words out. He pressed down harder. I flailed and fought, but garbed as he was in his armour it was like trying to move a mountain of steel.

He smiled down at me. 'When you wake, you will be chained over the fires below. I will rebuild Sevash brick by brick, and when I am done, you will be brought to me. Let us discover the limits of your immunity to magic.'

My vision was blackening around the edges. I pounded at his leg, his spiked greaves tearing my fists to ribbons. My terror battled against the desire to simply let go, to sleep and let it end. My final, enduring memory would be the cold, unremarkable face of the Abomination King.

The weight on my windpipe relented, and I found at last that I could breathe. My legs were no longer tangled in the chain of the morningstar. With the last of my strength, I backed away on my hands and knees, trying to put as much distance as possible between myself and the Abomination King.

He was no longer looking at me. His gaze was fixed towards the top of the pile of rubble, the glow of the crimson sky reflecting in his eyes, a peculiar expression playing about his face.

A phantom waited for us. A vengeful ghost broken free of the chains of death. A black silhouette, almost invisible against the darkness, brimming with cold, clinical murder. Locan.

CHAPTER 28

The Abomination King watched him warily. 'This does not concern you, Locan A'Shadow. This is between me and the Harkkens.'

'You know who I am then. Spares us a tiresome introduction.' Locan snorted and spat a long trail of saliva from his perch atop the ruins onto the polished black flagstones. 'I was coming to kill your girlfriend.' He eyed Halagrim's headless corpse. 'But I can see you've already taken care of that. Women. Can't live with them, can't come back from the dead without them. You're a cold cunt—' Locan paused, frowning. 'What do we call you, anyway? Your Abominable Majesty? Your Royal Abominableness? Doesn't trip off the tongue exactly. You must have had a name once.'

The Abomination King's eyes narrowed. 'You should be dead.'

'Look who's talking. And yeah, well. Ain't the first time someone's said that to me.' Locan took a few steps down the rubble. 'I just woke up. Guess old Dagin took one look at me and spat me back out.'

After a moment, the Abomination King's face quirked in

realisation. 'Of course. One death for one life. My rebirth was paid for with Halagrim's. You are of such little consequence that you weren't even needed.'

'As my father used to say.' Locan stretched his hands out, revealing his previously shattered wrists were seemingly uninjured. 'Even unbroke my bones.'

'The magic binding you died with Halagrim,' replied the Abomination King. He watched Locan carefully. 'You are whole, hale, and free to leave.'

'Suppose I ought to thank you for killing her then.' Locan was unarmed, of course, and his clever cloak with all its hidden blades was missing, but he began descending the rubble towards us. 'Now, don't think I'm not grateful, but I don't make a habit of thanking those I'm planning to kill. Looks a touch insincere.'

'Better men than you have tried and failed.' All the same, the Abomination King began to slowly spin his morningstar.

I was still retreating, and when I felt the rubble against my back, I got to my feet and began to climb, never taking my eyes off our foe.

The Abomination King's gaze swung to me. 'We are not finished, Cetrik. Run if you wish, but I will have you before you get beyond the first wall.' He returned his attention to Locan. 'You can still choose to walk away. I have servants who will escort you south to Guiland or north to Narlond, whichever you choose.'

'That's a generous offer to a man that's just returned to the land of the living and doesn't have any weapons,' said Locan. He raised a questioning eyebrow. 'Makes me wonder if you're a little bit afraid.'

A flush of anger crept up the Abomination King's cheeks. 'I have discovered truths beyond the comprehension of mortal men. I have dined in the depths of the Underrealm. I have traded barbs with Dagin himself. I have—'

'Let me just stop you there,' said Locan. 'If you can recall three seconds ago, I just came back from death myself. You know what I saw there? *Nothing.* No Underrealm, no Dagin, no demons dancing a jig around a ring of fire. You're filled with more shit than the imperial privy. You're not a visionary – there are drooling lunatics in asylums with more wits than you have.

'And if I stayed in the same place for four hundred years hidden behind thirteen walls and didn't learn anything, I'd have to be the stupidest cunt alive. I reckon if you left any man alone in a tower for four hundred years he'd at least discover the secret of an eternal erection or something. Give a woman four hundred years and she'd find a way for them to go without men entirely. You though' – Locan gave a bark of laughter – 'for all your preening and pride, what did you actually *do*? Turned a load of peasants and goblins into freaks. Tried to take Narlond four hundred years ago and got kicked in the balls by one fucking elf so hard you never left home again. Then you made up some shit about the Underrealm to try and make it seem like you've not spent centuries wasting your time and wanking over your own cleverness.'

I had seen Locan do this before – bombard his foes with insults and hope to put them in such a rage that he could put an end them easily – but he had not reckoned with the speed and ferocity of the Abomination King. In one rotation, the huge morningstar was travelling too fast to see, and Locan had to leap out of the way as its spiked head thundered into the rubble, sending up a choking cloud of dust and masonry.

When it settled, Locan had disappeared.

The Abomination King cursed, turning on the spot as he dragged his morningstar back, shortening the chain to a few feet and spinning it in tight circles to cover his front and rear. The shadows cast by the glow of the distant moon shrouded behind the Dreadveil were weak, which would slow Locan down, but I had seen him work with worse.

As a distraction, I rushed for where my sword had fallen,

clutching the pain of my broken rib. The morningstar came down so hard and fast that the flagstone shattered, and I had to leap back as the ground disintegrated into nothingness and nearly sent me tumbling into the pool of fire a thousand feet below. I watched as my sword fell, tumbling end over end into the magma.

But my ruse had worked. At the corner of my eye, the Abomination King turned barely in time to prevent Locan's knife finding the weak spot under his armpit, blocking the blade with his gauntlet and deflecting it over his shoulder. The knife shimmered silver, the same weapon Halagrim had used for her blood ritual. Inside his opponent's guard, Locan's leg went to lock around the back of the Abomination King's calf and bear him to the ground, but the sorcerer was quicker, side-stepping and driving the haft of his weapon into Locan's forehead. He retreated from Locan's blade, putting enough distance between them to take advantage of the long reach of his morningstar. Locan closed the gap, and almost immediately regretted it as the spiked head narrowly missed his knee, off target only because Locan chose that moment to slip into his foe's shadow. He re-emerged behind the Abomination King's back, but again the sorcerer was too quick, bringing the morningstar around on the backswing and forcing Locan into a retreat.

Locan's brush with death did not appear to have slowed him, but the Abomination King was faster and more agile than a man in such heavy plate had any right to be, and even a glancing blow from the morningstar would be enough to crush Locan's skull to powder. Locan had only the Abomination King's head and the supple mail at the joints of his armour to aim for.

Locan slipped into the shadows again to close the distance between them. His knife was fast as moonlight, pecking at his enemy's guard in a hundred different places, trying to position himself for a killing thrust. He could not let up for a moment – retreating would allow the Abomination King the full length of his morningstar to work with, and we had both seen his skill with it. Every time he threatened to retreat beyond the reach of Locan's knife, Locan would dive into the shadows and appear in the Abomination King's blind spot. Hoping to distract him, I rushed at the sorcerer's back, and almost immediately had to throw myself to the floor as the spiked ball came within inches of my skull, close enough that I felt the wind rush over my head.

They came to a stop together, the remains of a broken pillar serving to guard them from each other.

The Abomination King's morningstar was a spinning blur of darkness. 'Is that all you have?' He gave an acid laugh, twisting the weapon's head close enough to the ground to send sparks and mortar flying. 'I hoped for more from the most celebrated assassin of his age. I did always wonder whether anyone would ever send you after me. They would have been disappointed.'

'Clearly nobody thought your death was worth that sort of money.' Locan feinted to throw the knife, then slipped into shadows and reappeared atop the broken pillar, almost daring the Abomination King to swing for him.

'A true mercenary.' The Abomination King's mouth twisted. 'I can respect that. Deal only in gold, and you will never owe anything of true worth.'

I had come to my feet and was now inching around the edge where the flagstones met the rubble. In my fist, I clutched a lump of stone. If Locan could keep him talking, I could bring it down on the Abomination King's head and let Locan deal with the rest.

'But that's not all there is to you, is there?' The Abomination King's gaze glittered with malice. 'A mother who tried to kill you. A father who took his own life when he discovered what you were. No other family. Such a weight of gold paid for in death, and nobody to spend it on.'

Locan's lip curled. 'My past is an open book – why not tell me something I don't already know?'

'Very well.' The Abomination King paused, a silence full of meaning. I was behind him now. The rock was shaking in my fist as I battled to still my thumping heart. I crept towards his back. 'Farnella betrayed you.'

The change in Locan's face was like a storm passing over the sun. Farnella. The Rose of Rameon. A celebrated beauty who had cast aside all her family's riches to be with Locan. The only person from his days in the Dominion of whom Locan spoke with any fondness. 'That's not true,' he said. Nevertheless, I heard the tremor of doubt in his voice, caught the flicker of uncertainty in the darkening of his eyes. 'How the fuck would you know anyway?'

'I have always taken an interest in those with unusual magical talents.' The Abomination King's voice was sharp and sleek as silver. 'In my time, I have corresponded with many great men of Rameon. I have exchanged letters with senators and patricians of the old families and even members of the emperor's kin. Not all the world is so unimaginative as the Guilish. Your arrival in the city caused quite a stir – it was not long before men began to write to me of you. Who could fail to be fascinated by an assassin of such skill that he hides in the shadows themselves?'

His morningstar was beginning to spin again. I wanted to cry a warning to Locan, but I was within only a few steps of the Abomination King's back now. Locan was so intent upon his foe he did not even seem to have noticed me. 'It is no secret that Farnella had other lovers,' the Abomination King went on, his voice purring with amusement. 'You both did, after all – but the stories of you that she shared in other men's beds...' The morningstar was still close to him, its chain kept short, but spinning so fast that I feared I could not reach him without it taking my head off. 'I was almost embarrassed to read of it. The weeping and the insecurity and the fear, the agony at being rejected by your parents and the wild plotting against the emperor who stole your home from you. The drinking that you used to numb yourself. The night terrors when you went sober. She shared all of it. All those years you believed they feared you, and the whole of Rameon was laughing behind your back.'

'Lies,' said Locan. But he was not smiling or laughing now. The Abomination King's barbs had struck home. 'Even if any of that were true, Farnella—'

I saw what was about to occur before it happened. I broke into a run, heedless that the Abomination King might hear my heavy tread. The morningstar was a blur of darkness above him, when he unleashed its spiked head like a cannonball directly towards the pillar Locan was balanced on.

The column exploded in a spray of shards, directly below Locan's feet. He fell with it, the morningstar's backswing taking out the base and causing the whole thing to collapse. Locan recovered, somehow leaping clear and landing on his feet, but before he could reach for the shadows the Abomination King was on him, closing the distance between them and with both hands wrapping the adamantium chain of his morningstar around Locan's neck.

Locan's blade came up towards his foe's unprotected face, but the Abomination King was quicker, twisting the spare length of his chain and tangling it around Locan's arm, trapping the dagger between its adamantium links. Locan's left hand came up, grasping to gouge his assailant's eyes, but the Abomination King lifted him off the ground before he could find any purchase, locking their bodies together and suspending Locan in the air with the chain tangled around him like a constricting snake.

My rush forward brought me to within an arm's length of them, my makeshift weapon raised high, but the Abomination King must have sensed my approach, twisting to drive an armoured elbow into my face, knocking me to the floor and sending stars flashing across my vision.

Already, Locan's face was beginning to turn red, his eyes bulging as his legs swung ineffectual kicks against the Abomination King's heavy plate. The rock had slipped from my grasp when I struck the ground. Half-blinded and still dizzy from the blow, I rushed to my feet and leapt onto the Abomination King's back, grasping for his hold on the chain to try and free Locan. He staggered under my weight but remained upright.

He snarled in fury, twisting the chain tighter around Locan's neck. 'I gave you a choice, A'Shadow.' I strained against his grip, but the strength of his adamantium gauntlets refused to yield to me. 'When you reach the Underrealm, give Dagin my regards.'

Locan was still holding the dagger. It glittered among the remorseless black of the adamantium, tangled in the two men's death embrace. I reached for it and grasped it by the blade, releasing a scream as the razor-sharp edge broke the skin of my palm. I reversed the grip, nearly dropping it, and plunged it into the Abomination King's neck.

The hilt turned to molten metal as it penetrated his skin, and my scream became a howl as my already bloodied hand became an inferno of pain. The Abomination King was screaming too, his flesh mortifying to black as whatever sorcery protected him warred against the dagger's silver. His congealing blood crept up the blade towards me as if with a mind of its own, and I let go of the hilt, leaving it to sizzle and spit against the Abomination King's warding spells.

My intervention forced the Abomination King to weaken his grip on Locan to pull the dagger from his neck. I tried to leap clear, but found myself held fast where the sorcerer had managed to tangle the chain around my leg.

Locan's neck was bruised and bloodied where the adamantium had dug into his flesh, but the Abomination King's weakening hold allowed him to set his feet on the ground. He could still not free his arms, but he spat a globule of blood into the sorcerer's eye. 'Hold on tight, shithead,' Locan rasped from his ruined throat. 'You won't like where we're going.'

I knew a moment of terror as the ground fell away beneath us, leaving only a plummeting descent into darkness. Locan forced his way into the shadows, dragging me and the Abomination King with him.

We hurtled through a realm of indistinct blackness, shapes that might have been familiar rushing past before I could discern them, the ruins of Sevash no more than indistinct silhouettes far above us. The chains of the morningstar fell with us, but they had become as formless as the Abomination King's wraiths, writhing like worms feasting on the dead.

I had travelled through shadows with Locan only twice before. Both occasions had lasted less than an instant, a brief moment of terror followed by a dizzying, all-consuming vertigo when I was thrust back into the light. This was different – longer, but in the sense that time stretched into forever, its meaning thinned like fraying cloth. The darkness was all-encompassing, reducing the three of us to our essence, our frail bodies an abstract in a world where shadows reigned and physical form bowed to their will.

Another realm, one with no king worthy of the name, save for one man: Locan.

The Abomination King's mastery of magic might have prepared him better than most, but beyond the boundaries of earth and sky, Locan held the sorcerer's fate in his hands. Locan's fists pummelled him. The chains of the morningstar became one with his hands, turning themselves to Locan's will, becoming shadowy serpents that locked themselves around the Abomination King's limbs. The sorcerer threw a punch, a head-butt, sought to grab the ball of the morningstar and bludgeon Locan's skull, but the shadows reformed to thwart him, Locan shifting around him like water, that jagged lump of metal becoming an anchor that fixed our enemy in a sea of darkness.

That was how I understood events, at least. I was outside my comprehension of the world, and my mind sought to make what sense it could of the battle between them with the tools available to me. I was still locked in an embrace with them. I tried to help Locan, but all my senses were reversed, clouded. My fingers mutated before my eyes, dancing in the darkness like fronds of seaweed caught in an upstream.

And still we plummeted, beyond memory and time and the fiery pit below Sevash. I became one with shadows, unable to tell where we ended and the formless dark began.

And as I thought Locan meant for us to descend into forever, we struck the bottom. Our fall had seemed bone-breakingly fast, but when we landed it was as if the ground had always been there, only waiting for me to put my feet out.

I blinked, testing whether this was real. The world was a black curtain, dark beyond the depths of the sea.

At our feet, the Abomination King lay, tangled impossibly in the chain of his own morningstar, limbs rearranged like the pieces of an insoluble puzzle. He struggled, his cruel mouth spitting silent curses of fury, and the shadows rose around him, swallowing him.

'Huh. I didn't know I could do that.'

I looked at Locan. He had become darkness itself, the brightest light casting a silhouette so black that it seemed to swallow everything it touched. I looked down at myself, and there was nothing there.

'Where are we?' I asked. My voice floated away into the black ether.

'Shadows,' said Locan. He shrugged, sort of, or so my eyes and mind were telling me. 'Can't really put it any better than that.'

'Is this the Underrealm?'

'I hope not. Would hate for this cunt to be right.'

At our feet, the silhouette of the Abomination King

continued to struggle. Experimentally, Locan pointed at him, and a tendril of darkness spilled from his fingertip, becoming a silk-thin strand that began to thread its way around the sorcerer's form like a cocoon.

I tried to think of more I might ask Locan. There were answers here, if only I could think of the questions. My mind refused to conjure them for me, occupied with the inescapable sensation that I did not belong here. Nobody, living or dead, should have laid eyes upon this realm. I had to get out.

'Can we get back?' I asked.

'I can,' said Locan, threads of shadow still spooling from his finger. 'If I can find the way. Not sure about you. Might have to leave you here.'

Even through the cloud of confusion this place had diffused over my thoughts, my whole being was consumed with an existential dread. This was beyond life and death. I would be doomed to eternity here, one with the shadows, my consciousness unravelling thought by thought.

Then I realised that Locan was laughing silently to himself. I stepped forward to hit him, stumbled over the void, and found myself immediately back where I had begun.

'How can you even joke?' I hissed. 'How can you—'

'Relax,' said Locan, still chuckling. 'Just go back the way we came and you'll make it back to Sevash. I'll see you up there. Just want to make sure this arsehole won't be going anywhere for a couple of centuries.' The shadowy thread had reached the Abomination King's mouth, gagging him.

I looked up, in the sense that there was an up at all, and boundless blackness stared back at me. I could no more have returned to Midding than I could have swum to the moon. 'Locan, what do you mean?' Panic rose in my gut again. 'I can't—'

'For pissing sake, I'll help you.' Locan pulled free of the dark thread spooling from his fingers and tied it off, leaving our foe cocooned and hardly able to move an inch. Locan glided over to me and roughly grasped my arm, pointing it upwards at a slight angle. 'That way. I'll give you a push. Once you're back, you can think about what the quickest way of getting me a drink is. And by the way – I warned you about Hosten.' He turned his head towards the Abomination King and spat. 'Never trust a king.'

'Locan, wait—' I wanted to thank him for saving my life when he could have walked away and left me to the Abomination King – a few months earlier, I'm sure that's what he would have done – but before I could get the words out, Locan propelled me upward through the shadows, sending me hurtling through time and memory and death.

CHAPTER 29

I travelled in darkness. Less than darkness, for what is darkness when deprived of light by which to give it meaning? Without Locan to make sense of and give form to this realm of shadows, there was nothing. I could not even blink to check if it was simply that my eyes were closed – I had no eyes, no muscles by which to open and close them. I was pure consciousness, trapped outside of time and form, just a collection of rushing thoughts hurtling through forever.

I thought of Locan, the most recent recollection I had, to remind myself of existence and prevent my consciousness wandering to places I could not retrieve it. The whole of Guiland owed their lives to Locan A'Shadow, and there would not even be a body to prove it. As powerful as the Abomination King was in our own realm, in the realm of shadows the only master was Locan. The Abomination King would wait on his pleasure in its depths for eternity. When Locan and I were reunited, he would rebuke me in the fiercest terms for revealing our plans to Shaliya and leaving us at the mercy of Hosten and Halagrim. He would be right to. He had been right about a great many things.

Images of Shaliya flashed through my mind, every instant of her from when she had first met my eye across the common room of the Dwarf and Dragon to her last fatal encounter with Roddin, indelibly etched on my mind. I might float through this strange realm forever, searching for the shadow cast by her corpse, where our silhouettes could dance in the endless dark through eternity, fading into nothingness together.

At that thought, I felt my path alter slightly, a slight change in the pitch of silent hum that echoed through the darkness, the shadows responding to my desire.

Too painful. Too tempting. Too much to live for. The sun on my face and Morvolt between my legs. Food for my hunger and ale for my thirst. The smile of a pretty girl across a roaring fire. Locan, sneering and spitting and cursing. Rameon, the greatest city in the world, which I was yet to see.

And a dragon. I had once seen a dragon.

I swept up from the shadows into the cool yellow of a spring sun, the sweet scent of wildflowers in my nostrils and warm earth against my back.

I did not feel so groggy as I had when I had last travelled through the shadows with Locan. This felt like coming home. I flexed my fingers, testing them, letting them brush through the blades of grass and savouring the sensation.

For several minutes, I lay there, knowing the simple joy of living. The hunger in my belly and the dryness in my throat were to be savoured, proof that this was a world where those wants could be sated and when that feeling came it would be worth the discomfort. To my relief, the broken rib I had suffered at the hands of the Abomination King no longer plagued me – seemingly healed by my passage through the shadows.

My wonder at being alive so occupied me that it took me far longer than it should have to reach a very simple realisation: this was not Sevash. The ground was not brittle grey dust, and the warm, oppressive weight of the Dreadveil did not bathe the air in its crimson shroud.

I got to my feet, my delight at having returned to the world being swiftly replaced with the disturbing realisation that this was not a place I knew. Its barren stillness and rolling hills reminded me of Narlond. Grass carpeted the earth to the horizon at every point of the compass, with not even a tree by which I could take my bearings.

My brief deviation from the route Locan had set me on appeared to have put me hundreds of miles off course.

But it was not so cold as to be Narlond, and no flurrying northern snowstorms could be seen on the horizon. The sky was blue and the sun was lazily making its way across the highest point of its arc. This was not Narlond, and nor was it any part of Guiland I knew.

'Ho!'

The cry came from behind me. My feet were still numb from my reappearance, and I turned so fast that I nearly tripped over them.

A man was walking towards me, and to my shock I realised that I knew him. Pisspot, my one-time Pillars partner and the diminutive second mate of the *Red Fiend*, the few wispy blond hairs left on his head dancing in the stiff breeze.

'Pisspot!' I tried to run, stumbled, and forced myself to go more carefully. 'What are you doing here?' If the *Red Fiend* was here, I might not be as far off course as I had feared. This was perhaps one of Paleir's southern kingdoms.

'What am I doing here? What are you doing here?' Pisspot grabbed me in an embrace, then with wiry strength pulled me down into a headlock and began jabbing his knuckle into the top of my skull. I was so relieved to see him that I did not even try to free myself. 'Where have you been hiding? We thought you were dead!'

He released me and I stood up woozily. 'I was...' I blinked a few times, trying to arrange my thoughts, and began explaining to him why Locan and I had missed the *Red Fiend*'s departure, until Pisspot quickly interrupted me.

'Boy, we know all that! Why do you think we're here?' He grabbed me briskly by the elbow. 'Let's talk on the way back to the ship. The lads will be buzzing.'

I let him lead me, putting one foot in front of the other as best I could. 'But where are we?'

He looked at me strangely. 'Have you taken a blow to the noggin? You're the reason we're here! This is Midding!'

His shouted revelation disorientated me further. That wasn't possible. 'But... no... the Dreadveil—'

'The Dreadveil disappeared a fortnight ago – surely you noticed that? We got here over a week ago. Captain says we're here to get what plunder we can from Midding before the Guilanders turn up, but there's nothing here – we all know the reason we're sticking around is to find you.'

This was too much. My head was spinning so fast I thought I might fall over. Somehow, I had lost two weeks to the shadow realm. And if the Dreadveil was gone, did that mean the Abomination King was actually gone and it had not all been some near-death fever dream? Then where was Locan?

'Goblins' black bones,' said Pisspot when his words were met with only my bewildered silence. 'Have you spent the last two weeks pissed out of your head? You look like you've just woken up on the wrong ship after a night ashore.' He blew out his cheeks. 'Guess I'll have to explain everything. One of the Mór's men came to tell us that you and Locan were staying, so we sailed with the tide.' Pisspot scowled. 'Bloody liar, but I hope you won't blame us for trusting him. We had no idea what had been going on. Never trust a Palishman. The wind was against us though, blowing north like it had some place to be. Had to tack our way south – no easy task at the best of times stuck between the Dreadveil and the reefs, and you know the captain didn't want to be the man who scuttled his ship for the second time in a month. We weren't that far gone when we saw that dragon, gliding between the air and water like... well, like a sea dragon, I suppose.

'It caused a bit of a stir among the crew. All those who hadn't seen it over Tulbar wanted to chase it – how many times in his life is a man going to see a dragon? – and for all the captain likes to think he's got a black heart, he's soft as land-lubber shite really.' Pisspot winked at me. 'Don't tell him I said that. He turned us back north flying all the canvas we had – some of the lads were even holding their spare shirts off the side to try and give us a bit more speed.

'So we get back to Tulbar only a few days after we left, and there's pissing goblins running about everywhere. No sign of the Mór and no telling who's in charge—'

'He's dead,' I said. A small part of me had hoped that when Hosten reached Sevash and saw the evil of the place with his own eyes he would see his mistake and flee. But by then it had been too late. He had died a monster, another foul creation of Sevash. In all his learning of the Abomination King, he had never contemplated that such wickedness might fall upon him.

'Yeah?' said Pisspot. 'Well, that explains it. Anyway, helpful fellows that we are, we helped them get rid of the goblins. A few fled into the woods, but not enough to trouble anyone. That's when we get the tale of what happened to you and Locan out of that showy cunt Lenard, once we'd tied him to the mast and Shiv had whipped him a couple of times. His clothes ain't so fancy now. Well, we're a bit lost with what to do now – we can hardly sail into the Dreadveil after Locan, so the captain has us digging through the arena looking for you. Must have gone over a hundred corpses. Even thought we'd found you once, until Hanrik pulled down their trousers and we realised it was a girl!'

Pisspot gave a hearty laugh. 'I'm joking, I'm joking. Anyway, it wasn't long after that the Dreadveil disappeared. One moment it was there and the next it was folding in on itself, like someone was hauling on its halyard rope too fast. Before we knew it, there was nothing but clear blue sea all the width of the North Water. That's when the captain decided that you must have somehow followed Locan to Midding and we had to come find you both.' With a gleeful yelp, Pisspot leapt onto my back like a monkey, heedless of my fragile state, and planted a wet kiss on my cheek. 'You fucking brought the Dreadveil down! You bloody beauties! I'm desperate to know how you did it, but I'll wait till we're back aboard so the lads can all hear.' He laughed wildly and hopped down from my back. 'Anyway, what do you think to all that?'

'I think...' If the Dreadveil had disappeared, did that mean the Abomination King was gone forever? Was he gone beyond where even the magic of resurrection could touch him? Was being trapped in the shadows deader than dead? I would have to ask Locan when we reached the *Red Fiend*. My legs were swaying with exhaustion. 'I think I need to lie down.'

I stumbled, and Pisspot moved quickly to put himself under my arm. 'Come on,' he said, 'we're nearly back.' The ground was falling away towards a beach. 'A nip of rum and a nap and you'll be smooth sailing again. You'll have to tell us what happened first though.'

I was still trying to process all of what Pisspot had said. I was surprised Huretio had come searching for us, but Pisspot's presence was proof enough. 'Has Locan not told you?'

'No, didn't you hear what I said? We're still looking for him. Good thing we found you when we did – the captain said we'd give it just one more day.'

That was troubling. If I had been missing for two weeks, Locan would have had plenty of time to come back this way from Sevash by now. There were other ways he might have gone, but Midding's west coast was nearer than crossing either the Gulmid or the Midnar into Guiland or Narlond.

'But...' I was too exhausted to explain. I needed to get back to the *Red Fiend* and tell Huretio to send men to Sevash in search of Locan.

I stumbled along the beach, Pisspot keeping me upright and moving in a straight line. The *Red Fiend* was a hundred yards offshore, but there was a rowboat waiting for us. Huretio was standing alongside it, attentively studying something in his hand, turning it through his fingers.

At our approach he looked up from beneath his purple captain's hat and broke into a booming laugh. 'Cetrik! My boy!' His fierce embrace nearly sent me falling into the surf. 'You look like shit, my friend! Where have you been?' He slapped me roughly on the back several times, and the few crew members he was with followed suit, crowding around me in a cacophony of wholehearted greetings, jests about how they had almost left me, and rapid questions about what had happened to the Dreadveil.

A weak smile was all I could offer them in return. Somebody pressed a skin of rum into my hand, and thirsty as I was I took a long swig, nearly coughing half of it back up when I choked.

'Let the man breathe,' Huretio was demanding of his crew. 'Swarming round him like flies on a dog turd.' He wrapped an arm around my shoulders and steered me away along the shore. 'Cetrik, tell me everything. Where is Locan?'

'I...' There was no easy way to explain the realm of shadows. All I could say was, 'I don't know.'

Huretio frowned. 'But this is his dagger, is it not?'

It was then I noticed what Huretio had been studying in his hand. A slim, silver dagger, its hilt twisted and disfigured where it had melted against the Abomination King's skin. One of Locan's blades.

'It...' It made no sense. That the dagger should be here was another bewildering puzzle to add to my already overburdened mind. 'Yes.'

'Then perhaps he is still nearby,' said Huretio. He turned and called back to his crew, 'Search that way again!' He pointed along the beach. 'Go!'

My head was still spinning. That blade had been the only weapon Locan had – he would never have simply dropped it. Not unless somebody had taken it from him.

'I'll search as well,' I said, already turning to follow the *Red Fiend*'s crew. The sensation that something was not right filled me with sudden vigour. There would be time to rest later.

'My friend, you are exhausted.' Huretio steered me towards the rowboat. 'I did not spend a week hunting for you to let you trip and crack your head. I will row you back to the *Fiend*. Rest, and tomorrow—'

I shrugged Huretio's arm off me. 'Show me where you found it.'

'Do not worry about Locan. He is a born survivor. The world could tumble into the Underrealm, and you would find Locan stubbornly clinging to the edge. When he was your age, he was already—'

'Huretio.' I put the full force of my will into my words. 'Please.'

Huretio's brow furrowed as if he meant to disagree, but with a reluctant sigh he said, 'Fine. I will show you, but then you must rest.'

He led me along the waterline where the tide was lapping at the sand. I was shivering in the brisk coastal breeze, but I did not care. Over the water, a crowd of gulls were circling, cawing aimlessly to one another as they rode the air currents.

'Here,' said Huretio. He pointed to an area of beach that looked no different to any other. 'Half-buried in the sand like it had been there for days. We have scoured this beach half-a-hundred times and found nothing. I will search for one more day, but your friend could be anywhere. Perhaps he simply dropped it here when you arrived.'

I shook my head. 'We did not come this way.' I cursed the two weeks I had lost. Had Locan scoured Midding for me, as Huretio was now doing for him? My head was pounding, the agitated cawing of the circling gulls grating against my eardrums. I looked out over the water, searching for anything that might explain Locan's absence. I refused to believe he would willingly leave without me, not after he had fought the Abomination King to protect me.

'I know what you are thinking – he cannot have drowned,' said Huretio with forced patience. 'Our friend is a strong swimmer, and the tides around this coast are gentle. He—'

A shadow moved beneath the waves, and without waiting for Huretio to finish I threw myself into the sea.

The cold hit me like a hammer of ice. Huretio was crying out behind me, but I refused to heed him, ploughing into the water. The gulls had chosen this place to soar and squawk for a reason, and as my strokes lengthened and quickened, I saw it again, a black blur against the murk. I drove myself down into the water.

The silt from the seabed formed a curtain of dust across my vision, but my fingers brushed against a scrap of fabric. I grasped and pulled, but with my weakened state the body refused to budge an inch.

I surfaced, waving with both arms to the sailors watching me from the shoreline, Huretio staring after me as if I had lost control of my senses. Perhaps I had. 'Help!' I cried out to them. 'I need help!'

The body was so waterlogged and laden with stones that it took four strong swimmers to heave it from the water. I was a mess by then, a shivering wreck on the shoreline with my wet clothes lying in a pile at my feet and a cloak wrapped around my bare bones. Overhead, the birds continued to cry and caw, admonishing us for having claimed the meal that had been just beyond their reach. The grim-faced crew of *the Red Fiend* heaved the body onto the shoreline, and together we gathered around it.

The skin of his face was puckered and wrinkled from the water, pale from blood loss. An ugly gash in his neck revealed where the knife had slit his throat, letting the contents of his veins flood into the sea over the many days that had passed since his death. Men rifled through the pockets of his cloak, pulling free the heavy stones they had used to fix his body to the seabed where the weak tide would not dislodge it.

I had heard of the customs of the Odingr when they went a-reaving, coating the continent in fire and plunder and trafficked flesh. Without their own soil in which to bury their slain, they gave them to the sea, their second home. On their furthest voyages, it was said they could pass as many as five years without setting foot in their homeland, never returning until their vast holds were filled with loot.

'I know this man,' said Pisspot. 'I diced with him on Great Yex.'

'As if you can know that,' said Hanrik. 'He's been dead for days.'

But I had played Pillars with Pisspot, and the second mate's mind was as sharp as a straight razor. If he said he had seen this man before, I believed him. The Odingr we had met in the lands of King Wexl might have lingered there for weeks after we left, waiting for the weather to change. Perhaps they watched as the Dreadveil faded before their eyes, offering them smooth sailing all the way to the continent and beyond. How fortunate they must have felt to fall upon Locan on these barren shores, injured and weakened from his battle with the Abomination King. How many had it taken to subdue him? How many had he slain before they finally pummelled him into submission?

'They know who he is,' I said. Had I surfaced with Locan, the Odingr would have claimed me as well.

'Aye,' said Huretio. 'And they'll be sailing south as we speak with all the canvas they have. Big payday for them if they make it to Rameon.'

The emperor. When they went a-reaving, the way of the Odringr was to sell the slaves they claimed to whoever would pay the greatest weight of gold, and Emperor Vurash V's hatred of Locan was known in every corner of the continent. The Odingr would make all haste for the Dominion. They would reach the coast and sail their narrow, flat-bottomed vessel up the Afrates straight into the heart of the empire, where Locan would be sold like a cow to be slaughtered.

'We're going after them,' I said, 'aren't we?'

In the heavy silence, Huretio kissed his teeth, and for a moment I thought he would refuse me. 'Eh. We were sailing that way anyway.' He flashed a black-hearted grin. 'And I do love to spit in the emperor's face while I steal from his back pocket.' He raised his voice to the air. 'To the rowboats, you sons of whores! Last man aboard can stand guard while the rest of us feed the sharks with Odingr blood!'

I ran with them, in my exhilaration allowing myself to forget for a few moments what we were running for. We had hoped to reach Rameon as free men, but now Locan would go in chains as a gift for the emperor. Unless we could reach his captors first.

We sailed south with the wind at our backs, the *Red Fiend*'s sails all aloft as it skipped over the calm of the North Water like a flat stone, praying over every horizon that we would see the tall mast of an Odingr reaving ship.

At last, I was bound for Rameon. All that stood in my way was the rivers of Odingr blood we would have to spill to save Locan.

.   .   .

By the time we found Locan, however, the Odingr were long gone. To this day, I wonder if Huretio even believed it was possible to catch them. The *Red Fiend*'s captain ever hid his true purpose beneath layers of bluster. Some men keep their cards close to their chests, but Huretio was often playing a different game entirely.

Lost in all the excitement of the above, you are perhaps wondering what became of Morvolt, my horse. You will be relieved to know that the crew of the *Red Fiend* had not forgotten about him before their crossing from Tulbar. Morvolt was safe and well, back in his old cabin, where he and I shared a tearful reunion. Tearful for me, at least.

I was not prepared for how tired revisiting this tale would make me. Tired, and sad. I could go to my bed, and perhaps Shaliya will be waiting in my dreams, flaxen hair flowing like molten sunlight, bright blue eyes soft with forgiveness that I do not deserve.

And yet, for all my weariness, I do not believe sleep will find me this night. I find my thoughts racing to what came after the *Red Fiend* sailed from Midding. The pirate isle of Hortura. My fated encounter with Farnella, a beauty of beguiling smiles and honeyed promises, and the woman Locan had once loved. The great prison fortress of the Rook's Nest. The Dread King of the Muttalins and the Tragedy of Rameon.

But these are not tales to be scratched in parchment locked away inside one's study. These are tales to be told with a drink in my hand and a roaring fire at my feet. I ride now for the tavern, where I may write further or simply listen to tales of grief and glory, whether they be told by ploughmen or princes. And among the stories that reach my ear, I yearn most of all for any whisper of a dragon.

A LETTER FROM R.S. MOULE

Dear Reader,

Thank you for reading *The Assassin's Wrath*. If you enjoyed it, I would be sincerely grateful if you could leave a rating or review with your online bookseller.

If you are enjoying Legends of the Shadow and want to read something else with twisty politics, savage battles, and ancient magic, I thoroughly (and biasedly) recommend my previous series, the Erland Saga. Cetrik has done well to survive Narlond and Paleir, but I am not sure he would survive Erland.

If you have any thoughts you would like to share with me, I would love to hear from you. Please get in touch through any of the links to social media below. These are also a good way to stay notified of my new releases.

If you would like stay informed about the next book in the Legends of the Shadow series, just sign up at the following link. Your email address will never be shared, and you can unsubscribe at any time.

www.secondskybooks.com/rs-moule

Thank you again.

Roger Moule, May 2025

KEEP IN TOUCH WITH R.S. MOULE

instagram.com/rs_moule
x.com/RS_Moule

ACKNOWLEDGEMENTS

One of the difficulties with writing a book every six months is that this is where I inevitably end up thanking all the same people in a slightly different form of words. To that end, I am making an effort to thank by name those I have unfairly overlooked when writing the acknowledgements for previous books.

The Hotdogs (and their ever-expanding collection of chipolatas) – Alex, Katie, Alex, Michaela, Eamon, Charlotte, Nick, Laura, Nick, Lucy, Sophie, Andy, Tim, Catia, Harriet, Matty, Imi, Tom, Mark, Diana, Adam, Lauren. One of the many downsides of getting older is seeing less of you all, even those of you who still only live down the road. But good friends are like good books; you keep them forever.

The VIMVIPVIM crew – Charlie, Charlotte, Chris, and Jack. I don't go to the pub after work very often (not something I ever thought I'd say ten years ago), but when I do there's a good chance it's with some combination of you four. Thanks for making still having to work for a living bearable.

Akay and Kayleigh – board game, barbecue, and festival buddies, and the most portmanteau-able of all the couples I know.

As ever, my editor, Jack Renninson. Writing and editing this one was about as close as I've ever come to headbutting my keyboard. Thanks for not letting me despair. And everybody else at Second Sky who made this book possible.

Gabriel, my nephew, and of course his parents, Georgie and Dave. You don't get to choose your family, but if you could, I would certainly choose you. It is a joy and privilege to be an uncle.

My parents. I couldn't do any of it without you.

My cousin, Pat Collister, probably the first person to read my books after they are released. Thank you for your support. I am sorry about all the bad language.

Tinks – cat, writing companion, fearless explorer, queen of the house. I can't believe you are now old enough to drink.

Last but never least, my wife, Eloise. Writing is not the long-term plan; *we* are the long-term plan.

Roger Moule, May 2025

PUBLISHING TEAM

Turning a manuscript into a book requires the efforts of many people. The publishing team at Bookouture would like to acknowledge everyone who contributed to this publication.

Audio
Alba Proko
Melissa Tran
Sinead O'Connor

Commercial
Lauren Morrissette
Hannah Richmond
Imogen Allport

Cover design
Blacksheep

Data and analysis
Mark Alder
Mohamed Bussuri

Editorial
Jack Renninson
Melissa Tran

Copyeditor
Rhian McKay

Proofreader
Helen Hawkins

Marketing
Alex Crow
Melanie Price
Occy Carr
Cíara Rosney
Martyna Młynarska

Operations and distribution
Marina Valles
Stephanie Straub
Joe Morris

Production
Hannah Snetsinger
Mandy Kullar
Ria Clare
Nadia Michael

Publicity
Kim Nash
Noelle Holten
Jess Readett
Sarah Hardy

Rights and contracts
Peta Nightingale
Richard King
Saidah Graham

Dear Reader,

We'd love your attention for one more page to tell you about the crisis in children's reading, and what we can all do.

Studies have shown that reading for fun is the **single biggest predictor of a child's future life chances** – more than family circumstance, parents' educational background or income. It improves academic results, mental health, wealth, communication skills, ambition and happiness.

The number of children reading for fun is in rapid decline. Young people have a lot of competition for their time, and a worryingly high number do not have a single book at home.

Hachette works extensively with schools, libraries and literacy charities, but here are some ways we can all raise more readers:

- Reading to children for just 10 minutes a day makes a difference
- Don't give up if children aren't regular readers – there will be books for them!

- Visit bookshops and libraries to get recommendations
- Encourage them to listen to audiobooks
- Support school libraries
- Give books as gifts

There's a lot more information about how to encourage children to read on our websites: **www.RaisingReaders.co.uk** and **www.JoinRaisingReaders.com**.

Thank you for reading.

www.ingramcontent.com/pod-product-compliance
Lightning Source LLC
Chambersburg PA
CBHW031743180726
48283CB00005B/1645